HUSH MONEY

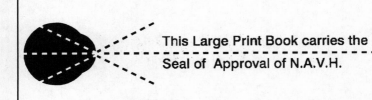

This Large Print Book carries the
Seal of Approval of N.A.V.H.

HUSH MONEY

CHUCK GREAVES

THORNDIKE PRESS
A part of Gale, Cengage Learning

WITHDRAWN

GALE
CENGAGE Learning®

Detroit • New York • San Francisco • New Haven, Conn • Waterville, Maine • London

GALE
CENGAGE Learning®

Copyright © 2012 by Charles J. Greaves.
Thorndike Press, a part of Gale, Cengage Learning.

LIBRARY OF CONGRESS CATALOGING-IN-PUBLICATION DATA

Greaves, Chuck.
  Hush money / by Chuck Greaves.
    pages ; cm. — (Thorndike Press large print reviewers' choice)
    ISBN 978-1-4104-5103-3 (hardcover) — ISBN 1-4104-5103-8 (hardcover)
  1. Attorneys—Fiction. 2. Show jumping—Fiction. 3. Horses—Fiction. 4. Insurance crimes—Fiction. 5. Murder—Investigation—Fiction. 6. Large type books. I. Title.
  PS3607.R42885H87 2012b
  813'.6—dc23   2012019255

Published in 2012 by arrangement with St. Martin's Press, LLC.

Printed in the United States of America
1 2 3 4 5 6 7 16 15 14 13 12

To *LYNDA LARSEN,*
for *EVERYTHING*

Man, surrounded by elements that concocted his ruin, by animals with speed and strength greater than his own, man was once a slave on earth; the horse made him king.

— HEPHREM HOUEL

Horse sense is the thing a horse has which keeps it from betting on people.

— W. C. FIELDS

PROLOGUE

I never cared much for horses. Then again, growing up in a Section 8 housing project in East L.A., my exposure was somewhat limited.

When I was a kid I had an uncle Louis, my mother's perennially unemployed older brother. Uncle Louis was a real railbird. He was partial to Hawaiian shirts, White Owl cigars, and cryptic, horse-related advice. Stuff like, "Always bet a gray mare in cold weather, kid." You'd see Uncle Louis on the street and ask him how's it going, and he'd say something like, "Good day at the track today. Found a sandwich and got a ride home." He was what you'd call a character.

Uncle Louis was a veteran of the Vietnam conflict, from which he'd somehow leveraged an imperceptible limp into a pronounced disability benefit. Since he never seemed to actually work, he showed up at our apartment a lot, usually around mealtime, to my mother's delight and my father's ineffable dismay. In the summers when school was out, he'd offer to take me to the park, or to a Dodger game, but we'd usually wind up shooting pool in some bar, or playing cards in some guy's apartment. Or else, of course, at the track.

Uncle Louis never had a credit card or a bank account. He cashed his VA checks at a strip club in Montebello, and he conducted his vague business affairs out of the front pocket of his trousers. When times were fat, he carried a roll of bills there, wrapped in a thick rubber band. When times were lean, he wore the rubber band on his wrist.

When I was sixteen, Uncle Louis won the Pick Six at Hollywood Park and promptly announced that he was moving to Hawaii in order to buy, of all things, a macadamia nut farm. It was around six months later that the Kona police fished his body out of Kealakekua Bay. There were no signs of foul play, they told my mother, except that his ears had been cut off.

The day before she got that call, I'd received a letter from Uncle Louis. Inside the envelope were a crisp hundred-dollar bill and a note scribbled on a yellowing bar napkin that read, "Let it ride."

Uncle Louis had let it ride, but to no avail.

The feds confiscated the farm — one acre of nuts surrounding four acres of marijuana — and my folks got stuck with his burial costs. Me, I kept the hundred.

While I never shared his passion for the ponies, I soon came to appreciate that the many hours we'd spent together at the track were anything but wasted. Uncle Louis was, after all, a student of life, as profound in his own way as Thoreau, or Kierkegaard, or any of the other hoary navel-gazers I'd later study in college.

My mother always said that Uncle Louis had missed his calling in life, and that he really should have gone to law school. So it was inevitable, perhaps, that I'd do exactly that.

And that horses, one day, would change my life forever.

1

It was a Thursday afternoon, almost five o'clock, and I was typing feverishly in the knowledge that by 5:01, Bernadette would be long gone. Reliability is a rare quality in a legal secretary, and when it came to quitting time, Bernie Catalano was a regular Old Faithful.

I was drafting a letter to the local claims manager of the Hartford Allied Insurance Company, which had issued a policy of health insurance to my client, Victor Tazerian. Victor was a fifty-four-year-old Armenian trash hauler whose leukemia was temporarily in remission. Hartford Allied, to the bewilderment of the Tazerian family, was refusing to pay for a new but promising medical procedure that involved harvesting and freezing Victor's own bone marrow while he was healthy, so that it later could be transplanted back into his body when the cancer made its inevitable return.

Hartford Allied reasoned that as long as the cancer was in remission, no surgery was warranted. In other words, they wouldn't pay for the procedure until Victor got sick again, and of course, once he got sick again, the procedure would be useless.

In the vernacular of my profession, this was called insurance bad faith — a state of affairs to which, in its many and varied forms, I was no stranger. As I'd tried to explain to Victor's sobbing wife Lina, the insurance industry operates in strict accordance with the three rules of American capitalism: invest someone else's money, make a profit, and try to keep both.

And so Victor Tazerian lay in a pre-op ward at the City of Hope National Medical Center awaiting a surgical procedure that costs more than he'll earn in a lifetime, while Hartford Allied's regional claims manager stood by his fax machine in Thousand Oaks waiting for a demand letter from me that we both knew he had no intention of honoring. Lina, meanwhile, sat by her telephone in Glendale wearing out her worry beads, while Bernadette, bless her heart, was eyeing the digital clock on her desk next to her car keys.

And that's the precise moment that Russ Dinsmoor chose to burst into my office and announce that Hush Puppy was dead.

I shot him a side glance and kept on typing.

"Shouldn't Buster Brown be notified?"

"Hush Puppy is a horse, you philistine. A very valuable horse belonging to Mrs. Everett, who, need I remind you, is a very valuable client of the firm."

None of which concerned me in the least, and so I ignored him, in the faint hope that he'd simply go away.

"I need you over at Fieldstone right away," he persisted. "Jared's out of town, and Sydney is *beside* herself with grief."

Sydney Everett, I knew by reputation, was one of the wealthiest old dowagers in Pasadena, a city positively freighted with women of a certain age who'd made their fortunes the old-fashioned way. Which is to say, by outliving their husbands. I also knew that a felicitously large percentage of these women happened to be clients of the city's oldest and snobbiest law firm, Henley & Hargrove, under whose yoke I presently toiled.

Jared would be Jared Henley, who, although not the brightest bulb in the Henley & Hargrove chandelier, was the only grandson of the firm's founder and, I surmised, the partner currently assigned to wipe when Mrs. Everett's nose started to run. Characteristically, however, Jared was vacationing in Cancún, or Bimini, or wherever it was that slow-witted grandchildren with trust funds went to mate with others of their kind.

"Why me?" I finally asked, glancing up from my screen. "I don't know a fetlock from a half nelson."

"Because there are two insurance adjusters out there as we speak, and we don't want there to be any trouble."

Deftly, painlessly, Russ Dinsmoor had sunk the hook.

"Trouble? Why would there be trouble?"

"I'll fill you in on the details later, Mac. For now, we must let slip the dogs of war!" He threw his hands skyward, then joined them together in prayer. "Please, big fella? For me?"

I caught a faint whiff of horse manure right there in my office, but I could see that Russ was genuinely concerned.

"All right already, I'm slipping. Just get out of here and let me finish this."

When I finally brought the letter out to Bernie, at exactly 4:59 P.M., she was sitting with her long legs crossed, filing her fingernails.

"Isn't that a little cliché?" I asked.

"No," she said, frowning at the clock. "It's a friggin' emery board."

■ ■ ■ ■

It was a ten-minute drive from Pasadena to the nearby suburb of Flintridge, a bucolic burg best known, where known at all, as the home of the NASA Jet Propulsion Laboratory. That's where they design and build all nature of moon rockets, Mars probes, and other esoteric space projects whose only societal benefit, as near as I could tell, was to keep Caltech graduates from defaulting on their student loans.

A quiet enclave of broad lawns and stately mansions, Flintridge had a reputation as one of the more affluent cities in the sprawling megalopolis of Southern California, a part of the world in which affluence, like Kardashians, seemed to be everywhere.

It was almost five thirty when I rolled the Wrangler up to the gatehouse of the Fieldstone Riding Club, and was there greeted by a wizened old codger with a clipboard. He wore what looked like the Gilbert and Sullivan interpretation of a military dress uniform, and I stifled an impulse to salute.

"Jack MacTaggart," I announced, "to see Sydney Everett."

He cast a dubious eye on the Jeep as he flipped through his list of authorized guests.

"Look, I'm probably not on there, but I'm Mrs. Everett's lawyer. From Henley and Hargrove."

I must have spoken the magic words, because he nodded and waved me through, pointing me past an emphatic MEMBERS ONLY sign and up a macadam driveway where the air seemed cooler somehow, laden as it was with the vaguely menthol scent of eucalyptus. The sun was low, the shadows were long, and the light filtering through the treetops was a glass-blown kind of opalescent amber.

I parked in an otherwise empty lot beside what looked like a sprawling hacienda, its walls of whitewashed plaster quaintly moldering under a mission tile roof. The clubhouse, like the rolling grounds it commanded, looked eerily deserted. I cut the engine, surveyed the surroundings, and did some quick arithmetic.

Even in a down real estate market, I figured that an unimproved half-acre lot in Flintridge, if you could find such a thing, went for a million bucks or so, depending on the location. This place looked to be over a hundred acres, and it sat in one of the tonier neighborhoods, bordered on the east by JPL and the parklands of the Arroyo Seco, and on the north by the lilac-colored foothills of the Angeles National Forest.

I didn't know how many members they had here, or the buy-in cost of a membership, but the breakup value of this place had to be enough to launch a couple of those satellites from across the road.

I shrugged into my suit jacket and set off on foot, following a dirt path that wended northward toward the hills. Songbirds were trilling in the massive oaks, and a red-tail hawk hung silently overhead. Not a bad place, I told myself, to spend your idle hours chasing foxes, or Democrats, or whatever they did around here for sport.

And then, as if a soundtrack to that reverie, I heard the rhythmic drum of hoofbeats, and I turned to see a young woman astride a gleaming black horse that grew in its approach to the approximate size of a mastodon. I stepped to one side, but she halted the thundering beast on a dime without so much as a tug on the reins. It was a pretty neat trick.

"You look lost," she informed me, flashing a smile from on high.

"Were the wing tips a giveaway?"

"They're not very practical around here, I'm afraid."

She had the wholesome good looks of a J. Crew catalog model, all dark eyebrows and high cheekbones. She wore a dirty polo shirt and khaki riding breeches that disappeared, just at the knee, into tall black boots. She was slender and tanned, and her hair spilled like a gusher of sweet crude from the back of a faded baseball cap.

I edged closer and reached up a hand.

"I'm Jack MacTaggart."

"Faith and begorra!" she laughed in a comic brogue as she leaned over to shake. "I'm Tara Flynn. And this" — she patted the big horse on its neck — "is Escalator."

I stepped back to regard the horse, which was ignoring us both and cropping at a strip of grass by the path. It was the largest living thing I'd seen outside of a zoo.

"Let me guess. Shetland pony?"

She smiled again.

"He's a Hanoverian, actually. But sweet like a pony."

"That's good," I said, "because if he ever gets testy, we'll have to call out the National Guard."

"Oh, he can be plenty testy. But a carrot usually does the trick."

The horse raised its head long enough to deposit some greenish slime on my pant leg. I scratched him lightly between the ears.

"I don't suppose you've seen a couple of beady-eyed weasels in business suits skulking about the place, have you?"

Her smile faded.

"Are you here about Hush Puppy?"

"That's right. I'm one of Mrs. Everett's lawyers."

She considered that for a moment, then gathered up the reins and turned the big horse ninety degrees to port. She pointed with her chin to some buildings off in the distance.

"If you head that way and look for Doc Wells's truck — it's a big white pickup — you'll find them all there." Then she added wistfully, "What a nightmare."

"I guess Mrs. Everett's pretty broken up about it?"

"Oh, I wouldn't count on that," she said, wheeling the horse around. "It was nice to meet you, Jack. I hope you're a good lawyer."

In the courtyard central to the four barns sat a white pickup truck, its tailgate down, alongside a silver Chevy compact and a burgundy Jaguar. Arrayed on the pickup's tailgate were what looked like instruments of persuasion from the Spanish Inquisition — tongs and calipers, blades and files, hooks and giant syringes. I heard the low murmur of voices emanating from the westernmost barn, so I headed in that direction, fishing a couple of business cards from my wallet as I walked.

They were gathered in the barn aisle beneath a neatly lettered sign that read HUSH PUPPY. There were five of them in all: the two suits, a kid in white coveralls I assumed was a groom, the veterinarian crouched in the doorway to the stall, and, by process of elimination, Sydney Everett, who was speaking into a small tape recorder held by the bigger of the suits.

I snatched it from his hand and toggled the Off button.

"Hey!" he barked. "What do you think you're doing?"

I popped the microcassette and slipped it into my pocket.

"I'm saving us both a lot of paperwork," I said, tossing the device to his startled sidekick. "And now I'm having a private word with my client."

I steered her by the elbow, out of the barn and into the courtyard, where even in the fading sunlight I could see that my preconception of Sydney Everett — that of a blue-rinse biddy with her eyeglasses on a chain — could not have been further off mark.

Although I made her for around sixty, she could have passed for forty-five by candlelight. She had sleek black hair, a full mouth, and rich olive skin that gave her an exotic, almost Mediterranean appearance. She too was dressed in riding attire — gleaming high boots with little silver spurs, tight black breeches, and a white cotton blouse that stretched to contain breasts of a shape and size not ordinarily found in nature.

She had the look of a woman who'd been around the block a few times, and who'd ended up buying the neighborhood.

"I admire a man of action," she informed me in a whiskey voice poured straight from the French Quarter.

"I'm Jack MacTaggart," I said, handing her a card as we walked. "Man of action."

She stopped to examine the card, and to give me the full head to toe.

"I was expecting Jared Henley," she said. "But I can't say I'm disappointed."

"I believe Jared's in Akron, for the big Star Trek convention. Russ Dinsmoor asked me to pinch hit."

She slipped the card into her breast pocket. It was a tight squeeze.

"Russell is just *so* thoughtful," she purred. "Was I being *dreadfully* foolish, giving a statement like that?"

"Did you tell them you were waiting for your lawyer?"

"Why of course. They were right there when I called Russell from my car."

"That figures. I would have had to go to court for an order excluding the statement."

"Oh, my. That wasn't very sporting of them."

"Look, Mrs. Everett —"

"Sydney, please."

"Sydney. Those men in there are not your friends, okay? Their only purpose in coming out here was to find some way to avoid paying your claim. You need to understand that right up front."

She nodded earnestly. "If you say so, Jack."

"Now look, we've only got a couple of minutes. Tell me everything you know about . . . what happened."

She cocked her hip and touched a manicured finger to her lips, a fleeting convergence of acrylic and collagen.

"Let's see. Enrique found Hush Puppy this morning, at feeding time. Enrique is the young man inside."

"Who was the last person to see the horse alive?"

She thought about that.

"I don't really know. I'd imagine it was Tara. Tara Flynn. She's the stable manager here at Fieldstone. She checks on the horses at night."

Lucky horses. "And when does she usually do that?"

"Oh, I don't know. Around six o'clock."

"And what time did Enrique find him this morning?"

"Around seven thirty. At least, that's what he said."

Which left a window of more than thirteen hours for the horse to turn belly-up.

"Had Hush Puppy been ill or . . . out of sorts in any way?"

She considered this for a moment, then shook her head.

"Not that I'm aware of, no. Of course, you'd have to ask Barbara."

Of course. "And who's Barbara?"

"Why, Barbara Hauser. Barbara *campaigned* Hush Puppy."

I crossed to the pickup's tailgate. In addition to the stuff laid out on display, there were clear plastic drawers with gauze and swabs and, in one of the compartments, a .45 caliber revolver. Doc Wells, it seemed, was not averse to a little old-school euthanasia.

Sydney followed me, positioning herself so that her outsized ordinance targeted the general vicinity of my nose. It was like staring into the grille of a '54 Buick.

"Look, Mrs. . . . . ah, Sydney. I have to

25

confess that I don't know a whole lot about horses, or what exactly one does with them at a place like Fieldstone. I assumed that you rode Hush Puppy because you owned him."

She thought this was amusing, the idea of a woman riding her own horse.

"No, I've never even sat on Hush Puppy, and I've had him for nearly four years. You see, Hush Puppy was a grand prix level show jumper. He and Barbara were working toward the Olympic trials in March."

"And where is Barbara now?"

"I think she's in San Juan Capistrano this week. Or is it Del Mar? You can check in the barn office. They'll have her schedule."

I knew that the suits would be getting antsy by now, and that I could get the details from Sydney later.

"Two more questions before we head on back. First, how large is the policy on Hush Puppy's life?"

"Oh, let's see," she said, her eyes rolling skyward. "I believe that it's two million dollars."

I nearly fell off the tailgate.

"What's your other question, Jack?"

"Forgive me for asking, but where were you between six o'clock last night and seven thirty this morning?"

26

Now a question like that can elicit any number of reactions from a client, ranging from surprise to mild annoyance to righteous indignation. Sydney Everett exhibited none of these.

"I had dinner at the Valley Hunt Club at seven, with friends from the Children's Hospital Guild. Plenty of witnesses there. Then several of us attended a concert at Descanso Gardens. The Pasadena Pops. They perform alfresco. If you haven't been, you should go. They're fabulous. That ended close to midnight. And then I went home. Alone. Tara called me at eight o'clock this morning, just as I was preparing to come for a hack. And that's it, I guess."

"And what about last night between six and seven?"

She thought for a moment.

"I believe I was bathing. Also alone."

Most people are uncomfortable looking you straight in the eye, even when telling the truth. They'll glance away, or study their shoes, or flick some lint from their shoulder. But not Sydney Everett. She delivered her alibi right to my face, her Bible-black eyes never once breaking contact. If she was lying as to her whereabouts, she was a natural. Or else she'd had plenty of practice.

"C'mon," I said, rising to my feet. "Let's

get this over with."

As we reentered the darkening barn, I noted that the groom, Enrique, was gone. The veterinarian, Dr. Wells, had just gotten to his feet and was brushing sawdust from the knees of his khakis. I was surprised to see that the good doctor was not much older than me.

The bigger of the two suits stepped forward to remonstrate, but I ignored him and offered a hand to the vet.

"Dr. Wells? I'm Jack MacTaggart. I'm Mrs. Everett's lawyer."

He shook my hand, showing no sign of the enmity that doctors will sometimes exhibit toward lawyers. He had a good face — clean-cut, lantern jaw, all-American handsome — and the crushing grip of a man with Popeye's forearms.

"Nice to meet you," he said. "I'm George Wells."

As he turned his attention to my client, placing a hand on her shoulder, I could see through the open door of the stall the lifeless body of a huge white horse.

"Sydney, I'm terribly sorry about the Pup," he said gently. "These things can happen, even to the healthiest of horses."

She lowered her eyes and nodded, disconsolate. Wells then addressed the rest of us, trading his warm bedside manner for the cold deportment of a clinician.

"All right, gentlemen. There are no signs of trauma, and we can safely rule out colic. I've taken blood, urine, fecal, and tissue samples. Pending the test results, I'm going to list the preliminary cause of death as cardiac failure of unknown etiology."

He regarded the suits.

"You can make transportation arrangements at the barn office. You'll have my final report when the lab work comes back, in around a week."

Wells then turned and slipped his arm around my client's shoulder — definitely a man of action — and together they walked into the courtyard, leaving me alone at last with my new best friends.

The younger of the two looked to be around twenty. He was pale and skinny, and he wore the kind of cheap suit that I associate with claims adjusters, car salesmen, and assistant managers at Sears. His boss was maybe thirty years older, and thought low fat was a village in Cambodia.

"Say, either of you boys ever heard of a composer named Al Fresco?"

"Gimme back my tape," growled Porky, extending a meaty hand.

"I don't think so," I told him, patting my

pocket. "But I'll tell you what. If you want, we could call the insurance commissioner's office and tell 'em you tried to take my client's recorded statement when you knew I was on my way over to meet with her. Got your cell phone handy?"

He scowled and scratched at his ear, thinking that one over.

"Okay, all right, forget it. Keep the goddamn tape. But we're still gonna need a statement."

"Yeah." The kid smirked. "We need to find out what she plans to do with those balloons she's smuggling."

Hardy har har. I handed the fat man my card. "You have any questions, you can call me. You want a statement, call your bank."

I left them with the carcass and headed outside, where a wine-colored twilight had descended on the Fieldstone Riding Club.

Wells was packing up his truck, while Mrs. Everett sat in her car with the engine idling, talking on the phone. As I approached, she put the Jag into gear and roared off, shouting, "Call me, sugar!" across the front seat. Through the swirling dust cloud, I could see that her vanity plate read HRS PLAY.

I was brushing off my jacket when Wells slammed the tailgate, hesitated, then started in my direction.

"I guess there's something you ought to know," he offered.

"After all these years," I said, "you'd think so."

"What?"

"Never mind. What should I know?"

"Well, I have a pretty good guess at what killed Sydney's horse."

He had my undivided attention.

"Yeah?"

"Yeah." He lowered his voice as he glanced toward the barn. "Don't hold me to it, but I'm pretty sure Hush Puppy was poisoned."

2

Russell Hale Dinsmoor was a product of the old school, a time and a place in which every lawyer in town knew just about every other lawyer in town.

In that bygone era, a lawyer's word was his bond, because his reputation was his most valued asset. Mendacity or incivility among lawyers was unheard of, because the chances were good that you'd be facing the same courtroom adversaries before the same judges over and over again, and because you probably belonged to the same clubs, or sat on the same boards, or drank in the same bars.

Nowadays, however, with a quarter-million attorneys in California alone, the practice of law has become all but anonymous, and this anonymity has spawned a pandemic of churlish behavior by and among lawyers the likes of which is rarely seen outside the preschool sandbox. Enamored of the sharp-practicing barristers of film and television, today's clients expect their attorneys — whom they're paying up to a thousand dollars an hour — to yield no quarter in pursuit of victory. As a result, even those lawyers unwilling to cross legal or ethical lines often have chalk on their shoes.

And so it was that my first encounter with Russell Dinsmoor, a scant two years ago, had been doubly noteworthy.

Dinsmoor had been retained as local counsel by a British insurance syndicate that had the misfortune of issuing a policy of health insurance to my client, an out-of-work longshoreman from Long Beach, one week before *he'd* had the misfortune of being diagnosed with stage three liver cancer. The syndicate was refusing to honor the policy, of course, but on the novel ground that my client had failed to disclose on his application for coverage a bout of adolescent bed-wetting.

I was on my own at the time, renting space in an office suite out on Wilshire in one of L.A.'s less glamorous neighborhoods. By then I was six years out of the night program at Loyola Law School, four of which I'd spent representing all nature of addled, addicted, and otherwise reprobate Angelinos as a Deputy Public Defender for the County of Los Angeles.

At the PD's office the hours were long, the supervising attorneys were indifferent, and the pay was a joke. But I got to try more than twenty criminal jury trials to verdict — the kind of courtroom mileage that the Yale and Harvard boys up in the glass towers on Bunker Hill could only dream about.

Then, when circumstances had required a hasty departure from the PD's office, I'd hung out a civil shingle on Wilshire. In contrast to criminal law, where life and liberty hang in the balance, civil lawyers fight over money. If nothing else, I told myself, it would be good training for married life.

I'd started with slip-and-falls and fender benders, and I'd soon worked my way up the legal food chain. And along the way I'd acquired a reputation for actually trying cases, rather than dancing the bluff-and-settle fandango that was the vocational norm.

In our longshoreman's case, I anticipated from the renowned Russell H. Dinsmoor the kinds of hardball tactics I'd come to expect of all insurance lawyers. Things like papers personally served on the Friday afternoon before a holiday weekend, obstreperous coaching of witnesses during depositions, and the need to file motions with the court to compel even the most basic pretrial discovery.

To my surprise, however, Dinsmoor was a horse of a different color. When a hearing in the case conflicted with my calendar, he stipulated to a continuance with no questions asked. When I needed additional time to respond to discovery, he not only agreed, but asked nothing in return. And yet, when an important substantive issue was in dispute, the old man proved tougher than a three-dollar steak.

Then, around six months into the case, a temp secretary sent Dinsmoor a fax that was supposed to go to my client. It was a long letter summarizing the deposition of the insurance company's urologist, in which I had critiqued the doctor's testimony, summarized the strengths and weaknesses of our case in general, and made suggestions for possible settlement strategies.

I had no idea that the fax had gone awry until it arrived in my mailbox three days later, along with a cover letter from Dinsmoor's secretary.

Dear Mr. MacTaggart:
The enclosed arrived by fax on Tuesday

afternoon. Mr. Dinsmoor, as you know, is in Memphis this week attending the annual meeting of the American College of Trial Lawyers. Upon receipt of your fax, I immediately recognized that a mistake had been made, and I telephoned Mr. Dinsmoor. He instructed me to return the fax to you, which I now do, and to assure you that nobody from this office has read or copied its contents. He also instructed me to tell you that you owe him dinner for two at the restaurant of his choice, payable at the conclusion of the case.

Sincerely,
Veronica Daley
Secretary to Russell H. Dinsmoor

The case never did settle, and the trial was held in March, before the Honorable Marshall T. Farnsworth at the old county courthouse on Hill Street.

My longshoreman, a nice-enough guy named Ted Burlingame, was a solid witness, testifying with obvious sincerity that he'd had no inkling of any health problems when he'd completed the insurance application. Although he'd admitted to telling a white lie elsewhere on the form — denying any prior medical history — he testified that he'd done so both because he was embar-

36

rassed, and because he'd figured that a brief episode of teenage bed-wetting had no bearing whatsoever on the issue of his adult health.

At least one juror was moved to tears when Ted described receiving the insurance syndicate's letter denying his transplant surgery, and how Ted and his wife had sat together at their kitchen table making plans for her future life without him.

I rested the plaintiff's case that afternoon, with that poignant image etched in the minds of the jury. Dinsmoor, to my surprise, rested his case a day later after first declining to cross-examine Ted, and then conducting only a perfunctory examination of his oncologist. I figured the old man had thrown in the towel in the face of my courtroom brilliance.

The next day, I delivered one of my better closing arguments, challenging the jury to send a message across the Atlantic to the syndicate bigwigs in London. I held the blank verdict form aloft and called it a memo to corporate headquarters. I said that if the syndicate wanted to do business in these United States of America, it had by God better learn basic American values of fair play and decency. Exhorting the jurors to act as the conscience of the entire nation,

I concluded by asking for damages sufficient to pay for the belated transplant, plus another million dollars to compensate Ted and his family for the emotional suffering they'd been forced to endure.

You could have heard a pin drop in the courtroom when Dinsmoor walked to the lectern to give his closing argument. His mood was somber, as though he was distracted by some sad and distant memory.

"You know," he began, cleaning his eyeglasses with the end of his necktie, "my father loved beef stew. Just loved it. And I remember one time, when I was around fifteen years old, my folks took me and my sister to Dad's favorite restaurant for his birthday. This was his favorite restaurant, mind you, because they had the best beef stew in town, and my father, as I said, loved his beef stew."

Dinsmoor put on the glasses, stuffed his hands into his pockets and started pacing in front of the jury box, seemingly lost in a pointless childhood reverie. I thought maybe he'd lost his marbles.

"And when the waitress came around to take our orders, sure enough, even though Dad asked her about the pot pie and asked her about the pork chops, he finally ordered the stew, just as we all knew he would. I remember that Dad was in rare form that night, excited like a kid on Christmas Eve. Not just because it was his birthday, mind you, but because he couldn't wait to dig into that beef stew, his favorite dish in the whole world, prepared by his favorite restaurant in the whole world."

Dinsmoor returned to the lectern.

"And when the waitress finally came back with our food, we all sort of watched Dad out of the corners of our eyes, because his excitement was infectious, and we all wanted to see the look on his face when he finally dipped his spoon into that great big, steaming bowl of stew. And it looked good too, brimming with potatoes and carrots and great big hunks of beef in a thick, hot gravy. Dad, he was practically trembling with anticipation when he scooped up a big, juicy piece of beef, eased it into his mouth . . . then spit it onto the table in disgust."

The jurors at this point were literally on the edges of their seats, as was old Judge Farnsworth, and I began to have a sinking feeling in my stomach.

Russ Dinsmoor had taken command of the courtroom.

" 'Waitress!' my father shouted. 'This meat is rancid! Take it back!' Well, the waitress just gave my father an insolent sort of look and she said, 'Well, sir, maybe *that* piece was rancid, but what about the rest of it? It looks perfectly good to me.' "

He slapped his palm on the lectern, and the jurors all jumped.

"And *that,* ladies and gentlemen, pretty much sums up the way I feel about the testimony of Mr. Burlingame in this lawsuit. Young Mr. MacTaggart here, like that waitress, expects you to swallow the rest of his client's story, despite the fact that by his own admission, Mr. Burlingame *lied* under penalty of perjury on his insurance application. Well, what about that? Are we going to overlook one bald-faced *lie* and accept the *rest* of this man's story? Is it our job to pick and choose what's true and good from what's false and rancid? Or are we entitled, like my father was entitled on the night of his birthday, to just send the *whole thing* back to where it came from?"

Although the trial had lasted a week, it took less than an hour for the jurors to return a defense verdict. It was the first, last, and only civil trial I'd ever lost, and I was devastated.

Two weeks later and still in a dark funk, I joined Dinsmoor for dinner at the Arroyo Chop House in Pasadena, where somewhere between his thirty-dollar filet mignon and his Grand Marnier soufflé, he all but knocked me out of my chair by offering me a job at Henley & Hargrove. He explained that the firm had been searching for a young trial lawyer to fill his shoes upon retirement, and that he thought I had the tools they'd been looking for.

The only thing more surprising to me than his offer was my acceptance. While I'd never aspired to partnership at a major law firm, with all its attendant bureaucracies, the reputation of Henley & Hargrove was not easily ignored. More important, the chance to work closely, even for a short while, with a trial lawyer of Russ Dinsmoor's stature presents itself but once in a lifetime.

We shook on it right then and there, whereupon Dinsmoor, draining the last of his vintage Bordeaux, handed me the biggest restaurant bill I'd ever seen in my life.

"Look at the bright side," he'd said cheerfully, dabbing his lips with a napkin. "At least I didn't order the beef stew."

And so it was that I found myself studying Russ's back as he stared out the windows of his corner office, lost in thought, his slender torso framed by the distant majesty of the San Gabriel Mountains. Russ's office was a

41

lot like his mind, which is to say, orderly but eccentric. His desk, as usual, was devoid of files or papers of any kind. His walls, in contrast, were a riot of diplomas and awards and photos of him grinning and gripping with assorted politicians and celebrity clients. He had an antique slot machine by the door, and a life-sized skeleton named Slim that served as a hat rack for Russ's gray fedora when not earning its keep as a courtroom exhibit.

Finally, after a full minute of silent rumination, he turned from the window and seemed startled to find that I was still sitting on his couch, awaiting his reaction to my report of last night's events at the Fieldstone Riding Club.

"Well," he said, "I don't see as though we have a problem yet, but the possibility of an ethical conflict certainly looms."

"More than a possibility, wouldn't you say? If Wells is right, we might have a duty to turn her in, or risk complicity in a crime."

Russ raised a cautionary finger. "Until this fellow Wells reaches a definitive conclusion as to cause of death, we've no grounds for suspecting Sydney of anything. She's innocent until proven otherwise."

"Many adjectives spring to mind in describing Sydney Everett," I told him, "but innocent isn't one of them."

He smiled. "Nevertheless, there's no ethical impediment as yet to assisting in the prosecution of her claim."

"And if Wells does conclude that Hush Puppy was greased?"

He winced at my word choice.

"Then if — and *only* if — there's evidence of her complicity, we could no longer represent her in the matter." He sighed. "That goes without saying."

I could see that Russ was pained by the thought of turning down work from Mrs. Everett. But I knew he'd find it more painful to be charged, at this stage of his career, with aiding and abetting a fraudulent insurance claim.

"Forgive me for stating the obvious, boss, but who else besides Sydney would have a motive to poison a million-dollar show horse?"

"If I were a younger man," he replied, slumping into his chair and extracting his pipe from a desk drawer, "that's a question I'd spend some time investigating."

Old Pasadena, the city's historic downtown, is widely known and frequently imitated as a model of urban renewal through historic preservation. Beginning in the 1980s, a group of visionary developers quietly bought up whole blocks of what was then the city's skid row. They evicted the junkies, sandblasted graffiti off the hundred-year-old brick, and *voilà,* a tourist mecca was born.

Where free-range winos once roamed darkened alleys drinking Thunderbird from brown paper bags, yuppies now sipped Chardonnay at sidewalk cafés. Out went the adult bookstores, the pawn shops, and the shot-and-a-beer taverns, and in came the multiscreen theaters and a parade of ubiquitous retailers like Banana Republic and Crate & Barrel and Victoria's Secret.

Ironically enough, there are more panhandlers, purse snatchers, and police in Old Pasadena today than before this so-called gentrification began. Plus you can't park your car downtown without tipping a valet or pumping half your paycheck into a meter. There are some who'd call this progress, but I'm not one of them.

So it was with a certain diffidence that I acceded to Tara Flynn's proposal that we meet at Cheval Blanc for dinner. The ersatz French bistro in the heart of Old Pasadena was a paean to all things trendy; a place where film agents and stock traders sipped single-malt Scotches while strutting for the attentions of waifish secretaries with shoulder tattoos.

I valeted the Jeep, waded through the Friday-night crowd, and found her perched on a stool at the bar, in a little black dress and pumps, nursing a margarita.

She was even more petite on a bar stool than she'd appeared on horseback and somehow, impossibly, more beautiful. Her crossed legs were slender and tanned and her hair, save for a few fugitive strands, was piled atop her head in a complicated sort of twisting maneuver. She was at once both cuddly and breathtaking — a sort of Gen Y Holly Golightly.

"I am, for your information," I announced over the din, wedging a bar-stool into the narrow space beside hers, earning looks from the circling pack.

"You are what?" she asked, unleashing that killer smile.

"A good lawyer. Just like you'd hoped."

Her face went blank, and then she remembered.

"Oh, right. Well, good for Sydney. Here's to her."

She lifted her glass and sipped.

"What is it, exactly, that you have against my client?"

"Well, let's see," she said, leaning in to be heard. "How do I explain this? In the horse world, there are basically two kinds of people. The first are people who genuinely love horses, and who ride for the sheer joy of it, all the time in awe of the fact that these huge, beautiful creatures trust you enough to let you just climb onto their backs and guide them around, asking nothing in return."

"That would be you, I presume."

"Very astute. And then there are people who like the *idea* of horseback riding, or the image I guess, but have no empathy or sense of wonder about the bond between horse and rider. To them, riding is just something that looked chic in a magazine. They have no interest in learning to communicate with their horse, and no interest whatsoever in their horse's feelings or well-being."

"And that would be Sydney?"

"No, I'm afraid not. Sydney Everett is in another category altogether. She's in it strictly for the money, which makes her toe-jam in my book."

She toasted again, and sipped.

"Is there money in horses?"

She thought that was funny.

"I know a woman who made a million dollars in show jumping. Know how?"

"No."

"By starting with two million. And owning a Hush Puppy or a Creole is even worse, what with all the training and special care and travel. The prize money doesn't begin to cover the overhead."

"What's a Creole?"

She set her glass down hard, splashing the bar. "You're joking, right?"

I showed her my palms. "Take pity. I'm new to all this."

She leaned in closer. "Creole was one of the best show jumpers the West Coast ever produced. Michael Martin won bronze at the Pan American Games on Creole in 2003, then Tamara Zwart rode him to a team silver at the 2004 Olympics. Then, around five years ago, just at the height of his career, Creole bowed a tendon at Indio, which would have put him out of competition for around a year or two at most." She licked the salt on her glass. "Except that he was found dead in his stall three weeks later."

I saw it coming then, and it wasn't a pretty sight.

"That's right," she said, her dark eyes blazing. "Rumor has it that Sydney collected a cool million on that one."

I managed a weak smile. "Anything else you know about my client that I should, but obviously don't?"

"As a matter of fact," she said, lowering her voice to a whisper. "Last week she canceled an appointment with her doctor, and Dow Corning stock fell five points."

I ordered the rib eye, a decision of which Tara clearly did not approve.

"If animals aren't meant to be eaten," I asked her, "then why are they made of meat?"

She ordered an arugula and watercress salad, of which even Escalator would have approved, and we proceeded to make the kind of small talk that, under ordinary circumstances, I try to avoid during a witness interview. I learned, for example, that she'd grown up in Marin County, north of San Francisco, where she and her late sister had ridden horses before they could walk, and where Tara had competed on her high school equestrian team.

I told her that my high school equestrian team was four guys shooting horse in the parking lot.

I also learned that she'd matriculated at Cal, but had dropped out to devote herself full time to riding. She'd trained in the Bay Area with a German guy whose name I was supposed to recognize, and then she'd made the move to L.A. five years ago, purchasing Escalator as a kind of reclamation project with money she'd earned giving lessons.

She'd been the stable manager at Fieldstone for almost four years now. While the pay was only so-so, she had full use of the club's facilities, plus she and Escalator got free room and board — he in a stall, and she in a dilapidated bungalow somewhere on the Fieldstone grounds.

"So, what does the stable manager do at a place like Fieldstone?" I asked, scanning the dessert menu.

"I order the hay and shavings. I schedule the manure removal . . ."

"Funny, that's the exact opposite of what I do."

She punched my arm. We were both a little drunk.

"I schedule the grooms, I coordinate each horse's feeding and medications, I make sure that each horse is tacked up and ready to ride when the owner wants to, and I make sure that each horse gets at least an hour of daily turnout."

"And you compete. Professionally?"

She nodded. "Last year I moved up to grand prix. That's the highest level in show jumping. The West Coast circuit is one of the best in the country. For years only Barbara Hauser represented Fieldstone in grand prix competition. Now, we sort of both do, although I'm the poor stepchild in the family."

"Meaning?"

"Meaning that the board of directors hasn't seen fit to sponsor me the way they do Barbara."

"Why not?"

"That's a good question. Ask your client."

She sounded more perplexed than bitter.

"Do you still give lessons? I might need a new hobby."

"I'm afraid you're out of luck. Barbara is the head riding instructor at Fieldstone. All of the other instructors report to her. I don't report to her."

She said this in a way that suggested she didn't want to report anything to Barbara Hauser, except maybe that Barbara's house was on fire.

The waitress returned, and I ordered an Irish coffee, in honor of my lovely dinner companion. She ordered chamomile tea, apropos of nothing.

"I take it Barbara competed on Hush Puppy."

She nodded. "At the major events she did."

"So what'll she do now?"

"I don't know. Learn to ride, I suppose."

She'd been twisting a loose strand of hair with her finger, but now she stopped.

"Actually, Barbara has plenty of other horses she can ride, but none is in the same league as the Pup."

"Will Barbara be around Fieldstone this weekend?"

"I think so. I'm pretty sure she's got lessons tomorrow. Why do you ask?"

"Because I'm a man of action. And I have an inquisitive nature."

She gave me an apprising look. "You'll like Barbara. Most men do. She's glamorous, she's beautiful, and she's got *scads* of money."

"Nope. Doesn't sound like my type."

She giggled. I liked making her giggle.

"I thought you said there was no money in horses."

"Not in horses, no. Barbara gets these, like, residual checks every month. She used to be on television."

"Unless she was on *Monday Night Football,* I probably missed her."

She smiled, tracing a circle on the tablecloth with her finger.

"She was on a daytime soap called *After Yesterday.* She played the slutty little blonde."

"Let me guess. It wasn't a stretch."

"Well," she said. "The blond part, maybe."

The drinks finally arrived. We cradled our cups, blowing steam into the empty space between us.

"Sydney says that you were the last person to see Hush Puppy alive."

She shrugged. "I walk the barns before dinner. There's a night groom, but he's usually busy cleaning tack."

"Did the horse seem all right to you?"

She thought about that. "There was nothing about his appearance or behavior that seemed out of the ordinary. If there was, I'd have called George."

"You did call George," I reminded her.

"When Enrique told me that Hush Puppy was down, I called his exchange. But by then, he was already dead."

"What happened next?"

"I called Sydney. Then, I assume, she called the insurance people. She probably has them on speed dial."

I set the cup down and folded my arms. "Do you really think my client's a horse killer?"

She studied me a long time before shaking her head.

"I don't know. But let me put it this way. I think she's *capable* of killing a horse. And that's the worst thing you'll hear me say about anybody."

We stood in line at the little valet stand on the sidewalk. The night had turned chill and I draped my jacket over her shoulders. She shivered and leaned her head into my chest, quietly humming along with the tinny music that played on the valet attendant's radio. It was a Mexican *ranchera* number, and she seemed to know the tune.

While the sidewalk teemed with strolling shoppers and the valets ferried a succession of Beemers and Benzes to the departing diners, we were like a tranquil little island in a rushing river of people and cars, horns and lights.

I reminded myself that this wasn't supposed to be a date. More like an interrogation, really, but it had somehow ended up here on the sidewalk, where I found my arm around her shoulders and my heartbeat in her ear, both of us in no hurry for the cars to arrive and the evening to end.

Then the Wrangler pulled to the curb, and the spell was broken. She handed back my jacket, and before I could speak she stepped quickly from the sidewalk and into the driver's seat, and the attendant slammed the little door behind her.

"Hey, wait a minute!" I protested, and she rolled down the window. Then a second Wrangler — also black — pulled up from behind. She read the look on my face, and turned, and then we both laughed. And then with the grinding of gears and the roar of her engine, she was gone. But her smile seemed to hang for a moment, disembodied in the night air like a Lewis Carroll apparition.

And then I blinked, and it too was gone.

3

Come sunrise, Sam had both paws on the bed and was nudging my arm with his cold, wet nose. Sam is half golden retriever and half drill sergeant, and sleeping in on weekends is against regimental policy.

My official title upon joining Henley & Hargrove was "Of Counsel," a flexible term that in my case meant I'd been hired in a probationary capacity, but with the tacit understanding that if I didn't grope the secretaries or steal from the petty cash, I'd make partner in a year.

In deference to that small uncertainty, I'd elected to rent when I'd moved up to Pasadena, settling into a cozy little cottage in a neighborhood of cozy cottages called Bungalow Heaven.

My house, like its neighbors, had a deep covered porch and two dormer windows that looked out over a sloping green lawn to a quiet and shaded street. The shingled exterior was UPS brown and girdled in gray river rock. The wooden shakes, the rock foundation, and the heavy beams at the eaves evoked a Yosemite Parkitecture that contrasted nicely with the stucco-and-aluminum orthodoxy of most L.A. suburbs.

Although I'd never before lived in Pasadena, I was no stranger to the environs. During my rookie rotation with the PD's office, I'd spent a month working the Northeast District courthouse on Walnut Street, and Sam and I had done a bit of hiking in the foothills north of town. Pasadena was the kind of sun-dappled oasis of palm trees, purple mountains, and Spanish missions depicted on Depression-era orange crate labels. And unlike most of Southern California, it had remained in many ways unchanged in the eight decades that followed.

I fed Sam his breakfast, then climbed into the shower. I do some of my best thinking in the shower, and today I was thinking I had at least one plausible answer to the question I'd posed to Russ Dinsmoor — the one about motive.

In the clarity of the steaming water, it occurred to me that Tara Flynn had a pretty good motive, not to mention the means and opportunity, to hasten Hush Puppy's demise.

■ ■ ■ ■

The office when I got there was Saturday-morning quiet, and Dinsmoor was nowhere to be found. Ever since Muriel's death, Russ generally spent his weekends reading, or puttering in his garden, or playing Jack Sparrow on a ratty old sailboat that he kept in Marina del Rey.

I powered up my computer and began composing him an e-mail, but then decided against it. For one thing, there was no way of knowing when Russ would actually read it. As far as I could tell, Russ only turned his computer on when his office was cold. And besides, what I had to say to him was better said in person.

I read through the Friday afternoon mail, dictated a few letters for Bernie to transcribe on Monday, then listened to my voice messages, of which there were three.

The first was from a lawyer requesting an extension of time to respond to some interrogatories. Routine stuff. The second was from the claims guy in Vic Tazerian's case, letting me know that he'd received my fax, but that their decision was unchanged, explanatory letter to follow. And so the dance of denial had begun.

The third message, to my surprise, was from Tara. It came in after midnight, and she sounded a little sleepy.

"Hello, Jack MacTaggart. I got your number from the Yellow Pages. Isn't it a little cheesy for a lawyer to advertise in the Yellow Pages? But I guess it's not advertising if it's just your name and phone number. I mean, it's not like '1-800-CAR WRECK' or anything, right? So I guess you're still okay. A girl can't be too careful.

"Anyway, I wanted to thank you for dinner, and for sharing your jacket. And if you're still interested in show jumping, I wanted to invite you to come out to the Equestrian Center in Burbank on Sunday. There's a fifty-thousand-dollar grand prix that starts at one o'clock, and I'll leave a ticket for you at the Will Call window. And if I win, then dinner's on me. How's that for a deal? So . . . that's about it. I hope you get this. All right, then. Sweet dreams."

I didn't need a mirror to tell me I had a stupid grin on my face. Uncle Louis always said that beauty was an overrated virtue. Well, what he'd actually said was, "Show me a beautiful woman, and I'll show you some guy who's tired of fucking her."

But Tara Flynn was more than just beautiful. She was also funny, headstrong, sexy,

58

compassionate, earthy, and just a little bit vulnerable. I think he would have liked her.

I sat for a minute to ponder my options. The most obvious, of course, was to pay a visit on Barbara Hauser at Fieldstone. I also wanted to confront Sydney, in person, about this Creole business, but I had no idea where to find her. So I logged into Omega, the firm's time-and-billing software program, in search of her account information.

I went straight to the active client list, and there, between EVAgen, LLC, and Ever Ready Construction, Inc., were all of Sydney Everett's vital statistics, including her home address, phone number, fax number, e-mail address, social security number, and cup size. Okay, maybe not her cup size.

I remembered the cassette tape as I waited for the down elevator. I had tossed it into my in-box on Friday morning, then forgot all about it. I considered waiting until Monday, but curiosity overtook me before the elevator did, so I retreated back to my office.

I slipped the microcassette into my Dictaphone, thumbed the Play button on the handset, and listened as the mellifluous tones of Porky's voice filled the little room.

"Today is Thursday, October the seventeenth, and we're here at the Fieldcrest

Riding Club in Flintridge, California —"

"Fieldstone."

That was Sydney.

"What?"

"The Fieldstone Riding Club. You said Field-crest. They make towels, I believe."

"The Fieldstone *Riding Club in Flintridge, California. This is Patrick Bowman of MLIC Risk Management on behalf of the Metropolitan Livestock Insurance Company. This is a recorded statement of . . . Mrs.?"*

"Mrs. is fine."

"Mrs. Sydney Everett, who is the owner of the insured animal. Mrs. Everett, do I have your permission to tape record this statement?"

"Do I have any choice?"

"Well, we need to get a statement."

"Then record away."

"Okay. Let's see. How long have you owned the insured animal?"

"I've owned Hush Puppy for almost four years. Is that right, George? Four years?"

"And when was the last time you saw the insured animal alive?"

"Well now, that's a good question. I'd say it was Tuesday afternoon that I was watching Barbara work him out. So the answer is Tuesday."

"Okay. And when's the last time anybody

saw the horse alive as far as you know?"

"Well, it must have been Barbara. She trains the horse for me. Barbara Hauser. H-A-U-S-E-R. She's one of the instructors here at the club. She rides him just about every day."

"Okay. Let's see. Was the horse sick or injured as far as you know? Hey!"

The tape went dead. I stared at the handset for the better part of a minute before ejecting the tape from the machine and placing it carefully into my bottom drawer.

That's the drawer that locks.

It was high noon when I reached the front gate at Fieldstone where, as a testament to my elevated social standing, Colonel Mustard emerged to greet me without his clipboard. He directed me to the stable office, where, he told me ominously, I should ask for Margaret Carlton, the weekend manager.

The office, when I found it, stood like a control tower at the center of a deluxe equestrian complex. It was a cubical building with windows on all sides, affording a 360-degree view of the trucks, trailers, horses, grooms, riders, children, and dogs that seemed to ebb and flow in tidal fashion between and among the surrounding barns.

Each of the windows was underscored by an old-fashioned planter box from which a profusion of colored flowers spilled. And above the blooms, like a spider at the center of her web, floated the head and shoulders of a smallish woman, her darting eyes alert to the activity around her.

The office door was open, but I knocked anyway.

"Come in," the woman said flatly, her voice a rusty hinge.

"Mrs. Carlton? My name's MacTaggart," I began, but she stopped me with an upraised palm as she lifted a microphone from the counter.

"Groom, please, to the west mounting block." Her amplified voice echoed among the barns.

"Lazy wetbacks," she thought aloud, her fingers drumming, her raptor's eyes probing the shadows. "We ought to deport the lot of 'em. Of course, they'd all be back in a week. They're like cockroaches that way."

She was a charmer all right.

Between the windows, the walls of the small office displayed framed photos of riders jumping beautiful horses over absurdly high fences. In a low trophy case was a folded Olympic flag, along with silver platters and loving cups of every shape and size. A filing cabinet, a chalkboard, and a small watercooler completed the inventory.

Leaning atop the cabinet was a framed poster commemorating something called the Silver Anniversary Fieldstone Grand Prix, featuring mirror images of leaping horse-and-rider combinations. On the left was the unmistakable profile of Tara Flynn, her jutting chin buried into Escalator's flying mane. On the right was a Nordic blonde astride a leaping white horse that I knew, somehow, to be Hush Puppy.

"Handsome poster, don't you think?"

Margaret Carlton was turned now in her chair. She was a wiry woman of beyond middle years, with sparse russet hair and thin orange lips.

"Indeed," I said, noting that the event was only two weeks away. "It makes me think that if I continue to walk the path of righteousness, I may one day be lucky enough to reincarnate as a saddle."

She frowned her disapproval, and I smiled brightly.

"Jack MacTaggart, to see Miss Barbara Hauser."

"Regarding?"

"Yes. Well, Barbara and I are collaborating on a plan to limit the number of Mexicans in the show-jumping industry, and I brought over some schematics for my Big Moat concept. It's all very exciting."

Her frown melted into a scowl. She didn't know what to make of me, and I didn't give a hang what she thought. As she was formulating a response, I spied over her shoulder the selfsame Nordic blonde walking a rust-colored horse down the ramp of an enormous trailer. I excused myself and followed.

Barbara Hauser wore tight blue jeans under black leather chaps that framed her shapely derriere in a fashion vaguely reminiscent of a *Playboy* centerfold Uncle Louis had once given me, and that I'd kept under my mattress for most of the sixth grade. She was half a head taller than Tara, but still couldn't have weighed a buck twenty soaking wet. Which, at the moment, didn't seem like a bad idea.

The trailer from which she'd emerged was a full-on eighteen-wheeler hitched to an idling Kenworth tractor, dark green with polished chrome, the door of which bore the inscription BARBARA HAUSER in flowing white script, above the words EQUESTRIAN ENTERPRISES, INC.

She held the horse's lead rope in one hand and a riding crop in the other. Her thick ponytail, the color of sun-bleached straw, swayed in rhythm with her walk.

"Barbara?"

She stopped the horse and turned, a

gloved hand shading her eyes.

"My name's Jack MacTaggart. Can I have a word?"

"Sure," she said. "What about?"

"I'm Sydney Everett's lawyer."

"With Henley and Hargrove?"

"That's right."

She turned on her heel and kept walking. "Come on over here, where we can talk in private."

She handed the rope to a passing groom and gestured with the crop to an open door.

It was a small tack room lined with wall-mounted saddles. The air was heavy with dust and leather, like an old baseball glove resurrected from the back of a closet. Beneath each saddle was a wooden chest, each chest emblazoned with the FRC logo.

As she entered behind me, a familiar voice rasped over the loudspeaker.

"Barbara, shall I call security?"

She stepped back into the sunlight, waving to the spider woman.

"No, Margaret, it's okay!" she called, then pulled the door behind her.

"I'm sorry to bother you," I began, "but I wanted to ask a few —"

She wheeled and jabbed the crop, like a fencer's foil, into my sternum. "Cut the bullshit! Where the fuck is Jared?"

I'm not the type to be easily surprised, but she had surprised me.

"Roswell, New Mexico," I told her, brushing aside the crop. "The big alien abduction symposium."

"Oh, you're a riot. What are you, the muscle? Well, I've got a message for him, *and* for you. *Nobody* fucks with Barbara Hauser, you got that? Not Jared Henley, not Sydney Everett, and certainly not the likes of *you!*"

The last pronoun she'd punctuated with another jab to my heart.

"Look," I said, moving the crop with my finger. "I can see that you're upset, which under the circumstances I can understand. But let me assure you, I have no idea what the hell you're talking about."

"I knew Sydney was fed up, but I never thought she was stupid! What did you Einsteins think the insurance people were gonna say? That horse was HSA tested two weeks ago! She's going down, dumbfuck, and so are you!"

"Listen very carefully," I said, struggling to control my voice. "First of all, I never even heard of Hush Puppy, or met Sydney Everett, until Thursday, okay? Secondly, if you think you know something about what happened, then I'd love to hear it. In fact, we can go to the police right now, and you can tell *them* about it. But whatever you do, don't you ever, and I mean *ever,* accuse me of wrongdoing, you got that, Blondie?"

We locked eyes for a moment, and then the set of her jaw softened as her weight sagged backward against the door.

"I'm sorry," she said, her head wagging. "I was totally out of line. This has been a really bad week for me. You have no idea."

She took a deep breath and managed a smile. "My therapist says I have anger issues."

"Tell your therapist they're contagious."

She smiled again, this time for real. "It's Jack, is it?"

"That's right."

"Where is Jared, really?"

"Why are Jared's whereabouts so important?"

She shrugged. "I don't know. He's the one who handles Sydney's legal affairs, isn't he?"

"Today that's me. Is there something you'd like to share?"

She examined one of the saddles, running her gloved finger along the stitching.

"I wish I had something to share. I was at the Oaks all week, down in Capistrano. I only heard about it yesterday. I think . . . well, I think I'm still in shock." Her eyes, newly moist under fluttering lashes, rolled to meet mine. "I guess I've been looking for someone to blame, Jack. I'm sorry it was you."

And with that she turned, yanked open the door, and stepped into the sunlight, the crop thrust forcefully into her seat pocket. She marched past the semi and toward the barn office, where over her shoulder I could see Margaret Carlton speaking urgently into a telephone.

I shaded my eyes and followed the crop, wagging as it was like a metronome in time with her walk. And unlike her acting, her rhythm was damn near perfect.

Flint Canyon Road ran in serpentine fashion through an oak-studded ravine that was dry as yet, awaiting arrival of the winter rains. At irregular intervals, imposing gates marked the entrances to hillside estates whose slate or mission tile roofs were sometimes visible above the treetops. I passed a car with Armed Response emblazoned on its doors, the driver craning his neck to read my plate.

It was the kind of neighborhood where the nannies pushed the strollers, the trainers walked the dogs, and even the coyotes had some kind of pedigree.

The entrance to the Everett estate was like the others, only more so. Bracketed by ten-foot pillars of hewn granite, the elaborately filigreed gate looked like something copied from the Palace at Versailles. Or possibly vice versa.

On one side was a push-button call box, and on the other, to my surprise, was a sign for the Flintridge Realty Company. I maneuvered the Wrangler and pushed the intercom. After a moment, the voice of a man spoke, as through a paper towel tube.

"May I help you?"

"Jack MacTaggart for Mrs. Everett."

"Who?"

"Mrs. Everett."

"No, who's calling please?"

"MacTaggart!"

"Are you expected?"

As a matter of fact, I wasn't.

"Define expected."

"I beg your pardon?"

"I'm with Flintridge Realty!"

Okay, so I fibbed. But the gates glided open, allowing me to ascend a long and shaded driveway to a parking area hard by an enormous stone fountain. From there, a brick walkway crossed a wide emerald lawn and rose to the front doors of the largest private residence I'd ever seen in my life —

a three-story castle done up in old brick and ivy, and topped by a gray slate roof.

The look was go-to-hell British aristo-cratic, complete with gables, turrets, leaded glass galore, and a dozen or so wrought-iron balconies, and it was only slightly smaller than the American Airlines terminal at LAX.

As I mounted the steps, one of the front doors opened and a slight Asian man of sixty or so years stepped out to greet me. He wore a good blue suit with the jacket buttoned, and he carried himself with the haughty air of a Beverly Hills maître d'.

"Mr. MacTaggart," he pronounced. "Do come in. I'll alert Mrs. Everett to your ar-rival."

He led me through a large and empty foyer to a sitting room, which was likewise mostly empty but for one couch, one coffee table, and one side chair, all draped in sheets, and with carpet rings marking where the other furniture had been. He gestured to the couch, and I sat facing the treetop view across the canyon, while he set off to find the lady of the manor.

When he'd returned a minute later, he cleared his throat and gestured for me to follow. We passed back through the foyer, then up a marble staircase to the second-floor landing. From there we followed a long hallway, where hooks and nails in the wood-paneled walls attested to the absence of artwork. A Styrofoam packing peanut crunched underfoot.

"Where are we going?"

"To the gymnasium, sir."

As we approached the hallway's end, I could hear the muffled rhythm of music. The houseman knocked loudly on the paneled double doors, then opened one without waiting for a response.

My ears were assaulted by the thumping bass line of a disco-era standard as I stepped into what had once been the ballroom; a cavernous, two-story space with a polished parquet floor and an elaborate gilt ceiling. The door closed firmly behind me.

Sunlight flooded the room from French doors open at the far end, reflecting off the mirrored panels that formed the other walls. Exercise machines loitered here and there as in an avant-garde sculpture garden, while chrome barbells rested on low steel racks. Meanwhile, Donna Summer's sonic vocals were loud enough to loosen a filling.

Sydney Everett sat hunched over the handlebars of an electronic exercise bicycle, pedaling hard in time with the music. She wore a sports bra and some kind of bicycle shorts, both originally white, both now soaked to the color of wet newsprint. Her gleaming back was tanned and remarkably well-toned, and her snakelike vertebrae rippled with her effort.

I walked to the stereo cabinet and jabbed at the Power button, silencing Donna in mid-wail. The silence, as they say, was deafening.

"So, you're in the real estate game now!" she called without turning.

My footfalls echoed as I walked.

"This is L.A. Everyone's in the real estate game, one way or another."

As I reached the machine she stopped pedaling and pushed a button on the console. Numbers flashed and a tone sounded. She studied the readout for a moment, then turned on the seat to face me.

Her hair had been twisted into a knot, but a few strands had worked themselves free and now clung to the sides of her neck. Her face was shining, and the rise and fall of her breasts strained the fabric of her top to the point of material failure.

"Speaking of real estate, how big is this place, anyway?"

"Nine bedrooms," she breathed, "depending on how you count."

"I count sequentially."

72

She looked at me and smiled.

"I'm sure you do."

"And how many children did it take to fill nine bedrooms?"

"Dear boy," she said, untangling herself from the machine. "Children cause stretch marks."

She'd plucked the towel from the handlebars, and now she dabbed at her face as we walked. I followed her onto the balcony, where a pitcher of ice water and a lone crystal goblet were waiting on a wicker table.

"I thought you had sons," I said, trying hard to admire only the canyon view as she leaned over to pour.

"No, Jack. Harold had sons. Four of them. You can't pin them on me. Would you like a drink? An eye-opener, perhaps?"

She drained her glass, then she refilled it and did it again. Over the rim of the glass, she was watching me watching her.

"Looks like you're getting ready to move."

She set down the glass and dabbed at her mouth with the towel.

"Please don't tell Russell. Not yet, anyway. He'll be upset that I didn't ask him to review the contract."

"Where are you going?"

"A condo. Over on Orange Grove."

As condo locations went, Pasadena's Orange Grove Boulevard was still in the high-rent district, but it was area codes removed from this place.

"Do you know the difference between a condominium and gonorrhea?" I asked her.

She arched an eyebrow. "No, tell me."

"Nowadays, you can get rid of gonorrhea."

She laughed at that.

"As much as I've enjoyed this house," she said, gesturing, "it's a bit *much,* if you know what I mean. Since Harold died, I've felt like I'm haunting the place. Downsizing will be a welcome change."

"What about all the furniture?"

She shrugged. "What I can't use or consign, I'm placing in storage."

"Remind me to buy stock in Public Storage."

Still facing me, she leaned back with both elbows resting on the railing, her nipples visibly erect in the cool canyon air. Not that I'd ever notice such a thing.

"Where did Russell find you, anyway? You don't seem to fit the Henley and Hargrove mold. You're much too . . . I don't know. *Vigorous.*"

"You mean rough around the edges."

"Perhaps." She studied my edges. "But that's nothing to be ashamed of. I was as

74

rough as they come, before I met Harold. Then, over the years, I don't know. We bought this house. A new wardrobe. Club memberships. Charity boards. The edges may smooth, but it's a thin veneer. What counts is what's in here," she said, tapping a lacquered fingernail against her pneumatic cleavage, oblivious to the irony of the gesture.

"So where did you and Harold first meet?"

She pouted theatrically.

"Now you're just being polite. I liked you better when you were rough."

She moved forward as she said this, stopping only when her breasts, like the oversized fenders of a small yacht, had firmly docked with my rib cage.

"Is that why you came here, Jack? To *pump* me for information?"

I don't know if she expected me to fall over backward or to take her up in my arms, and the truth be told, I damn near did both.

"You flatter me, Mrs. Everett. You're a very handsome and accomplished woman. But at the risk of sounding trite, you are old enough to be my mother."

"Wasn't it Freud who said that all boys secretly want to sleep with their mothers?"

"No," I told her. "That was my Uncle Louis. And it was cheerleaders."

She laughed again as she eased herself backward.

"You're precious, do you know that? I *was* a cheerleader. First in Baton Rouge, then at Southern Cal. Only they called us Song Girls then. *That's* where I met Harold."

"And what was he, captain of the football team?"

"Goodness, no. He was chairman of the board of trustees. It was quite a scandal at the time." She sighed. "But when Harold set his mind on something, he could be very persuasive. His boys hated me, of course. They still do. They made all sorts of threats about the estate, but Russell took care of that. I still miss him terribly. Harold, I mean. But that's not why you came all the way out here, is it, Jack?"

I scraped back a chair and sat.

"No, ma'am. I came to ask you about Creole."

She retrieved the glass and carried it to the railing.

"What about Creole?"

"What about him? Did it ever occur to you that Creole was something I should have known about?"

She flushed ever so slightly.

"It never occurred to me that he was something you *didn't* know about. Russell

76

certainly knew. And Jared certainly knew. Don't they include you in the meetings, sugar?"

Touché.

"Insurance companies don't believe in co-incidences, Mrs. Everett. And normally, neither do I."

"Sydney. Then you both have a lot to learn."

"Did they fight you on the last claim?"

"I wouldn't call it a *fight* exactly. There were some delays, of course. Some letters. Jared handled it."

I raised my eyebrows. The expression "Jared handled it" wasn't one you heard every day.

"Was there an autopsy?"

"It's called a necropsy, sugar. And yes, there was. But they found . . . well, no reason to deny the claim."

"And what will the necropsy show this time?"

She flushed again, deeper.

"I'll tell you what it *won't* show. It won't show any wrongdoing on *my* part. And if you don't believe that, then maybe I am speaking to the wrong lawyer."

"Okay," I said. "I'm sorry. But that's the kind of heat you can expect with this claim. Of course, Jared will be back soon, and I'll understand if —"

"No," she cut me off. "I'd rather you handle it. I meant what I said before. I like your style, Jack. And I hope I didn't —"

"Forget it. When I said I was flattered, I meant it."

She cast her eyes downward, the better to contemplate her two-hundred-dollar Nike cross-trainers.

"Tell me something. Why'd you tell Bowman that you'd seen Barbara ride Hush Puppy on Tuesday? Barbara says she was out of town all week."

She came over and sat, looking earnest.

"Did I say that? Isn't that just the *silliest* thing? I must have been in shock. You see, that's *exactly* why I need you to be there for me, Jack."

Like a trick knee, Sydney Everett's Bourbon Street drawl seemed to come and go without warning. Right now she was wall-to-wall y'all.

"Don't get me wrong," she continued. "Jared's a capable enough young man. But he *is* rather young. And you know I think the *world* of Russell. I mean, Russell could talk a possum out of a magnolia tree. But sometimes he just isn't, I don't know, *tough* enough. Do you know what I mean?"

She was wrong, of course, about Dins-

78

moor. As for Jared Henley, his problem wasn't youth. He was, in fact, only a couple years younger than me. Jared's problem was that he was born on third base and thinks he hit a triple.

"Okay," I said. "If I'm going to represent you, then I'll need your help with something. Who else besides you might have had a motive to kill your horse?"

"*Kill* Hush Puppy? Who would want to do such a thing?"

"I don't know. That's what I'm asking you."

"And you think *I* had a reason to do so?"

"Offhand, I can think of two million reasons."

She started to respond, her eyes flashing anger, but she settled instead on a sigh of resignation.

"You have a lot to learn about horses, Jack. And about people. We stable over two hundred head at Fieldstone at any given time. I'll bet if you checked the records, you'd see that three or four horses die every year, for all kinds of reasons. Injury, colic, old age. There's no reason for you, or the insurance company, or anyone else to think that . . . that this is unusual. You heard George. Sometimes these things *happen*."

"I heard Wells rule out both injury and

colic, whatever that is."

She shrugged, as if to say, Life is a Mystery. "You say you've spoken with Barbara? What did she tell you?"

"She seemed angry. At you, I think."

She sat up and splayed a hand at her throat.

"At *me?* Why me?"

"She didn't say, exactly. Oh, but she did say that you were fed up."

"Fed up? Fed up with what?"

"I don't know. I was hoping you could tell me. I was also hoping —"

But before I could finish the thought, the butler appeared in the doorway and loudly cleared his throat.

"Very sorry to interrupt, ma'am, but your tea begins in one hour."

"Oh, dear. Thank you, Lim. I'll be right along."

He nodded and withdrew, and Sydney placed a hand on my forearm.

"If you're going to be my lawyer, Jack, the first thing I'll need is your help in giving Hush Puppy a proper burial. I've given the matter a great deal of thought. I'll clear it with the other board members, but you'll have to deal with the authorities. You can't plant a tree these days without getting a permit from somebody or other."

"A burial at Fieldstone?"

"Exactly."

"You mean his ashes, I assume."

"I most certainly do not."

"All right," I said without conviction.

"Good." She draped the towel over her neck as she stood, and I followed her into the ballroom, where Lim lurked behind the curtains like a player in a B movie. I wondered how long he'd been listening. Then, at the doors leading to the hallway, she stopped and turned to face me, offering her hand.

"Tell me the truth, Jack, and please don't be modest. Do you win all the cases you handle?"

"Let me put it this way," I said, taking it. "I've never come in worse than second."

4

The Los Angeles Equestrian Center isn't really in Los Angeles, but rather in Burbank, near the spot where Western Avenue dead-ends into the L.A. River. Which isn't really a river, but more like an open concrete culvert that carries L.A.'s gray water and other urban effluent past towering walls of graffiti on a long, snaking journey toward the Pacific Ocean.

I'd never been to this part of town before, and I could see no compelling reason to return. The homes were small and tired, with swaybacked barns and dusty riding rings visible through broken fences. It was an urban equestrian neighborhood that must have known better days.

In the strip malls along Western, feed and tack stores rubbed shoulders with the usual assortment of taco joints, nail parlors, and donut shops. And once on Riverside Drive, old vaqueros in straw cowboy hats rode stringy horses two abreast toward forgotten roundups in the cracked gutter of the roadway.

I turned off of Riverside, joining the line of late-model cars inching toward the Equestrian Center's entrance. There a bridle path crossed the driveway, forcing you to wait for a gap in the Sunday afternoon rent-a-horse traffic to finally pass under a soaring wooden archway. And then, as if by magic, you entered another world.

White board fencing surrounded rolling green lawns. Spotless white buildings, neatly trimmed in green, sat in nests of colorful flowers. Long hedgerows divided lawns from pastures, and pastures from riding arenas. It was as though a little slice of Virginia horse country had been uprooted and gently planted on the hardscrabble banks of the L.A. River.

I paid my money to park, and was swept by the tide of traffic to an outlying dirt lot. My original plan had been to find a shady spot for the Jeep, crack the windows, and leave Sam inside with a bowl of water. But I'd seen enough dogs on leashes to conclude that he might actually be welcome, and so we set out together, following the crush of spectators toward the big white tents, the country and western music, and the smell of grilling meats.

I announced our arrival at the Will Call window, where a leather-skinned woman in turquoise jewelry, like one of those Incan mummies you see in *National Geographic,* handed me a small white envelope in which I found both an admission ticket and a lunch coupon. When I asked her if my golden retriever was welcome inside, she rasped, "Honey, if he don't scare the horses, he's welcomer'n Brad Pitt in my bathtub."

The atmosphere outside the gates was charged and festive, like that of a small county fair. There were outdoor bars, and food tents, and vendors in freestanding trailers selling all nature of equine paraphernalia, from ten-thousand-dollar French saddles to two-dollar horseshoe earrings. There was also a big display of Ford pickup trucks, alongside an area showcasing new horse trailers of every shape and size.

The crowd was overwhelmingly female — an even mixture of western cowgirls and English huntswomen — with a sprinkling of stallions mixed in for color. The latter, I noticed, seemed to congregate by the bars and the trucks. I also noticed that many of the teen and preteen girls had come dressed to ride, in tan breeches and high boots, which must be the horseshow equivalent of bringing your baseball glove to Dodger Stadium.

It was a sunny day, unseasonably warm for mid-October, and I wore a Loyola T-shirt over khaki shorts and sneakers, plus a Dodger cap and sunglasses, all of which made Sam and I look like we'd taken a wrong turn on our way to the Glendale Galleria. Even so, several of the girls stopped to pet and coo at Sam, which always happened when we were out together in public. Sam was a canine Cary Grant, and females of every species turned weak-kneed in his presence.

As we circled the grounds, I spied a booth hawking the wares of the Metropolitan Livestock Insurance Company of Baltimore, Maryland. The booth was manned by a perky young cowgirl in a denim dress and pigtails, whose job was to smile at the passersby and hand out folded brochures. According to their literature, Met Livestock offered "Equine Mortality and Major Medical insurance at rates unmatched by our competition."

Unbidden, the young proprietress launched into a speech that she'd obviously memorized for the occasion.

"Equine mortality insurance protects your investment in the event of death, theft, or humane destruction necessitated by accident, illness, or injury. Have you protected your investment, sir?"

"Well," I told her, "I put the hardtop on and locked all the doors."

That seemed to please her. "That's downright smart of you, sir."

When I asked her about Met Livestock's track record for paying claims, she said, "I don't know nothin' about no track records. But if you sign up for coverage today, you qualify for a chance to win that trailer over yonder."

I bought a five-dollar beer and led Sam to the entry gate, where I was handed a program and directed to one of the round tables that flanked two sides of a beautifully manicured lawn. The tables were draped in white linen with bright floral centerpieces and oversized umbrellas. Across the way, on the north side of the lawn, two grandstands swelled with the general admission spectators.

The area between the tables and the grandstand was around seventy yards square, and was dotted with riotously colorful jumps. They were delicate, almost sculptural affairs consisting of white or candy-striped poles resting between tall white standards, all of them decorated with potted plants and huge bouquets of brilliant flowers. One of the jumps had gigantic fiberglass Budweiser bottles as standards, lending a distinctly corn dog touch to an otherwise haute cuisine affair.

There were two gleaming Jaguars, themselves festooned in flowers, parked at opposite corners of the lawn. Each car came equipped with a toothsome model in evening dress, waving to the late arrivals.

A stately woman and two young girls, both dressed to ride, were already at the table when we arrived. Sam, after enduring the obligatory fawning and petting, settled down in the shade, and I asked the mom whether it was too late to bet the daily double.

Monica Stern was one of the huntswomen. She wore a wide-brim straw hat, big designer sunglasses, and lots of understated jewelry. She offered a firm hand and introduced her daughters as Rebecca, age fourteen, and Courtney, age twelve. Rebecca was the spitting image of her mother, a coltish young heartbreaker with a mane of chestnut hair and pale green eyes, while kid sister Courtney was apple-cheeked and pudgy. They were from Palos Verdes Estates, down in the South Bay, and I didn't have to see it to know that they'd driven up in a

Range Rover.

After the introductions and small talk, I confessed to Courtney that I was new to all of this, and she took pity on my ignorance.

"Inside the program," she explained in the kind of singsong cadence one normally reserves for foreigners or imbeciles, "there's a list of the horses and riders, and that's called the order of start."

"The order of go, stupid," said big sister Rebecca, earning an arched eyebrow from her mother.

"What ever. They have, like, a lottery to see who goes first. See?"

I found the sheet, which listed each horse, each rider, and each owner, followed by little boxes for keeping score. There were twenty-four entries in the competition, including Escalator and Tara Flynn, at number twenty-one. Number thirteen in the program was Hush Puppy and Barbara Hauser, owned by Mrs. Harold Everett of Flintridge, California.

A waitress stopped to ask if I'd seen the menu. I ordered three hot dogs, potato chips, and, not wishing to risk an arched eyebrow from Monica Stern, an iced tea.

"How come *I* can't have a hot dog?" Courtney complained to her mother.

"Because they're made from dead pigs,

dear," she replied evenly.

"And they're gross," added Rebecca, drawing no reproach this time from her mother.

The PA announcer welcomed us in a rumbling baritone to the Los Angeles Equestrian Center's Fall Classic Horse Show, just as two sequined cowgirls on matching pintos galloped onto the field trailing huge American flags. We all stood, Sam included, as a big-haired blonde stepped to the mic and warbled a Nashville version of the national anthem that wasn't too bad, finishing to polite applause and more galloping by the flag girls.

I asked Courtney for help in keeping score.

"It's really easy. If the horse knocks down a rail, it's four faults. If the horse refuses a jump, it's five faults."

"Four," said Rebecca, eyes rolling.

"Whatever. See the big clock? If you go over the time allowed, it's like a point for every second. Anyway, the rider with the fewest faults wins. And if more than one rider goes clear, there's a jump-off."

"How many faults," I asked, "for jumping onto the hood of the Jag?"

The first competitors had entered on course, and Darth Vader introduced them as "Liz Kelly on Highmeadow Farms' Superfly." They walked around for a while, then stopped, then started off at a canter.

The horse was brilliant white, the rider equally splendid in a red hunting jacket. They circled a couple of jumps at leisure, then tripped an electronic eye that started the big digital clock. The milling crowd fell totally silent.

"She's really good," hissed Courtney in a stage whisper.

They sailed over the first jump, surged forward, and jumped the next two in quick succession. Then they cut a sharp turn and jumped, turned again, then jumped three in close combination to a smattering of applause from the crowd, myself included. There was a tension in the air that seemed to build with every jump.

After two more efforts, they galloped toward a low white board and long-jumped over a water trough, sending up a splash where the horse's hoof had landed in the drink. A judge raised his flag, and the crowd released a collective groan.

"Toes in the pool!" exclaimed Courtney.

They continued undaunted, galloping and twisting, surging and flying over the remaining obstacles, around fifteen in all. By the time they'd tripped the electronic eye to finish, they'd knocked down two rails, plus the water foul. The crowd broke into applause.

"Twelve faults!" announced Courtney.

"She should have done four strides to the oxer, and she *totally* chipped in at the Liverpool," said Rebecca to her mother, who nodded in agreement.

The next rider was already on course. His name was Estrada, from Puerto Rico, and he easily weighed two hundred pounds. Monica, reading my mind, offered, "Show jumping, dressage, and three day are the only Olympic events in which men and women compete head-to-head."

Estrada stormed the course, finishing with eight jumping faults and two time penalties, which Courtney dutifully noted on her score sheet.

It was a star-studded field. There were former Olympians, current national team members, and past winners of this and that international grand prix. As each horse cleared the jumps without fault, the tension would build and the crowd would hold its collective breath. Then a rail would fall, and the balloon would suddenly deflate. Of the next ten riders, only one — an American with the unlikely name of Calico Simms — completed the course without fault, to whoops and thunderous applause.

After each round, Rebecca and her mother would critique the performance, finding fault with this or that approach, distance, or hand position. It was like watching a Yankee game from the Steinbrenner family box.

After the first dozen riders had gone, there was a break in the action. Then the PA man somberly announced, "Ladies and gentlemen, your attention please. The Los Angeles Equestrian Center joins the entire Southern California equestrian community in mourning the tragic passing of Hush Puppy, our defending Fall Classic champion."

There was a collective gasp from the crowd.

"Hush Puppy was a ten-year-old Holsteiner stallion owned by Mrs. Harold Everett of the Fieldstone Riding Club in Flintridge, California. Please join us in a moment of silence in memory of this great champion."

The audience fell silent, with many removing hats from bowed heads. When the competition finally resumed, the crowd was still abuzz.

Rebecca asked, "Oh my God, Mom! What happened?"

Monica shook her head. "I don't know, honey." She turned to me. "Hush Puppy was one of the finest horses we have. It's a huge loss for the sport. And for the U.S. Olympic effort."

And maybe, I told myself, for the Metropolitan Livestock Insurance Company.

By the time Escalator pranced onto the grass, only Simms and one other rider — a skinny guy from Brazil — had posted clear rounds. My palms were actually sweating as Tara steered him to the center of the field, backed a few steps, then took off at a slow canter.

She wore a black helmet and a fitted black jacket trimmed in gold, and Escalator wore a black-and-gold saddle pad and a matching doohicky on his ears. As she circled, the announcer rumbled, "Next on course is last year's Southern California rookie-of-the-year Tara Flynn on the twelve-year-old Hanoverian gelding, Escalator." There was a smattering of tepid applause.

The big horse sailed easily over the first three jumps, turned slowly, jumped clear again, then rounded toward the triple combination. I had a grip on the edge of the table as Escalator surged forward and jumped, strode, jumped, strode, and jumped again, barely brushing the third rail with a hind foot. The pole seemed to bounce in its cups and rock forward, but it stayed in place. The crowd gasped at first, then clapped.

Tara took Escalator wide and turned him like an aircraft carrier, nearly sideswiping one of the Jags. Then she spurred the big horse forward, clearing the next two obstacles with room to spare. As they turned toward the water trough she checked him, straightened his head, and thundered forward. He cleared the water with ease, checked up sharply, then cleared another double combination.

The big horse seemed to be gaining strength, with Tara battling for control. The crowd, meanwhile, had started oohing and cheering with every effort.

They circled to the far side of the field and jumped a combination along the fence, then cut diagonally across the center and floated over two more jumps, Escalator's hind legs kicking high into the air. He was tossing his head now, rooting at the bit, and Tara had to wrestle him into the final turn. There were only two more jumps to go.

The penultimate obstacle was a double-wide job with a small water trough below. Several horses had clipped the second rail, but Escalator cleared it easily as he thundered to the final jump, which consisted of the big beer bottles separated by white board planks. Tara checked him once, then checked again hard, releasing his head at the very last second. He sailed clear, and the crowd went wild.

"And it's three for the jump-off!" bellowed the announcer, and the spectators roared again. Tara, meanwhile, downshifted to a trot, then to a walk, thumping Escalator's gleaming neck as they exited through the gate.

"How about that?" I asked Rebecca, who'd managed to find fault with all the other riders.

"She was lucky. He's obviously too much horse for her. For starters, he needs a much stronger bit. Don't you think?"

Monica nodded. "A horse that size won't fare well in the jump-off."

"*I* think he's a beautiful horse," Courtney said, reading my face.

After the last three riders had finished, each with multiple faults, there was another break as the grounds crew rushed onto the course to reconfigure the jumps. I fed Sam his hot dog, and he indulged Courtney in another round of petting.

I asked her how the jump-off works.

"They race against the clock," she said, giggling as Sam lapped at her face. "The fastest clear round wins. And the course is much shorter. Only six or seven jumps.

You'll see."

After visiting our respective restrooms, Sam and I returned to find that the course had indeed been radically transformed. Many of the jumps were gone altogether, while others had been arranged into new combinations. And one of the Jaguars was now parked, amid a fresh explosion of flowers, smack in the middle of the action.

When the crowd was finally settled, the PA man announced, "Ladies and gentlemen, please welcome back on course our first competitor in today's jump-off, entry number one hundred seventeen, Calico Simms on Rocky Mountain Farms' Blue Zircon."

The horse was a dappled gray, and its rider wore a matching gray helmet with a sparkling red stripe. They stopped at the edge of the course while Simms surveyed the altered landscape. Then an electronic tone sounded and they started off in a loping canter, gathering speed as they approached the electronic eye.

By the time the clock was tripped, the horse was at full gallop. They jumped, turned sharply, jumped a double combination, then turned so sharply that the horse actually slipped on the beaten-down turf. The crowd gasped, but the horse steadied itself and bolted forward through a line of three jumps, then turned a sharp half-circle to another double combination. Finally, they looped a tight arc around the Jaguar and raced to the Budweiser jump, which they cleared to thunderous applause. The clock registered 37.21 seconds.

"Zero faults, thirty-seven point twenty-one seconds," Courtney intoned as she marked her sheet.

"Too slow," said Rebecca. "You'll see."

Monica added, "If you want to compare rounds, she landed off the last combination at exactly thirty-two seconds."

Next on course was the Brazilian, Diego Dos Santos, who was the reigning world champion and Olympic gold medalist. Tall and angular, he wore a pea green jacket with blue trim, and his chestnut-colored horse wore a matching saddle pad. Eden du Boilary seemed smaller and finer than the other horses, which I guessed would be an advantage on the twisting speed course.

And so it was. The little horse was sure-footed and catlike in the turns, essentially replicating Blue Zircon's performance, but with greater precision. When they touched ground at the final combination, the clock read thirty seconds flat. By the time they'd circled the car and cleared the beer bottles,

35.01 showed on the scoreboard, and the crowd roared its approval.

"See?" said Rebecca in triumph. "That's your winner."

Courtney glanced my way before marking her sheet. "We'll see."

As Tara trotted on course, Escalator reared up and bolted forward, giving two big bucks with his hind end. Tara somehow stayed on board, steadied him, and then brought him under control. The crowd tittered and whistled.

"What did I tell you?" said Rebecca. "She'll be lucky to stay in the tack."

"Ladies and gentlemen, our final rider on course is entry number one hundred twenty-one, Tara Flynn on Escalator. The time to beat is thirty-five point zero one seconds."

They were trotting now, Tara studying the new geometry as the crowd fell totally silent. Then the tone sounded and she stopped, backed three steps, and started off in a canter. The horse was fussing and throwing its head, but Tara pointed him to the first jump and kicked.

Escalator attacked the course like a thrashing shark, surging forward, jumping, turning and jumping again, with Tara's chin buried in his mane. Twice it looked as though he'd miss a jump altogether, only to have Tara yank his head at the last second. She appeared to be compensating for Escalator's size and long stride by taking the jumps at dangerously sharp angles, to the amazement and delight of the crowd. But despite her efforts, they still landed off the last combination at thirty-two seconds. Good for second place, perhaps, but not the blue ribbon.

And then Tara did something wonderful. While the other riders had looped around the Jaguar, as their horses' momentum required, Tara cut *inside* the car, kicking up a plume of flowers, and took Escalator through the last jump on two quick strides at an angle that rocked one of the standards. But the bottle remained upright, and the planks stayed in their cups, and the scoreboard clock froze at 35.00.

It took the crowd a moment to react. At first it appeared as though she'd lost control and gone careening off course. There was a collective gasp, then stunned silence, and then, finally, an explosive roar that rocked the grandstand, and may have startled seagulls off the beach out in Santa Monica.

I jumped and shouted, and Sam was barking, and we were both drowned out by the crowd, and by the announcer bellowing, *"Unbelievable! Tara Flynn and Escalator!*

Thirty-five seconds! What a round!"

The crowd remained standing as Tara brought Escalator back to a trot, and even from across the field I could see her hundred-watt smile light up the grandstand.

She was soon joined on course by Simms and Dos Santos, who shook her hand in turn and trotted their mounts over to the Jaguar. Some officials and photographers had gathered there, and ribbons were pinned to the horses' bridles: yellow on Blue Zircon, red on Eden, and finally, a big blue number on Escalator, who tried his best to bite at the trailing streamers. Tara was handed flowers and a folded blanket, and they all posed for pictures next to the car.

After all of that, the loudspeakers blasted Van Halen's "Jump" and the three horses cantered the perimeter of the field, ribbons streaming, to thunderous applause that followed them like a wave. As the procession passed our table, our eyes met and she shouted something over her shoulder that was lost in the din.

At the far end of the field, Simms and Dos Santos peeled off, leaving Tara to take a solo victory lap.

"Ladies and gentlemen, let's have a big L.A.E.C. round of applause for our new Fall Classic champions, Tara Flynn and Escalator!"

Again the crowd roared. Tara raised the flowers like a sword, allowing Escalator to charge the fence line at a gallop. Then, when they approached our table, she drew the horse up sharply and walked him to the railing. I doffed my hat and bowed, and she laughed as she stretched to hand me the bouquet.

"Come over to the barn!" she shouted, as Courtney clambered over her sister to paw at Escalator's neck.

By the time Tara had finished her lap, the applause had quieted and the buzzing crowd, like a thing unplugged, was filing for the exits.

There were tables set up at the entrance to the barn complex, behind which the three jump-off finalists were holding court for their fans, mostly teenaged girls, who waited patiently to have their programs autographed. Although it was Tara who'd taken the blue ribbon, I noticed that the line for the Brazilian, Dos Santos, was twice as long as the other two combined.

Tara had shed her helmet and jacket, and she was perched on the edge of a canvas chair, sipping bottled water and chatting with each of the girls in turn. A woman stood over her shoulder, jotting notes into a spiral notebook.

Sam and I ducked in behind a woman who was shepherding her daughter, a pudgy doppelganger, to the head of the line. When it was our turn at the front, I slid the program onto the table and Tara signed it before looking up.

"Thanks. I've been a huge fan, ever since Thursday."

She beamed, touching a hand to her throat.

"A huge fan," she said, "would have brought me flowers."

"Now that you mention it, I did have some flowers. But I gave them to a girl."

"A cute girl?"

"Very cute."

"How cute, exactly?"

"Well, when the braces come off, she'll be the prettiest sixth grader in Palos Verdes."

She noticed the leash, and her eyes followed it downward.

"And who's *this* big sweetie?" she enthused, leaning forward to look. Sam took this as an invitation to push his way under the table and clamber into her lap.

"Tara, Sam. Sam, Tara."

She buried her face in his ruff, and he reciprocated by nosing his way into her open shirtfront. He was a chip off the old block.

"C'mon, junior. Autographs only."

The reporter watched with detached amusement. "I can see you're busy, Tara, but one last question. What happened with Hush Puppy? Anything you can tell our readers?"

She nodded to me. "Here's the man to ask. This is Mrs. Everett's lawyer."

The woman offered a hand. "Hi. I'm Gwen Hickey, from the *Chronicle.*"

"Jared Henley." I smiled. *"Travel and Leisure."*

"What can you tell our readers about Hush Puppy, Jared?"

"He's dead."

"So we've heard. What was the cause?"

"He didn't say."

She looked at Tara, who shrugged.

"Well, what did the vet say?"

"Something about cardiac failure of unknown etiology. That means his heart stopped, but they don't know why."

She jotted some notes. "Anything else you can tell us?"

"Yeah. Never order iced tea at the Equestrian Center. I think they make it with old sweat socks."

It was right about then that Diego Dos

Santos stood up, stretched languidly, and ambled over to join us. He was still wearing his boots, his tighty-whitey riding pants, and a sweat-stained shirt in robin's egg blue. He was taller than I'd expected, but thin as a coat hanger, and he had a face that a romance novelist would probably describe as darkly handsome.

"You know, Tara," he said in a thick, Ricky Ricardo accent. "I never like to lose, but it's less difficult somehow losing to a beautiful woman. That was a very clever ride. Very clever, and very bold. Let me buy you dinner tonight. I'm intrigued by bold and clever women."

She turned in her seat to face him. "That's very sweet of you, Diego, but I already have plans for this evening."

He glanced at me across the table. "Break them. I'm flying to Belgium tomorrow, and this will be our only chance to get to know each other better."

"Thanks again, but no thanks."

He moved directly behind her, placing both hands on her shoulders. "All right then," he said, looking me square in the eye. "We can skip dinner, and we'll order room service at my hotel."

I reached across the table and grabbed his forearm, holding it upright like a broken umbrella as he tried to pull away.

"How'd you like to fly to Belgium without an airplane, Diego?"

"Let go of me! Who are you? This is an assault!"

"No. Technically, this is a battery. But I'd be more than happy to demonstrate an assault."

"Let go of me!"

This time it was more of a plea than a demand, so I set him free, and he stalked off toward the barns, rubbing his wrist and muttering over his shoulder in Portuguese. Or maybe it was Flemish. I was never very good with languages.

5

Lina Tazerian was sobbing again, her great bulk quivering under a floral-print house-dress. I walked to the credenza at the far end of the conference room and returned with a box of tissues.

"Oh, Mr. MacTaggart," she wheezed, blowing her nose loudly, "what are we going to do? Victor is not looking well again, and I'm afraid for him now very much."

"What we're going to do, Lina, is to get a lawsuit on file right away in order to obtain what's called an injunction, which is a court order requiring that Hartford Allied pay for the surgery. But first we'll need to find a doctor who's an expert in the field, and who has no financial stake in the outcome of the case. If we can get an expert declaration stating that this is a proven, nonexperimental treatment modality, then the court might — and I emphasize *might* — make Hartford Allied pay."

Her eyes, shining with hope and fear, looked up into mine.

"But how are we going to pay for such a doctor? And where will we find him?"

Both were good questions. Finding an oncologist with expertise in bone marrow transplantation shouldn't be difficult. Both UCLA and USC had outstanding cancer research facilities, as did the City of Hope, where Victor was currently in residence. Finding a doctor willing to take a stand against one of the nation's largest health insurance companies, however, was another matter entirely.

But that's where Russ's connections in the medical and insurance communities might come in handy. As for the cost, well, Henley & Hargrove would just have to front it, and hope that their soon-to-be partner doesn't bring home the silver medal.

"Lina, I don't know the answers to those questions yet," I told her. "And even if we find the right doctor, you have to understand that the court could still turn us down. That part is beyond our control. But the one thing I can promise you is that I'll do everything in my power to help Victor."

Her eyes welled up again, but she managed a tight smile.

"I know you will, Mr. MacTaggart. Victor

and I thank God for you every night." She took up my hand and pressed it against her sodden cheek. "God bless you."

One benefit of practicing in a firm like Henley & Hargrove was the abundance of associates, paralegals, and law clerks who stood ready and willing to tackle any task, no matter how complex or mundane, at any hour of the day, night, or weekend. Associates are salaried lawyers, usually in their first years of practice, who struggle mightily to impress their seniors in the hope that they, too, will one day be judged worthy of admission to the partnership.

There's a story, perhaps apocryphal, that's told about Thomas Dewey, the former governor of New York who nearly thwarted Harry Truman's reelection to the White House in 1948. Dewey in his later years founded a large and successful New York law firm that still bears his name. One Saturday morning, so the story goes, an associate was doing research in the firm's library when the telephone rang. To the young lawyer's chagrin it was Mr. Dewey himself, calling to say that he absolutely needed some research done immediately, and that he wanted a memo on his desk on Monday morning.

The associate's heart sank. He already had a project that would require him to work through the weekend. "Sir," he said, his voice quavering, "I'm afraid I'm just too busy to help you." Too busy? "Young man," said Dewey, his voice rising, "do you know to whom you're speaking?" Without missing a beat, the young lawyer replied, "Yes, sir, I do. But do *you* know to whom *you're* speaking?" Dewey was apoplectic. "No!" he barked. "Good," said the young lawyer, hanging up the phone.

Henley & Hargrove was blessed with a brace of top-notch associates, but none better than Marta Suarez — a petite force of nature who'd graduated first in her class at USC Law School. Barely twenty-six years of age, Marta had assisted me in the past, and she'd impressed me both with her limitless energy and with her preternatural poise in some very sticky situations.

It's said that in law school they teach you metalurgy, but that in practice you learn how to weld. Marta was book smart for sure, but for a doctor's daughter who'd taken her silver spoon to the best private schools, she was street savvy as well. I'd dubbed her Mayday, and the nickname had stuck. She was a welder.

I called her into my office and gave her

the lowdown on the Tazerian case. Her job would be to prepare a draft complaint and draft applications for both a temporary restraining order and a preliminary injunction. This would involve reading the Hartford Allied policy, researching some coverage issues, analyzing questions of jurisdiction, venue and federal law preemption, and ultimately preparing a declaration for our expert to sign.

And I needed it all by yesterday. In addition to whatever else was already on her plate.

"No problem," she said gamely, pushing her glasses up the bridge of her nose. "Anything else?"

"Anything more and we'll have to clone you. You can get the file from Bernie, and call me if you have any questions. And hey, Mayday, let me ask you something."

She looked up from her notes. "Yes?"

"A hypothetical. Let's say you're middle-aged and rich. Really rich, okay?"

"Okay so far."

"And let's say you own some horses, including one really valuable horse. It's worth . . . well, it's worth a lot."

"What, a racehorse?"

"No, it's a sport horse. It jumps over

fences. But it's a potential Olympic champion."

"All right."

"Why would you want to kill your horse?"

She gave the matter some thought.

"Because it clashed with my handbag?"

Did I mention that Mayday could be irreverent? When she saw I was serious, she set her legal pad aside.

"Okay, let's see. Do I have insurance on my horse?"

"Yes, you do. Lots of insurance. Only you're rich, so the money doesn't matter."

She tapped her pencil against her chin. "Well then, my horse must have been sick, and I was putting it out of its misery."

"Nope. Your horse was healthy as a horse."

"Then it was probably my husband's horse, and when I caught him in bed with the upstairs maid, I don't know, I just snapped."

I smiled. "Sorry, no husband."

She folded her arms. "Okay. In that case, I'm going to have to challenge your premise."

"Good," I said. "What part of my premise?"

"Either I'm not as rich as you think I am," she said, "or else I just didn't do it."

■ ■ ■ ■

Although the lunch hour had come and gone, Dinsmoor had returned none of my voice messages, even though Veronica had assured me that he was, in fact, somewhere in the building. So on a hunch I rode the elevator down to the basement, where the firm's closed files are stored. And sure enough, there I found him, seated at a corner table with the contents of a storage box spread out before him.

He glanced up when he heard me. His look was sheepish, as though he'd been caught red-handed in the act of some guilty pleasure.

"Ever heard of Max Hennigan?" he asked me before I could speak, removing his pipe and setting it carefully on the table.

Max Hennigan was a legendary San Francisco trial lawyer from back in the days of waistcoats and watch fobs. Clarence Darrow, Louis Nizer, and Max Hennigan are the sepia-toned standards by which today's trial lawyers are measured. "Of course."

"Had a trial with him when I was a young whelp. Just about your age. He was around seventy, maybe seventy-five years old, but still meaner than a one-eyed badger. He scared the hell out of me. Scared the judge, too."

"You had a case against Max Hennigan? What kind of case?" I pulled up a chair and sat.

"It wasn't *against* him, exactly. It was a securities case. Insider trading. I was defending a young stockbroker who, according to the government indictment, had made a fortune on tips from a golfing buddy who was a corporate muckety-muck. Hennigan was defending the brokerage that employed him. We were cocounsel, in a manner of speaking."

Cocounsel with Max Hennigan. Just when you thought you'd heard all of Russ's war stories, there was always a better one.

"And?"

"And," he said, leaning back to savor the memory, "it was kind of like being in a knife fight while getting leg-humped by a rottweiler. Hennigan was on my side as long as it was a convenient place to be. But I knew he was liable to turn on me at the drop of a hat. Fortunately, it never came to that. Here."

He handed me a document from the box. Yellow in color and brittle as onion skin, it bore the title "Judgment on General Verdict." Sure enough, it showed Russell H.

113

Dinsmoor on behalf of somebody named Vernon Soule, and Maxwell R. Hennigan on behalf of the firm of Merrill Lynch, Pierce, Fenner and Beane. And of course, it was a defense verdict.

"If memory serves," he said, "I used the old cat-in-the box closing."

"The what?"

"Come now, my boy. You were a public defender. Didn't they teach you anything?"

"They taught us that if you use the Music Center parking lot, you get free in-and-out privileges on Thursdays."

He smiled and closed his eyes.

"The case boiled down to whether my man knew that the information he was getting was nonpublic. There was circumstantial evidence that he knew. To win the case, we had to convince the jury that there was reasonable doubt. So, in my closing argument, I told them, 'What if we take a cardboard box, place a mouse in the box, then place a cat in the box and close the box up overnight. The next morning, when we open up the box, and the cat is still there but the mouse is gone, well, that would be *circumstantial* evidence that the cat ate the mouse, right?' They all agreed that was right.

" 'Now,' I said, 'let's suppose we take the same box, put in another mouse, put in the cat, and close it up overnight. When we open the box the next morning, sure enough, the cat is still there and the mouse is gone. Only this time,' I said, 'there's a little mouse-sized hole down in the corner of the box. That hole,' I told them, 'is reasonable doubt. Now let's talk about the holes in the government's case.' "

I shook my head as I handed him back his trophy.

"What are you doing down here anyway?"

"I'm reviewing closed files. That's what my time sheet will say." He gestured toward the file boxes towering behind him. "Truth is, I'm taking a little stroll down memory lane."

He was soft-soaping me, of course, and had been from the moment I'd entered the room. Russ Dinsmoor, as Sydney Everett had averred, could talk a dog off a meat wagon.

I tried to look stern. "You know damn well I've been looking for you."

He laced his hands behind his head. "You don't say."

"Look, you asked me to do you a favor. It's bad enough you've got me working for Catherine the Great over there. Don't smirk, I'm serious. But then you didn't give me all the facts, and that made me step on

115

my dick. And I don't like stepping on my dick in public. And if I'd seen you on Saturday, I'd have kicked you in the shorts, I don't care how old and decrepit you are."

He was grinning now from ear to ear.

"You know," he said, "there's many a man would give their eyeteeth to spend time with Sydney Everett."

"Any man who'd give up teeth to be with Sydney probably wears dentures. And you know that's not the issue."

He sighed.

"Look, Jack, if I'd told you about the other horse, you'd have jumped straight to the conclusion that she's guilty. As indeed, you apparently have. My hope was that with an *open* mind, you'd learn something useful to her case. If I caused you any embarrassment, I'm sorry. I truly am."

We eyed each other across the table. Russ was thin and hawk-faced, and his eyes were the color of running water. A widower who'd lost his only child in Vietnam, Russ's impending retirement owed itself to considerations less actuarial than medical — a congestive heart condition that had already required a quadruple bypass. He was a solitary man living on borrowed time, outwardly stoic and good-natured, but keenly aware of his own mortality.

116

All of which helped to explain why, from my first day on the job, Russ had taken it upon himself to act as my surrogate parent, guardian angel, and parish priest. He'd tutored me not just in the law, but in being the kind of lawyer who brings credit to himself, his firm, and his profession. Along the way, he'd become my biggest booster, but also my harshest critic. I'd learned more carrying his briefcase for the past six months than I'd learned in four years of law school and nearly six years of practice, both public and private.

"Did you know that she's selling her house?"

"No," he said, his smile fading. "I didn't know that. Did she say why?"

"Something about Harold's ghost haunting the hallowed halls. She's moving down to Orange Grove, but don't let on that I told you, because she swore me to secrecy. She also lied to the claims adjuster about the last person to see the horse alive. Hush Puppy, that is. Then she lied to me about lying to him. That's a lot of lying from someone I've only known for a couple of days."

He made a grunting sound.

"What's more, I've concluded that she's not very well liked at the Fieldstone Riding

Club. Not by the hired help, anyway. Bottom line, she may be a charming lady, and she's certainly interesting to look at, but you might want to rethink the firm's involvement with her at this point."

He looked right through me to the far wall, as he often did when moving the chess pieces around in his head. After a full minute of this he finally said, as much to himself as to me, "You don't suppose the old girl actually *did* it?"

Russ, I could see, was in the throes of a common racetrack malady that Uncle Louis called the triumph of hope over experience. As much as we all relished the Perry Mason fantasy of trumping the odds and exonerating a seemingly guilty client, it was invariably just that — a fantasy. I thought about Wells, and about Tara. I thought about Barbara Hauser, and about Creole. But most of all, I thought about that two-million-dollar mortality policy. You didn't need a map to see that all roads led to Mount Everett.

And then it dawned on me that that had been the whole point of Russ's little story about the cat and the mouse, about circumstantial evidence and reasonable doubt. And so I asked myself the question that his parable had invited: Could there be a mouse-sized hole out there somewhere that I was overlooking?

Russ gave me the name of a doctor who might provide a declaration in the Tazerian matter. His name was Heinrich Wagner, and his medical specialty was something called genetic biology.

Although a Yale man himself, Russ was a member of a civic group called the Caltech Associates, where he'd heard Wagner lecture on the promise of genetic engineering in the battle against cancer. Russ had later used him as an expert in a medical malpractice case, and he described Wagner as a cross between Albert Einstein and Walter Cronkite, meaning that although the good doctor had more degrees than a thermometer, he could still speak to jurors in kitchen-table English.

It was late afternoon when I rang Wagner's lab at the Pasadena campus. After introducing myself and exchanging the standard pleasantries, I inquired if he might be willing to consult on a case involving bone marrow transplantation as a treatment for leukemia. He asked some good questions, checked his appointment calendar, and agreed at least to look at the medical records.

He said that as a favor to Russ, he'd charge me nothing if he concluded that he couldn't be of help. Otherwise, he'd bill me $500 an hour for all the time he spent, starting ten minutes ago. I thought that was decent of him, and I told him so. I also told him that my associate, Ms. Suarez, would deliver a copy of Vic's file to the lab before closing.

With that behind me, I asked Bernie to pull up Jared Henley's old file on the Creole claim. She soon reported back that there was no file in storage, and no index card to suggest that a file had ever been placed in storage. Which was strange, since the claim had been resolved nearly five years earlier.

Kim Noffinger, Jared's secretary, remembered the case but knew nothing about the file, other than that it wasn't in any of the cabinets outside of Jared's office. Although a missing file was not without precedent at Henley & Hargrove, it was a rare enough occurrence to merit a raised eyebrow. I asked Bernie to keep looking.

For my next order of business, I logged onto the Flintridge Realty Web site. The listings were ordered by price, and Sydney's was tops on the page.

Under an aerial photograph and the heading Jewel in Flint Canyon, the sales pitch read:

Extraordinary craftsmanship and the finest materials and finishes are in evidence throughout this Tudor jewel on three acres overlooking scenic Flint Canyon. This astonishing 8,500-square-foot residence features nine bedrooms, ten baths, five fireplaces, a gourmet kitchen and other custom details too numerous to mention. MLS 128503. Offered at $8,250,000.

Well, I figured, good for Sydney. Eight mil would buy her a whole lot of condo in this market. With enough left over to pay our bill.

Which brought me, at last, to matters of the heart.

After our victory dinner at the Chop House, where we'd toasted her waxing of the Brazilian, Tara had talked me into surrendering custody of Sam for the day. This, in turn, had necessitated surrendering to her my house keys. I owed her a call.

"Hello, this is Tara."

"Zees is Diego," I said in my smarmiest *Mask of Zorro* accent. "I am at zee airport, and I want you to know zat zees ees our last

chance to have Cinnabons togezair before I
fly to Belgium."

She giggled. "Throw in a latte, Diego, and
I'm yours."

"You're way too easy."

"Don't count on it."

"Seriously," I said, lowering my voice,
"one of my neighbors called this morning
to say that a beautiful young woman was
carrying my flat-screen television out to her
car. That wasn't you, was it?"

"Don't laugh, mister. I have your dog."

"Prove it."

"Say hello to your daddy, Sam."

There was some rustling, followed by an
all-too-familiar panting.

"I'm introducing him to the horses. So far
he's been a perfect gentleman."

"Sure you've got the right dog?"

She said something to Sam that I didn't
catch.

"Okay. What'll it take to ransom him
back?"

"Well, for starters, I noticed a barbecue
grill on your back porch."

"You mean Old Sparky?"

"I'm thinking Sam is worth at least a
grilled veggie dinner. Maybe some zucchini?"

"In the old West," I told her, "they hanged

men for grilling zucchini."

"If Sam and I happened to be in the neighborhood with a Jeep full of groceries, what might be a good time to drop by?"

"Well, let's see. *Monday Night Football* kicks off at six."

"I knew it! A true romantic."

"Oh, but you've got my TV. Okay, make it six thirty. And Tara?"

"Yes?"

"If a steak should happen to fall into your shopping cart, give it a good home."

No sooner did I hang up on Tara than Bernie buzzed to inform me that a Patrick Bowman had called and had left an 800 number. This, in my experience, was rarely a good sign.

"*Welcome to the Metropolitan Livestock Insurance Company's automated voice mail system,*" answered a beatific female voice. "*All calls may be monitored for quality assurance. Please listen carefully to the following options, as our menu has changed.* Para continuar en Español, marque numero uno. *For information about purchasing a Metropolitan Livestock insurance policy, please press two. If you are already a Metropolitan Livestock policy holder and wish to renew, change, or cancel your coverage, please press three. For all new claims, please press four. For all exist-*

ing claims, please press five. If you know your party's four-digit extension, you may enter it at any time. For our company directory, please press six. For all other inquiries —"

I pressed six. It was her again.

"Welcome to the Metropolitan Livestock Insurance Company's employee telephone directory. If you know your party's four-digit extension, you may enter it at any time. Otherwise, please enter the first five letters of the last name of the person you are calling."

I entered A-S-S-H-O.

"Sorry, that's an invalid entry. Please try again."

B-O-W-M-A.

The phone rang, then rang again.

"Bowman!" barked a familiar voice, through what might have been an egg salad sandwich.

"Welcome to the Henley and Hargrove automated voice mail system," I intoned. "You have the right to remain silent, but if you choose to give up that right, please stay on the line. To speak with Mr. Hargrove, please press one. To speak with a lawyer who's still living, please press two."

"Oh, it's you. I've got your client's file right here. It just came back from our *fraud* unit. When can I take her statement?"

"First of all, you're a real prick for leaving

me an 800 number. Give me your direct dial, or you'll never hear from me again."

There was sunshine in his voice. "Geez, MacTaggart, did I do that? I usually give that to the bill collectors." He recited the number.

"As far as a statement, how about 'no comment'?"

"Looks like I'm headed for court then."

"You mean the food court?"

"No, wise guy, I mean the Superior Court."

"Let me make a little suggestion. How about we both knock off the posturing, and wait for the lab results. Once we have those, and the necropsy report, then we'll each have a better idea of where we stand. Fair enough?"

"All right," he said grudgingly. "Fair enough."

"And there's one more thing. My client wants her horse back. There's going to be a burial service out at Fieldstone."

That was a new one on him. "No shit," he said. "Glad you told me."

"Where's the carcass now?"

"Chino Hills. We use the veterinary hospital out there."

"Do us both a favor, will ya? Call and tell 'em that on this case, neatness counts."

On my way to the elevators, I had what you might call an irresistible impulse, compelling a short detour up to the ninth floor, and to Jared Henley's office. His door was ajar, and Kim had left for the day, so, being a man of action, I popped in for a look.

It was a big office — too big for his modest seniority — and on the best side of the building, looking north onto the ornate dome of City Hall.

On the wall inside the door hung several framed documents, including a *Golf Digest* cover autographed by Phil Mickelson and an old *Sports Illustrated* cover autographed by Tyra Banks. Below these, symbolically enough, hung Jared's diploma from the Stanford Law School, the alma mater of three generations of Pasadena Henleys.

Jared's grandfather, William T. Henley, had cofounded the firm of Henley & Hargrove back in 1910, and his son Morris, Jared's father, was still the managing partner, a post he'd held for more than twenty years.

Although now well into his sixties, Morris Henley was still a prodigious rainmaker who could charm the pants — wallet included — off of the stingiest CEO. He could also be short and condescending to those he considered his lessers, a vast universe that included most of the firm's lawyers and all of the office staff. A great bull of a man, scowling and florid, he remained by all accounts one of the sharpest business lawyers in California.

In many ways, Morris and Russ were like oil and water, which made their long partnership all the more remarkable. Russ was a traditionalist who venerated the law as a profession — a calling more akin to a secular priesthood than a business. Morris, on the other hand, had a merchant's heart, and he ran the firm with both eyes fixed on the bottom line.

One could only assume that the Henley family was a major benefactor of the Stanford Law School. There was no other explanation for how a ten-volt intellect like Jared had ever matriculated to, let alone graduated from, one of the finest law schools in America. But graduate he did, in what Russ described as the half of the class that makes the top half possible.

I knew that Jared had begun his career at Henley & Hargrove as a litigator, until Russ had politely suggested to Morris that his son's talents must lie elsewhere than in a courtroom. As a consequence, Jared now split his time equally between the corporate department, working under his father's sheltering wing, and various Club Med locations throughout the northern hemisphere.

I sat in Jared's calfskin swivel, and I slid his top drawer open. Inside was the usual assortment of pens, pencils, paper clips, Post-it pads, and the like, all fully stocked and neatly arranged. Of the two lower drawers, one held a hand mirror, a spring-operated grip strengthener, and a dog-eared membership roster from the Annandale Golf Club.

The other drawer was locked.

Neither Jared's desktop nor his in-box was encumbered by files, mail, memos, or paperwork of any kind, and the desk's only adornments were a Tiffany-style lamp, a heavy brass letter opener, and three framed photos arrayed on the outer perimeter.

One photo depicted a golf outing in which Jared clenched a fat Cohiba robusto in his teeth as he and two playing partners leaned on their drivers, grinning for the camera.

The next captured Jared in a scarlet mortarboard and gown, posing alongside his beaming father with the arched façade of the Stanford Law School clearly visible in the background. It was the first evidence

I'd seen that Morris Henley could actually smile.

In the last photo, a horse and rider hurtled a low fence in what looked like one of the oval arenas at Fieldstone. That one I picked up for closer inspection. It was Jared all right, in tall boots and a quilted vest, his shoulders tipped over the arching neck of a brown horse. He actually looked good, which shouldn't have surprised me, since looking good was the central tenet of Jared's personal creed.

I was just rising to leave when something back in the first photo caught my attention. I lifted the frame and snapped on the lamp for a better look. Sure enough, the cartoon forearms were a dead giveaway. The big guy on Jared's left, his chiseled face obscured by Oakley shades and a Ping ball cap, was none other than George Wells, DVM.

I didn't recognize the third guy in the picture. He was a short, pockmarked Asian man in a bucket hat, and he appeared neither handsome nor stylish, and thus oddly out of place in Jared Henley's small orbit of privilege.

And just then, as a shadow darkened the doorway, I found myself face-to-face with the very real and glowering visage of Morris Henley.

"Looking for something, MacTaggart?"

I set down the photo. "As a matter of fact, I was. We seem to be missing a file, and I thought it might be in here somewhere."

"Well," he said, "if it's not in that photograph, perhaps you should try looking through the wastebasket next."

I cleared my throat and stood.

"In the future, young man, if you need something from Jared's office, and if neither he nor Kimberly is available, then send them an e-mail. If it's urgent, you can call Mrs. Petrov. If none of them is available, you can call me personally. Are we clear on that?"

"Perfectly."

"Good. Is there anything further we need to discuss?"

"No, sir."

I sidled through the doorway and shrank down the hallway toward the elevators, his eyes burning blisters in the center of my back.

6

Tara brought a red wine, which went nicely with my steak.

And while I wasn't sure about grilling the zucchini, she proclaimed it to be delicious, and on that I took her word. She'd even brought a butcher's bone for Sam, who'd lain curled at her feet as we sat in the flickering darkness watching the Bears and Packers trade snot bubbles on the not-yet-frozen tundra of Lambeau Field.

Tara had insisted we watch the game, but I'd turned it off after her third comment about how good so-and-so's butt looked in tight pants.

"What do they wear under those pants, anyway?" she'd asked.

"Sorry, but I'm sworn to secrecy. Article two, section five of the Guy's Code. If I told you, I'd have to kill you."

We were on the sofa now, her head on a pillow in my lap. The wine was almost gone, the fire was down to embers, and Sam had dragged himself, tottering and somnolent after his big day at the barn, over to his favorite armchair.

"What's HSA testing?"

"What?"

"A little birdie told me that Hush Puppy had been HSA tested two weeks before he died."

"Oh," she said. "That's the U.S. Equestrian Federation. It used to be called the American Horse Show Association. The HSA."

"They do, what, random drug testing?"

"They're a regulatory body. They blood-test at the bigger shows. Not always, but sometimes."

"Do you think Wells might want those results? As some kind of baseline?"

She half rolled to face me. "He doesn't need them, sweetie. George took blood from all the horses last month. Testing for West Nile virus."

We hadn't really talked about Hush Puppy since our dinner at Cheval Blanc, in part because talking to civilians about pending cases is a slippery slope. Anything that Sydney may have told me is protected by the attorney-client privilege, and anything I learned from Russ, or that I figured out from my own investigative efforts, is protected by the attorney work-product doctrine.

Technically speaking, disclosure of a privileged communication to a third person like Tara, without the need to know, would result in a waiver of the privilege. If for some reason I was ever placed under oath, I'd either have to cop to the leak, or else commit perjury.

"He seems like a decent guy."

"George? He's a prince," she said sleepily, turning toward the fire.

"I'll bet he's a big hit with the ladies."

She rolled again, this time with an enigmatic smile. "I doubt that very much."

"What's so funny?"

"Well, for one thing, George is gay."

"Get out of town. How do you know?"

"Article five, section one of the Gal's Code. If I told you, I'd have to kill you."

She seemed very pleased with herself.

"What else did Barbara say?"

"Who says I spoke with Barbara?"

"Oh, I heard Margaret Carlton raving about some lunatic who'd barged into the office and insulted her, and then accosted Barbara in a tack room."

"I'd buy that guy a beer."

"It had a ring of familiarity."

"First of all, I deny it was me. Secondly, if it was me, I didn't really insult her. And thirdly, if it was me and if I did insult her, she deserved to be insulted."

"So," she purred, not letting it go. "What did you learn in the tack room?"

"Two things. First, that Barbara's a lousy actress. Second, that she thinks Sydney killed Hush Puppy."

"There you go. Case closed."

"Speaking of Barbara, do you own a pair of those black leather chaps? Because that, I believe, is a fashion statement that should be made more often."

She sat up and hit me with a pillow.

"Did you know that Sydney wants to bury Hush Puppy at Fieldstone?"

She smothered her face in the pillow, muffling a scream.

"What?"

"Nothing. She makes me crazy, that's all. First she has him killed, then she has to make a big show of how much she cared about him. I know she's your client, sweetie, but she makes me want to puke."

And that's where I left it, figuring nothing good would come from any further mention of Sydney Everett, or Hush Puppy, or especially Barbara Hauser. So we finished the wine, and I tossed another log onto the fire, and just as I was executing a headfirst slide into second base, the telephone rang.

I ignored it, but Tara did not.

"Answer," she breathed.

I lifted the receiver to a loud clunking noise, like a dropped handset, and to soft jazz playing in the background. Then I heard a familiar voice.

"H'llo, Jack," Sydney Everett slurred. "Whatcha doin' home on a beautiful night like this?"

"Hello, Mrs. Everett," I replied warily, shrugging my shoulders at Tara, who draped my shirt over her head as she fled into the bedroom. "What a pleasant surprise. What can I do for you?"

"Don't get me started on that subject, sugar. I could think of a thing or two, but you're 'parently not interested. Am I right?"

"Mrs. Everett, don't confuse discretion with disinterest."

She thought about that for a moment, while a saxophone riffed in the silence.

"Oh, you're a smooth one. That's why you're my lawyer. You are my lawyer, aren't you, sugar?"

"I am your lawyer, Mrs. Everett."

"Sydney." She whispered, "Do you know what I'm wearing right now?"

I could see this was going nowhere.

"Sydney. Maybe it would be better if we talked in the morning. You could call me at the office."

"You said you were gonna take care of me. Russell always took care of me. Even Jared took care of me."

"As will I. I'm usually in by around eight thirty."

She sighed heavily. "Don't you ever get lonely, Jack? Don't you ever just . . . miss people?"

"Everybody gets lonely, Sydney. You know that. Everybody does."

Silence. "Yeah, me too. Sometimes I get so lonely, I just want to cry."

"Look, Sydney, you should get some rest. I'll bet whatever's got you down won't seem so bad in the morning."

There was more silence. And then the line went dead.

The denial notice from the Hartford Allied Insurance Company arrived on Tuesday morning. The certified letter, dated on Monday, was from a National Claims Specialist in Connecticut who again cited the policy's exclusion for experimental treatments. The letter was short and coldly polite, concluding with, "our review of your recent correspondence and the Insured's medical file compels us to sustain the preliminary determination that Policy Exclusion III (d) (3) (iv) applies, and precludes Coverage for the subject Treatment."

This was insurance-speak for "Have a nice life, Mr. Tazerian." Or what's left of it, anyway.

I sounded the general quarters, and spent the rest of the morning with Mayday. Our strategy called for an end-run around the formal trial process by trying to get a judge to issue a mandatory injunction — a court order for immediate coverage on the ground that Vic's life was in imminent danger. I had no illusions, however, that getting such an order would be anything but a long shot.

Mayday had done her part, working all night to draft the documents. Only Heinrich Wagner's declaration was needed to complete the package, and so we called him together from my office.

"Wagner here."

"Dr. Wagner, this is Jack MacTaggart, and I've got you on the speakerphone because my colleague Marta Suarez is here. I believe you met yesterday."

"Yes, lovely girl. Hello, Marta."

"Hello, Heinrich," she chirped.

"We were wondering if you'd had a chance to review Mr. Tazerian's records."

There was a pause while papers were shuffled somewhere on the Caltech campus.

"Yes, I've read them. Very unfortunate case. Acute lymphoblastic leukemia with reciprocal translocation of the MLL gene. Very nasty stuff."

"And what about the transplant procedure? Is it likely to work?"

I held my breath in the silence that followed.

"Yes," he said finally, "I think maybe so. Let me explain."

I nodded to Mayday, who started writing.

"This type of leukemia occurs when the bone marrow malfunctions, and defective or immature blood cells are produced. These cells interfere with the production of normal blood cells. They have to be eliminated, either by chemotherapy or by radiation. The problem, of course, is that radiation or chemotherapy also kills the healthy cells, not to mention the bone marrow itself. So, a transplant becomes necessary. Transplantation allows for aggressive treatment with chemotherapy or radiation, followed by replacement of the damaged bone marrow. Are you following me so far?"

Marta, the doctor's daughter, nodded.

"Perfectly," I said. "Please continue."

"The problem with transplantation is that

the body's immune system will attack and destroy the donor marrow. That process is called rejection."

"Yes, I'm quite familiar with that in my personal life."

He gave a little chuckle. "Unless the patient is lucky enough to have an identical twin, the chances of rejection are quite high, because of the difficulty in obtaining a good genetic match."

"Hence a transplant from yourself to yourself."

"Exactly. That process is called an autologous transplant. It used to be strictly theoretical. Nowadays, however, there have been tremendous advances in the techniques used to purge the marrow before it's reintroduced to the donor. The chances of a successful transplant are actually quite high. And I'd be very happy to provide a declaration to that effect."

And I'd be very happy to have it. So Mayday hurried off with her notes, and I volunteered to deliver the declaration personally, after lunch, to Wagner's laboratory at Caltech.

The next item on my to-do list bore the notation Headstone Riding Club, which I'd scribbled on Monday morning in reference to a certain equine funeral.

There are no form books or practice guides in the library for this kind of assignment. It would involve phone time spent with a succession of petty bureaucrats, then processing a ream of forms, requests, applications, and waivers.

While I had every intention of leaving that to Mayday, I would need to report some progress to Sydney. So I stiffed in a call to the general business office at Fieldstone, and as the telephone rang, I offered a silent prayer that Margaret Carlton didn't haunt that house as well.

To my relief, a chipper young woman named Sally answered. I introduced myself, and I explained the reason for my call.

"Oh, yes," she said, "we've been waiting to hear from you. The board approved the interment ceremony yesterday."

Proving, I thought, that there's a euphemism for everything. Even lowering a dead horse into a hole with a crane.

"If there's anything I can do to assist," she continued, "please let me know. I've been placed in charge of the arrangements at this end."

"Should I offer congratulations or condolences?"

She chuckled. "All in a day's work."

"You'll be hearing from my colleague,

Miss Suarez. Later in the week, I suspect."

"That will be lovely. Oh, and Mr. Mac-Taggart? I hesitate to even bring this up under the circumstances, but a proviso attached to the board's approval was that Mrs. Everett bring her dues and her boarding fees current. Some of the board members felt that it was only appropriate."

"Sure, I'll let her know. How much are we talking about?"

I heard the *clickity-clack* of fingernails on a keyboard.

"Let's see," she said. "August, September, and now October. Waiving the interest, of course, the total would be eight thousand five hundred dollars."

So much for any notion I might have entertained about riding. I'd have to find a more affordable hobby. Smoking crack, for instance.

"I'll be sure to tell her."

"Thank you," she replied pleasantly. "That will be most appreciated."

The first thing that surprises you about the California Institute of Technology is that it's not very large — maybe four square blocks in total. And the undergraduate population is likewise small, numbering fewer than a thousand. Somehow you'd expect a larger physical presence from what is arguably the greatest academic institution on the face of planet Earth.

It was at Caltech that Linus Pauling described the nature of the chemical bond, that Carl Anderson discovered antimatter, and that Charles Richter invented the science of earthquake study. And with thirty other Nobel laureates having served on the Caltech faculty, those guys didn't have to eat lunch by themselves.

I'd learned all of this, and more, as Russ's sometimes guest at the Caltech Atheneum, which is the on-campus faculty restaurant. Viewed from the street, the Atheneum is an ornate confection of carved stone archways and marble balustrades. On the inside, the wood-paneled walls and thick Persian carpets transport you to another place and time.

The waitstaff at the Atheneum consisted of undergraduate students on work-study, and all wore plastic lapel tags with their first names and academic majors. Russ and I were once served chicken Kiev by Judy, Theoretical Physics. I'd told Russ that it was the one joint in town where you couldn't say that the waitress was no rocket scientist, because many of them actually were.

A gaggle of pimply undergraduates was exiting the Beckman building as I approached, and they directed me to the second floor, southwest corner, where I met with a windowless metal door and a sign that read:

LABORATORY B-211
BRIAN HUANG, M.D., PH.D,
HEINRICH WAGNER, M.D., PH.D
EVAGEN, LLC

I knocked loudly, to no response. Entering unbidden, I was disappointed to find no bubbling beakers, or arcing electrodes, or cages of shrieking monkeys — just a large, oatmeal-colored room bathed in a sterile white fluorescence.

There were lab tables with sinks in the center of the room, and modular steel bookshelves on the side-wall beyond. Along the street-side wall was a row of low filing cabinets. The only glassware in sight was a coffeepot, warming itself on one of the tables.

By the wall opposite the windows were two steelcase desks, battleship gray, set ten feet apart and facing into the room. Between them hung the lab's only adornment, an enormous Periodic Table of the Elements, several of which, it occurred to me then, may have been created in this very building.

A laptop was open on one of the desks, casting a ghostly bluish glow onto Vic Tazerian's medical records. Wagner's desk was spartan — just the computer, the records, a telephone, a chipped coffee mug bristling with pencils, and a photo in a laminate frame.

The picture, slightly faded, showed the young doctor in a Blues Brothers suit and muttonchop sideburns. His wife, who may have been Eva, wore an ankle-length dress and open-toed sandals. They both sported heavy Clark Kent eyeglasses. In the background was a cityscape that could have been Vienna or Prague, or maybe even Baltimore.

In contrast with Wagner's desk, Dr. Huang's was positively festive. There were crystal paperweights, an antique porcelain inkwell, and three silver frames holding photos of Asian children of various ages. Or maybe the same child at different ages.

In the center of the desktop was a stack of mail that included the latest issues of *Fortune, Time,* and *Scientific American,* and atop the stack was a paperweight — an intricately carved dragon in milky green jade.

I heard a toilet flush, and after a moment Heinrich Wagner emerged from a side door drying his hands on a towel. He was tall and lanky, and twenty years older than the man in the photograph. His hair was ash-gray now, and the Elvis sideburns had been pared to academic orthodoxy.

"Mr. MacTaggart? Sorry to keep you waiting."

I set down my briefcase and accepted his hand.

"Please, call me Jack. From the looks of things, you're working on something important, so I'll try not to take much of your time."

He folded himself behind his desk, studying the computer screen.

"Oh, this is just a little program I'm writing for an NIH research project. Do you write software?"

"Are you kidding? My uncle used to say there are three kinds of people in the world — those who understand math and those who don't."

He looked at me over his glasses.

"Say, that's pretty good. Mind if I use it in a lecture I'm giving?"

"Help yourself. I know he won't mind."

He pecked at the keyboard, frowned at the result, and then closed the lid.

"There, that should hold. So, you have a declaration for me to sign?"

I sat at the other desk and drew a folder from my briefcase.

"I understand you've gone over this with Miss Suarez, but I'd still like you to read it carefully. Some day your deposition might be taken, and you'll want to testify that you read every word."

He accepted the document and scanned it quickly. It was four pages in length, covering his qualifications, the materials he'd reviewed, his opinions, and their bases. The opinions were, first, that Vic was an excellent candidate for the surgery, and second, that advances in medical science had made the surgery almost routine. When he'd finished reading, he opened a drawer and removed a ballpoint pen, then signed the declaration without comment.

"Here you go," he said. "I hope it's of some use to you. And to Mr. Tazerian, of course."

I returned the file to my briefcase.

"So, what will happen next?"

"We've already phoned the insurer to tell them that we're going in ex parte tomorrow morning, for an order compelling them to pay for Vic's surgery. The judge will either grant that motion or deny it. If he denies it, he'll do so either because he doesn't believe we're entitled to the relief we're seeking —

that's called a denial with prejudice — or because he thinks there's still time, and he wants to give the carrier a chance to file papers in opposition. That's called a denial without prejudice, meaning that he still may grant the motion, but just not yet. And if that's the case, the judge might allow the carrier's counsel to take your deposition. If that happens, we'd want you to be available right away — maybe as early as next week. Is that possible?"

I could see this was turning into a bigger commitment than he thought he'd made.

"No, that's fine. I'll make the time if I have to."

"Thank you, we appreciate that. I assume you've given a deposition before?"

"Oh, yes. Twice as an expert witness, and once in connection with a car accident."

"You know the routine then. But if there's to be a depo in this case, we'll meet beforehand to prepare, okay?"

He nodded. "That's fine."

I closed the briefcase and stood.

"I'll get out of your hair. Thanks again for all your help."

"My pleasure." He stood, and we shook hands. "Good luck to you, and please give my regards to Mr. Dinsmoor."

On my drive back to the office, I dialed

Tara on her cell. Her voice when she answered was obscured by a rumbling noise in the background.

"Hello?"

"Tara, this is Jack. Can you hear me?"

"Wait a minute," she said, and the engine noise quit. I realized then that it was a tractor, and that Tara had been driving it. "Better?"

"Much better. I'm sorry to bother you, but I have an important question. Highly confidential, okay?"

"I already told you, sweetie. You were wonderful."

"I'm being serious now."

"Sorry. Confidential and serious."

"Fieldstone is a membership club, right? So the members own the club's assets, including the real estate, right?"

"That's right, the equity members do."

"And Sydney's an equity member, right?"

"As a board member, she'd have to be. Why?"

"I'll explain later, but here's my question. Wouldn't her membership be worth a small fortune? I mean, all that property . . ."

"The answer is, yes and no. On paper at least, all the equity members are real estate rich. But it would take a majority vote to shut down the club and sell the assets. And

148

with over a hundred members who ride, that will never happen. And the memberships are nontransferable. So if an equity member quits the club, they get nothing."

"That settles it," I told her. "I'm withdrawing my application."

"I'm sure Margaret Carlton will be crushed."

"Great. Can I come watch?"

7

I'd explained to Tara that I needed the night alone in order to prepare for tomorrow's hearing, and after collecting the final paperwork from Mayday, I drove through the In-N-Out on Walnut on my way to Bungalow Heaven.

A hearing like this, in federal court no less, would be a crap shoot. We wouldn't know the identity of the judge until we filed the complaint in the morning, since new cases are assigned on a random basis using a computer program, known colloquially as the Wheel. We'd then march upstairs to the courtroom and insert ourselves into the judge's already busy calendar. The judge would have to read all the paperwork on the spot, maybe with a courtroom full of lawyers or a jury waiting in the hallway, and then issue an immediate ruling.

There are fifty or so federal judges in downtown Los Angeles, and they varied widely in their political and judicial philosophies, not to mention in their intellectual capabilities and judicial temperaments. I personally rated judges on a two-axis scale, based on their brains and their courtroom demeanor. Under my system, all judges fell into one of four categories: smart and pleasant, dumb but pleasant, smart but unpleasant, and dumb and unpleasant.

In the federal system, judges are appointed with lifetime tenure. By this, the founding fathers hoped to keep the judicial branch above politics and immune to the mood swings of a fickle electorate. But the practical result was, no matter how dumb or unpleasant a judge might be, he can sit on the bench and make lawyers miserable forever, or at least until his estate plan matures. Which explains why some federal judges in L.A. have been around since Christ was a corporal.

Moreover, once a case is assigned to a federal judge, you're stuck with that judge for the duration, and there's no mechanism for getting the matter reassigned. So, much like the coin toss in sudden-death overtime, the spin of the Wheel often determines the outcome of your case. Which isn't fair, of course, but as Uncle Louis would say, fair is the place where they hold the pie-eating contest.

It was eight thirty by the time I'd finished my courtroom preparations. Sam was asleep in his chair, Van Morrison was getting all bluesy on the stereo, and everything should have been right with the world. Yet I found myself oddly disquieted, my thoughts not on Vic Tazerian, but on matters closer to home.

Barbara Hauser had said that she knew Sydney Everett was fed up. Sydney, who owed over eight grand to the club on whose board of directors she sits, had tried to place Barbara at the scene of the crime, yet continued to deny that a crime had occurred. And Barbara, for her part, blamed not just Sydney for Hush Puppy's death, but Jared Henley as well.

And in the midst of these dark ruminations, it was, strangely enough, the polished chrome image of an eighteen-wheel Kenworth semi that nudged the tumblers into place.

There were no lights in the darkened parking structure. My space, along with those of the other Henley & Hargrove lawyers, was on the second level, so I doused my headlights and navigated the up ramp by memory.

The structure was all but empty at this hour, but for one car still conspicuously in its place. Morris Henley's black Cadillac sat like a steel panther, coiled and menacing in the reflected glow of the street-level neon. I cruised slowly past, up to the third level, and chose a space marked RESERVED FOR BANK EMPLOYEES ONLY. Mine was the only vehicle in sight.

Sanchez, as I'd hoped, was away from his desk in the building lobby. As night watchmen went, Sanchez ranked somewhere between Barney Fife and Barney the purple dinosaur. Conventional wisdom had him spending most nights asleep on a couch in the bank, but he could just as easily have been upstairs somewhere, checking on the cleaning crew. Wherever he was, he'd left a sign-in sheet on a portable stand by the elevators. I bypassed both, however, crossing to the recessed doorway that led into the stairwell.

The stairwell was dim, with only emergency lighting to show the way. I muted my footsteps as best I could on the bare concrete stairs.

I was breathing through my mouth by the fifth floor, sweating by the seventh, and I had my hands on my knees by the time I reached the ninth-floor landing, where I paused in the malachite glow of an EXIT sign to devise a rudimentary strategy.

The floor was rectangular, with the lawyers' offices forming the outer perimeter. Interior to these, the secretarial carrels were separated from the view offices by low partitions and a wide, carpeted hallway. The floor's central core, moving east to west, consisted of the elevator lobby, the men's restroom, a copy center, the word processing center, and the women's restroom. Then a narrow north-south corridor bisected the floor, separating these from the bookkeeping department and the open-stack library.

Morris Henley's office occupied the southeast corner of the floor, catty-corner to the library, while Jared's office was to the north. My first destination — the bookkeeping department — lay roughly midway between them.

A stairwell fire door separated the landing where I now stood from the wood-paneled elevator lobby beyond. Once I stepped through that door, two things would happen, and neither of them was good.

First, the door would lock behind me, and I'd be trapped in the elevator lobby unless I entered my personal four-digit security code into the lock mechanism on one of the two doors leading into the office proper. Second, during the brief interval that I was inside the elevator lobby, my image would appear on a closed-circuit television monitor wall-mounted in the bookkeeping department. And both, not incidentally, would leave a permanent record of my visit.

But these were manageable risks. Unless Morris was standing in bookkeeping and watching the monitor, I'd be safe for now. As for later, nobody would bother to read the door logs or watch the videotape unless there was a reason to do so, like an office theft. And I didn't plan to leave any evidence of the theft I had in mind.

I filled my lungs and pushed through the fire door, then strolled casually past the security camera to the north-side door, where I entered my code. When the lock mechanism blinked from red to green, I slipped into the hallway.

So far, so good.

The hallway in which I now stood was eerily deserted, and I crept its carpeted length for a read on Morris's whereabouts. Through the duck-blind of library shelving, I saw a light bar under his office door, and I pictured him inside, seated on his throne of human skulls, finalizing a deal to convert the local orphanage into condos.

I backtracked to the central hallway and turned right, then right again, pushing through the heavy glass door to the bookkeeping department.

It was a narrow room, long and windowless but for the doors at either end. In the bluish glow of the closed-circuit television monitor, with its flickering, split-screen image of the elevator lobbies on eight and nine, I could just make out the filing cabinets on the left-hand wall and the desks along the right, which combined to form the room's center aisle.

The farthest of the desks was the imperial domain of Nicky Petrov, the firm's office manager. Mrs. Petrov was in charge of the bookkeeping department and all of its functions. She was also the de facto head of human resources and office services. If you ran out of paper clips at Henley & Hargrove, you called Mrs. Petrov. If you needed to approve secretarial overtime, you called Mrs. Petrov. If you wanted to know which wine to serve with grilled zucchini, you called Mrs. Petrov.

It was Mrs. Petrov who, on my first day in the office, walked me through all of the firm's systems and procedures. She introduced me to Bernadette, assigned me my parking space, activated my computer, and programmed my telephone. And then, from a jailer's ring that she kept in the top drawer of her desk, she'd handed me the key to my office desk.

And, as I recalled, she'd kept the duplicate.

I edged forward into darkness, feeling my way down the aisle, tracing my hand along the fourth and final desk until I found the drawer, slid it open, and did a Stevie Wonder impression as I felt for the cold necklace of keys.

Jared's door was ajar, and I closed it quietly behind me, fumbling for the pull-chain to his Tiffany lamp, which threw a scrim of jewel-colored light onto the office walls.

All was as I'd left it, except for two neat piles on the desktop. One consisted of magazines, continuing-education flyers, and junk mail, while the other appeared to be business correspondence — each letter opened and paper-clipped to its envelope.

I stripped off my sweatshirt and laid it at the base of the door, and then I settled into Jared's chair. There were more than fifty keys on Nicky's ring, each bearing an embossed, three-digit number of no determinable significance. I chose one at random, and under the watchful eyes of Phil and

Tyra, I bent to what I expected would be a long task.

Except that the lower-left drawer, locked only yesterday, tonight rolled easily open.

I moved the lamp closer. Inside the drawer were what appeared to be Jared's personal files, alphabetically arrayed. Most of the file tabs, beginning with Annandale, were hand-labeled, but a few were typewritten. There were maybe twenty files in all.

The Everett/Creole file, not surprisingly, had a typewritten label. Below this title were the words "Insurance Claim," and below that was the bookkeeping account number.

I doused the light, snugged the file into my waistband, and covered it with the knotted arms of my sweatshirt. After giving the office a final once-over, I took the keys and moved quickly to the elevator lobby, leaving yet another electronic fingerprint as I exited past the camera and through the stairwell fire door.

My heart was beating now, and it wasn't just the stairs. It was, I realized, the same feeling I experienced whenever a jury filed back into the courtroom, and I rose for the reading of the verdict.

I closed my office door and set the file on the blotter. I sat for a moment and studied it, the manila cover faded with age, the corners scuffed and frayed by frequent use.

I moved and angled my desk lamp. And then, my fingers wriggling like a safecracker's, I opened the file.

Mounted on one side were the file's original contents — a stack of hole-punched correspondence pertaining to the old insurance claim. Bottommost was a demand letter from Jared that he appeared to have copied from a form book. Next came some back-and-forth sparring with a claims adjuster, and then a letter transmitting Creole's necropsy report, with copy attached. The official cause of death, I noted with interest, was "Idiopathic Cardiac Arrest," meaning that the true cause was never determined.

The final letter transmitted the settlement check, a copy of which was likewise attached. Both the letter and the check were dated more than four years ago. The check was payable to Sydney Everett, in the sum of $1,004,250. The million would have represented the policy limit, and the balance would have been interest that had accrued while the claim was pending.

None of this, however, was what I'd come looking for.

Hole-punched and mounted on the other side of the file were bank statements that I recognized as coming from a non-IOLTA account. As a general proposition, whenever a lawyer holds money that belongs to a client, California law requires that it be deposited into the firm's client trust account. The Henley & Hargrove trust account, for example, might contain as much as half a million dollars in pooled funds at any given time, mostly from client retainers. Under California law, interest on lawyers' trust accounts — IOLTA for short — belonged neither to the lawyer nor the client, but was paid into something called the Legal Services Trust Fund, which the State Bar then used to fund legal services for the indigent.

But a lesser-known provision of California law allowed lawyers to open separate, interest-bearing accounts in trust for their clients, free from the IOLTA strictures, whenever the lawyer expected to hold client funds for any substantial length of time.

And that's exactly what Jared had done for Sydney Everett. And by so doing, he'd effectively removed the account, and any funds flowing through the account, from the books and records of Henley & Hargrove.

The account, I saw, had been opened at First Pasadena Bank, headquartered downstairs, with the oldest of the statements dated four years ago, roughly two months after the Creole settlement had funded. The statement reflected both an initial deposit and a final account balance of ten thousand dollars. Each month thereafter, the sum of $110,000.00 had been wire-transferred into the account, then promptly removed from the account, both by check and by wire. At the end of each month, the same balance — ten thousand dollars — remained.

The last of the fifty-odd statements was only three weeks old, for the period ending September 30 of this year.

Stapled to each of the monthly bank statements were the wire-transfer confirmations, each pair reflecting funds electronically entering and leaving the account. Like the statements themselves, the earliest confirmations were four years old, while the latest were from last month.

I fanned the stack, examining the wire confirmations at random. The top sheet in each pair listed Flintridge Bank as the payor, for the account of Sydney Everett, for credit to the account of Sydney Everett, c/o Jared Henley, trustee. The bottom sheet listed First Pasadena Bank as the payor, for the account of Sydney Everett, c/o Jared Henley, trustee, for credit to the account of

161

Barbara Hauser Equestrian Enterprises.

Each of the monthly wires from Sydney was in the sum of $110,000. Each of the monthly wires to Barbara was in the sum of $100,000. The difference in each case, ten grand per month, had left the account by check. And I didn't need an accountant to figure out where they'd gone.

By my calculation, the file in my hands evidenced not less than four Class A felonies.

The first, of course, was extortion. For more than four years, Barbara had been blackmailing Sydney to the tune of over a million dollars a year — not to mention the use of Hush Puppy, not to mention whatever other goodies they'd managed to finagle from Fieldstone — all to ensure Barbara's silence.

The second crime was insurance fraud. Sydney wouldn't be paying that kind of hush money unless she had, in fact, hastened Creole's death and then somehow gotten caught.

The third crime — two crimes, really — were chargeable to Jared; for being an accessory both to the initial insurance fraud and to the subsequent extortion.

The fourth and final felony — insurance fraud again — was a crime in progress. Sydney had obviously reached the end of her rope, and figured that the insurance on Hush Puppy's life was just the ticket to getting back on her feet. And, perhaps not incidentally, to shafting Barbara in the process.

It was a train wreck, pure and simple; a steaming pile of greed and stupidity rising nine stories over Colorado Boulevard. And sitting atop the pile, his propeller-beanie spinning in the breeze, was William T. Henley's only grandson.

The big machine whirred and glowed in the darkened space, and I kept waiting for a tap on the shoulder that never came. The whole operation — from warming up the copier, to removing the staples, to hand-feeding the pages, to restapling them together — took less than twenty minutes, but it somehow felt like hours.

I swung by my office to lock up the copies, then reentered the ninth floor as before, via the stairwell, only this time heading straight for Jared's office. There I replaced the original file, taking pains to leave everything exactly as I'd found it. Then I tiptoed back to bookkeeping, and I returned the keys to Mrs. Petrov's desk.

And it was only then, with the checkered

flag plainly in sight, that the wheels began to wobble.

Movement on the closed-circuit monitor froze me where I stood, and I glimpsed Morris Henley's bullet head passing through the north hallway door. My mind raced. While I might have been able to explain my presence in the office, I had about as much business in the bookkeeping department as I did in Jared's wastebasket.

I considered a mad dash toward reception, but quickly ruled that out. Even if he didn't see me, Morris would almost certainly hear my footsteps, which would lead to a review of the door logs and the videotape. My only option was retreat, down the darkened aisle and into the printer closet at the far end of the room, where I pulled the door closed just as Morris burst in from the hallway and snapped on the lights.

I watched through the little window as Morris rooted through the file cabinets with the ferocity of a bomb-sniffing dog. I guessed he was assembling the month's unpaid accounts, copies of which he would later circulate to the responsible attorneys along with terse tidings of woe, since Morris Henley regarded any account more than sixty days past due as a kind of personal affront.

He slammed the last drawer shut and carried a thick stack of files to the far desk. I watched his back now, his broad shoulders bent to the task, the pinkish flesh above his shirt collar puckered like the back of a baby's knee.

After ten minutes of this, I saw the computer monitor, the corner of which was barely visible over his shoulder, blink to life. Within moments, the big Omega printer beside me started to whirr, bathing my dark little cocoon in a greenish, night-vision fluorescence.

I turned from the window in search of a hiding place, just as wide sheets of green-bar paper began streaming from the printer, the sound of their parturition filling the closet like the engines of a DC-10. Morris rose from the desk and turned in my direction. I cursed under my breath.

And then I noticed the fire alarm.

The metallic box, no larger than a cigarette pack, was mounted on the wall by the printer. I untied my sweatshirt, wrapped my fist, and punched out the little glass window. And when I flipped the switch inside, bedlam erupted on all points of the compass.

An ear-splitting buzz accompanied the blinding flash-pop of halogen lights mounted in the high corners of the room. With my fingers in my ears and my heart in my throat, I waited for the door to open, and when it didn't, I turned again to the window in time to see Morris's barn-sized back retreating to the desk.

After a few jabs at the keyboard, he gathered the files to his chest and hurried to the hallway door, where he paused for a long moment amid the flashing lights and general pandemonium. Turning his gaze back into the room, he appeared to lift his nose in the air, like a feral animal scenting distant prey. Then he tripped the light switch, plunging the room back into darkness, and moved down the hallway in the stroboscopic stutter of a silent film villain.

I tore through both doors, then down the hallway and through the elevator lobby, the stairwell fire door slamming behind me as I bounded downward, spurred by the knowledge that the disabled elevators would force anyone still in the building — Morris included — to exit the same way.

At the ground-floor door I halted, catching my breath and listening to the echo of slamming doors and shuffling feet above me. Then I gathered myself and strolled casually into the lobby.

Sanchez was back at his desk, talking

excitedly into the telephone as people crowded around him. I ducked through the exit doors, into the cold night air, and strode quickly to the parking structure.

Safely in the Jeep, I listened for the sound of the fire engines, and as the pounding in my chest quieted, I laughed out loud at the absurdity of what I'd done.

And it was only then, as I revved the engine and backed into the cavernous darkness, that I noticed my sweatshirt.

Or rather, that I wasn't wearing it.

8

Morning found me at the clerk's window in the old federal courthouse on Spring Street, awaiting the spin of the Wheel. Behind me stood a baby-faced assassin named Donald Carlisle, who'd been dispatched on behalf of the Hartford Allied Insurance Company. Carlisle was thumbing his BlackBerry rather than reading the sheaf of paperwork I'd just handed him, and that alone was enough to piss me off.

"You know you're wasting our time here," he informed me.

"Is that right?"

"C'mon, pal. There isn't a judge in town who'd order a half-million-dollar medical procedure on an ex parte application, and you know it."

Carlisle was from Plimpton, Simmons & Stark, one of the biggest firms in L.A., not to mention New York, London, Brussels, Hong Kong, and around a dozen other world capitals where the firm had offices. His three-button cashmere suit bespoke eastern prep school, Ivy League undergrad, maybe Harvard or Yale Law, and his haircut and briefcase both were new and expensive. He wore one of those Rolex scuba watches, big as a Skol can and waterproof to five hundred meters, but I'd wager that the closest he'd ever come to a dive boat was the smoked salmon he'd had with his morning bagel.

"Gosh, maybe you're right," I told him. "Let me call my client and tell him to pick out a coffin, and then you and I can go across the street and have cappuccinos."

Carlisle glanced up long enough to roll his eyes.

The clerk returned to the window, and with the zeal of a Soviet-era customs agent began file-stamping my papers. When he shoved the stack across the counter, he said, "Eighth floor, Judge Spencer."

My heart sank, and I could see the trace of a smile crinkling the corners of Carlisle's eyes.

The Honorable Amos Spencer was around a hundred years old, and he was best known for two things. The first was imposing stiff monetary sanctions against lawyers who displeased him in some fashion, like, for example, by appearing in his courtroom. The second was imposing draconian sentences on criminal defendants — far in excess of the federal sentencing guidelines, which, despite their name, are pretty much mandatory.

As a consequence of both predilections, Spencer had the dubious distinction of being the District Court judge most frequently reversed by the Ninth Circuit Court of Appeals. And that he was said to regard as a badge of honor. In one notorious case, the appellate court had advised him, in a blistering published opinion, to consider anger management counseling.

By reputation at least, Spencer was, on my two-axis scale, dumber than an Irish setter and about as pleasant as a colonoscopy. But I wasn't about to throw in the towel. As Uncle Louis would say, sicker dogs have lived.

I collected my paperwork and started toward the elevators. "Coming, Junior?"

"You go ahead," Carlisle replied. "I've got to call my office with the good news."

When I entered his courtroom, Spencer was on the bench with a jury in the box. I signaled to the clerk and quietly handed her the papers. The bailiff, a beefy federal marshal, glared as though I'd farted in church.

The clerk scanned the papers, double-checked the filing stamps, then nodded toward the rows of empty seats, where I parked myself and waited. Carlisle arrived a few minutes later and took a seat on the opposite side of the aisle. I think he actually winked at the court reporter, a cute little Latina in a short skirt and heels. He was a cocky little bastard.

It was a criminal trial in progress, and an FBI haircut was on the witness stand. The prosecuting attorney asked him a series of grossly leading questions, to which every defense objection was promptly and sharply overruled. This went on for forty minutes, until Spencer looked up at the clock and announced the morning break.

As he left the bench, I watched the clerk intercept him with my papers. The old judge looked at them like he'd been handed a dead animal, then he scowled in my direction before ducking through the door to his chambers, his black robe trailing like a windblown shroud.

The break, normally around ten minutes, stretched to half an hour. The bailiff had escorted the jurors into the hallway, so Carlisle and I were the only civilians left in the courtroom. He stood at the bar, chatting up the court reporter, while I sat rehearsing how to break the bad news to Lina.

I'd had better mornings. For starters, I'd gotten only a few hours of fitful sleep. Then, at first light, I'd driven to the office only to find my sweatshirt gone. And then, and this was the capper, Sanchez informed me that the fire department wanted copies of the security-cam tapes from the ninth floor. Drawing Amos Spencer in the litigation lottery completed the superfecta.

A buzzer sounded two angry bursts, jolting me from my reverie, and the reporter teetered back to her machine. Seconds later, Spencer reappeared and climbed onto the bench. He pulled his microphone close, wrapping a pair of rimless spectacles over his ears.

"Tazerian versus Hartford Allied Insurance Company, docket number 437622 ASRx," he read without preamble. "Ex parte application for a temporary restraining order and a preliminary injunction. Counsel, state your appearances."

By the time he'd finished the sentence, both Carlisle and I had passed through the gate to the lectern, where we took turns leaning into the single microphone.

"Jack MacTaggart for the plaintiff, Mr. Tazerian," I announced.

"Good morning, Your Honor. Donald Hudson Carlisle of Plimpton, Simmons & Stark for the defendant and responding party, Hartford Allied." He'd said all of this while looking directly at the court reporter, and he'd punctuated the sentence with a wink.

The judge hadn't noticed, however, as he continued to flip through the papers. I imagined him searching for a typographic error that would justify remanding me into custody.

Finally, and without looking up from his reading, he said to Carlisle, "Counsel, I assume your client opposes this application?"

"Yes, Your Honor."

"Pray tell me why."

Carlisle shot his cuffs.

"First of all, from a purely procedural standpoint, there's been no showing that any irreparable harm will come to Mr. Tazerius if the TRO is denied and my client is given twenty days to present a formal, written opposition. But the court needn't reach that issue today because, substantively, there's no basis whatsoever for the requested injunction. As the court knows, mandatory injunctions are disfavored. In this case, the

Hartford Allied policy clearly states that experimental treatments are excluded from coverage. Our senior medical staff in Connecticut carefully analyzed this transplant procedure and determined that it was both experimental in nature and unlikely to be of any therapeutic benefit to the insured. Under the plain language of the insurance contract, that determination is conclusive."

Carlisle looked to the ceiling, a sigh in his voice.

"As Your Honor knows, group health insurance plans are priced with these exclusions in mind. As much as Hartford Allied would love to see all of its clients receive every treatment ever devised by the imagination of medical science, that just wouldn't be fair to the other policyholders. They count on us to be there, and also to be solvent, when *they* need treatment. There has to be some limits on what any one individual can demand of the plan. If not, premiums would rise to the point where nobody could afford insurance, and that would be . . . well, a national health crisis.

"For all of these reasons, Your Honor, we respectfully submit that the court should not only deny the requested restraining order, but summarily deny the injunction as well, and dismiss the case forthwith."

And with that, plus a smirk in my direction, he stepped aside.

It was a good, lawyerly argument. I thought he might have overplayed it a bit with the national health crisis, but the old man had listened carefully, and even seemed to nod a time or two.

But Donald Carlisle had made two big mistakes, and that left me an opening.

Spencer turned his watery eyes on me. "Mr. . . . MacTaggart. Anything you'd like to say for the record?"

I stepped to the mic and placed both hands on the lectern.

"Victor Tazerian, Your Honor, is a trash man. He earns thirty thousand dollars a year. Without this insurance, he cannot afford this treatment, and without this treatment, he'll be dead before Easter.

"There is only a very small window of opportunity for this surgery to be effective. We cannot wait a few months, or even a few weeks, for a decision to be made in this case. Any delay would be tantamount to a death warrant for Mr. Tazerian.

"The fact that the Hartford Allied policy states that the company's medical decisions are final is irrelevant to these proceedings, as the court well knows. Every contract, and especially insurance contracts, come with

175

an implied covenant of good faith and fair dealing. You, Your Honor, not Hartford Allied, decides whether that covenant has been honored in this case, or whether it has been breached.

"And in that regard, the court might like to know that I made a formal, written demand on Hartford Allied to pay for this procedure on Thursday evening. Their claims management in Connecticut rejected our demand on Friday evening. With all due respect to Mr. Carlisle, I'm skeptical that their 'senior medical staff' made any analysis, careful or otherwise, about this procedure. In fact, I'd wager that the only analysis performed by Hartford Allied was by its claims personnel, and that the only factor they considered was the cost of the surgery."

Carlisle at that point tried to shoulder me away from the lectern, but he came up short in the shoulder department. Spencer stared him down like a weasel in a wind tunnel.

"Let him finish!" he snapped. "This isn't the roller derby."

"Heinrich Wagner," I continued, "is a world-renowned expert in the field of leukemia research. You have his declaration. In Dr. Wagner's opinion, the surgery in question is not experimental by any stretch of the imagination, and Mr. Tazerian is, in fact, an excellent candidate for that surgery. Simply put, it will save his life.

"In closing, I would only note that Hartford Allied is a publicly traded company. Their net pretax profits last year were over three *billion* dollars. So we can all sleep easily tonight in the knowledge that this procedure isn't going to break their piggy bank, and it certainly isn't going to trigger any national health crisis. It will, however, save the life of a trash man from Glendale, and it's on his behalf that I respectfully urge this court to issue the requested order."

Except for the one outburst, Spencer's face had been a mask throughout my argument, impossible to read. He seemed to listen, but he didn't frown, smile, or otherwise telegraph his feelings. I clung to the lectern and held my breath.

First he grunted. Then, when he finally spoke, it was to Carlisle.

"Counsel, what are the names of these doctors in Connecticut you say reviewed this man's medical file?"

Carlisle licked his lips.

"I don't know their *names,* Your Honor. I deal with the general counsel's office in Hartford. But I've been assured —"

Spencer cut him off.

"You'll produce these doctors, whoever

they are, for deposition here in Los Angeles next week. At *your* client's expense. Tell 'em that's a cost of doing business out here on the left coast. You, Mr. MacTaggart, will produce this Dr. Wagner for his deposition. Now you two go out in the hallway and work out the scheduling. Then I want you both back here next Friday . . ."

He turned to his clerk, who chimed, "November first."

"November the first, at nine A.M. You can each submit a declaration by four o'clock on Thursday afternoon, not to exceed five pages, summarizing the depositions. Exchange them by fax."

He shuffled the papers on his desk.

"The application for a temporary restraining order is denied, *without* prejudice. Time is shortened so that the hearing on the application for a preliminary injunction and a permanent injunction is now set for November the first at nine A.M., in this courtroom. Is notice waived?"

"Notice waived," I intoned. Carlisle, visibly shaken, said nothing.

"Plaintiff to give notice!" snapped the old judge, tossing my papers onto the clerk's desk with a thud. "Now get my jury back in here!"

Like most lawyers, I've been known to

make my best arguments in the car on the way back from the courthouse. But not today. Today I just cranked up the stereo, rolled down the windows, and savored the experience.

Carlisle's first mistake had been telling Amos Spencer that under the terms of the policy, the insurance company — and not Amos Spencer — had the last word on coverage. That was the rhetorical equivalent of waving a red flag in front of a bull.

His second mistake, the fatal one, was serving up that "senior medical staff in Connecticut" canard. I don't know if he'd made that up himself, or if he was just reciting the script they'd given him to work from. Either way, he'd never have screwed that pooch if he'd taken the time to read my declaration instead of pricing Bordeaux futures on his BlackBerry. And that little boo-boo had put Donald Hudson Carlisle squarely behind the eight ball.

I half expected a squad of cops or a phalanx of fire marshals awaiting me in the lobby, but all I found was the familiar face of Maurice Jackson, the day man.

As a young puncher with more courage than talent, Mo Jackson had fought the best middleweights of his generation, including the legendary Tony Zale, and he had the face to prove it. I always addressed him as Champ, an honorific that never failed to produce a gap-toothed grin.

I stopped at his desk, to see if he'd heard anything about the fire alarm.

"No, suh," he rasped. "Sanchez done handled it las night."

"Thanks, Champ. Let me know if you hear anything."

I was happy to see no crime-scene tape on my office door, and no fingerprint powder on my desk. Less felicitous was the note from Bernie that read: Nail appt. at 11:00. Early lunch. Back at one. xoxox.

What's more, and less felicitous still, the prodigal son had apparently returned, as I had voice messages both from Jared Henley and from George Wells.

The message from Jared was short and breezy. "Little bird says you're looking for me, sport. I'll be here all day." There was a wistful note there at the end.

The message from Wells was also short, but was anything but breezy. "This is George Wells. I just got the lab results back, and we need to talk." He left both his office and his cell phone numbers.

My first call, however, was to Lina Tazerian. At first she thought we'd lost the case, and she began to sob. I explained to her that a denial without prejudice was the best result we could have hoped for, and that we had a better than decent shot at getting the injunction next week. I'm not sure she understood the rationale, but she finally said that if I was happy, she'd be happy too.

My next call was to Mayday. She wanted a blow-by-blow of the hearing, and she whooped with delight at the outcome. I asked her to call her pal Heinrich, and then to order a transcript of the hearing. I wanted a permanent record of Carlisle's argument, in case Amos Spencer's memory proved as short as his temper.

I reached Wells on his cell phone. From the crowd noise in the background, I guessed he was at the racetrack at Santa Anita. Wherever he was, he had to shout to be heard.

"Halicephalobus deletrix," he said.

"Hali-what?"

"It's a parasite. *Halicephalobus deletrix.* It's very rare, and very fatal. It was present in both the blood and fecal samples."

"So that means he wasn't poisoned?"

There was a pregnant pause.

"Wait a minute," he said. There followed a sound of movement, and the crowd noise suddenly quieted.

"That's better. Can you hear me?"

"Yeah, fine."

"Okay, here's the deal. The parasite is a nematode. It lives in the soil, or in water. Clinically, the fatality rate from equine infestation is one hundred percent. By that I mean that every reported case of infestation in horses has resulted in fatality."

"Okay."

"But here's the rub. If it were present in either the soil or water at Fieldstone, then other horses would be infected as well. But they aren't."

"How do you know that?"

"Because they'd be dead too. It's not only fatal, it's also fast-acting."

He paused to let this all sink in.

"Infestation typically occurs through the mouth or nose, or through an open wound. Hush Puppy had no open wounds. The necropsy will tell us whether the parasite was present in the mouth or nasal passages. But I can tell you right now, that's very unlikely."

"Why's that?"

"Because that would mean it entered his system through his feed or water. And if it did, then other horses would almost certainly be infected. Maybe people as well. And they'd be dead too."

Yikes.

"If he wasn't infected through food or water, or through an open wound, then how?"

There was another pause.

"Based on what we know," he said, "parasitic infestation was almost certainly induced by hypodermic injection."

"Okay," I said, still pacing. "Here's the way I see it. Sydney kills Creole and somehow gets caught by Barbara Hauser. Barbara blackmails Sydney. Jared handled the insurance claim, so Sydney runs to Jared. Her first mistake. Jared not only counsels her to pay, he offers to facilitate. For a small fee, apparently."

Russ looked a little queasy. On his desk were the copies I'd made of the purloined bank records.

"Sydney takes Jared's advice, which is her second mistake. She also agrees to buy Hush Puppy, so that Barbara can gallop to Olympic glory. And that's the backstory, as they say in Hollywood.

"Now we fast-forward a few years. The Everett fortune is waning, but not Sydney's lifestyle, which if you haven't noticed, is rather extravagant. So, she starts borrowing from Peter to pay Paul, and pretty soon she's upside down. And then one day she wakes up and says to herself, 'Hey, wait a minute, if Barbara were to finger me for Creole, I could turn around and finger her for blackmail, and we could both go live in a gated community.' Which she knows that Barbara, having developed a taste for the finer things, would never risk. So to hell with Barbara, she figures, and to hell with Jared too. She's strapped for cash, and she needs a fresh start."

Russ rose and crossed to the windows.

"So, she does what any pillar of the community would do under the circumstances. She puts a hit on Hush Puppy, then she hires Henley and Hargrove to make sure the claim gets paid. Did I miss anything?"

For a long while Russ said nothing. Then again, he had a lot to digest.

I'd told him the whole story — about my first dinner with Tara, my meeting with Barbara, and my phone call to Sally. I'd told him about the tape recording, the missing file, Sydney's drunken phone call, and my escapade in bookkeeping.

Last but not least, I'd told him about the deadly little parasites, halitosis dandruff. The only things I'd held back were my personal involvement with Tara and my still-missing sweatshirt, the former out of fear

184

he'd disapprove, and the latter because it was my problem to deal with.

As he studied the distant mountains, I couldn't tell whose predicament was paining Russ more — Sydney's or Jared's. Sydney, after all, was a longtime client who owed her wealth, now largely dissipated, to an epic probate battle Russ had waged against her rapacious stepsons. As for Jared, whatever his myriad shortcomings, he was still the son of Russ's longtime partner, not to mention a Dinsmoor protégé at the time of the events in question.

When Russ finally spoke, his voice was hollow.

"I've known Jared since he was in diapers, you know."

That sounded like a preamble, but he left it hanging.

"Was that before or after law school?"

He shot me a look that said he was in no mood for jokes.

"Sorry. If it's any consolation, he at least kept it off the Henley and Hargrove books. Up until now, at least, we could all plead ignorance."

This was cold comfort. Once Jared had learned of the blackmail scheme, which was a crime in progress, his ethical obligation was to advise Sydney to report both her involvement and Barbara's to the authorities, and to withdraw from her representation if she failed to do either. At a minimum, he should have run, not walked, to consult with Russ. Instead he'd acted on his own misguided judgment, and in the process had become an accessory. And the shrapnel from that bombshell, if it ever hit the press, would leave a lot of people bleeding.

Russ was in his chair now, tapping his pipe in his palm.

"Jared was a new lawyer then. I suppose if Sydney came to him and told him in confidence about the blackmail, he may have thought he was duty-bound to keep it a secret. Evidence was never the boy's strong suit."

Russ was trying to give Morris Henley's only son the benefit of the doubt. Which is not what I'd like to give him.

"As for the payments," Russ continued, "Jared probably thought that using a non-IOLTA account would insulate the firm from his conduct. That's something, at least."

"You're right, that was thoughtful. He really earned those monthly service fees."

Russ sighed. "That's an unhappy fact, I'll grant you that."

I wasn't quite sure where this was heading. Or maybe I was, but I was in no mood to go there.

Russ read my face. "Judge not lest ye be judged," he said. "Didn't I read that someplace?"

"Yeah. The same place where it says thou shalt not kill and thou shalt not steal."

He didn't respond. His mind, I could tell, had already jumped several moves ahead.

"The question now," he finally said, "is how best to extricate them both from this little quagmire."

"You can't be serious."

He raised an eyebrow.

"Don't forget, he's still my partner, and she's still our client. Not for long, perhaps, but that depends."

"Depends on what?"

"On their side of the story. There are generally two."

There was a note of reproach in his voice that surprised me under the circumstances. After all, Jared had just earned his black belt in stupid, and Sydney, whatever her self-inflicted travails, was a serial horse killer.

"We're looking at three or four felonies here," I reminded him.

He nodded. "Not to mention a possible disbarment, and a public scandal. I understand the stakes, Jack. That's exactly why we need to proceed with caution, avoid leaping to facile conclusions, and above all else, refrain from making matters worse than they already are."

I didn't see how matters could get any worse, but I was new here.

"What about the insurance claim?"

He grunted. "It sounds to me like they'll deny it, once they get the report from this Wells fellow. That should put an end to that. If Sydney wants to pursue it further, well, then we'll have to confront her with this other business."

He sighed again, heavily. "I suppose we'll have to confront her anyway, at some point."

"And Jared?"

Russ reclined in his chair, clamping the pipe stem in his teeth, and I could hear the wheels turning.

"Let me speak to his father. After forty years, I owe him that much. Why don't you avoid Jared for a day or two, if that's possible. Then, if he asks about Sydney or the pending claim, just give him a status report and play dumb. You should be convincing at that."

He was smiling now, which I found oddly comforting. Having done the heavy lifting up until now, it was nice to have someone else shouldering the load.

"He knows I've been looking for his Creole file."

"Then ask him for it. I'll be interested to hear what he says. Just don't let on that you've already seen it. Or that you know anything about . . . any of this."

He squared the papers into a pile.

"What about Sydney? Do I tell her about Wells?"

He thought about that.

"Why don't you put her off as well, until we've met again. Give me a chance to think this through and speak with Morris. I'm the one who got you into this. Let me take it from here."

I stood to leave.

"You've considered, of course, that Morris already knows about this?"

He looked up, surprised.

"No, I have not. Why would you say such a thing?"

I told him how Morris had reacted upon seeing me in Jared's office. The same office, I reminded him, where the evidence had been stashed. "Plus," I continued, "you yourself told me that Morris knows the serial number of every dollar the firm's ever made."

"Hence the non-IOLTA account."

"And Morris never noticed the bank statements coming to Jared every month?"

I could tell he wasn't buying it.

"Let me see if I follow your reasoning. In order to help a client he hasn't worked with in years, and whom he doesn't particularly like, by the way, Morris Henley has been risking professional scandal, financial ruin, and criminal prosecution, all so that his son could add an extra ten thousand dollars to his monthly partnership draw?"

He was right, of course — it made no sense. The firm was Morris Henley's life, and his family's legacy. However much he may dote on Jared, the risk-reward was ridiculous.

"You're sure you don't want me there when you talk to Morris?"

"I believe I'll keep you out of this. I'll tell him that I made inquiries when I learned she was selling the house. And, that I obtained copies of the bank records somehow, after discovering the account."

"How'd you discover the account?"

"By deductive reasoning, the same as you." He smiled. "You don't have a monopoly on inquisitiveness."

"You don't need to cover for me. I'm a big boy, you know."

He pointed his pipe in my direction.

"You know, Jack, I'm not going to be around forever. To make a career at this firm, you're going to have to earn Morris Henley's respect. Breaking and entering, setting off fire alarms?" He shook his head. "A less perspicacious man might get the wrong impression."

Back in my office, after looking up "perspicacious" in the dictionary, I called Tara to confirm our dinner for Friday, which she'd insisted on hosting. Something about fresh seaweed at the farmer's market.

"And what about Sam?" she asked. "Does he eat table scraps?"

"Does Sydney Everett sleep on her back?"

She groaned. "That's awful."

"That's very perspicacious of you."

As I passed through the building lobby, Sanchez jumped to his feet and motioned me over.

"Señor Jack," he whispered. "The fire marshal called again. What should I tell him?"

It was only then that I realized Sanchez had been counting on me, as the first person to whom he'd spoken that morning, to bring him the security tape.

"Bad news," I said gravely, clapping a hand on his shoulder. "The system was down last night. There is no tape."

He nodded and reached for the phone.

9

I'd spent a lifetime avoiding people like Jared Henley, and for two whole days, despite a half-dozen increasingly strident voice messages, I had put my experience to good use. By Friday morning, however, I knew the time had finally come.

I did a double take in the building lobby as I passed the security desk. Neatly folded next to Mo Jackson's telephone was my missing sweatshirt, looking every bit like the cheese wedge that it was. I had to assume there was a fire investigator lurking somewhere nearby, hoping that anyone dumb enough to leave it behind would be dumb enough to come back and claim it. But today, that wouldn't be me.

Kim Noffinger studied her computer screen with the intensity of a NORAD wing commander repulsing a cruise missile attack.

"Try the red jack on the black queen," I

suggested.

She looked up and smiled. "Where were you when I needed you?"

I leaned in to see that it was chess, not solitaire.

"Is he busy?"

She rolled her eyes and stroked the keyboard. "Check."

I found Jared in his swivel chair, his tasseled loafers propped on the edge of the desk. He was busy all right, cleaning his fingernails with the letter opener. He wore a salmon-pink dress shirt, designer jeans, and a suntan that suggested six weeks adrift in an open lifeboat.

Jared Henley wasn't as big as his father, and he must have inherited his hair from his mother's side of the merger. But he had the unmistakable block head and Roman nose of the Henley clan, softened in his case by pale blue eyes and a cherubic mouth, lending an air of infantile petulance to an otherwise handsome face.

It was, according to Bernie, the kind of face you wanted to slap, just on general principles.

"MacTaggart! Christ, I thought you were avoiding me." He waved the opener at one of his client chairs, both of which were laden with boxes and bags of what appeared to be golfing paraphernalia. "Move that crap and have a seat."

I set a stack of sherbet-colored shirts on the floor.

"I see they've probated the Bing Crosby estate."

He laughed, swinging his feet to the floor. "Duty-free shopping. I figure the flight delay cost me around two grand."

I settled into the chair. "Did you get that shirt in the airport?"

He looked at his chest to make sure. "You like it?"

"Did you buy the matching skirt?"

He laughed again, but with less enthusiasm.

"Is it my imagination," I said, "or do you get more vacation time than the rest of us working stiffs?"

"I was attending a seminar," he said defensively. "Boss's orders. Not that it's any of your business."

"Let me guess. 'Selected Issues in Subtropical Recreation'?"

He set the letter opener on the desk.

"I suppose I should thank you," he said, scooting his chair forward, "for helping out with Sydney."

"So you've heard."

He nodded. "Poor old broad. She paid a

bundle for that horse."

"You know what they say. Losing one horse is tragic, but losing two is just plain careless."

He nodded. "Yeah, I get the picture. The insurance people are not gonna like it."

"As a matter of fact, they don't like it. By the way, Mrs. Everett has asked me and Russ to handle the claim."

That surprised him. "C'mon, sport. What do you know about horses?"

"As much as you know about insurance litigation. Anyway, you were out of town."

"Fine," he said. "No skin off my nose." He took up the letter opener and gestured to his little pile of mail, which, I noticed, appeared largely untouched. "I've got more on my plate than I can handle anyway."

Truer words were never spoken.

"We've been looking for your old Creole file. Bernie said there was no card in the system."

"No shit? I'll have Kimmy look for it."

"She already has. It's not closed, and it's not in your drawers."

He stroked his chin, as though to demonstrate that he was bringing all of his intellectual firepower to the issue of the missing file.

"Can you think of anyplace else it might be?"

"Did you check with Dinsmoor?"

"Yes, I did."

"What about the basement? Maybe the card just got lost."

"Sorry, still cold."

"What's that supposed to mean?"

To avoid lifting him from his chair by the collar, I walked to the windows, where I watched the first winter storm clouds building over the mountains. I pictured Jared's body hurtling through space toward the pavement below.

"Hey," he said, "I know! Did you check in that little file-processing room? All kinds of shit gets lost in there."

"How about your desk?"

"What?"

I turned to face him.

"Your desk. Bottom left drawer, the one that locks. Maybe you put it there and forgot all about it."

"No way," he said.

"Humor me."

With that he abandoned any pretense of bonhomie. He looked, in fact, as though he'd like to poke me in the nose.

"All right," he said, digging into his pocket for a key case. "Suit yourself."

He unlocked the drawer and pulled it open.

"Satisfied?"

I walked around to see that his personal files were all there, their alphabetic tabs raised like hackles down the center of the drawer.

And that the Creole file was gone.

Russ would be upset, I knew, but I couldn't see that I'd done any real harm. The cat was already out of the bag, or the box, or wherever the cat had been, and it was only a matter of time before Jared found out. Besides which, the guy just pissed me off.

Outside of Russ's office, Veronica Daley was busily relabeling a tall stack of files.

"Is he around?"

Veronica was in her fifties, or maybe her thirties. A church-mouse spinster with limp brown hair and a perpetual head cold, her life revolved, as far as I could tell, around the care and feeding of three Siamese cats and one aging Pasadena barrister.

"You just missed him," she sniffled. "He said he had errands to run, and that he might not be back until Monday."

"Do you know if he met with Morris yesterday? Or this morning?"

From beneath the files she unearthed a

calendar book and flipped a page. To my knowledge, Russ was the only lawyer in the firm who still kept his appointments on paper.

"It's not in his day book."

"What does he have for today?"

She rescanned the page. "He had a lunch with Judge West, but he had me cancel that. And a haircut at two, also canceled. And that's pretty much it."

"Did he say where he was going?"

She shook her head. "You could try his cell phone, I suppose."

She gave a little shrug. We both knew that reaching Russ by cell phone was like trying to contact space aliens with radio messages broadcast from Earth.

"If he calls in, would you tell him I'm looking for him? It's semi-important."

"Is there anything I can do?"

"Yes," I told her, "you can stop wearing that perfume. It's driving me wild."

I did try Russ's cell, but of course got no answer. I tried his home as well, with the same result. I left messages on both, asking that he call and stressing that it was urgent. Other than that, there was nothing I could think to do.

Not that it really mattered at this point. As far as I was concerned, *l'affaire* Creole was no longer my problem. Russ would huddle with Morris, and together they'd find some way to extricate Jared's Footjoy from the shit-pile — an exercise with which Morris, I would guess, was all too familiar.

As for Sydney, her insurance claim was a dead letter, and if there was a God in heaven, she'd get what she had coming. Or then again, maybe she wouldn't. The truth is, I didn't give a rat's red ass. If Russ wasn't outraged by what I'd uncovered, then I wasn't going to lose sleep over it either. Whatever happened from here on, I was all too happy to watch it unfold from the sidelines.

I went to check on Mayday, who reported that she'd sweet-talked the Flintridge city manager into expediting a special use permit for Hush Puppy's interment ceremony, an event that Mayday had dubbed the Big Dig. She said the guy had all but ejaculated when she'd told him it would be a personal favor to Mrs. Everett. Mayday had put him in touch with Fieldstone, and the baton was now safely in Sally's competent hands.

Mayday had also gotten deposition dates from Heinrich Wagner. I asked her to coordinate that through Bernie, and to call Donald Carlisle's office directly. She nodded, scribbling notes on a legal pad.

"How's my hypothetical horse?" she asked as she wrote.

"Still dead, I'm afraid."

"Gone, alas, but not forgotten."

She opened a drawer and extracted a glossy magazine called *The Chronicle of the Horse.* She turned it around and laid it open to a dog-eared page.

The article, by Gwen Hickey, was headlined "Sudden Death for a Champion."

"Shit."

"I got it from a friend. She's into horses, and she knew we represent Mrs. Everett. I thought you might be interested."

I scanned the article, which filled four six-inch columns. It mostly recounted Hush Puppy's illustrious career, and it included a quotation from Sydney, who'd said, "Hush Puppy was a great champion and a wonderful friend, and his death was a crushing blow, both to me personally and to horse lovers everywhere."

Tara was right; it made you want to puke.

"Did she really kill her own horse?" Mayday whispered, her eyes wide with wonder.

"Of course not. Well, maybe."

I finished reading the article. It concluded with:

Although the cause of death was not immediately known, attorney Jared Henley, legal counsel to Mrs. Everett, cited "cardiac failure of unknown etiology."

Necropsy results are pending.

So much for a quiet ending. Although the article made no mention of Creole, it wouldn't take Woodward and Bernstein to make the connection once the necropsy results became public.

Russ would need to know about this as well.

The season's first rain blew forgotten smells across the sidewalk — ozone and pebbles, earthworms and dust. It drummed my umbrella and it pixilated the idling Wrangler's headlights as I crouched to dial the combination.

The lock gave with a *snap,* and gravity, or maybe the wind, wrenched the chain-link gate from my fingers. I splashed back to the Jeep.

Tara's solution to my late arrival was to divert me to the back service gate, which was used to move trailers through the Fieldstone grounds during shows. She'd said it was the fastest route to her little bungalow, which sounded good at the time.

She'd failed to mention that the rain would turn the earthen driveway to oozing muck.

The beating wipers carved glimpses of an open landscape dominated by sagging oak trees, and the driveway topped out onto a paved parking lot where a row of horse trailers shimmered.

Tara's house was obscured by a row of hedges, the lights from her windows glowing like storm lanterns in the raging darkness. I spied her Jeep out front, huddled beside a battered F-150 pickup. I parked alongside the truck, honked once to herald our arrival, and opened the passenger door for Sam. The smell of wood smoke greeted our dash for the porch, where Tara stood now backlit in the open doorway.

"Isn't it wonderful?" she squealed, clapping her hands in delight.

She kissed me on tiptoes, then bent to welcome Sam, who buried his head in her crotch and whimpered.

"Let's get you out of those wet clothes and into a dry martini," she vamped in a thick Sean Connery brogue.

She poured them from a silver shaker. "A Flynn family recipe," she answered before I could ask.

Tara had gone all out for the evening. There were candles glowing on the tables and logs crackling in the old stone fireplace. Enya wafted from the stereo, while a savory aroma from the kitchen permeated the entire house.

Sam walked an inspection lap before settling by the hearth, ignoring the yellow eyes that tracked his movements from the mantel.

"Stanley and Livingstone," said Tara, following my gaze. "Aren't they the sweetest things?"

"I don't know. Let's grill one up and find out."

"Please tell me you like cats."

"On the advice of counsel, I'm invoking my constitutional right against self-incrimination."

"Well," she said, tilting her glass to the firelight. "The night is young. Maybe I'll teach you a thing or two before it's over."

I drank to that.

Tara wore jeans for the occasion, plus a flimsy black top and gray sweat socks. Her hair was down but pulled back on the sides and fastened behind her head with a silver clip, a style that gave her the look of a Moorish princess.

"When does the next tour depart?"

She smiled. "Turn around. This is it, plus

the bedroom. And that's a separate admission."

The room was cozy-small, with dark wood
walls and an open-beamed ceiling. There
was a couch by the fireplace, some bookshelves and a table in one corner, and a
small antique desk in the other. On the wall
opposite the fireplace was an open kitchen-
ette with a Formica counter.

The décor was shabby-chic equestrian. All
of the framed photos — on the desk, the
end table, and the bookshelves — were of
horses, or of riders, or of horses and riders
in varying combinations. A blanket with the
Budweiser logo was draped over the sofa
back. The magazines arrayed on the coffee
table were all equine in nature, and included, I noticed, *The Chronicle of the Horse.*

The only secular artifacts were a vase of
roses on the table, and a pair of family
photos on the mantel.

"Your parents?"

Stanley edged backward as I moved toward the fire. Or maybe it was Livingstone.
Tara came and stood beside me.

"Sean and Dierdre Flynn, themselves."

Her father, she had told me, was some
kind of Silicon Valley executive, and he
looked the part with his tight gray hair, steel
glasses, and a face made for television. But

Tara clearly favored her mother, who could easily have been a model. In the photo she was leaning into her husband, her dark hair swept over one shoulder. They were in dinner dress, at twilight, sitting at an outdoor table with maybe a golf course in the background.

Dierdre Flynn had Tara's black Irish cheekbones and full eyebrows, but also a square jaw with a faint cleft to the chin. She wore a low-cut dress and a necklace of sparkling stones. The look in her eye was challenging, maybe defiant.

"She's very beautiful," I observed.

Tara said nothing.

The other photo was in black and white; two small girls in Sunday dresses, perched on a hay bale. Both wore identical patent leather shoes and pageboy haircuts, and even I couldn't distinguish between Tara and her late sister.

"Whenever I'm feeling too happy," she said, leaning against me, "I look at that picture, and it brings me back to Earth."

Which was a very Catholic thing to say.

"You never told me the story."

She moved away. Her voice, when she spoke again, came from the sofa.

"You've heard the term Irish twins? Well, Keira was the youngest, by ten months. We were close, of course, but . . . different. I was the little lady, playing house and dress up, and she was the tomboy in cowboy boots. Reckless. Always getting dirty, always getting hurt."

I replaced the photo and turned to face her, the fire warm at my back.

"She was by far the better rider. Completely fearless around horses. She was always out at the barn, always riding bareback. Always challenging me to races."

She reached for the shaker and topped off her glass.

"We were forbidden to ride on Sundays. My mother said they were good Catholic horses, you see. But Keira was so willful. One Sunday, when I was ten years old, Keira disappeared from the house, and I knew she'd gone down to the barn. So I snuck away to look for her. I wanted to bring her home before she got into trouble."

As she lifted her glass, a tear rolled down her cheek.

"Look, Tara, you don't have to . . ."

"No, it's all right." She studied her drink. "Only when I got to the barn, the horses were all there. I called for her, but she didn't answer. And then I found her horse's bridle, lying in the dirt. We never saw her alive again."

"Don't," I said.

She wiped her cheek with her wrist.

"A neighbor saw the car, but he couldn't describe the driver. He told the police that Keira was carrying a bucket of carrots when she got in. And that when the car drove away, the driver threw the bucket out the window."

Me and my big mouth.

"Get your heels down."

"Make him quit it!"

"He can't help it, he's trotting. When he trots, you bounce."

"I'm bouncing into the soprano section!"

"That's because you're not posting. Post!"

"Posting is worse!"

Tara made a clucking noise and the horse trotted faster.

"Shit!"

"Chin up, heels down, stop complaining," she said. "Just keep the horse between you and the ground."

I was glad somebody was enjoying this. I know it wasn't me.

What I was doing, per Tara's instruction, was trying to rock my pelvis forward in time with the rise of the horse's outside shoulder. But every third stride or so I'd lose the rhythm, and the pommel of the saddle would remind me why whoever had invented the automobile had become a very rich man.

"Are you all right?"

"Are there paramedics on call?"

"Whoa, boy," she said, and the big horse, whose name was Iroquois, broke stride to a walk, then slowed to a stop. From the center of the circle Tara gathered in the line, making loops as she approached.

"Well," she said, patting the horse by way of apology, "as first lessons go, I've seen worse."

"Oh, yeah? Where?"

"I once worked at a summer camp for special needs children."

I dropped my feet from the irons and slid gingerly to the ground.

"And what's with these saddles? How's a man supposed to rope cattle in this thing?"

She was securing the stirrups to the sides of the saddle which, being of the English variety, looked more like a bar stool than one of the big Barcaloungers that ferried Gary Cooper and John Wayne across the prairies of the American West.

"We cover cattle roping in the second lesson," she said, grabbing my shirtfront and pulling me in for a kiss. "You did good. Really."

It was high noon on Saturday, and we stood in a muddy clearing across the road from Fieldstone, among the big eucalyptus, oak, and sycamore trees of the Hahamongna Watershed Park. The Hahamongna were an ancient Tongva Indian tribe who used to hunt and gather here in the Arroyo Seco before there were flood control channels and golf courses and a football stadium called the Rose Bowl. I'm pretty sure there are no Hahamongna left anymore, since we were standing in a park, and not the parking lot of a casino.

Tara led the big horse back to the little public stable from which we'd borrowed him. I limped along beside her.

"Are you okay?"

"I'll let you know when the other testicle descends."

"You'd be a lot more comfortable in riding breeches."

"You mean those bun-huggers with the little knee patches? I don't think so."

"Trust me, you'd look cute in bun-huggers. When's your birthday?"

We dropped off the horse and continued on to our Jeeps, which we'd left by the park entrance. The impromptu lesson had been Tara's idea, in response to a crack I'd made over breakfast to the effect that shouldn't the horses be the ones who got the ribbons instead of the riders?

That had gotten her Irish up. Then, when I'd confessed that the next horse I rode would be my first — or at least, my first without a coin slot in its head — she'd dared me to cowboy up.

"So," she said as we walked, "if I put you on Escalator and sent you out there next Sunday, how do you think you'd make out?"

"I doubt I could get him over a jump."

"No offense, sweetie, but I doubt you could get him into the ring."

"Insult to injury."

"Would you agree now that the rider deserves a little credit?"

"More than a little. Mea culpa."

"Now then," she said, her point made, "would you rather have an ice pack on your crotch or a late lunch?"

"I think I saw that movie once, at a bachelor party."

She ignored this.

"The kitchen's still open at the club. That is, if you're willing to risk being seen together."

"That depends. Any chance of running into Margaret Carlton?"

"Unlikely. She'll be at the barn office."

"What about Barbara Hauser?"

She gave me a sideways look.

"And what about Sydney? My boss says I'm supposed to be avoiding her."

"Your boss is a smart man."

We drove past the guard shack, where Tara waved without slowing and I drafted behind, snapping off a crisp salute.

We parked behind the clubhouse and entered through a rear door. Inside the kitchen, three teenaged girls stood washing a stack of dishes in assembly-line fashion while chattering away in Spanish. We placed our orders with the cook, a stout doyenne whom Tara introduced as Maritza Jimenez. The two of them proceeded to converse in rapid-fire Spanish. At one point Maritza glanced at me and the two of them giggled, as did the chorus by the sink.

"Another hidden talent," I observed as we passed through a large fireplace room and onto the patio.

"Maritza is my *madrina.* She's always looking out for me."

"Does that mean my food might be poisoned?"

Only two of the patio tables were occupied; one by a pair of giggling teens, and the other by Sydney Everett. Sydney was flanked by a pair of turkey-necked crones who might have been sisters, and she did a double take when she saw me. I gave a little wave.

An enormous oak tree rose from the center of the patio, dwarfing the tables around it. And although it must have been eighty degrees in the sun, the shade was cooler than the look in Sydney's eye.

"Hey," I asked Tara, "what's Irish and stays out all night in the rain?"

"I'm not sure I want to know."

"Patty O'Furniture."

She chose a table in sunlight, with a clear view of the main riding ring below. A lesson was in progress, and Barbara Hauser stood rotating like a lighthouse, calling instruction to a circling student. I took the chair that put my back to Sydney's table.

"Is this awkward for you?"

"No, don't be silly. Blink twice if she goes for the knife."

A waiter appeared, and Tara ordered cervezas. Behind me, chairs scraped on flagstone and murmured goodbyes were spoken. I followed Sydney's approach to our table in Tara's eyes.

"Hello, Jack. Hello, Tara. What a surprise to see you here. Together."

She was wearing the same basic riding outfit she'd worn at our first meeting, to the same general effect.

"Hello, Sydney. Would you care to join us?"

She pulled back a chair and sat. "Delighted."

We all regarded one another in silence. A breeze sent fallen oak leaves skittering across the flagstones.

"Beautiful day, isn't it?" I offered.

"I know. You two were discussing Hush Puppy's interment service."

"Actually," Tara said, "we were just discussing cutlery."

I cleared my throat. "You'll be happy to know that the city has agreed to issue a special use permit."

"They already have, sugar. We've scheduled the service for Wednesday morning. We'll gather at sunrise. I do hope you're planning to attend."

Tara sat upright in her chair.

"You mean *this* Wednesday?"

"Precisely."

"But you can't do that! We'll be right in the middle of show prep. Do you have any idea what that involves?"

Sydney was rearranging the sugar packets in their little plastic holder. "Having chaired the show committee for many years, Tara dear, I believe I do."

"Then you know that the entire crew will

214

be working overtime. We'll be setting up the grandstands, moving in the vendors and caterers, bringing in the trailers. Not to mention reworking the footing, dressing the jumps, and putting out a dozen other last-minute fires. And you plan to hold a *funeral* service in the middle of that?"

"It's only fitting, don't you think? Hush Puppy always loved the hustle and bustle of a big show."

While Tara smoldered, it occurred to me that if Sally had scheduled the service for Wednesday, then she expected to have Hush Puppy's remains by then. Which meant that the necropsy was probably finished.

"If not the service," said Sydney, satisfied now with her ministrations, "pray tell, what does bring you two together?"

"Philately," I said. "Tara's promised to show me her stamp collection."

"I believe it's pronounced 'fellatio,' Jack. And if Tara collects stamps, then I'm the queen of England."

Tara jumped to her feet, her fists clenched.

"How *dare* you speak to me that way!"

"I'm not aware that I was speaking to you at all, dear."

There was a sudden commotion in the ring below. We all turned to see Barbara's student on the ground with his horse galloping loose, its reins and stirrups flapping.

Tara was already running. She scrambled down the ivy-covered embankment and vaulted the railing. I leapt to my feet and followed.

Tara ignored the crumpled rider, and took an angle on the horse. It was bucking now, wide-eyed and frantic, spurred by the bouncing stirrups. As she approached with her arms aloft, the horse suddenly wheeled, galloping straight in my direction. His tail was raised like a battle ensign, and his flared nostrils came at me like the muzzle of a twelve-gauge shotgun.

I sidestepped the charge and grabbed at the reins, holding on long enough to spin the horse around. But the braided leather seared my palm, and a sickening *pop* tore my shoulder loose from the socket. I dropped to my knees, struck by a lightning bolt of pain.

The horse stood stunned and blowing as Tara grabbed the bridle. She touched its neck and murmured something soft, and the snorting animal's eyes began to focus.

"I've got him, Barbara! Jack, are you all right? *Jack!*"

I was not all right. One glance confirmed that my right shoulder was no longer visible, my right hand hanging limply a good eight inches below its counterpart. I must have gone into shock at that point, because I felt no pain.

A hand touched gently on my head.

"Don't move, Jack. Just breathe."

Tara's voice was distant, as from the wrong end of a megaphone. There were more words spoken, and then I heard her shout, *"Call nine-one-one! We need an ambulance right now!"* And then things got a little fuzzy.

"Everything's going to be fine, sweetie. Don't you worry. Just focus on breathing. That's it. Just breathe."

I sat in the ambulance for a long time with my arm strapped to my side and a cold pack taped to my shoulder. Just as I thought they might have forgotten about me, the rear doors swung open and a gurney was lifted into the space at my feet, strapped to which, like a miniature Frankenstein's monster, was the fallen rider.

His neck was immobilized in a hard plastic collar that cupped his chin and held his head at attention. His face and shirtfront were streaked with dirt and an IV tube snaked from his arm to a plastic bag that the paramedic was attaching to a hook on the roof.

"Hang in there, buddy," the EMT said, although it wasn't clear which of us he was addressing. "We'll be rolling in a minute."

The man on the gurney was pale but conscious, and when he rolled his eyes to look at me, he managed a little smile, as if to say, what a fine pair of buckaroos we are. He was an Asian gentleman in his middle fifties, and despite the neck brace and the odd context, I recognized him immediately.

From the golfing photo on Jared Henley's desk.

10

Veronica Daley's eyes, mournful on the best of days, today were dark and anguished.

"The clerk in department fifty-seven called to ask whether Mr. Dinsmoor was on his way. He missed the nine o'clock calendar call. I tried his cell phone and his home, but there was no answer." She snatched at a tissue and added superfluously, "It's not like him to be late to court."

I started to say that Russ hadn't returned my calls from Friday, but caught myself in time.

"What did he have on calendar?"

"Just a status conference, in the Hudson matter."

That, at least, was good news. In the history of Western jurisprudence, no lawyer was ever executed for missing a status conference. At worst, the court would put the matter over to another date and impose a light monetary sanction. But in Russ's case, even that was unlikely.

Only when she'd finished blowing her nose did Veronica notice the arm.

"Oh, Jack! What happened to you?"

"Old bowling injury. Just call the clerk in fifty-seven and tell them we're sorry. Tell them we can either get somebody down there in thirty minutes, or else the court can put the matter over."

"I already did that. They put it over to next week. But I'm worried about Mr. Dinsmoor, Jack. Where could he be?"

It was an excellent question. Since Russ wasn't great about checking phone messages, I hadn't lost any sleep over the weekend. But missing a court appearance was something else entirely.

I forced a smile. "I wouldn't worry. He probably spent the weekend out on the boat and overslept, that's all. What's his next appointment today?"

She consulted his book.

"Nothing, really. A lunch date at the University Club."

I still didn't know if Russ had met with Morris, and I wasn't about to canvass the Henley family to find out. Besides which, I had other fish to fry. Mayday had scheduled the Hartford Allied depositions for tomorrow, and Heinrich's deposition for Thursday. That meant I had today to prepare for the former, and that I'd have to meet with Wagner sometime Wednesday afternoon, following the Big Dig. Between the depositions, Hush Puppy's funeral, preparing Wagner, Thursday's briefing deadline, Friday's hearing, and whatever fallout remained from Sydney's insurance claim, my hands were full.

Or hand, as the case may be.

Surgery, thankfully, had not been necessary. But after an interminable wait in the crowded ER, the docs had been kind enough to knock me out before popping the shoulder into place. And they'd insisted I wear a sling-like contraption of elastic and Velcro to keep it that way for the next couple weeks.

When I'd awakened in the recovery room, Tara was at my bedside, wearing a brave but worried look. I'd croaked a lame joke about being in heaven, and she'd told me to savor the moment, because I'd probably never experience it again.

According to Tara, Brian Huang had been discharged an hour earlier, with a lightly sprained neck and a badly bruised ego. She'd described him as a newer member of the club, and she was greatly impressed by my concern for his well-being.

After my discharge, we'd found an all-night rental agency, where I'd bagged a two-door Toyota with an automatic transmission. As for my Wrangler, Tara promised to keep it at her place and give it a good home until my arm was fully healed. When Agnes, the woman behind the Enterprise counter, had voiced concerns about the shoulder, I'd assured her that if I was well enough to escape from prison, I was well enough to drive a car.

Back home in Bungalow Heaven, in the wee hours of the morning, Sam had growled at the brace but was otherwise glad to see the old man, and the feeling was mutual. He was a little less forgiving when we both discovered that you can't open a dog food can with one hand.

I'd spent my entire Sunday on the couch with Sam, watching football and eating Advils like salted peanuts. Tara arrived toward evening and grilled me a steak dinner, which only confirmed how pathetic I must have looked. I apologized for imposing a hiatus on sleepovers, but she'd told me to look at the bright side. I still had one good hand to keep me company.

Back down on the eighth floor, Bernadette knocked, then stopped in the doorway.

"What happened to *you?*"

As was her custom on Monday mornings, Bernie was an hour late. If it wasn't car trouble or boyfriend trouble, it was a sick cat or a dying parent. Or sometimes the other way around. After six months, I'd learned to quit asking. Today she looked as though she'd gotten two hours' sleep and had put her makeup on in the car, possibly with a stick.

I frowned at my watch. "Isn't that my line?"

She gave a dismissive wave. "Oh, it's just Lance. He's *such* an asshole. That man would fuck a snake if somebody held the head."

Lance was Bernie's oft-wayward boyfriend.

She gestured with her chin. "So what's with the arm? You get in a beef or something?"

"Yeah. You should see the other guy."

"Oh, come on. Everyone's gonna ask me. Don't force me to make up a story, 'cuz you might not like it."

"Tell 'em I sprained it filling out your late slips."

She made a face.

"Go get your coffee, then call Mayday for some calendar updates. We'll need a conference room and a court reporter tomorrow, for two doctors' depositions."

She was still pouting as I closed the door in her face.

The morning mail included a copy of George Wells's report to Bowman. He'd kept it short and sweet, stating only that the cause of Hush Puppy's death had been "multiple organ failure incident to parasitic infestation by *halicephalobus deletrix*." He'd been kind enough not to mention the likely method of delivery.

But that small blessing was short-lived, since the mail also included a thick FedEx package from the Metropolitan Livestock Insurance Company of Baltimore, Maryland. Inside was the necropsy report, along with a cover letter from one Antonio Rizzardi, vice-president of claims. Mr. Rizzardi regretted to inform me, as counsel for policy owner Sydney Everett, that my client's claim had been denied under Article A ("Coverage"), section 1(a) of the policy, on the grounds that the cause of death of the insured animal was other than "accident, injury, sickness, or disease," and also under Article B ("Exclusions"), section 5(b), on the grounds that there is no coverage for "any act committed by You or at Your direction . . . with the intent to cause a Loss."

The report itself was nine pages long, and

consisted mostly of laboratory reports. There was an executive summary at the end, entitled Findings and Conclusions, that basically mirrored Wells's report, but with the added dagger that "the absence of *deletrix* in the mouth, throat, esophagus, and nasal passages confirms that infestation occurred other than by environmental contamination."

And so the jig was up. My normal practice would have been to forward both reports to Sydney, probably by messenger. But instead I set them aside, pending further instructions from Russ.

The Caltech Web site, as you'd expect, was state of the art. I hunted and pecked my way from the home page to the faculty profiles, and there I found the blemished but jovial face of Brian Yee-Horn Huang, M.D., Ph.D. According to his bio, Huang had been a research fellow and a professor of cellular biology for the past seven years, and his credentials were, even amid the pantheon of the Caltech faculty, pretty remarkable.

He'd received his undergraduate degree in chemical engineering from China's University of Science and Technology at age nineteen, before defecting to the United

States during the last throes of the cold war. He'd then earned a doctorate in biochemistry from MIT and a medical degree from Johns Hopkins. His list of publications covered three single-spaced pages, and his list of honors and awards was nearly as long.

I found what I was after on the fifth page of his résumé, amid a recitation of private research grants and corporate affiliations. The entry identified Huang as the president and cofounder of EVAgen, LLC, which was described as "an emerging leader in the application of recombinant technologies to the prevention and treatment of equine viral arteritis and related conditions." The good doctor appeared to have taken to capitalism like a Peking duck to water.

I wasn't overly surprised when Tara told me that the man in the ambulance was, in fact, Heinrich Wagner's lab partner. In fact, it all seemed to fit. I'd first seen EVAgen on the firm's active client list when I was looking for Sydney's address. When I saw it again on the lab door, I'd assumed that Russ had done work for his friend Wagner, or had maybe referred Wagner to the corporate department for some business advice. But something in Huang's eyes, looking up at me from the gurney, had reminded me of the photos I'd seen on the other desk in

Wagner's lab. And knowing that he'd been on a golf outing with Jared had closed the loop.

My curiosity now piqued, I left the Internet and logged on to Omega, where I located the client data for EVAgen, LLC. The billing address wasn't at Caltech, but rather on Oak Grove Drive in Flintridge. That had a familiar ring. I Googled yellow pages.com and found the listing for the Fieldstone Riding Club, also on Oak Grove. That would put EVAgen's corporate headquarters somewhere nearby, and I guessed it wasn't in the Hahamongna Watershed Park.

I knew from Russ that Caltech managed the Jet Propulsion Laboratory under a long-term contract with NASA. I also knew that a lot of the NASA space jockeys had offices and laboratories both at the open Caltech campus and behind the gates of fortress JPL. What I didn't know was that some of them, apparently, were running private ventures while on the government's payroll.

I was returning from the restroom when I remembered Veronica Daley. A quick trip up to nine found her still stewing in her cubicle.

"Anything yet?"

"No," she said, almost tearfully. "And now

I'm really worried, Jack. I've left a half-dozen messages, on both phones. What do you think I should do? I've already canceled his lunch."

I consulted my watch. It was ten minutes past noon.

"You've checked the entire office?"

"Of course. Nobody knows where he is or where he might be."

"Including the basement?"

She reproached me with her hound dog eyes. "He's not in the office, Jack."

Everyone at Henley & Hargrove knew that Veronica was overly protective of Russ, and that she could be as much a Chicken Little as a mother hen. Only now, she had me worried as well.

"Tell you what. Let me take a run out to his house. I could use the fresh air."

"Oh, Jack. Are you sure? What about your arm?"

"I'll take it with me."

For as long as I could remember, the words "San Marino" had been synonymous with old money in Southern California, and driving down the wide and shaded boulevards, past Spanish- and Mediterranean-style mansions, you couldn't escape the feeling of having entered a sort of time capsule.

But here, as in so many neighborhoods in Los Angeles, appearances were deceiving. Behind the iron gates and beneath the red-tile roofs, tensions bubbled, and immigration was the hot blue flame that roiled the waters. But this being San Marino, it was an immigration issue with a twist.

Over the past couple of decades, a new breed of superrich newcomers from Taiwan and Hong Kong had changed the face of San Marino, for better or worse, making it one of the few Asian majority cities in America. I could remember Russ telling a story about a Chinese gentleman who rang his doorbell one evening and offered to buy his house, on the spot, for the cash that his assistant carried in a Louis Vuitton suitcase.

"More than I could spend in a lifetime," Russ had chuckled, wagging his head at the memory. So sudden and frenzied was the Asian influx that many longtime residents could tell a similar story.

In many of the stately homes, so-called parachute kids, deposited Stateside by their Chinese parents, fended for themselves on generous allowances wire-transferred from overseas. And while the average SAT score improved precipitously at San Marino High, the rise came in direct proportion to the decline in the football program.

Russ, for his part, was sanguine about the demographic shift. Others were less so. Many of the old families, in fact, had fled San Marino for other communities. I once heard a silver-haired client say to Russ, "Let's hope the last white family to leave Chan Marino remembers to take the flag."

It was twelve thirty when I rolled the rented Toyota to the curb chez Dinsmoor. The modest old house sat at the crest of a low knoll, screened from the street by an enormous sycamore tree whose fallen leaves littered the sloping lawn. I reached over to shove the transmission into park and then, awkwardly, to extract the keys from the ignition.

The house looked lifeless, in contrast with its neighbor to the west — a cheery Colonial whose front porch hosted a pre-Halloween convergence of ghosts, scarecrows, and jack-o'-lanterns. Russ's neighbors to the east lived behind a ten-foot hedge that formed a protective stockade against the world, their driveway blocked by iron gates and flanked by giant stone dragons.

I hiked Russ's driveway to the garage, detached and recessed from the main house, its high windowpanes clouded by grime. Standing on tiptoes, I could make out the vague contours of Russ's Mercedes, a nearly vintage SL coupe that had been, I knew, a gift from Muriel on their twentieth wedding anniversary.

At the front of the house, the screen door was propped ajar by a slag-heap of mail and newspapers. Sunday's editions of both the *Times* and the *Star-News* were bound in nylon twine, with Monday's papers sprawled loosely atop the whole. I rang the doorbell, and without waiting for a response, I rattled the handle.

I returned to the garage. It was separated from the house by a gated path leading, I knew, to the big sloping backyard where Russ had hosted a Sunday barbecue for the firm's summer law clerks only a couple of months earlier. I unlatched the gate and circled to the back door, but it too was locked. I banged loudly on the glass and called his name, then waited and did it again. Then I pulled out my cell phone and dialed, listening as the phone rang, unanswered, inside the darkened house.

Thanks to Uncle Louis, I could actually open a door like this with a credit card, but it was an operation that required one hand more than was presently at my disposal.

And then I spied a life-sized stone bunny, crouching in the ferns by my feet. If Russ were inside, alive but unconscious, I knew

231

he'd forgive me for what I was about to do. I hefted the bunny to my shoulder, then turned and heaved him crashing through one of the door panes.

I slid the latch and hipped the door wide, glass shards crunching underfoot. The flying bunny rested against a sofa leg near a deep gouge in the hardwood floor. Other than this, the room was neat and tidy, and I stood for a moment in the half-light, listening to the clock on the mantelpiece.

"Russ?"

The living room opened to a large kitchen, where there were signs, at least, of human habitation. Dishes were stacked in the sink, and a half-full water glass rested on the tiled island. There was a stale odor of mildew in the air.

"Russ?"

I searched the house. A hallway led past a pair of guest bedrooms to a large and cozy den. There a paperback novel — a Philip Roth — lay pup-tented on a side table by an easy chair. Beside the book, in a heavy crystal ashtray, lay Russ's pipe, cold and empty. A matchbox from the Chop House completed the tableau.

Bookshelves lined the walls from floor to ceiling, and peppered among the books were framed photos of Russ, and of Muriel, and of Russ, Jr., juxtaposed with an assortment of travel mementos and crystal figurines.

The photos were mostly old, their colors faded as though shot through a bluish filter. There was a high school graduation, and a young man in uniform. There was a father and son playing catch in the backyard, Russ lean and muscular in a white T-shirt, a lock of dark hair spilling onto his forehead.

I lingered for a while, looking at the pictures and scanning the book titles, when a silver-framed photo grabbed my attention. It was a black-and-white shot of me and Russ, briefcases in hand, marching in tandem down the Grand Avenue steps of the L.A. County courthouse. A television reporter, off-camera, had thrust a microphone in front of Russ, who was speaking as he walked, his eyes downcast.

I'd never seen the photo, but I remembered the scene. I'd accompanied Russ to court on behalf of a talk show host who'd been stalked by a fan with a history of mental illness. There had been a small article about the hearing in the next day's paper, but no photograph. Russ must have gotten the picture from the photographer somehow, but he'd never mentioned it to me.

I left the den and returned to the kitchen, then walked the opposite hallway toward the master suite. And it was there that a murmured conversation stopped me cold. I flattened against the wall, listening to the muted voices of two men arguing.

I like to think that with two functioning arms, I'd have simply knocked down the door and let the chips fall or the fur fly. But as it was, I tiptoed back to the living room and quietly lifted the iron fireplace poker off its hook by the mantel.

I crept down the hallway, paused for a breath, then kicked the door wide. It slammed into a table and shattered something glass. I stepped into the room and there, staring me in the face, was Russ's king-sized bed, rumpled but empty.

On the nightstand, a clock radio played an interview program on public radio.

After searching the closets and master bath, I returned again to the kitchen. Below the picture window framing the big sycamore was a little built-in desk, and on the desk were a pad, a pencil cup, a chunky telephone, and a pea-sized light blinking urgently on an old-fashioned answering machine.

In for a penny, I figured, in for a pound.

There were four messages in total, each

preceded by a robotic voice reciting the date and time. The first consisted of five seconds of silence, then a dial tone. The second, third, and fourth were all from Veronica Daley, each sounding more plaintive than the last.

Missing, I realized, was the message I'd left for Russ on Friday morning.

The telephone itself, being of an older vintage, had no call history or other visible memory functions. The notepad was blank, and the drawer below held only a Yellow Pages, some postage stamps, and an open box of paper clips.

And so, on the theory that I'd done enough damage for one afternoon, I exited the way I'd come, taking care to replace the poker on its hook and return the bunny, more or less intact, to its rightful place in the garden.

Had I seen anything suspicious, I would have called the police. As it was, I simply called Veronica, assuring her that all appeared to be well. Well, that is, if you overlooked the fact that Russ hadn't been home for at least two days, and yet his car was still in the garage. But she allayed that concern, explaining that Russ owned a second vehicle, an older Jeep Wagoneer that had once belonged to Muriel. She said she'd keep looking.

So instead of fretting about Russ Dinsmoor's well-being, I spent the drive back to the office, and the rest of Monday afternoon, wondering where he might have gone.

And nursing a vague hope that the Stickley lamp I'd broken in the bedroom was only a reproduction.

11

Depositions are a form of cross-examination, and the goal of cross-examination, at least in the gospel of Russell Dinsmoor, is to lead the witness by the nose down a narrow chute and into a very small pen. Once inside the pen, the witness is presented with a Hobson's choice — a question that if answered "yes" constitutes a fatal admission, but that if answered "no" exposes the witness as the prevaricating fool we already knew him to be.

An experienced witness senses the chute, and will kick and fight to avoid the pen. This is a sport unto itself and can, under the right circumstances, lead to hours of diverting amusement. Dr. Herbert Zelman, the second of Hartford Allied's Connecticut show ponies, was not an experienced witness, and as a result, he spent most of Tuesday morning in a series of very tight places.

Dr. Zelman had every reason to be uncomfortable. After first admitting that he had not, in fact, had an opportunity to read the Tazerian medical records until *after* the denial letter had been mailed, the good doctor was nonetheless struggling to justify, with an exhausting display of semantic gymnastics, Hartford Allied's refusal to cover Vic's surgery.

Meanwhile, other than mumbling a few desultory objections, Donald Carlisle comported himself like a mensch, quietly thumbing his BlackBerry while wearing the face of a man passing a kidney stone.

At around eleven thirty, as I was about to offer Dr. Zelman a change of underwear, Bernie interrupted with a loud knock and a meaningful look, curling a bloodred fingernail in my direction. I proposed a ten-minute recess and followed her into the hallway.

"This had better be good," I grumbled.

"There's a couple of cops asking for you. I parked 'em in the north conference room."

A line like that rarely portends good news, and was doubly unwelcome under the circumstances. It was just my luck to be handcuffed and perp-walked to the elevators in full view of my new colleagues, the office staff, and Donald fucking Carlisle.

"Two, you say?"

"Well, three altogether, but two are definitely cops."

"Is the third a fireman?"

"A fireman? How should I know?"

"Well, was he wearing a big rubber coat and a funny hat?"

She put a hand on her hip.

"Okay. Tell them I'll be there in a minute, and offer them some coffee. Then get Mayday to my office, pronto."

I tracked Carlisle to the men's room, where I found him talking Dr. Zelman off a ledge, metaphorically speaking, through the door of one of the stalls. I told them that an emergency had arisen, and that my colleague, Ms. Suarez, would have to finish the deposition in my place.

Back in my office, I set the scene for Mayday and gave her some quick pointers on how to close out the witness should I be detained. I avoided the word "incarcerated," so as not to cause undue concern.

There were three of them all right, all sitting at the conference room table behind Styrofoam coffee cups. Since I was expecting Pasadena officers in blue, I was surprised to see a trio of business suits, and even more surprised that one of them came with a familiar face.

"Hello, Mac."

"Hello, Gabe. A little outside your jurisdiction, aren't you?"

Gabriel Montoya was an assistant district attorney who, when last our paths had crossed, was working out of the Santa Monica courthouse. We'd had a couple of cases there, back in my public defender days. As prosecutors went, Gabe was reasonable, intelligent, and a real stand-up guy. Which made him a minority of one in the DA's office.

He'd added a few pounds since I'd seen him last, but the handshake was still warm, and the smile still genuine.

"Jack MacTaggart," he said formally, nodding to his cohorts, "these are detectives Tom Parker and Nick Griegas, LAPD."

Neither man stood or smiled. Parker, the senior of the two, had probably been a linebacker in high school, maybe thirty years and fifty pounds ago. His sandy hair was thinning now, showing patches of scalp above a fleshy face and small, angry eyes.

His partner, Griegas, was younger than me, tall and trim, with the polished good looks of an East L.A. politician.

Gabe addressed himself to Griegas.

"Jack's one of your homeboys, Nick. Roosevelt High, right?"

Griegas looked surprised. "You must be

240

one of the Guadalajara MacTaggarts."

It didn't take a genius to figure out that an assistant DA and two LAPD detectives weren't here to discuss a false fire alarm. "So," I said, "to what do I owe —"

"What happened to your arm?" Parker interrupted, in a tone that suggested more than just idle curiosity.

Hearing his voice, and focusing again in on his meat-slab face, I realized there was something familiar about the big man. Like maybe I'd cross-examined him once, and he hadn't liked it.

"Dislocated shoulder," I told him. "Horse accident."

"Horse accident," he repeated, turning to his partner. "What happened, Counselor, you fall off your polo pony?"

And it was then, in a feculent flash of memory, that I placed Detective Thomas Parker of the LAPD's elite robbery-homicide division.

"Actually, I was in a threesome with your wife, Parker, when the horse fell out of bed."

He darkened from pink to red as he rose from his chair. Gabe stepped forward with both hands raised.

"Hold on. Wait a minute. Everybody chill. Jack, you're not helping things here."

"If someone would tell me what we're do-

ing here, then maybe I could be more helpful."

"Try burglary for starters," snapped Parker, leaning two ham-sized fists on the table,
"and spoiling a crime scene. And maybe
homicide before we're through."

"What are you talking about?"

The sneer returned. "Neighbors reported
a guy with his arm in a sling breaking into a
residence in San Marino yesterday, and your
prints are all over the scene." He leaned in
closer. "What's the matter, Counselor? Cat
got your tongue?"

"What homicide?"

Gabe turned and nodded to Griegas, who
produced a manila envelope from his briefcase. He handed it to Gabe, who held it for
a moment, then slid it across the table.

There were six photos in all, each eight-
by-ten in vivid color. Russ was dressed in a
black sweater, khaki slacks, and black canvas
shoes. From the position of his body, it
looked as though he might have fallen
backward out of the sailboat's cockpit and
come to rest on the deck with his head near
the aft railing. I didn't see any blood, but
his face was swollen, his complexion pale
and waxy.

He was obviously dead.

There was a moment there where I'd

neglected to breathe, and I slumped into my chair like a guy who'd been sucker punched. By way of a standing eight count, Gabe gathered up the photos like a dealer preparing to shuffle.

"When?" I croaked.

It was Griegas who spoke, in the staccato rhythm of a man reciting what he'd already memorized.

"We took the call from the MDR Station yesterday, late afternoon. Guy there noticed the hatch doors were open on his neighbor's sailboat, so he went over to investigate. That would have been Monday, at around noon. The ME estimates he died on Saturday night. COD as yet undetermined."

All of which meant that Russ's body had lain in the sun, like a fish on a dock, for nearly two days. And that's what started the tears.

Gabe came around and put a hand on my shoulder.

"Take it easy, cowboy. We need you to answer a few questions."

I stood and walked to the credenza, brushing past Parker, and helped myself to some tissues.

"Whatever I can do, Gabe. You name it."

Griegas consulted a small notebook he pulled from an inside pocket.

"There were four messages on his cell phone, and they all came from this office. Three were from someone named Veronica. We assume that's his secretary."

"Yeah. Veronica Daley."

"The fourth call — the first in time — was from you. You said it was urgent that he call you right away."

That would have been Friday morning, just after he'd left the office.

"What was so urgent, Jack?"

"Nothing important. We'd had a hearing in a case, that's all. I wanted to report what happened."

Parker and Griegas shared a look.

"You realize he was a heart patient, right? He'd had bypass surgery."

"Yeah," said Griegas. "I know. We saw the scar."

"And the meds in his bathroom," Parker added. "Where we also found your prints."

The picture came into focus. A neighboring boat owner had found Russ's body and called the sheriff, which has jurisdiction over the marina. They, for some reason, called in robbery-homicide. Who had, in turn, found my message on Russ's cell phone, and then picked up a residential burglary report from the San Marino PD. Me again, conveniently leaving my prints all over the dead man's house. And like all California lawyers, my prints were on file in the state database.

"So what makes this a homicide investigation?"

Parker and Griegas shared another glance, then both looked to Gabe. He thought for a moment and nodded. It was Griegas who explained.

"We have reason to believe the victim's body was moved onto the boat after he died."

"What reason?"

"This is bullshit!" exploded Parker, slamming a fist on the table. "I say we run his ass downtown!"

Now I was the one on my feet.

"You listen to me, Parker. Your victim happens to be my friend. When he missed a court appearance on Monday, I went to his house for a look. I found his car in the garage and two days' worth of newspapers out front, so I broke into the house. As for my whereabouts on Saturday night, I was at Huntington Memorial with a tube down my throat. So save the act for someone who gives a shit."

"What was on the message machine?" Griegas demanded.

"You first. What makes you think his body

was moved to the boat?"

Parker started to protest, but Gabe cut him off.

"Forensics found fibers from his clothes in the back of his vehicle, in the cargo area. Also some blanket fibers on his clothes that don't match anything in the Wagoneer or the house. Plus, they estimate that the body was only in the sun for around five or six hours."

I processed all of this, then turned to Griegas.

"There were three calls from Veronica, that's all. And a hang up."

"What sequence?" he asked, making notes.

"The hang up was first. That was Saturday night, at nine-something. Veronica's calls were all on Monday morning."

"And he erased 'em!" Parker yelped to Gabe, his tone all wounded indignation. "For that alone we should book him and print him."

"You don't have to print me, Parker. Just go home and dust your wife's ass."

This time, neither Gabe nor Griegas could stop him. He grabbed for my throat as I stiff-armed his face, twisting to protect the shoulder. We glanced off the windows and into a potted ficus before Griegas finally got an arm-bar under his chin. Parker's eyes were wild, his face the color of a fresh bruise.

"You cocksucker!" he gasped as Griegas wrestled him backward to a chair.

"That's enough!" Gabe barked. "Both of you, knock it off!"

I straightened my collar. My shoulder was pulsing like a sore tooth, but I wasn't about to give Parker the satisfaction of showing it. We glared at each other across the polished glass tabletop while Gabe used a wad of tissues to mop the coffee.

When the oxygen finally returned to the room, I addressed myself to Griegas.

"For what it's worth, Detective, I called Russ at home on Friday morning, just after he'd left the office. That message *wasn't* on the machine."

Griegas found his notebook on the floor and made an entry. "What time, exactly?"

"Before noon. Right after my cell phone message."

I glanced over at Parker, who appeared to have regained his composure. Maybe he was thinking about the Internal Affairs investigation that would follow from a citizen assault complaint. Then again, maybe he was just resting up for another charge.

"Where'd you find his cell phone?"

I'd put the question to Gabe, but it was

Griegas who answered.

"It was in the old Benz, in the garage. In the glove compartment."

I nodded, adding another small tile to the mosaic.

"Okay, let's assume you guys are right about the body being moved. What makes you think the house was the crime scene?"

This time Gabe answered.

"There was blunt force trauma to the back of the head, which left a bruise. Which means he was still alive at the time. At first, we assumed the bruise came from a fall. You know, a head strike."

"Which could have happened anywhere."

"That's what we thought," Parker growled, a smile creasing his lips. "Until we found your prints on the poker."

The L.A. Coroner's office is on Mission Road, hard by the old County-USC Medical Center. We drove in Gabe's Volvo, while Griegas and Parker lingered like a bad smell at Henley & Hargrove to question Veronica and drink the free coffee.

I'd requested some privacy while giving Veronica the news, but Parker wouldn't have it, fearing that we might, as he'd put it, collude on our alibis. So Gabe served as a witness when I called her into my office.

I gave it to her straight and she took it hard, sobbing, "I knew something was wrong! I *knew* it! I could *feel* it!"

After she'd had a good cry, I explained to her that the detectives wanted to ask her a few questions, and that I had to accompany Mr. Montoya to identify the remains. Which was a poor turn of phrase, and she'd started crying all over again. And if Gabe hadn't been there with us, I probably would have joined her.

When she'd finally composed herself, I'd asked her if Russ had any family that we should notify. She confirmed my understanding that his only sister had died childless several years earlier. I'd suggested she send a short e-mail to the partners, and I promised to check back with her before the end of the day.

When you get right down to it, there are only four ways to die: by homicide, suicide, accident, or natural causes. Assuming Parker wasn't blowing smoke just to watch me blink, then someone had taken great pains to try to make the first way look like the last. And that, more so even than the fact of Russ's death, was what gnawed at the pit of my stomach.

As we transitioned from Arroyo Parkway onto the southbound 110, it was Gabe who broke the uneasy silence.

"I'm sorry about Parker. I didn't realize he still had such a hard-on for you."

I rolled my eyes, but his were still on the road.

"You and this Dinsmoor were pretty close, I take it."

"Yeah. You could say that."

"It's funny, I recognized your voice on the message right away. Slew said you'd gone with some white-shoe firm up in Pasadena. Small world."

"Too small for my taste."

It took him a second to get my meaning.

"Oh, yeah. I guess so. I would've given you a heads-up, but it's Parker's investigation. I'm just along to referee."

The midday traffic was light, and we reached the Dodger Stadium exit in less than ten minutes. The same drive in the morning for the eight thirty calendar call took at least forty-five. It was a drive I'd shared with Russ at least a dozen times.

"I've heard of this Dinsmoor, right? He was some kind of big-shot trial lawyer."

"He was the best I've ever seen."

Gabe could tell I was in no mood for chitchat, so we rode in silence until the off-ramp for the Golden State. I pulled the business card from my pocket and studied the little embossed gold shield.

"Parker doesn't really think I'm a suspect, does he?"

"Tom Parker is a linear thinker, Jack. Dead body, head strike, phone message, break-in, prints in the house, prints on the poker. What do you expect him to think?"

"You forgot one other thing."

He glanced across the seat. "I don't know, Jack. I don't think Parker's that kind of cop."

"You mean the blue kind?"

He didn't respond.

"What about you?" I turned in the seat to face him. "What do you think?"

"Me? Off the record? I think the tool-mark guys will confirm what I've said all along, which is that Dinsmoor hit his head on the floor, or maybe on the deck, when he passed out. And if you say you were in the hospital on Saturday night, then you were in the fucking hospital. And I'm sorry for your loss, buddy, I mean that. I'd have bet the farm on a heart attack, except for the forensics."

"He could have crawled back there for any reason. Maybe to put the seats down."

"Maybe. But what about the exposure? It was nice and sunny on Sunday."

"I wouldn't know. I spent the whole day on the couch."

"Alone?"

"Does my dog count?"

"Will he take a polygraph?"

Traffic was light on the Golden State, and we soon exited at Mission Road. The hospital loomed in the distance like an old Soviet prison.

"It doesn't matter at the end of the day whether Parker makes you for a suspect or not. You're still the guy who crapped on the crime scene. He's a real stickler about his crime scenes."

"If I contaminated the scene, nobody's gonna feel worse about it than me. Trust me, I'm a lawyer."

Gabe grinned. "Yeah. I'm from the government, and I'm here to help."

We pulled into the Official Vehicles Only lot, where Gabe flashed his creds to an attendant at the gate and then trolled for a spot in the shade.

"There's one other thing," he said. "At the marina, all the slip tenants have their own parking spaces. It's part of the rent. Only we found the Wagoneer parked in the wrong space. Maybe nothing, but still."

"Aren't the boats behind a fence or something?"

"They are, and there are keypad locks on all the gates. But every wino and parrothead down there seems to know the combos, plus people are coming and going all day, and they prop the gates open to carry groceries and stuff. There's a million places you could hide. We've got a couple of uniforms asking questions, but I'm not holding my breath. And by the way, you'll be happy to know that your prints aren't on the lock or the gate, or anywhere on the Wagoneer or the boat."

The Los Angeles County Department of Coroner, as it's officially known, performs more than six thousand autopsies every year, which, for the mathematically inclined, averages out to more than sixteen per day, including Christmas and Valentine's Day. Especially Valentine's Day. I'd actually witnessed an autopsy once, as part of a child neglect–manslaughter case I'd been assigned to defend, and it was a memory I would have preferred not to revisit.

Gabe signed us in at reception, from which we were escorted by an efficient young Asian woman with serious eyeglasses down some stairs to the mezzanine. There a cinder-block corridor took us past a series of closed doors. We passed a group of teenagers with droopy pants and sideways hats led by a fat man in scrubs, all heading back in the direction from which we'd come. Some of the kids looked like they'd just stepped off a roller coaster at Magic Mountain.

"Field trip," whispered Gabe. "First-time offenders."

The corridor led to double doors, and beyond those to an open room reeking of sour milk and disinfectant. An array of large stainless steel drawers took up the far wall. There were six autopsy tables in the center of the room and all, thankfully, were empty. It was a slow day for murder in Los Angeles.

The air-conditioning was cranked on full, and the room was cold enough to hang meat. All of which explained why Melissa, who was our assistant medical examiner, wore a heavy turtleneck sweater in eighty-degree weather.

She went to a filing cabinet and found the right paperwork, then she walked us to a little dressing area. There she put on a blue apron, latex gloves, and the kind of plastic shower cap you get at the Holiday Inn.

"Been here before?" asked Gabe, watching her back.

"Once."

Melissa rejoined us and proffered a jar of Vick's. Gabe declined, and I followed suit. Melissa dipped a finger and dabbed a spot under each nostril, like a penitent blessing herself with holy water. She replaced the jar, slipped a blue surgical mask over her ears, and led us past the tables to the wall. Using both hands, and leaning all of her ninety-five pounds into the effort, she rolled one of the big drawers open.

"Stand back, please," were the first words she'd spoken since we'd left reception.

I was expecting to see a body lying peacefully under a white sheet, the way the dead are always depicted on television. So it was especially jarring to see Russ stark naked and curled on his side, pale as candle wax, with plastic bags on his hands. The stench of ripe death kicked me in the stomach, and I covered my face with my hand.

Both Gabe and Melissa were looking at me, out of concern I thought, until I realized they were waiting for an ID. I nodded, and she scribbled something on the clipboard.

Ten minutes later, we were outside in the fresh air.

I spotted the news van first. It was parked curbside at an odd angle, its microwave antenna fully extended. Next to the van were two figures — a slob in a baseball cap and a blow-dried blonde in a business suit, the latter twirling a cordless microphone. A large video camera rested on the sidewalk, and big boy grabbed for it as the gate started to move.

"Jesus Christ," I muttered, and Gabe followed my eyes to the street.

By the time the gate had fully opened, the blonde was standing in the center of the driveway, forcing Gabe to stop. She came around to the driver's side brandishing the microphone like a weapon.

"Terina Webb, Channel Nine Action News!" she announced, thrusting the mic into the open window. "We're here outside the coroner's office with assistant district attorney Gabriel Montoya. Gabe, what can you tell us about the death of Russell Dinsmoor?"

Gabe stood on the brake, but he left the car in drive. As he squared his shoulders to the camera, I leaned back into my seat.

"Hello, Terina. Unfortunately, there's nothing to report as yet. We were just here to identify the remains. Our investigation is ongoing."

As she retracted the mic to ask another question, Gabe hit the gas and we bounced onto southbound Marengo. I'd made the mistake of glancing in her direction as the car lurched forward, and our eyes had held for less than a second.

"Sorry about that," Gabe said. "Did she make you?"

"Yeah, I think so."

"Shit."

We rode in silence for several blocks, and when Gabe's cell phone rang, I actually jumped.

"Montoya."

He listened and nodded, grunted, then listened some more.

"Okay, thanks. I told you. Yeah. I'll meet you in an hour."

He leaned back and clipped the phone to his belt. "You want the good news first or the bad?"

"I could use some good."

"Okay. The fireplace poker wasn't scrubbed or smeared, and the only residue they found was soot. And, they lifted your prints off the clock radio in the bedroom. So it looks like maybe your alibi isn't total bullshit."

"Is that you talking, or Parker?"

"That was me."

"Okay, what's the bad?"

"They found a transfer on the kitchen floor that they're pretty sure is a head strike."

I was staring straight ahead, numbly watching the hood of the Volvo gobble up the yellow line as we neared the freeway overpass.

"It gets worse," Gabe continued. "There were no eyewitnesses at the marina, and no security cams on the parking lot, the gate, or the dock. Remind me to park my yacht in a better neighborhood."

"Moor."

"More what?"

"You moor a yacht. You park a car."

"Excuse me, professor."

We took the on-ramp at Soto and headed east on the Santa Monica freeway. It wasn't yet three, but the traffic through downtown was already approaching gridlock.

"Okay, Gabe. If the neighbors saw me and called the cops, why didn't anybody see a body being carried in a blanket from the house out to the garage?"

He thought for a moment.

"Because it was dark."

"Exactly. So either he was moved on Saturday night and left in the Wagoneer to rot for twenty-four hours, or he lay on the kitchen floor all day Sunday, then was moved."

"Assuming the perps were the movers," Gabe replied, following my thinking, "then why would they take that kind of risk?"

"That's a good question, but here's a better one. Why would they move the goddamn body in the first place?"

By the time we'd reached the office, it still wasn't clear whether my status had been upgraded from prime suspect to crime-solving ally. In any event, Gabe promised to call me as soon as they'd established the cause of death. More important, he promised to do what he could to keep Tom Parker's attention focused on Russell Dinsmoor, and off of Jack MacTaggart.

12

I rode the elevator to nine, but instead of finding a deposition still in progress, I saw through a gap in the blinds that the conference room was crowded with people. Those who didn't have seats were pressed against the walls, and all were facing the head of the table, where Morris Henley stood with a somber mien, gripping a chair back with both hands. Margot, the ninth-floor receptionist, confirmed that the deposition had ended half an hour ago, and that an emergency partners' meeting was now in progress.

I walked the hallway to Russ's corner, but Veronica's desk was empty. And although Russ's door was open, I had neither the time nor the stomach to poke around inside.

Back down on eight, Bernie was holding court amid a gaggle of secretaries, all of them chattering in low tones, and when she saw me coming, she broke free and closed like a heat-seeking missile. I gestured to my office, and shut the door behind us.

"Where have you been? Everybody's been looking for you!"

"I was at the coroner's office, thank you."

"You could have told me! Was it awful?"

"Was what awful?"

"You know. All the bites."

"What are you talking about?"

"We heard Mr. Dinsmoor was eaten by a shark."

"Oh, for God's sake. Sit down, please."

She did, and I punched up my e-mail as I spoke.

"First of all, nobody was eaten by anything. Russ had a heart attack on his boat over the weekend, that's all. Unfortunately, the outcome was the same."

She seemed disappointed to learn that Russ had met so prosaic an end.

"Not even one bite?"

"Not even a nibble. Now tell me what happened after I left."

"Let's see. The two cops had Veronica in the north conference room. I don't know what happened in there, but the tree got all busted up. Then the big one stayed for a while and made phone calls, while the cute one went with Veronica to Mr. Dinsmoor's office. Then, around ten minutes later, the big one joined them there. When they both finally left, Veronica was crying. That was, like, forty minutes ago. Then she came here looking for you. So did Marta, by the way. And there's a partners' meeting upstairs, like, right now, and you're invited. Plus, your phone hasn't stopped ringing all afternoon."

I had e-mails from both Veronica and Mayday, plus several from the partners who were closest to Russ. But all of those could wait.

"Where's Veronica now?"

"She's up in the meeting, I think."

"Shit."

"What's wrong?"

"What isn't?"

My late appearance sent a charge through the conference room, and several of the lawyers crowded around to variously console and question me, both about Russ and about my arm. Morris rapped his knuckles on the table, calling for order.

"All right, everybody. Quiet, please! Let's get an update from Jack."

He ceded his position at the head of the table, and from there I turned to face my new colleagues, many of whom I knew only casually, and a few of whom I knew barely at all. I noted Jared Henley's presence in the chair directly opposite from where his father had stood. Veronica Daley sat to my right, clutching a fistful of tissues, her face a road map of anguish and despair.

"First of all," I said to Morris, "if you can spare Veronica, Bernie's been looking for her."

He nodded in Veronica's direction, and she practically bolted to the door.

"Okay," I continued, addressing the room. "I've just returned from the coroner's office, and I'm very sorry to have to confirm that Russ Dinsmoor died over the weekend, on his boat, probably from a heart attack. There will be an autopsy, but for now that's the working hypothesis."

There was an eruption of murmurs and cross talk, forcing Morris to raise his voice.

"People! Order, please!"

Jared spoke up from the far end of the table.

"Why are the police investigating a heart attack? They were here for two hours, making a big scene. That's not the kind of image Henley and Hargrove likes to project to its clients, Jack."

All of this he'd said without a trace of irony.

"It so happens that I know the assistant

DA who's working the case. He assures me that whenever there's a body found in public, they have to conduct an investigation. It's strictly routine."

That sounded convincing enough, and everyone seemed to be buying it.

"But there's something else you need to be aware of. There was a television crew from Channel Nine News waiting outside the coroner's office. The press, for whatever reason, thinks there's a story here. So be forewarned."

This triggered another outburst. There's nothing like the scent of a little press coverage to start a lawyer salivating. It was Russ who'd said that the most dangerous place you can stand in a courtroom is between a lawyer and a reporter's microphone. To a probate or business lawyer, who rarely ventures outside his own office, the prospect of a TV appearance was like a Coast Guard cutter to a castaway.

I waited a while before rapping my own knuckles on the table.

"In conclusion," I announced, waiting for quiet, "let me say this. Everybody in this room has known Russ a lot longer than I have, so forgive me for being presumptuous. But my understanding is that Russ outlived his entire family. Which means it'll be up to the firm, and especially Veronica, to make the funeral arrangements. So please, let's give her our full support as well as our sympathy. And Morris," I added, turning to face him, "I'm more than happy to ride herd on whatever cases Russ was handling."

Morris put a hand on my good shoulder as he reclaimed his place at the table.

"Thank you, Jack. We all know how close you were to Russ, and what a shock this must be for you. Hell, for all of us. Before you arrived, I announced that Jared would be serving as the new chair of the litigation department. I know I speak for him when I say that your full support will be welcome during this difficult period of transition."

Jared's eyes were locked onto mine as his father spoke. And try though he probably did, he still couldn't keep the smirk off his fatuous face.

Veronica Daley's e-mail was addressed to Attorneys and Staff, and was headed simply, "Russell H. Dinsmoor."

I'm sorry to have to report to you all that Mr. Dinsmoor passed away this weekend, and that we only learned of his death today. Mr. MacTaggart has gone to identify the body. When I have more information about the funeral arrangements, I will pass it along to everybody.

I found her in Russ's office, sitting in Russ's chair and rummaging through one of his desk drawers. I rapped "Shave and a Haircut" on the door frame.

"Anybody home?"

A look of relief flooded her face.

"Oh, Jack. Thank heavens."

She stood, and we hugged. Or at least we did what passes for a hug when there are only three arms available for the undertaking.

She closed the door and gestured to Russ's chair.

"Sit, please."

I sat, but on the edge of the little side couch. She started to join me, then said, "Oh, wait a minute," and hurried back out.

The office was in uncharacteristic disarray, with files cluttering the desk and floor. Yet even amid the chaos, it seemed somehow emptier, as though the spirit of the place had departed along with the man. I walked to the slot machine, inserted a token from the till, and pulled the lever. The tumblers hummed and spun, then froze in rapid sequence. Two sevens and a cherry.

"That old machine." Veronica sighed, shutting the door behind her. "What will become of it?"

She handed me an envelope with the Henley & Hargrove logo embossed in the corner. It was large and white, and my name was written in block letters across the front. I recognized Russ's handwriting.

"What's this?"

"I don't know. Mr. Dinsmoor said that if anything ever happened to him, I was to give that to you. There was another one, which I've already given to Mr. Henley."

"When did he do this?"

"It was August, I remember that. Just after that barbecue he hosted for the summer clerks."

I sat down and patted the couch beside me. Veronica wore a pale blue skirt with a matching jacket, and her hands were crossed primly in her lap. Her eyes were pink and raw. I reached over and took her hand in mine.

"How are you holding up?"

She nodded gamely. "Okay, I guess."

"How did it go with the police?"

She shrugged. "They asked a lot of questions. Like, did Mr. Dinsmoor have any enemies? Was he acting strangely? Had he received threats? Things like that. Oh, and they wanted to know if you two were friends, and whether you'd had a falling-out."

"Let me guess. That would have been Parker, the bigger one."

She nodded. "I think it was."

"What happened when they brought you here?"

Her eyes swept the office. "Let's see. They wanted to look at his calendar. Then they asked me to open his e-mail."

"Did you give them a printout?"

She nodded. "Yes. The current message screen, the sent messages, and the trash."

"Would you mind printing for me what you gave to them?"

"Of course." She rose and crossed to the desk. "Just give me a second."

I stood by the windows. A large bird, a falcon perhaps, circled the dome of city hall. It too looked to be searching for something lost.

The printer sprang to life, and Veronica gathered up the pages, punching the stapler with a closed fist.

"Here they are."

"Thanks."

She slumped into the chair and blew the hair from her eyes. "Is there anything else I can do?"

I studied the pages she'd printed, looking

for anything out of the ordinary.

"I know Russ was technophobic, but had you ever seen him use the Internet for anything? Research, maybe?"

"I don't know about research, but I showed him how to use Google once." She looked at the screen. "The icon is still on his desktop."

"Did the police look at that?"

"No. They never asked."

That surprised me. If Gabe had stayed behind, he wouldn't have missed it.

"What are all these files?" I asked, nodding to the overall clutter.

"After I sent out my e-mail, Morris and Jared Henley came by. They closed the door and went through Mr. Dinsmoor's drawers, and they took some of his files with them. These were left behind. I guess I'm supposed to put them back."

"Have you seen a file I left with Russ on Thursday? Unmarked? It had some bank statements in it?"

"No," she said, logging off the computer. "I'm sure there was nothing like that."

I had twelve voice messages, ten of which, including the one from Morris, were internal calls. Most were brief expressions of shock or condolence.

The message from Morris said that he'd just gotten Veronica's e-mail, and that I should come see him as soon as possible. But after the meeting upstairs, I considered that obligation fulfilled.

The first of the outside calls was from Tara, at 2:05 P.M. She'd asked after my arm, and said that she'd bring a pizza at six. She said she had news.

The second outside call came in at 3:30 P.M., while Gabe and I had been mired in traffic on the Pasadena Freeway.

Hello, Jack? This is Terina Webb, from Channel Nine Action News. You remember me, I hope? I thought that was you in the car with Gabe, and now I see that you and Russell Dinsmoor were law partners. I'd like to speak with you as soon as possible, and I'm on deadline for the six o'clock broadcast. Please call me right away, will you? It'll be good to talk to you again.

She'd left her office and cell phone numbers. I deleted the message without writing them down.

Veronica's printouts consisted of messages Russ had either sent or received in the last ten days, including those that had been deleted during that time. They showed the name of the e-mail sender and recipient, a reference line, and the date and time of each message.

Most were internal postings that I'd also received, group mailings addressed to Attorneys or Litigation. Others came from individual lawyers, including a couple from me. There were a few outside messages as well, but all looked to be business-related. None appeared to have any bearing on his whereabouts or death.

The big white envelope contained two documents, each blue-backed and printed on heavy bond paper, each with the word COPY rubber-stamped at the bottom.

The first was entitled "Fourth Amendment and Complete Restatement of the Last Will and Testament of Russell Hale Dinsmoor." The second was entitled "Third Amendment and Complete Restatement of the Dinsmoor Family Trust." Both documents were dated in August.

The first was what the estate planning drones called a pour-over will. It simply recited that after the gift of any automobiles he might own at the time of his death to the American Red Cross, the rest and residue of Russ's property and estate would pass to the trustee of the Dinsmoor Family Trust, "to be added to and become a part of the corpus of the trust estate thereunder and to be held, administered, and distributed according to the terms and provisions thereof."

The second document was the declaration of trust, which, thanks to the will, effectively disposed of his entire estate. Once again, the beneficiaries were various local and national charities, with two notable exceptions. The first was a cash bequest of $50,000 to Veronica Daley, should she survive him, "in appreciation for her friendship and many years of loyal and dedicated service."

And then, according to the trust instrument, "that certain real property located in the County of Los Angeles, State of California, commonly known as 31 Sycamore Lane, San Marino, California, together with all fixtures, appliances, furniture, furnishings, books, personal possessions, and effects contained therein at the time of the Settlor's death," were to be distributed by the trustee, free of trust, "to Jack MacTaggart, provided that he survives the Settlor hereof."

And the trustee of the trust, the person charged with its execution following the death of the settlor, was none other than Russ's longtime friend and partner, Morris Henley.

The first two stories on the six o'clock edition of Channel 9 Action News involved a brush fire in Malibu and a police pursuit in Compton that ended in gunfire. Both were covered by the Channel 9 Top Chopper Team, and both featured bird's-eye footage of conflagration, crashes, and carnage, thereby honoring the first commandment of TV journalism, which is that if it burns or bleeds, it leads.

Next came a commercial break, followed by the news anchor's lead-in to what he termed, "a shocking and gruesome discovery aboard a sailboat in Marina del Rey." For that, we went to reporter Terina Webb, standing by at the marina.

It was a live shot, with what I assumed to be Russ's sailboat bobbing and clanging softly in the background. Darkness had settled on the marina, and a brisk onshore breeze was forcing Terina Webb, supernaturally luminous in the klieg lights, to hold her microphone and notes in one hand so that she could manage her hairdo with the other.

"Thank you, Paul. I'm here in Marina del Rey where police today confirmed that the body

273

discovered yesterday on the deck of this sailboat, the Sloophole, *is that of Pasadena attorney Russell Hale Dinsmoor. Dinsmoor, age seventy-six, was a former president of the Los Angeles County Bar Association, and was well known throughout the city's legal community for his work in a number of high-profile cases, including his defense of then mayor Warren Burkett in the so-called Harborgate bid-rigging scandal."*

As she spoke, Russ's smiling visage suddenly materialized in the upper-right quadrant of the screen. It was a stock head shot that looked to have been taken around ten years ago.

"I spoke earlier today with Henry Glassman, a neighboring boat owner who made the gruesome discovery."

The scene jumped to an unshaven man in a polo shirt sporting sunglasses and a bad comb-over. He was seated on a wooden pylon in broad daylight, speaking into a handheld microphone. A line of masts swayed drunkenly in the background.

"I just come down to get some stuff off my boat when I looked over and saw that the hatch was open next door, which was strange because I've never seen the guy here during the week. So I went over to check it out, and

that's when I saw the body just lying on the deck."

The picture then shifted to Gabe in the Volvo, speaking into the camera without sound. My face, in profile, was barely visible in the shadows. Terina Webb spoke in a voice-over.

"In a Channel Nine exclusive, police sources have confirmed to this reporter that Dinsmoor's death is under investigation as a possible homicide, and representatives of the District Attorney's office today visited the County Coroner to inspect the body of the deceased."

Gabe's voice suddenly picked up in mid-sentence.

". . . investigation is ongoing."

Then it was back to the live shot on the dock.

"And in a final twist to an already bizarre story, the man we just saw seated in the car next to Assistant District Attorney Gabriel Montoya was none other than Jack MacTaggart. You'll recall that MacTaggart, now a partner of Russell Dinsmoor, was the lawyer whose defense of alleged Koreatown shooter Tyrell Lewis led to a police department shutdown three years ago when Lewis, shortly after his release from custody, fatally wounded LAPD Detective Raymond Rizzo. You can bet

we'll be following this story closely as it unfolds. Back to you, Paul."

I hit the power button on the remote, and we sat on the couch in silence. In my case, it was angry silence.

Tara looked from me to the screen and back again.

"What does it all mean, sweetie?"

It was a simple question with a very complicated answer.

To the civilian public, the Raymond Rizzo affair was one of those news stories that grabs the headlines for a week or two, then winds up at the bottom of the birdcage. But to those in L.A. law enforcement — and to the lawyers, politicians, and press who move in its tight and incestuous orbit — it was a story with legs, as the day's events had clearly demonstrated.

I stood and paced as I spoke.

"I told you I used to be a public defender, right? Well, once upon a time, around three years ago, I was assigned to defend a young man who'd been accused of shooting a woman who ran a little supermarket in Koreatown. It was my first capital case, and it got a lot of play in the press because the woman was very well liked in her community. Plus, the shooting was captured on a surveillance videotape."

"I think I remember seeing that on TV."

Which she probably had. The jumpy black-and-white footage of the assailant in a hooded sweatshirt shooting Evelyn Kim for sport after she'd already emptied the cash register had run for days on the local news outlets. As did footage of the candlelight vigil outside Kim's market, and the weekend march through Koreatown demanding more and better police protection.

If it bleeds, it leads.

"My client was a kid named Tyrell Lewis, a gangbanger with a long list of priors. And while the surveillance video made for good television, it was pretty much useless as evidence, because the shooter's face never turned toward the camera.

"The DA charged Lewis because a storefront preacher named Mustafa Burrell had made a tape recording of a phone conversation he'd had with Lewis, in which Lewis had copped to the shooting. Other than some weak circumstantial evidence and the aforementioned rap sheet, the telephone confession was the sum total of the DA's case."

Tara sat back on the sofa and crossed her legs, Yogi-style.

"The DA was under a lot of pressure to convict. And because it was a capital crime,

I had a budget that allowed me to hire an investigator. We focused on this character Burrell. Long story short, Burrell was a self-ordained minister with a rap sheet longer than Lewis's, not to mention a professional snitch who'd worked with the DA before. This was like the fourth or fifth time he'd done the same thing — telephoned a high-profile suspect under the pretext of offering spiritual guidance, and then talked him into a taped confession."

Tara frowned. "Isn't it illegal to tape-record somebody without permission?"

"Or without telling them, yes. But that doesn't make the tape itself inadmissible. You see, the Fourth Amendment protects against illegal searches and seizures by government actors, not by private citizens. If Burrell had been a cop or a prosecutor, then the confession would have been tossed like a lit match. But Burrell was a civilian."

Tara furrowed her brow, troubled by the distinction.

"Anyway, I brought a motion to exclude the tape on the ground that Burrell *wasn't* a civilian. Maybe the first time he'd done it, acting on his own dime, okay. But the cops were using the guy as a tool to skirt both the Fourth Amendment and the Miranda strictures. That was my argument, anyway.

And we backed it up by showing that Burrell, despite his own probationary status, had never been arrested or prosecuted for any of these illegal phone calls. Plus we showed that he'd been in contact with Tom Slewzyski, the assistant DA who was prosecuting Lewis, right before the tape was made."

"So the district attorney put him up to it."

I shrugged. "I thought so, and the judge agreed. He ruled the tape inadmissible on the ground that Burrell was, in essence, a government agent. No tape, so no confession. And without the confession, Lewis walked, making me king-for-a-day at the PD's office."

"But did he actually shoot the woman in the market?"

"I don't know. Probably."

Tara, I could see, found this outcome less than satisfying.

"But you have to ask yourself, which is the greater evil? That one guilty man goes free, or that the government is allowed to systematically flaunt the Constitution?"

"Do I have to answer that?"

"That's a tough one, huh? Well, not for me it wasn't. Not at the time, anyway."

She shifted her position to make room on

the couch.

"So then, who's Raymond Rizzo?"

I returned to my place and sat.

"Ray Rizzo was an LAPD robbery-homicide detective. Truth is, I never met the man. But one day, he and his partner were investigating an armed robbery out in Inglewood when Rizzo was killed by a shotgun blast through a closed garage door. He was wearing a vest, but the shot severed the femoral artery. He bled to death right there on the sidewalk."

"Don't tell me."

I nodded. "Tyrell Lewis murdered Ray Rizzo exactly twelve days after I'd sprung him from custody. Now ask me why I remember that it was twelve days."

"Why?"

"Because a few days after Rizzo's murder, every cop in L.A. reported to work wearing a black button with the number twelve in dripping red ink. As did every one of the four thousand sworn officers statewide who attended Rizzo's funeral."

"Oh, Jack."

"At the time Rizzo was killed, the police union happened to be working without a contract, and there hadn't been an LAPD fatality in over two years."

Her look was blank. "I don't understand."

"Neither did I, at first. Anyway, the chief ordered the officers to stop wearing the buttons, but they refused. Then, when the officers were threatened with disciplinary action, the union staged a walkout. It was the only time in the history of the Los Angeles Police Department that every officer in uniform below the rank of lieutenant failed to report to work. Needless to say, it got the chief's attention, and the buttons stayed."

Tara nodded vaguely. "I remember that."

"It didn't take long for every politician in the state to jump on the union's bandwagon. They demanded to know how a guy who'd already confessed to a murder could be walking around Inglewood with a sawed-off shotgun."

She put a hand on my face.

"Was it awful for you?"

I shrugged. "I actually attended Rizzo's funeral. Looking for absolution, maybe, I don't know. But the union turned it into a circus. At one point I counted seven on-camera interviews being conducted simultaneously. There was even a radio station there doing a mobile broadcast, handing out T-shirts with a big red target superimposed over Lewis's mug shot. Those were a big hit with the cops."

As I described it to Tara, Ray Rizzo's

funeral came back to me like it was yesterday. It was held at Forest Lawn, across from the Warner Brothers lot in Burbank. I could still picture his widow, in a black dress and veil, flanked by two school-aged boys as she received the flag and badge while the still cameras flashed. I found out later that the boys were neighbors, as the couple was both childless and separated.

I also remembered the helicopter flyover, the twenty-one gun salute, and the bagpipes, which struck me as a peculiar choice for the funeral of an Italian American cop. The union had kicked out all the stops. The only things missing were the Ferris wheel and the bearded lady.

Lastly, I remembered the pallbearers as they carried the flag-draped coffin from the hearse to the grave site, all stepping in time to a lone snare drum. There were six of them, all in their dress blues, with white gloves and little black bands on their shields. The two in front were the chief himself, with his gold stars twinkling in the sun, and the union president, the detective who just happened to have been Raymond Rizzo's partner.

"Parker," said Tara.

I nodded. "Himself."

She sat in silence, studying the hands in her lap.

"Whatever happened to Lewis?" she finally asked.

"He was tried and convicted of Rizzo's murder. He got the death penalty, which in California means a lifetime spent in appellate purgatory. Only Lewis somehow managed to hang himself in the shower room at the Twin Towers. Or so the sheriff claimed. I don't think anybody pulled a muscle investigating it."

Tara said nothing.

"The union got their contract extension, plus a fat ten percent raise. Slewzyski, the ADA, got a promotion. And the judge who'd ordered Lewis released lost his bid for reelection, which happens in L.A. about as often as a snowstorm. The union pumped over a hundred grand into the campaign."

She took my hand in both of hers.

"And what happened to Jack MacTaggart?"

I smiled weakly.

"That shmuck? He'd already resigned, the day Ray Rizzo was killed."

She rocked onto her knees and hugged me, her face warm against my neck.

"Hey," I said, remembering. "What about you? What was your news?"

"It's nothing. It can wait."

"No, c'mon. What is it?"

I eased her away and she twisted a finger through her hair.

"It's no big deal," she said quietly. "It's just that I got fired today."

13

By rights I should have been catatonic, but my thoughts were still racing, bouncing off my bedroom walls long after the lights were out.

When the day had begun, my only concerns had been a bum shoulder, a couple of depositions, and a possible citation from the fire department. I'd still had a boss, Tara'd still had a job, and Raymond Rizzo had been but an old and fading memory.

How quickly things can change.

Staring at the darkened ceiling, I twisted and retwisted the facts I'd gleaned from Gabe into a dozen different shapes, like trying to solve a Rubik's Cube, and always with the same frustrating result.

Russ had left the office on Friday morning, his destination unknown. He'd canceled his appointments, so he expected to be gone all day. He'd left his cell phone off and in the car, which was not unusual. At some point he'd gotten my phone message at home, but he hadn't returned it.

He'd died on Saturday night. We'd know the cause of death soon enough, but whatever it was, he'd suffered a blow to the head while still alive, probably from a fall to the floor in his kitchen. He'd either lain on the floor all Saturday night and all day Sunday, or his body had been moved on Saturday night and held somewhere, probably in the back of his Wagoneer, for more than twenty-four hours.

The body had been moved, at night, by at least two people who wanted it out of the house in San Marino. They'd carried it to the Wagoneer in a blanket they'd brought for that purpose. They'd worn gloves, left no clues, and had taken the time to close up the house and garage before they'd left.

Therefore, they were careful.

Whoever they were, they'd known that Russ kept a boat in the marina, and that he often went there on weekends. They'd either found a key to the boat in the house or they already had a copy of their own. They'd known the boat's location, but not the location of his parking space.

Therefore, they were fallible.

They'd traveled to the marina in at least two vehicles, the Wagoneer and a getaway car. They'd moved the body to the boat late Sunday night, when the slips were dark and likely to be deserted. They must have known the gate combination before they'd arrived, and that their movements wouldn't be captured by any surveillance camera.

They'd planned ahead, but maybe not too far ahead.

Joe Comb-over had discovered the body midday Monday, after it had lain in the sun for only six or seven hours. So whoever they were, they wanted the body to be found. And not next year, in a shallow grave outside Barstow, but right away, and in broad daylight. They thought that whatever the real cause of death, they'd disguised it well enough to pass for a heart attack, and that no one would ever be the wiser.

They were overconfident.

These were the things I knew, or could deduce from the things that were known. But without more, anything else was rank speculation. And that included both the identity of the killers and the motive for their crime.

Once I'd worn grooves in my brain thinking about Russ, I rolled onto my good side and thought about Tara.

She'd been called onto the carpet and told that her services were no longer required.

She was expected to perform her duties through the end of the horse show, and then to be off the Fieldstone property within ten days.

When she'd demanded an explanation, she was told that unsanitary barn conditions had resulted in Hush Puppy's death, and that the board had come within one vote of imposing a quarantine and canceling the show altogether. That would have been a major scandal, not to mention a financial catastrophe, and somebody's head had to roll. Margaret Carlton, with help from Barbara Hauser, would serve as interim barn manager until a full-time replacement could be hired.

Tara had been fatalistic, but I was furious, since the decision had Sydney Everett's fingerprints all over it. She must have gotten hold of George Wells's report, and she was turning the evidence of her own culpability against Tara. Worse yet, I suspected that none of it would have happened if we hadn't eaten lunch together on Saturday at Fieldstone.

And finally, like Scrooge's third ghost, there was the small matter of my career. I still didn't know if Russ had ever met with Morris, but given Jared's charge to head the litigation department, I had to assume not.

Which meant that it fell to me to inform the managing partner that his son was a criminal. Even with proof in hand, that would be no easy task. But with Russ gone, and with both files missing, I had nothing to back up the charge.

It was well after midnight when I finally dozed, and that's when the dream began.

I was walking up a hill, at dawn, through a heavy mist. Up ahead, a group of mourners was dressed in black, their backs all turned as though to a frigid wind. Bagpipes keened somewhere in the distance, and a lone snare drum played a steady march.

The slope grew steeper somehow, and suddenly I was fatigued, stepping in time to the drum but making no progress. I fell to my knees, and when I finally did reach the others, they parted to reveal a huge rectangular grave, as deep as it was wide.

I crawled to the edge for a look at the big white horse, but there was no horse to be seen. Instead there was the tiny body of a man, curled on its side, as pale and naked as a drowned bird. And when the wind blew harder, the man's skin began to peel away, like a birch tree shedding its bark.

I woke in a sweat, my shoulder hot and throbbing. Outside the window, a bone-colored light chalked the eastern sky. The digital readout on the alarm, which I'd set for five o'clock, read 4:57 A.M.

Sam lifted his head, and whimpered, and then lay back to sleep.

There was no portentous mist awaiting me at Fieldstone; just a light fall breeze, a diamond-blue sky, and a low sun throwing long shadows across the blacktop.

The entrance gates, previously utilitarian affairs, had been transformed since the weekend into a riot of fall colors — sunflowers and Indian corn, orange ribbon and gnarled gourds — all of it wrapped and woven onto naked grapevines to form enormous wreaths.

The guard shack was empty, but a barricade of straw bales deflected traffic away from the main parking lot and onto a short side road that opened to a grass field where parking attendants in green Fieldstone jackets waved the late-arriving mourners into spaces along a stretch of white board fencing.

I parked the Toyota and followed two middle-aged couples as they hurried in the direction from which we'd come, down the side road and around the barricades to the main lot and clubhouse.

The grounds crew was out in force, mowing lawns, hauling hoses, and pushing wheelbarrows full of pumpkins and potted plants. A front-end loader, school bus yellow, trucked manure from the barns. In the field beyond the hedges, blanketed horses blew steaming breath onto the dew-slicked grass while grooms loitered by their sides, chatting and twirling their lead ropes.

The clubhouse parking lot had been converted into a bazaar of white canvas booths, where vendors either worked on their displays or gathered in small groups to drink coffee and eye the members passing somberly through their midst. I followed my escorts across the lot and over the patio, then through a hedgerow, and onto a rolling green lawn.

There was no crane in sight, but there was a mound of topsoil visible around a hundred yards uphill from where the crowd had gathered beneath a towering oak. I scanned the faces as I approached, noting several that I recognized.

The first was Sydney, in a black knit outfit, receiving air kisses and hand squeezes from the late arrivals. The second was Barbara Hauser, standing at the other side of the gathering, her hair loose and glowing in the dappled sunlight. And somewhere in the middle, like a fungus clinging to the big tree itself, leaned a hawk-eyed Margaret Carlton, watching over the rim of a Styrofoam cup.

It was a prosperous-looking group, the men in suits or tweed sport coats and the women mostly in dresses. Black and navy seemed to be the colors of choice, although Barbara was conspicuous in a white blouse and jeans. It could have passed for a charity event, or maybe a political fundraiser, except for the grim faces and the muted conversation.

Since many of the guests were drinking coffee, I traced the source to a table draped in white, where two silver urns flanked open boxes of breakfast pastries. I triangulated my approach so that I was screened from both Sydney's and Margaret's views.

"Here. Let me help with that."

The offer came from a strawberry blonde, who reached over to work the lever above my cup. There was something about her voice that was vaguely familiar.

"You wouldn't be Sally, by any chance?"

She straightened to her full height, which was nearly six feet in flats. Her hair was back and her face, pale and freckled, fell somewhere midspectrum between plain and pretty.

"Yes, Sally Cates." She started to offer a

hand, then quickly withdrew it. It was an awkward gesture, followed by a flush of color on her cheek. "You must be Mr. Mac-Taggart."

"Guilty as charged."

She nodded to the arm. "I'm very sorry about your accident." Then in a stage whisper, she added, "I had to fill out all the paperwork for our insurance company."

"I hope you made it more sensational than it really was."

"Oh, absolutely. Don't be surprised if Paramount calls about a film option."

We drifted from the table as we spoke. On a low rise just a short distance from the gathering were velvet ropes that stretched theater-style between portable brass stands.

"What time's the matinee?"

She followed my eyes up the hill.

"I imagine we'll start once Mrs. Everett is finished on the red carpet."

There was a snarky tone in her voice that I hadn't heard on the phone.

"I suppose I should thank you, Mr. Mac-Taggart, for helping make this possible."

"Trust me when I tell you that the credit belongs entirely to Sydney."

Then I spotted Jared. He and Barbara were standing apart from the crowd, Barbara's eyes downcast, her head nodding earnestly as she listened to his monologue. Again, Sally followed my gaze.

"Someone you'd like to meet?"

"Isn't that the girl from *After Yesterday*? The slutty little blonde?"

"Her name's Barbara Hauser. She's one of our jumper trainers."

"If you'll excuse me," I said. "I've never missed an episode."

Jared wore a navy suit with a sky-blue tie and a matching pocket square. He raised a finger to Barbara as I approached.

"Hello, sport! Thought I might see you here. You two have met, I think."

Barbara smiled. "Yes, of course. I believe you owe me a dollar, Mr. MacTaggart."

"I do?"

"That's what they charge for a nine-one-one call, isn't it?"

"I think those are free. But if I'm wrong, just add it to Sydney's account."

The smile wavered, but only for a moment.

"All right, I'll do that." She gestured toward my arm with her cup. "Is that as bad as it looks?"

I shrugged both shoulders and tried not to wince. "I look on the bright side. If I were a horse, they'd have put me down."

"That," she said, winking at Jared, "would

depend on your breeding potential."

They appeared awfully cozy together, considering my last encounter with Barbara.

"It's nice to see that you two have buried the hatchet."

"What's that supposed to mean?" Jared demanded.

Barbara placed a hand on Jared's arm. "Mr. MacTaggart is referring to a little misunderstanding we had earlier." Then she added, "Before all the facts were known."

"Are all the facts known? Why am I always the last to find out?"

"Didn't you hear?" she said. "There was a parasitic outbreak in the stallion barn. Standing water, apparently. We're lucky only one horse died. It could have been a lot worse."

"Not for the horse that died."

A familiar sound wafted down from above, and all eyes turned toward a man in full Scottish regalia skylighted on the ridge. The tune he played was slow and mournful, but then again, "Zip-a-Dee-Doo-Dah" would sound slow and mournful on the bagpipes.

Barbara poured her coffee onto the grass. "Showtime," she said.

It wasn't until we'd all reached the ropes that I finally saw Tara. She was standing at the foot of the huge grave, staring blankly into the abyss. She wore a flannel shirt over jeans and work boots, a pair of calfskin gloves dangling from her seat pocket. I thought of Cinderella, on a break from cleaning her evil stepmother's house, peering in at the party.

I moved beside her, and she reached her arm around my waist. She neither spoke nor looked in my direction.

The hole that we both now faced was maybe ten feet deep, with sheer vertical walls and perfectly squared corners. Inside lay the white horse's body, tightly wrapped in heavy, double-ply plastic. A bouquet of red roses leaned against his belly, obscuring the broad bandage encircling his midsection. Adorning the bouquet was a single blue competition ribbon.

From our vantage, the horse looked like a child's toy, or maybe a Christmas tree ornament that had been dropped in the dirt and forgotten. The arriving guests took turns leaning over the ropes, shaking their heads and murmuring.

Once the crowd had fully assembled, the bagpipes quieted and a silver-haired gentleman stepped over the rope at the head of the grave, clearing his throat for attention.

First he welcomed us to what he called "a bittersweet celebration of an extraordinary life." Glancing at notes, he recited Hush Puppy's numerous awards and accomplishments, and he praised Barbara Hauser for having, as he put it, "taken greatness and molded it into legend."

As he droned on, I scanned the faces of the other mourners. Jared was over by Sydney now, and both stared into the grave. Margaret Carlton stood with her arms crossed, watching the speaker. And when I came to Barbara Hauser, our eyes locked across the chasm and she smiled like an atheist during Thanksgiving grace.

When the eulogy was finished, Sydney stepped over the rope with a helping hand from Jared. Her eyes were red and her voice was choked with what seemed like genuine emotion.

"I just want to thank all of you, my dearest friends, for joining me here today," she began, sniffling and dabbing with a handkerchief. "This means so much to me, and to my beloved Hush Puppy. *Our* Hush Puppy."

I could feel Tara stiffen.

"I'm afraid I don't have Michael's way with words, so let me just say this. The bond between horse and owner is a special thing, a *spiritual* thing. So while God in his infinite wisdom may have taken Hush Puppy from us prematurely, his memory will live in my heart forever. And now, with this lovely memorial, I hope that he will live in your hearts as well, and in those of generations to come. Thank you all so very much."

She'd rushed the ending, burying her face in the handkerchief, and when she stepped back over the rope, Jared was there to give her hand a squeeze. Michael, the first speaker, stepped forward into her place.

"Ladies and gentlemen, that concludes the formal portion of this morning's program. On Sydney's behalf, I want to thank you all for coming. There are refreshments on the table, so please feel free to linger. And when you do leave, please be mindful of the show preparations."

And with that, the crowd splintered and melted down the slope, some heading toward the food and some toward the clubhouse beyond.

Tara made no move to leave, and in fact, she tightened her grip on my waist. After a minute or so, we were alone where we stood, and I finally turned to face her. She continued staring numbly into the grave.

"Are you all right?"

She didn't respond, and it seemed she was lost in the spectral fog of my dream.

"I know," I said. "Sydney's full of beans, and this was all a big farce. You were right about that. Why don't we —"

"You don't understand," she finally said, looking up with shining eyes.

"What are you talking about?"

She wiped her nose on the sleeve of her shirt.

"The horse in the grave," she said, gesturing. "That isn't Hush Puppy."

"You mean he isn't even *dead?*"

We were walking now, down the hill toward the clubhouse, heads turning as we passed the crowd at the table. She waited until we were out of earshot before responding.

"Hush Puppy's dead all right. I saw him in his stall, remember? And so did George. It's just that the horse back there isn't him."

"Are you sure? I mean, it was pretty dark down there. And with the plastic and all?"

She stopped and turned to face me.

"I've groomed that horse a thousand times, okay? I've picked his feet, pulled his mane, clipped his coat, and cleaned his sheath. I know Hush Puppy. And that poor animal, whoever it was, isn't Hush Puppy!"

She marched off toward the clubhouse, her work gloves flapping a wordless farewell. I hurried to catch up.

"Hold on, wait a minute. Do you think

anybody else noticed?"

"I don't know. I doubt it."

There was a clutch of members milling on the patio, while others were gathered by the doors leading into the fireplace room. I could see Sally Cates, her head above the crowd, watching us as we approached.

"Wait a minute, for Christ sake!" I grabbed Tara by the arm and turned her to face me. "Where are you going?"

"I'm getting to the bottom of this!"

"Wait, honey. Hold on a minute." I took her elbow and steered her into the field. "Let's think this through."

She resisted at first, then leaned her head into my chest. I held her close, watching as more heads turned in our direction. I guided her around a low hillock facing away from the clubhouse, and there we sat on a log.

"How did that horse, whoever it is, get into the grave in the first place?"

"I don't know. They worked on the excavation last night. I tried to stay out of it, this whole rotten thing. The main office handled it. I just assumed the body was delivered from . . . wherever."

"A vet hospital in Chino Hills."

"Okay. Well, it hadn't arrived by the time I left."

"When was that?"

"I don't know. Five thirty."

Common sense dictated that we start from the end and work our way backwards, following the chain of custody.

"Who would have actually put the body into the grave?"

"Rudolfo would have supervised. He's in charge of grounds."

"Can you talk to him and find out? We need to track the body from the time it arrived at Fieldstone until the time it went into the ground, okay?"

She nodded. "Okay."

"Tell me something else. When a horse dies, who transports the body? Is there like an ambulance service or something that you call?"

"No, not really. There are a couple of haulers who have closed trucks with winches. We keep a list in the barn office."

"Would there be any kind of record of who delivered the body last night?"

She thought about that.

"There'd be an invoice, certainly. In the main office."

"Where in the main office?"

She turned to face me, her mood lightening.

"I'm not sure, but I'll bet I could find it.

If I had five minutes in there alone."

I stood and looked toward the clubhouse. There were a dozen people still on the patio, with more drifting down from above.

"How many people work in that office?"

"It depends. Usually just Sally and the bookkeeper. Sometimes Maritza. She does odd jobs when she's not in the kitchen. But with the show starting tomorrow, it'll be busy all weekend."

From the ridge above came the rumble of heavy machinery. The front-end loader was moving toward the dirt mound, while two guys with shovels stood by the grave. A third was clearing the velvet ropes.

"Now's obviously not the time. But I could come back at lunch, and try to lure Sally out of the office."

"No, sweetie, you've got enough to deal with. Let me handle it. I'll call you later and let you know."

"I don't want to get you into more trouble."

She smiled weakly. "What are they going to do, fire me?"

As I headed to my car, past the booths in the parking lot, a familiar voice called out from behind.

"Jack? Jack! May I have a word please?"

Sydney stood in the shaded portico between the patio and the double-doors to the clubhouse. She leaned on one hip, smoking a cigarette.

My first instinct was to keep walking, but Russ's admonition — the one about judging — slowed me to a halt. I turned and moved in her direction.

"Hello, Sydney."

"You weren't going to leave without saying hello?"

"I believe I just did."

She stamped out her smoke and strolled into the sunlight, gesturing for me to follow. She walked to the far corner of the patio, away from the others, before turning again to face me.

"You have some explaining to do," she said quietly.

"Speak for yourself."

"I beg your pardon. What have I done to deserve this kind of treatment? First you bait me in front of the staff, then you don't even *bother* to tell me that you've had George's report for *days*. And now, today of all days, you ignore me completely and parade around in public with that . . . that guttersnipe."

"Do me a favor, Mrs. Everett, and spare me the homily. I know all about you and

Barbara and Jared and Creole."

She raised a hand to her face, as if she'd been slapped.

"And I know it was you who had Tara fired, which was petty even for someone as small as you. I also have a necropsy report on my desk that proves you had Hush Puppy killed. So don't presume to lecture *me,* thank you."

"How dare you —"

"And as for that guttersnipe, she's worth ten of you on your best day. So you know what? Fuck you, Sydney. Fuck this club, fuck all your snobby friends, and fuck the horse you rode in on."

I left her on the patio, slack-jawed, and stalked toward my car. I was only thirty feet clear when the shouting began.

"How dare you speak to me that way! I'll call Russell and have you fired, you . . . you Blue-beard! You peasant!"

All heads now turned in Sydney's direction, and so did mine.

"For your information," I told her, "Russ Dinsmoor is dead. And so is your phony insurance claim."

14

There were three news vans waiting at the curb, and their doors flew open as I rounded the corner from the parking structure. A familiar face led the charge, with the others in close pursuit.

"Jack! It's Terina Webb, Channel Nine Action News!"

I kept my head down and ducked into the lobby before they could get a shot. Mo Jackson stood at his desk, his arms folded, watching the show.

I noticed the sweatshirt still hadn't been claimed.

"They been out there all mornin'," he said, shaking his head in amazement. "Lotta fuss about a false alarm."

I told him, "If any of them tries to enter the building, shoot to kill."

When the elevator doors opened on nine, who should I see but Detective Tom Parker, sharing a chummy farewell with Morris

Henley. Both reacted like they'd been caught holding hands in the men's room.

"MacTaggart," said Morris. "You're here."

"You've gotta be somewhere."

He cleared his throat and adjusted his necktie.

"I'd like a word with you in my office, if you don't mind."

Margot handed Parker his parking validation, and the big man sauntered past me with a boxer's glare.

"Oh, Detective," I said as he stood by the elevators. "Gabe said he left a sweatshirt downstairs in the lobby. He asked if you could pick it up for him."

Morris Henley's corner office may have lacked the mountain views, but it was the largest on the floor by far. And the view wasn't exactly shabby, looking eastward along Colorado Boulevard. Come New Year's Day, he'd have the best seat in the house for the Rose Parade. He would, that is, if he took the time to look up from the year-end financials.

The office decor was Man-Cave Revival — heavy mahogany furniture with green leather and brass rivets. And in place of the industrial wall-to-wall that covered the rest of the ninth floor, Morris had installed hardwood flooring, which he'd then smothered with a thick Persian carpet.

His Stanford diploma was framed in mahogany, to match the furniture. Sunlight had faded the sheepskin to the same pale yellow as the legal pads stacked neatly on the corner of a desk that was big enough to land fighter jets. On the wall opposite the desk was a huge oil painting, a plein air landscape of hills and trees in a heavy gilt frame.

If God were a lawyer, I thought, His office would look something like this.

I sat in one of the client chairs, feeling like a middle-school miscreant summoned to the principal's office. Morris, meanwhile, made a big show of setting aside his work before forming a steeple with his fingers.

"First of all," he began, "I know you're probably upset with my decision to appoint Jared to chair the litigation department. Perhaps you thought that you were a more deserving candidate. I want you to know that I'm not insensitive to your feelings in this regard. You and Russ were obviously close, and he was certainly grooming you as his successor."

He laced his fingers into a sausage ladder that he rested on the edge of the desk.

"As the firm's managing partner, however,

it was my duty to consider a host of other factors. For one thing, you're a relative newcomer here and, lest we forget, not yet a partner. And to many of your colleagues, MacTaggart, you're something of an enigma. Frankly, there are times when I number myself in their company. For another thing, I would have grave concerns about the productivity of the department with you in charge, undertaking all of this pro bono and contingency-fee litigation. Russ was well aware of my feelings on that subject."

He pronounced the words "pro bono" and "contingency" as though they were synonyms for welfare and socialism.

"Jared, on the other hand, is a known quantity. He's been with the firm since his graduation from the Stanford Law School, and he's well-respected by his peers. Moreover, he shares my philosophy about departmental productivity. And, having had the pleasure of supervising his work, I can assure you that he is well up to the task."

That Morris hadn't a clue what Jared was up to, or as to his standing among his peers, was painfully obvious, but now was probably not the time to educate him.

"I understand perfectly, Morris. Naming

Russ's successor is entirely your prerogative."

He leaned back in his chair, which groaned under his weight.

"I'm glad we can agree on that. As my father used to say, there are two things that are essential to the success of a law firm. The first is profitability. And I don't recall what the second one is."

He chuckled at his little witticism, but when I failed to reciprocate, he cleared his throat and continued.

"Now then. Jared and I have reviewed Russ's files, and there appear to be several court dates upcoming. Until Jared can disengage fully from his other commitments, we'll be counting on you to make sure that nothing falls through the cracks. I've asked Jared to prepare a memo to that effect, and you should have it on your desk by this afternoon. Are there any questions about that?"

"Nope."

"Good. And while we're on the subject, Jared mentioned something about an insurance claim for Mrs. Everett, but we didn't see that file in Russ's office. What's the status of that matter?"

"You never discussed that with Russ?"

He frowned. "No, why would I?"

"The status," I told him, "is that I've got it covered."

He folded his arms, leaving the frown in place.

"Harry Everett was a personal friend, MacTaggart. He leveraged a wildcat well in Signal Hill into the largest independent oil company in California, smack on the heels of the Great Depression. But that wife of his . . ." He shook his great bison head. "For every dollar Harry earned, she managed to spend two. There wasn't a charity in town she didn't underwrite or a fund-raiser she didn't attend. A gold digger and a social climber, if you want my opinion."

"Love is blind," I reminded him.

"Love," he snorted. "Don't make me laugh."

As he said this, he produced from a drawer an envelope, large and white. From it he extracted two blue-backed documents and arranged them side by side in the center of his blotter. He then produced what looked like a letter, as yet unfolded, that was paper-clipped to its envelope.

"The main reason I asked you here is to discuss Russ Dinsmoor's estate plan. These documents are his Will and his living trust. I've been named executor of the estate, and successor trustee of the trust. And these" —

he leaned and handed me the letter — "are excerpts from the trust instrument, along with a letter from me to you. Trustee to beneficiary, as it were. Take a moment and read them."

The letter was indeed from Morris, informing me that I was a beneficiary under the trust of Russell H. Dinsmoor, and that as such I was entitled to receive a copy of the trust terms affecting my interest. It also warned that I could not bring an action to contest the trust later than 120 days from the date on which I'd received personal delivery of the letter and its enclosure.

The enclosure consisted of two Xeroxed pages from the trust instrument, setting forth Russ's bequest of the house and its contents to me.

"Okay, I've read it."

He studied my face, then leaned back in his chair.

"The trustee of a trust has many responsibilities, MacTaggart, not the least of which is to preserve the trust corpus until all potential challenges have been resolved. And that brings us to Detective Parker, with whom you're apparently well acquainted. When I watched the news last evening, I learned that the police are conducting a homicide investigation. A small detail you neglected to mention in your report to the partners."

"Bernie's working on a shark-attack theory. I didn't mention that either."

Morris was stone-faced.

"This morning I telephoned the authorities, and I was referred to Detective Parker. He was most eager that we meet. I've now learned that not only is there a homicide investigation underway, but that you yourself are what he called a 'person of interest' in that investigation."

I sat up straight. "That's bullshit, and Parker knows it."

Morris's voice was soothing, even if his look was not.

"Calm yourself, son. I'm sure it's all a misunderstanding. But under the circumstances, I hope you can appreciate that I'd be in breach of my fiduciary duties as a trustee if I took any steps to transfer title to the property in question until all of this is resolved. The probate code makes it quite clear that anyone complicit in the death of the settlor is disqualified from receiving trust property. So you see, regardless of how absurd the allegation, my hands are tied."

His hands, actually, were flipped palms-up.

"Did you tell Parker about the bequest?"

He nodded. "I did, in confidence. I also told him that the very idea of a Henley and Hargrove attorney having any involvement in any sort of criminal activity is preposterous."

I found Morris's opinion on that subject somehow less than comforting.

"Are we finished here?"

I picked up the letter and crossed to the door, where his voice stopped me in my tracks.

"A word to the wise, MacTaggart. According to Detective Parker, you've been interfering with his investigation. He tells me that you broke into the Dinsmoor residence and that you compromised a crime scene. I don't know what you were thinking, but that's not the way that a prospective Henley and Hargrove partner comports himself. So in the future, you're to stay out of the way and let the police do their job, is that understood?"

He rose from the chair, leaning both fists on the desk.

"And let me be perfectly clear. That's not a request. That's an order."

"I've looked everywhere, and I haven't found any file like the one you described."

Veronica was slumped in Russ's chair,

looking none the better for her night's rest. Her eyes, moist and raw when last we'd met, today were dark and sunken.

"Do me a favor? Fire up that computer. There's something I want to see."

She pivoted and bent to the task.

"When did you first introduce Russ to Google?"

"Oh, I'd say a month ago. Maybe six weeks. I remember, he said something about a cartoon character . . . what was the name? Snoopy Smith?"

The Google home page filled the screen, toy-balloon letters against a stark white background. I rounded the desk to look over her shoulder.

"When you demonstrated it, do you remember what you might have used as a search term?"

She hesitated. "No, I wouldn't . . . oh, wait! I think we looked for newspaper sites. He was surprised to learn that you could get the news online for free. He said it was no wonder all the papers were going out of business."

"Type in the letter 'a.' "

She typed a lowercase "a" in the dialog box, and nothing else happened. The cursor blinked numbly, inviting further input.

"Now try 'b.' "

She backspaced and replaced the "a" with a "b," with the same result.

"Go through the whole alphabet like that."

The exercise took but a few minutes. The first letter to produce a response was "l," which expanded automatically into "los angeles times." The next was "n," which yielded "new york times." The last was "s," which produced two hits — "secretary of state california" and "snuffy smith."

"That's it," she said, stroking the "z" key.

"Do you remember showing him the secretary of state's Web site?"

"No, I'm sure I didn't. Why would I do that?"

I bent down and kissed her on the cheek.

"Was that helpful?"

"Maybe not," I told her. "But I've been waiting a long time for an excuse to do that."

There were three documents sitting on my desk. The first was Mayday's declaration, describing the second half of the Zelman deposition, with relevant excerpts attached.

The second document was a draft declaration for my signature, attached to which were three partial transcripts. Two reflected the doctors' admissions that neither had seen Vic Tazerian's medical records until after the denial letter was written. The third was an excerpt from the court hearing on Thursday, in which Donald Carlisle had stuck his foot so far into his client's mouth that two Connecticut doctors couldn't extract it.

The third document was a memorandum from Jared, which read, "Have put Dinsmoor files on Kim's desk. At earliest convenience, please review to determine appearances to be covered, then handle. Report all hearing results and required follow-up by memorandum. Also, advise forthwith as to any media-sensitive matters."

"Asshole."

I put my voice messages on speaker. There were nine calls in all, five of which were from local news outlets including channels 5, 9, and 13, plus the *Times* and L.A.'s legal newspaper, the *Daily Journal*. I jotted the last number down.

Of the other messages, three pertained to pending cases, including one from Pat Bowman.

The call from Gabe Montoya had come in at 7:35 A.M.

Hey, Jack, it's Gabe. I saw the news last night, and I'm really sorry. I should have just run her over, but the D.A. has a policy about cooperating with the press. Anyway, I'm sorry.

So here's a makeup. I just found out that Parker is headed over to talk to your boss, who apparently called downtown and asked for the detective in charge. I hope that helps. I'll talk to you later, buddy. De minimus non curat lex.

The sign-off was a legal maxim, in Latin, meaning the law doesn't concern itself with trifling matters. It was Gabe's way of saying that I shouldn't sweat the small stuff.

We sat at one of the lab tables, with the periodic table as our backdrop and the Tazerian medical records as our centerpiece. Since Heinrich Wagner had given an expert deposition before, and since he'd been prepped by Dinsmoor himself, my little refresher had been as much for Mayday's benefit as for the doctor's.

"Will this case go to trial?" Wagner asked when we'd finished.

"No, I don't think so. If the judge grants the injunction, that should effectively end the case."

"And if he denies it?"

"Then Vic will die, and the Hartford Allied blimp can fly another lap around the Rose Bowl."

Mayday interrupted.

"If we win on Friday, won't they just file

317

an interlocutory appeal? They could try to run out the clock that way."

"I don't think so. Even assuming it were an appealable order, the only issue would be whether the trial court's decision was supported by substantial evidence. That's a very high bar for them to overcome. Plus, the appeal wouldn't stay the order anyway, so the case would be moot by the time it was heard. Lastly, an appeal would run the risk that their conduct would be criticized in a published opinion, and that would be a disaster for a company so conscious of its image. No, I'd say Friday is come to Jesus for Hartford Allied."

"Or for Mr. Tazerian."

"Well," said Wagner, "they can question me all they want, but I'm not going to change my opinion. You can be assured of that."

"Thanks, Doc. I'm sorry it came to this, but we want you to know how very much we appreciate your help."

"Not a problem. Like I said before, anything for a colleague of Russ Dinsmoor."

I don't know if it was my face or Mayday's, but Wagner saw it immediately.

"Did I say something . . . ?"

I glanced at Mayday. "You haven't heard. I'm sorry, I should have said something earlier. I'm afraid that Russ passed away over the weekend. It was all very sudden."

Wagner blanched, rising unsteadily to his feet.

"Are you all right?"

"Yes, I'm fine. It's just . . . as you said, so sudden."

"He'd had a history of heart problems."

"Is that so? I didn't know that." He shook his head. "And he looked so well on Friday."

"Friday?" I leapt from my seat. "What do you mean Friday?"

"I mean . . . I met with him here on Friday. He seemed perfectly well. In fact . . ."

"Doctor Wagner, this is extremely important," I said, trying to control my excitement. "Why did you meet? Whose idea was it?"

"Objection, compound," said Mayday. Wagner looked at her, then back to me.

"He rang me up, Friday morning. Said he had something urgent to discuss. That he didn't want to speak over the telephone. So I invited him here."

"When? What time did he arrive?"

"I don't know. In the afternoon. I'd say two thirty, maybe three o'clock."

"And what did he want to talk about? Please, Doctor, it's very important."

"He wanted to know about EVAgen. About Dr. Huang's work."

"And?"

"And I told him it was a start-up venture that Brian had formed. Something to do with vector control. Viruses. That's Brian's specialty."

I felt the hairs rise on the back of my neck. "I checked the Caltech Web site. It said that EVAgen was involved with equine something-or-other. Something that sounds like arthritis but isn't."

"You mean equine viral arteritis. At first, perhaps, but the company is much more than that. It's aroused all sorts of venture capital interest."

"Why? What else are they working on?"

"I'm afraid I don't know. I'm not involved with EVAgen, and I've never felt it was my place to ask. Confidentiality agreements are pretty standard in biotech deals. Most of Brian's work is conducted at his lab at JPL. We've no real security here on campus, and because of the CDC implications —"

"The what?"

Mayday answered. "The Centers for Disease Control and Prevention. It's part of the Department of Health and Human Services."

"That's right," said Wagner. "And they

require a level of security that we simply can't accommodate here at the university."

"And you discussed all of this with Russ on Friday?"

"He wanted to know about EVAgen. Who else was involved in the company, who Brian's partners were."

"And?"

"I told him I didn't know. I suggested he ask Brian."

"Did you put him in touch with Dr. Huang?"

"No, I'm afraid you have it backwards. It was Brian who introduced Russ to me."

"Wait a minute. I thought you met Russ through the Caltech Associates."

"I did. Brian was one of his sponsors. Russ was Brian's guest at the lecture where we first met."

Now I was the one looking lost.

"So how did Russ and Brian meet?"

"Don't you know?" Again Wagner looked from me to Mayday. "Brian and Russ are next-door neighbors."

15

I thumbed my cell phone while Mayday drove. As the number rang, I studied the little map that Heinrich had torn from his campus directory. It was a bird's-eye view of the entire JPL facility, which consisted of more than a dozen buildings spread over a hundred hillside acres. He'd circled the location of Brian Huang's laboratory, a freestanding structure on the northwest corner of the map.

"Montoya."

"Gabe, it's Jack. We need to talk, and I mean now."

"Shoot."

"No, I mean in person. I have new information about Dinsmoor's whereabouts on Friday, and maybe the germ of a theory. About motive."

There was silence on the line before Gabe responded.

"You know the Parkway Grill on Arroyo?

I'll meet you at the bar in twenty . . . oh, shit. With traffic, make it forty minutes."

"From Santa Monica," I said, "we'd better make it an hour and a half."

"No, man. I'm downtown. In fact, Griegas and Parker are heading my way. See you there."

The line went dead.

"I don't suppose you plan to tell me what this is all about?"

I turned and studied Mayday in profile, considering.

"In college," I finally told her, "I took a survey course in psychology. I don't remember much from the class, but for some reason I remember one particular study about the impact of television on people's perceptions of the world. They'd have people fill out a questionnaire that asked things like, 'How many times in your life do you think you'll witness a shooting?' Stuff like that. And people who watched little or no television were pretty accurate in their perceptions of the world. But people who watched a lot of television overestimated the amount of violence and death they'd encounter in their lifetimes."

"I suppose that depends where you grow up."

"I suppose. Anyway, one of the questions

asked, 'What is the likelihood that you'll ever see a dead body in public?' or something like that. And it occurred to me that I'd never seen a dead body, period, except once at an autopsy, and once at my mother's funeral. And I grew up in East L.A., thank you, and I worked in the criminal justice system."

"The point being?"

"The point being that in the last two weeks, I've seen one dead man and two dead horses. And until ten minutes ago, it never even occurred to me that they all might be connected."

Back in her office, Mayday worked the keyboard while I watched. The home page of the California Secretary of State's Web site blinked onto the screen.

"Now what?"

There were icons for Election and Voter Information, for Campaign and Lobbying Information, and a catchall for Other Services. There was also an icon called the California Business Portal, which sounded like a good place to start.

"Go there," I said, pointing.

She clicked, and the next screen that appeared had more than a dozen hyperlinked headings, including Business Entities,

Forms, Samples, and Fees. Below these was a cascading list of subheadings.

"Try Limited Liability Companies."

She did, and another screen appeared, this one busier than the last. Along the margin ran a menu of further destinations, one of which was Records Order Form: Certificates, Copies, and Status Reports. Technology, I thought, was a wonderful thing.

"Let's order some records."

The next screen was a pdf file, signaling the end of our online odyssey. The document was entitled Business Entities Records Request. Among the available records were Statement of Information documents, including the original, the most recent, and any changes. These were the public filings that would show the ownership of a limited liability company like EVAgen, LLC.

"Jeez," I said. "This will take days to process."

"Not if we use DataCheck."

The name was vaguely familiar. "What's DataCheck?"

"It's a service up in Sacramento that takes orders by phone or e-mail, then hand-walks your document request through the bureaucracy. They then either snail mail or e-mail you the results, depending on the urgency. All the corporate guys use them."

"How long would something like that take?"

"If we called them now, we'd probably have the documents by tomorrow afternoon."

Which wasn't bad, but if my hunch was right, it was too long to wait. And then I remembered where I'd seen the name DataCheck before.

"Forget it. Come with me."

We swung past my office, then rode the elevator to nine. Veronica was at her desk, and once again, it was clear that she'd been crying.

"Oh, Jack!"

I waved her into Russ's office, shutting the door when all of us were inside.

"You knew, didn't you?"

"Congratulations. You deserve every penny."

She shook her head and dabbed at her nose with a tissue.

"Did you and Morris discuss the funeral?"

"I called over to All Saints. We've arranged it for Monday."

I handed her the slip of paper I'd been carrying.

"Call the *Daily Journal* when we're finished. They called earlier about Russ, and they may be running a story. I'm sure they'd be happy to print something about the service."

"I was hoping you'd agree to speak," she said, looking up from the slip. "I know Russ would have wanted that."

"I'd be honored. On one condition."

"What's that?"

"If I hear any bagpipes, all bets are off."

I handed her the printouts that she'd given me on Tuesday.

"Russ received an e-mail on Friday morning from a company called DataCheck. It's in his trash bin. See it?"

She flipped to the entry.

"Okay."

"Could you find that message and print it, including the attachments?"

"Of course. Is it important?"

"I think it might be."

She looked at Mayday, then moved to the desk. We waited while she booted up the computer and made her way to the repository of deleted e-mails. After a minute, the printer began to hum.

We drove west on Union, then south on Arroyo Parkway. The shops and restaurants were already starting to fill, and our progress was slowed by too many cars trolling for too few parking spaces. Pasadena, I'd come to understand, was a Hahamongna Indian word meaning "many cars."

Mayday finally broke the silence.

"Okay. We know from the secretary of state's records that Brian Yee-Horn Huang and the Jared Henley Living Trust are the co-owners of EVAgen, LLC. I still don't understand what it means."

I was silent for a couple of blocks.

"In a trial," I finally answered, "the jury doesn't always get the evidence in a nice, chronological sequence. Sometimes the cop testifies first about the crime scene. Then the neighbor testifies about the barking dog. Then the wife testifies about the gun in the dresser drawer."

"You've been very didactic of late."

I smiled. "In your opening statement, you might tell the jury that evidence comes from the witness stand like the pieces of a jigsaw puzzle, and that it's not until the end of the trial that all the pieces fall into place. Which is why the jurors need to keep an open mind throughout the trial, right up until the very end. And they should think of your opening statement as the picture on the front of the puzzle box. First you describe the final picture to them in your opening, and then, through witnesses and documents, you put all the pieces together."

"Let me guess. We're like the jurors who don't have all the pieces yet."

"Exactly."

She gave me a look. "Okay, what pieces do we have?"

I wasn't sure how deeply I wanted Mayday involved in all of this. Then again, having allowed the camel's nose into the tent, I wasn't entirely sure I could keep her out.

"That's a long story. For right now, all you need to know is that Gabe Montoya is an assistant district attorney, and he's a friend. He's working the investigation with a cop named Parker, who is not a friend."

"And what does the picture on the box look like so far?"

"Jumbled. But at the center of it all is a murder."

"Wait. Are we talking about Mr. Dinsmoor now, or about Mrs. Everett's horse?"

"That," I said, "is an excellent question."

The Parkway Grill was an old brick warehouse, all English ivy and skylights, converted into one of Pasadena's most chichi restaurants. It was the kind of joint where aspiring actors served you duck-and-goat-cheese pizza with a Cabernet reduction sauce for twenty bucks a throw.

It was after five when we arrived, and the

valets were already stacking the cars three deep in the parking lot. In the marquee spaces up front were a vintage Ferrari and a couple of Porsches. Mayday's Lexus would earn us a spot somewhere within hailing distance. Gabe's Volvo, on the other hand, was probably back by the Dumpsters.

As for the man himself, we found him at a little table in the bar area, sipping a jewel-colored concoction from a martini glass. We dragged over chairs, and I did the introductions.

"Does your husband know you drink those?" I nodded toward his glass.

"Don't start. It's a Cosmopolitan."

The waitress arrived, and I ordered a Bud. Mayday requested a Chardonnay, and Gabe reloaded on the Cosmo.

"You drink three of those, you get a gift certificate to Victoria's Secret."

"Screw you, Mac. What's your germ of a theory?"

"Actually," I told him, "germs *are* my theory. Or viruses, anyway. Did we learn anything from the autopsy yet?"

"No toxicology yet." He glanced at Mayday. "The stomach cavity was clean. No pills, no overdose. That's all we know so far. Oh, and the only prints in the house were yours, Dinsmoor's, and the housekeeper's."

The waitress returned with a dish of little bean pods that required, happily, two hands to eat.

"Marta and I just met with a doctor at Caltech. He's an expert witness for us in a case, and tomorrow's his deposition. I was originally referred to him by Dinsmoor. Turns out, he met with Dinsmoor on Friday afternoon, over at Caltech, which makes him the last person I know to see Russ alive."

That got his attention. "Okay."

I removed the folded pages from my pocket and tossed them onto the table.

"These are all the e-mails Russ sent and received over the last ten days. Parker already has this. One's from a company called DataCheck. See it? They do public records searches, like at the secretary of state's office in Sacramento. The last page is a document they e-mailed to Russ on Friday morning, just before he left the office."

Gabe took the page and tilted it toward the light.

"So what the hell is EVAgen, LLC?"

"It's a company that does biomedical research. Viruses, apparently. Brian Huang shares a lab at Caltech with our expert, whose name is Wagner. Anyway, Wagner says

Russ came to see him on Friday to talk about Huang. Huang and this EVAgen company."

"And what's the Jared Henley Living Trust?"

I looked at Mayday.

"It's the reason I called you instead of Parker."

Gabe peered over the top of the page. "C'mon, Mac. You know I can't withhold anything."

"I know, but here's my proffer. Jared Henley is one of the junior partners at my firm. His father's the guy Parker met with this morning, our managing partner."

Gabe nodded. "Parker liked him. Said he was very forthcoming."

"Did you know Parker told him I was a person of interest?"

"Oh, Christ. I'm sorry, Jack."

"Not your fault. Anyway, Jared Henley is Morris Henley's son."

Mayday added, "The idiot son you keep locked in the attic."

"I get the picture. He's a legacy."

"You remember my call to Russ's cell phone on Friday? How I said it was urgent?"

"Yeah?"

"Well, I fibbed. The call wasn't about a court hearing. It was about Jared Henley.

I'd uncovered some dirty laundry a few days earlier, and the call was a follow-up."

"And how dirty was this laundry, exactly?"

I glanced around the bar before leaning in closer.

"I'd learned that Jared has been acting as a conduit for extortion payments from a client to a blackmailer. And I'm pretty sure Russ had the evidence with him in his briefcase when he left on Friday."

I looked over at Mayday, whose frown told me she was learning more today than how to prepare a witness for deposition.

"Okay," said Gabe, letting it marinate. "So you think Dinsmoor's visit with Wagner on Friday loops back to Jared Henley because of this EVAgen? Or am I missing something?"

My cell phone interrupted, and I excused myself and rose. It was Tara, and she was excited.

"I got it!" she said.

"Talk to me."

"The driver who delivered the body is named Joaquin Salazar, and I've never heard of him. He's not somebody the club ever uses."

"Did you get a phone number?"

"Yes. Do you have a pen?"

"I don't even have a hand. Can we meet

in a little while?"

"Okay, but I haven't schooled Escalator yet. Can you come over? If I'm not in the main ring, I'll be at the barn office. I'll have my phone on, so just call me."

"I'll see you in an hour. Keep your heels down."

The drinks had arrived at the table, and Gabe had his wallet out. Not to pay, of course, but to show Mayday some photos of his boys. As workaholics went, Gabe was a world-class father.

"Yes, there's more to the story," I said, resuming my seat, "but here's where it gets a little murky. EVAgen has something to do with horses. Or horse viruses, anyway. Jared is a member at the Fieldstone Riding Club, up in Flintridge, and so is this Dr. Huang. And Huang has an office at the Jet Propulsion Laboratory, which is right across the road from Fieldstone. Plus, the blackmail thing went down at Fieldstone."

He took a minute to process the information.

"That's it?"

I sipped my beer and considered how much more I could say without violating any privileges. Or sounding like a lunatic.

"Here's the kicker. We find out today that Huang lives in San Marino, right next door to Russ's house."

Gabe waited for more, and I could see that he still wasn't hooked.

"Don't you see? Huang could have come and gone from the house without raising an eyebrow from the neighbors. Plus, we wondered why anybody would go to the trouble of moving the body? Well, Huang had a reason — to move the crime scene clear across town, and hope it never traced back to San Marino."

"Until you brought it back, by breaking and entering."

"Exactly."

He tasted his drink and considered it.

"You think Huang was tied up in the blackmail thing?"

"No, I don't. I don't know where he fits in, but he fits."

Gabe frowned into the pink mirror of his Cosmo.

"Does this Jared character know that Dinsmoor was wise to the blackmail?"

"That's the sixty-four-thousand-dollar question. The answer again is, I don't know. Russ was gonna speak to the father, but I don't think he made it."

"You think the kid somehow found out, and got to Dinsmoor first? The kid and his business partner Huang? All for what was in Dinsmoor's briefcase? I don't know, man. There's a lot of holes in that cheese."

"Maybe. But if the autopsy turns up some exotic virus, you heard it here first."

Gabe drained his glass, checked his watch, and then tucked the papers into his pocket.

"Okay, Counsel, here's what I'm prepared to do. I'll see if I can steer Parker toward this Jared without making it obvious. As for Huang, I'll tell Parker about your meeting with Wagner and let him run with it. What's Wagner's first name?"

"Heinrich," replied Mayday.

"Heinrich. Okay. And as for the blackmail thing, I never heard it from you. But if we need it later, you'd better think of a way to serve it up fresh."

"Thanks, Gabe."

"No, thank you. Who ever knew that civil practice could be so interesting?"

He stood to leave.

"Oh, and one other thing. Does Jared know that *you're* wise to the blackmail thing? Because if he does, and if your theory isn't as half-assed as it sounds" — he nodded at my arm — "then you might want to think about packing a piece in that holster, cowboy."

Mayday dropped me at the curb, but I

walked past the lobby doors and straight for the parking structure.

It was after six when I arrived at Fieldstone, and a violet dusk was settling over the grounds. I drove straight to the grass parking field, then hoofed it back to the clubhouse. The main ring below the patio was overlit by floodlights, and there a lone rider cantered graceful loops between the jumps.

I followed a path down to the covered grandstand area and sat to watch Tara and Escalator work, their shadows a shifting compass rose in the glare of the lights. The jumps were dressed with flowers now, plus straw bales, pumpkins, and other seasonal adornments in shades of burnt orange and yellow, all of it lending a fantastic quality to the scene, as though I'd stumbled into a young girl's equestrian dreamscape.

Tara turned Escalator at the far end of the ring and pointed him on a diagonal line through the center of the maze. They jumped three of the low obstacles in quick succession, turned sharply, then jumped two more along the far rail. Escalator broke from a canter, then down to a walk, his nose finally stretching to the ground. I started to clap, and Tara's smile lit up the far corner of the arena.

"Bravo!"

She gave a little bow, then pointed toward the exit gate.

By the time I'd made my way there, she and Escalator had already circuited the arena, and still the big horse blew clouds of frost into the cool night air, his dark coat wet and shining in the lights.

"Open sesame!" she called as they approached.

Once onto the grass, Tara let the irons drop and swung herself lightly to the ground, looping the reins over the horse's ears. She kissed me, her face all damp and warm, then secured the stirrups in place. She wore the same shirt and jeans as this morning, with her crop tucked snugly into the waistband of her chaps. The chaps were tan leather and fringed at the legs, with the name TARA embroidered on back between a pair of green shamrocks.

"Ready to take on the world?"

"He feels pretty good right now. Ask me again on Sunday."

She led Escalator by the reins into the darkened field.

"Aren't you freezing?"

"No, are you kidding? It feels great. How's the arm?"

I gave it a shrug, and this time I didn't

wince. "Did you talk to Ronaldo?"

"Rudolfo," she corrected. "He said the carcass arrived at around six o'clock, already wrapped in plastic. They directed the driver up to the grave site, and he lowered it in with his winch. He didn't recognize the driver. Then they directed him to the main office to drop off the invoice."

"If only we had that darned invoice."

I could see her smile in the darkness.

"I had Maritza run into the office, screaming that there was a rat in the kitchen. Everybody ran out, and I slipped in. The payables were in a folder on Sally's desk."

"Did they catch her?"

"Catch who?"

"Margaret Carlton. In the kitchen."

She pretended not to hear.

"Funny thing, though. The delivery charge was only a hundred dollars. It would normally cost around five hundred to haul a horse out to Chino."

"So next time, hire that guy."

"Next time," she said, "Margaret and Barbara can hire whoever they want."

We were on a bridle path now, passing below the stallion barns where Hush Puppy had lived and died. Tara and I walked abreast, with Escalator bobbing behind like a great big dog on a leash. Up ahead, lights from the main barns shone like a beacon off a ceiling of low clouds.

"Ever heard of something called EVA? Equine viral arteritis?"

She stopped. "Of course. Why?"

"What is it, exactly?"

"It's a virus. A very contagious virus, and if it gets into your barn, it spreads like wildfire. The symptoms are flulike. High fever, loss of appetite. But the worst is spontaneous abortion in pregnant mares. It can devastate a breeding barn."

"Is there no cure?"

"Quarantine and rest is usually all it takes. For mares and geldings, that is. But for some reason I don't think anyone fully understands, a stallion that's been exposed to EVA becomes a lifetime carrier. It's a career-ending diagnosis for a breeding stallion."

"And there's no vaccine or anything?"

"Yes, there is. Almost all breeding farms vaccinate. Why are you asking these questions?"

"You remember Dr. Huang, for whom I bravely risked life and limb? That's apparently his field of expertise."

"What is?"

"EVA."

"I thought he was a rocket scientist."

"He is. But he runs a company on the side called EVAgen. Ever heard of it?"

"No. Should I?"

"I don't suppose Hush Puppy ever had this EVA, did he?"

She considered it. "I don't think so. But the person to ask would be George."

We entered the main quadrangle, where a groom in dirty coveralls rushed over to loosen Escalator's bridle and drop the bit from his mouth. He slipped the bridle over one shoulder, then looped a nylon halter over the horse's nose and neck, all in what looked like a single motion. The whole exchange lasted about five seconds, and was executed with the precision of a NASCAR pit stop.

As the groom led Escalator away, I followed Tara toward the barn office. Once inside, she kicked the door closed and drew a folded sheet from her pocket.

"Do you want to call, or shall I?"

The invoice was the kind you'd tear off a preprinted pad, with the name Joaquin Salazar on top, above the words Specialty Cartage Services. There was a printed phone number and a P.O. box address in Duarte. Below these, in what appeared a hurried scrawl, was a date followed by the notation "One-Way Delivery $100."

"He may not speak too good the English," I said. "Can you put him on speaker?"

She jabbed a button on the telephone, and a dial tone filled the little room. Then she punched in the number, and we waited through two and a half rings.

"Hello?"

"Hello," she said, "is this Mr. Salazar?"

"Yes. Who is calling, please?"

"Mr. Salazar, this is Margaret Carlton from the Fieldstone Riding Club. You delivered an animal here from Chino Hills on Tuesday night. Hello?"

There was a long silence on the line. Finally, he said, "No, ma'am, there has been some mistake. That wasn't me."

"Well, we're processing an invoice here, and it's got your name on it. For a hundred dollars? Does that ring a bell?"

"Yes, that's right. A hundred dollars."

Tara looked at me and shrugged.

"Mr. Salazar," I interjected. "Did you or did you not deliver a dead horse to the Fieldstone Riding Club on Tuesday?"

"I did, yes, sir."

"Where did you pick up the dead horse that you delivered to Fieldstone?"

"Is there some kind of problem?"

"No, sir. Just tell us where you picked it up. That's all we need to know."

There was another, longer pause. And then came the dial tone.

16

The offices of Plimpton, Simmons & Stark occupy the top six floors of the Library Tower, L.A.'s tallest high-rise. Mayday and I rode together in my rented Toyota, with Heinrich following in his Prius hybrid. And since I'd left my arm brace at home today, I had both of my hands on the wheel.

At the entrance to the underground structure, we were met by two rent-a-cops manning a check point. They asked us our business, then requested permission to search the trunk of our car. I told them it was okay, but to be really careful of the nitroglycerine. They didn't think that was funny.

In the building lobby — three echoing stories of chrome and black marble — we were made to line up between velvet ropes in order to show our picture IDs and have our names cross-checked against a list of authorized visitors. We were each then issued a clip-on magnetic tag that was scanned at another checkpoint by the elevators. There a guard escorted us to the elevator car, using his own key card to activate the console of buttons.

The events of September 11, 2001, may be a distant memory to many here on the West Coast, but the security industry that blossomed in its aftermath was showing every sign of immortality. I had no doubt that the theatrics downstairs were less about security than about impressing the friends and intimidating the foes of the building's many law firm tenants.

"I don't know why the security's so tight in the lobby," I told Heinrich as we ascended, "when they're just going to strip-search us upstairs."

The penthouse reception area was attended by three winsome twenty-somethings perched behind a marble console, each wearing a hands-free headset and dark, serious eyeliner. I announced our arrival, and we were offered our choice of coffee, tea, or sparkling water. As a joke I asked for a decaf mocha latte, and the girl replied, "Yes, sir, please have a seat."

The furniture was all chrome and black leather, arranged into four seating areas. At the center of each was a low glass table, and on each table there were six different newspapers arrayed in two neat rows, including *Der Spiegel* and *Le Monde.* I checked, and all were today's editions.

There also hung at each seating area a huge abstract painting, all drips and smears of black and gray paint in a stainless steel frame. We sat and took in the airplane-level view that stretched from downtown to the Pacific Ocean some twenty miles distant, and it occurred to me that in summertime, when smog choked the high-rise canyons of downtown L.A., the view would look less like an aerial photograph and more like one of the paintings.

After we'd cooled our heels for the prescribed interval, a woman in a bloodred business suit materialized and announced, "Mr. MacTaggart? Mr. Stark would like a word with you in private, if he may."

Thomas Lewellen Stark, otherwise known as the Pope, was the managing partner and éminence grise of the Los Angeles outpost of Plimpton, Simmons & Stark. He was a former president of the State Bar of California, a former president of the American Bar Association, and a former undersecretary of state under both Democratic and Republican presidents. Long a legendary L.A. power broker, he'd gained some measure of national fame by negotiating the release of hostages from the U.S. Embassy in Libya in the late 1980s.

I had no idea to what I owed the honor or, for that matter, what the honor might portend, but I rose to follow her, signaling for Mayday to join me.

We passed down a hallway to a glass-walled conference room, and there a tomahawk-faced gentleman with silver hair and unnaturally perfect teeth rose to greet us. On the table before him sat a gilt-edged cup and saucer, and at the table next to him, looking every bit as white as the china, sat Donald Hudson Carlisle.

"Mr. MacTaggart? Very good to know you. Please, come and sit. I'm Tom Stark, and I believe you've met Mr. Carlisle."

The old man wore an impeccable gray suit with a starched white shirt and pocket square, gold cuff links, and the kind of wide rep tie that went out with the Reagan administration. He gestured to some chairs opposite from Carlisle.

"Please make yourselves comfortable. Has anybody offered you a beverage? We make the best coffee in Los Angeles. It's the only reason I was persuaded to support the NAFTA treaty, but that's just between you and me."

"You're lucky," I told him. "The coffee at

our place, if they served it in prison, there'd be a riot."

He flashed a smile, just to show that he appreciated a sparkling wit.

"I'll get right to cases, Mr. MacTaggart. Carlisle here tells me that you and he are having trouble ironing out your differences in an insurance matter. It may be presumptuous of me, but I thought that if I could convince Sadat and Begin to shake hands, then maybe I could be of some help to you in getting this thing settled to everybody's satisfaction."

Thus was revealed the price of admission to the papal audience. Carlisle must have sent up a rescue flare after last week's hearing, and Hartford Allied must pull enough weight to merit an intervention from the top of the letterhead. And my role, presumably, was to kiss the old man's ring and be grateful for whatever indulgences he might deign to offer.

Before I could respond to his overture, there was a knock on the door and the red suit returned, this time with a little pushcart on which sat a china cup, saucer, and silver spoon, which she proceeded to set on the table before me. There was one of those little sticks of rock-candy sugar resting on the saucer.

"Decaf mocha latte," she said before turning to leave, and Stark gave me a look that may or may not have called my manhood into question. I cleared my throat.

"I certainly appreciate your offer, Mr. Stark. Our problem is, I have a client who'll be dead in a few months, and you've got a client that won't pay for the only treatment that can save him. If you can find a middle ground there, we should send you back to Gaza."

He chuckled softly.

"Oh, there's always a middle ground, young man. If I've learned anything from fifty years of practice, I've learned that." He leaned back in his chair. "For example. Suppose you two agree to submit the issue to binding arbitration. I mean, do you really want a matter of life and death decided by six people too dumb to avoid jury duty? You could have a final resolution in a couple of months. Maybe a couple of weeks. Otherwise, this has the potential to drag through the trial and appellate courts for *years*." He leaned forward again and winked a bushy eyebrow. "And while I can't promise anything, I might even persuade our people to pay for the arbitrator."

You couldn't help but admire the way in which the old fixer had brandished both the carrot and the stick. I hoped Mayday was taking notes. And while I would have loved to hang around and spar a few rounds, just to say that I had, Henley & Hargrove wasn't paying Heinrich Wagner five bills an hour just to sit out in the lobby and read *Der Spiegel.*

"Mr. Stark, there's nothing in this world I would enjoy more than to put your client in front of a jury, dumb or otherwise. Unfortunately, I expect the court to deny me that pleasure tomorrow morning at around nine fifteen. So if you don't mind, I believe we have a deposition scheduled."

Thomas Lewellen Stark was not accustomed to impertinence. Not on his home court anyway, and certainly not from the likes of me. His eyes still twinkled, but the smile tightened into a thin, red gash.

"I wouldn't be too certain of that, young man. You see, I've known Amos Spencer since we were on the Law Review together at Boalt, and I've never known him to be much of a plaintiff's judge. As a matter of fact, we were just lunching together at Chancery Club, and I recall him railing about all the frivolous tort cases clogging his docket. No, sir, I wouldn't be too cocksure if I were in your shoes."

I rose, and Mayday did likewise.

"Thank you for your time, Mr. Stark. But we appear to have differing views on how the system works. And for all of our sakes, let's hope yours is wrong."

His voice stopped us at the door.

"Once you walk through that door, young man, all settlement discussions are over. So please, save the false bravado. As you yourself said, we're talking about a man's life here. What if you're mistaken about tomorrow? Have you considered that? Are you prepared to have a man's *life* on your conscience?"

I turned to face them both.

"Don't you worry about me, Mr. Stark. My conscience is clear. Then again, I've never had to shill for an insurance company."

It was nearly two o'clock when we descended to the lobby to turn in our badges. After the Kabuki theater with Stark, the deposition itself had been anticlimatic, and Heinrich had acquitted himself well. I asked Mayday if she'd mind catching a ride back in the Prius while I stayed behind to scout out some real coffee, and to make an important phone call.

"Bowman here," the fat man intoned.

"Hello, Pat. It's Jack MacTaggart. You got

351

a second?"

"Hey, MacTaggart, I'm sorry about that letter. I thought they were gonna send the report to me first. I would have —"

"Forget it. Listen, I'm downtown right now, and I'd like to drop by your office. Can you spare a few minutes?"

I could hear the wheels turning.

"Uh, yeah, I guess so. Sure. I'll be here."

"Relax, I'm not armed. I just need to ask you a couple of questions. I'll be there in fifteen minutes."

The address was on Wilshire, not far from my old stomping grounds. It was a squalid block of storefronts in a seedy part of town, and Bowman's building appeared right at home with its surroundings.

It was a two-story shoe box with a bumper-scarred archway leading into a central courtyard. Half the spaces in the cracked parking lot were empty, and of the half-dozen cars that were there, one was up on blocks.

A building directory hung in the hallway, advising that MLIC Risk Management was on the second floor, in suite 210. The concrete stairwell smelled like cat piss, and there were no cats in sight.

The second-floor hallway was open to the courtyard, and the cantilevered walkway flexed under my weight, enough for Bowman to hear me coming and greet me at the door. He wore blue gabardine pants and a matching vest that didn't begin to cover his gut. With a fez and fly whisk, he could have doubled for Sydney Greenstreet in *Casablanca.*

"Hello, MacTaggart. Welcome to Hancock Park South." He stood aside and made a gesture for me to enter.

I'd had the feeling on the phone that Bowman wasn't used to receiving visitors, and one look inside his office had confirmed it. It was little more than a repository for the file boxes that lined its walls from floor to ceiling, all on the verge of collapsing onto a conference table that itself sagged under the weight of another dozen boxes. There was a desk on the far side of the room beside a yellowed ficus. On the desk were a telephone, some more files, and an old desktop computer.

"I'd offer you an espresso, but I gave my staff the day off. Just clear off one of those chairs and make yourself cozy."

He kicked a file box over to the threshold to prop the door open. A weak draft from the parking lot cut the odor of mold and dust and rustled some of the papers.

I surveyed the towering boxes. Each bore

a name and policy number in black Magic Marker.

"Are these all Met Livestock files? You guys must write a lot of insurance."

He followed my eyes to the ceiling.

"Last time I checked, we had about half the equine market in Southern California. You'd be amazed how many horses there are in L.A."

"And you handle all the claims investigations yourself?"

"Just for L.A. County. Me and Billy, that is. You met him at Fieldcrest. He can be a wiseass, but he's basically a good kid."

Bowman sat heavily in the chair opposite mine. "I hope you realize I could get in trouble for this. Are we off the record?"

"You are if I am."

He grunted. "Okay, what can I do you for?"

"Two things. First of all, you said that Hush Puppy's remains were at a vet clinic in Chino Hills. I'd like the name of the clinic, and a person to contact there."

"Why, was there a problem? I told the girl your people were gonna call."

"Oh, the horse was delivered all right, but I guess there was an issue about the charge."

Which was technically true, according to Tara.

He pushed to his feet again and crossed to the desk, from which he withdrew a brick of business cards bound with a rubber band. He thumbed through the cards until he found the one he was looking for.

"Here," he said, tossing the card onto the table, "you can keep it. The office girl is named Violet."

I slipped the card into my pocket while he eased back into his chair.

"What's the second thing?"

"I want to know what else you've got on my client."

"What do you mean?"

"I read the necropsy report. You guys wouldn't risk a bad faith claim on that alone."

He shifted in his chair, studying me.

"She's in hock up to her hooters, you know."

"I guessed as much. But that still doesn't cut it."

He ran a hand across his mouth. "Okay, what the hell. You'd get it in discovery anyway."

He rose without speaking and dug through one of the file boxes on the table. I could see the word "Everett" on the side, followed by a claim number.

He removed a binder from the box and

set it on the table. Then he snapped the rings open and handed me a sheet of paper. It was a photocopy of an e-mail that had been printed and three-hole punched.

The message had originated from MLIC Call Center, and was addressed to MLIC Old Business. The author was identified as Operator 047, and the message read, "A man named Henley," followed by the firm's phone number, "enquires if policy CA99-12116 is still current and in force."

The date on the message was October 11, a week before Hush Puppy's death.

"Did you talk to him?"

"Are you kidding? Unless it's a new business call, or unless the caller already has a name or an extension number, all calls made to the 800 number roll to our call center in Sri Lanka, wherever that is. Near India's ass-hole, I think." He gestured at our surroundings. "Anything to save a buck for our policyholders, that's our motto. Anyway, some dot-head down there forwarded the message to our old business unit in L.A."

"Did somebody there call him back?"

"Apparently not." He took the sheet and studied it. "Maybe because the caller's name didn't match the name on the policy. You'll notice he didn't identify himself as a lawyer. Then again, maybe it just fell through the cracks." He shrugged. "For whatever reason, there was no further action noted."

The fact that the owner's lawyer had called to check on the policy status a week before the insured animal turned belly-up stank to high heaven. That, combined with Sydney's financial condition, combined with her claims history, combined with the necropsy results, had made the case for denial.

Bowman withdrew a little booklet from the storage box. It was a membership directory from the Fieldstone Riding Club.

"Not only did he handle her last claim," he said, brandishing the roster, "but he's a member of the goddamn club."

"That e-mail is hearsay," I told him. "To get that call into evidence, you'd have to fly the operator over to testify."

He shrugged. "I'm no lawyer, but I know we do it all the time. The tape's admissible as a business record."

"Tape? You mean they tape-record these calls?"

"Hell, yes. Some of these people barely speak English. Wait a minute."

Bowman rummaged through the box again, this time extracting a cassette tape in a hard plastic case. There was a date and a claim number printed on the label.

"Once we catch a claim, the first thing we do is check the call log on the policy. If there was a recent call, we put a trace on the tape. This time we got lucky."

I remembered my call to Bowman on the 800 number: "All calls may be monitored for quality assurance."

"You got a tape player here?"

"Not for this size, no. But what's the difference? We know what it says."

"Can I borrow this to make a copy?"

He smiled, wagging a finger. "Now, now, MacTaggart. I may be jolly, but I'm not Santa Claus. Not that I don't trust you. It's just that the wife's gotten used to three squares and the satellite dish, if you know what I mean."

I reached into my pocket and peeled off a pair of twenties. "How about this? I'll pay you to make me a copy. Like you said, I'd get it in discovery anyway."

Bowman looked at the bills, and I could see him calculating how many Krispy Kremes they'd buy. It must have been enough.

"Come to think of it, you owe me for a tape anyway. There's a Radio Shack down the street. I'll have a copy by tomorrow. But if the shit ever hits the fan, you didn't get it from me."

Violet and I chatted amiably as I inched the Toyota northbound through the rush-hour gridlock.

"If I had your file number, I'd certainly give it to you. Trust me, I'm a lawyer. This would have been Tuesday afternoon, to the Fieldstone Riding Club. The owner's name was Everett. The horse's name was Hush Puppy."

"I'd sure like to help you," she responded, "but it's like, without a file number, I wouldn't even know where to start looking."

I detected, in the youthful nonchalance of her elocution, the polished steel of a tongue stud.

"Violet. A gentleman named Patrick Bowman from the Metropolitan Livestock Insurance Company called there sometime last week, and he spoke to you personally. He requested that the remains of this particular horse be preserved and delivered back to the Fieldstone Riding Club for a burial service. Does any of that ring a bell?"

"Whoa, I remember that! Wait a second."

And with that I was placed on hold for the third time in the conversation. Not that it mattered, since I'd moved less than a hundred yards during that time.

"I found it!" she returned, breathless. "There's a cover sheet, and a necropsy report, and a whole bunch of other stuff. So, like, what do you need?"

"Is there any kind of receipt or bill of lading that documents the disposition of the horse's remains?"

"What?"

"Any paperwork that shows what happened to the horse's body after they finished the necropsy?"

"Wait a minute . . . hold on . . . there's a release and disposition form and a receipt for delivery. Is that what you need?"

"That's exactly what I need. Now, do you have a pen handy?"

"Wait, hold on. Okay, shoot."

I respelled my name, gave her the office phone and fax, and made her repeat them back to me. She promised that the records would arrive before I did. In this traffic, I'd told her, Thanksgiving would arrive before I did.

In a tight black body suit with painted orange stripes, Bernadette looked like Tony the Tiger's trailer-park girlfriend. To this she'd added a striped tail and orange ears on a plastic hair band. All of which meant that today was either Halloween or laundry day at the Catalano household.

She pouted when she saw me coming.

"What are you supposed to be?" she demanded.

"I'm a person of interest."

"To who?"

"To whom. Did a fax come for me?"

"I don't know, but I'll check."

She bared her teeth and made a clawing motion, then turned and padded off toward the copy center, twirling her tail as she walked.

There were several voice messages awaiting my arrival. They included two calls from Sydney, plus an update from Mayday, the latter informing me that she'd faxed off our declarations to Carlisle and that a messenger had delivered the originals directly to Judge Spencer's courtroom for tomorrow's hearing.

I considered calling Sydney, but concluded I'd neither the interest in nor the energy for another lecture on funereal etiquette.

I was sorting through the day's mail when a knock sounded.

"Come in!"

It was Bernie again. She tossed some

papers onto my desk.

"There's a bunch of us going to El Cholo after work, if you'd like to join us. Some have already left." She fluttered her eyelashes as she turned. "The ones whom have the nice bosses."

The faxed documents all bore the logo of the Chino Hills Veterinary Associates. The first was a cover sheet with a handwritten notation reading, "Good luck! Love, Violet." The "i" in Violet was dotted with a little heart.

The second document was entitled "Receipt for Delivery," and it identified an outfit called Jesse Vigil Carting and Hauling — and not Joaquin Salazar — as the party to whom Hush Puppy's remains had been released. Moreover, the date of the exchange was Monday, and not the Tuesday afternoon before the service. At the bottom of the receipt was a scrawled signature that looked to be Jesse Vigil's, but with no accompanying address or telephone number.

The final document, two pages in length and dated the previous Friday, was entitled "Release and Disposition." It was basically an authorization form, allowing the clinic to release the horse's remains to Jesse Vigil. It was difficult to read the document, both because the type was small, and because it appeared to have been faxed and refaxed several times.

The form identified Hush Puppy by name, Sydney Everett as the owner/ insured, George Wells, DVM, as the attending veterinarian, and the Metropolitan Livestock Insurance Company as the clinic's client.

And at the bottom of the form, blurry but legible, was the signature of the person who'd authorized the release.

The person's name was Tara Flynn.

17

I'm not sure why I was still driving the Toyota. Maybe it was for the plastic wood trim or the imitation leather seats. Then again, maybe it was because retrieving the Wrangler would have meant facing Tara.

Traffic was Friday-morning light, and Mayday and I arrived at Spring Street with more than twenty minutes to spare. We parked in the underground lot on Main and joined the nervous stream of dark-suited lawyers zombie-shuffling toward the old United States Courthouse.

Outside the doors to Amos Spencer's courtroom, the day's schedule had already been posted. There was no longer a trial in progress, and there were only three matters on the morning calendar. Our case, *Tazerian v. Hartford Allied,* was in the leadoff spot, and next to the case name appeared the printed words "Continued Hearing on Application for TRO and Preliminary and

Permanent Injunctions." Next to this appeared the handwritten addendum, "And Order to Show Cause re: Sanctions."

There were a few lawyers already in the courtroom, including Carlisle in the front row chatting nervously with a middle-aged guy I didn't recognize. I motioned for Mayday to grab a seat, and I passed through the gate to present my business card to the clerk. On the way back I nodded in Carlisle's direction, but he didn't seem to notice.

Mayday had Carlisle's faxed declaration in her lap, and she handed it to me as I sat. Despite the schedule that Judge Spencer had established, the declaration hadn't arrived until after midnight, meaning that we hadn't laid eyes on it until this morning. Mayday had read it to herself on the drive down, and had assured me that it contained nothing of concern. Now I took a moment to read it for myself.

The only nuggets Carlisle had managed to mine from his deposition of Heinrich Wagner were that Wagner had once before been retained as an expert witness by our firm, and that Wagner, although a medical doctor by education, had no hands-on experience in treating leukemia patients. But these were popgun puffs compared to the mortar rounds we'd rained on the Hartford Allied doctors.

As I finished the last paragraph, Mayday nudged my knee, and I looked up to find Carlisle and his colleague looming above me in the center aisle. The older lawyer smiled and reached out a hand.

"Jack MacTaggart? I'm Fred Pollard. Can we step outside and chat?"

The courtroom clock read eight fifty, so I rose and followed after them, gesturing for Mayday to join us. Carlisle and Pollard walked a short distance down the marble hallway and stopped by the water fountain, where Carlisle bent to wet his whistle.

"First of all," said Pollard as we joined them, "I've been brought into this case to try to get it resolved, one way or the other. And I can tell you from personal experience that going forward with this hearing is not the best option for your client. In fact, back when I headed up the office, we used to call Amos Spencer the Cyclone. And not because he can be angry and long-winded, both of which are true. It was because he could change direction without warning, and just when you thought you were in the driver's seat, boom, your case was in toothpicks and your client was hanging upsidedown in a tree. If I've seen that happen once, I've seen it a dozen times."

Pollard had a pleasing accent, like maybe he'd grown up in Memphis or Charleston, but there was nothing soft about his message. First off, he was telling me he had once served as United States Attorney for the Central District of California, meaning he'd been the head federal prosecutor for all of L.A., Orange, San Bernardino, Riverside, Ventura, Santa Barbara, and San Luis Obispo counties — an area that in both geography and population was larger than forty or so states. Second, he wanted me to know that this was now his case, not Don Carlisle's, and that if I wanted a fight, I'd better be ready to step up to the heavyweight division. Third, he wanted to make sure I understood that he and the judge had a long history together, and given Spencer's famously pro-prosecution bent, I'm sure it had been a happy one. Last, and probably most important, he was warning me that, although I might think I held all the aces, there was still a wild card somewhere in the deck.

"Now I know you've already spoken with Tom Stark about this," he continued, "but I think you should reconsider the benefits of taking this case to binding arbitration. I've talked to our client, and I can assure you that they're willing not only to arbitrate, but also to pay all the associated costs. And that includes your fee."

"What?"

He nodded. "That's right. I'm talking about a big payday for you, Counsel, win or lose. From where I'm standing, that sounds like a pretty good offer, especially in light of the alternative." He tipped his head toward the door we'd just exited.

Pollard's offer was an insult on several levels, and I'm sure that to Mayday, I looked like one of those cartoon thermometers that grows redder and redder until it bursts.

"If you spoke with Stark," I said, "then you know we've already rejected his offer of binding arbitration. And let's face it, Fred, nothing's happened since then to make your case any stronger."

Carlisle interrupted, "Oh, yeah? We found out that Dr. Wagner's your in-house expert."

We all ignored him, and I continued addressing Pollard.

"We both know your client has one of the worst track records in the industry for paying claims. They hide behind ERISA, and they hide behind big firms like yours, and they use the Vic Tazerians of the world like Kleenex. This case is a textbook example, and frankly, it makes me sick. First you ignored the treating doctors, then you let the bean counters make the medical decisions, and then, when you finally got called to account, you tried to lie your way out of it."

Carlisle interrupted again. "Who are you calling a liar, you two-bit ambulance chaser?"

I took a step in his direction and he stumbled backward, goosing himself on the water fountain.

"Shut up. The grown-ups are talking."

I turned back to Pollard.

"You want a settlement proposal? Here's my offer to you. First, honor your insurance contract and pay for the surgery. Second, apologize to Mr. Tazerian and his family for what you've put them through. Third, identify the people in Hartford who denied his claim and fire them all. And fourth, figure out who it was that cooked up the fairy tale Carlisle spun for the court last week, and fire them too. That offer's good for thirty seconds, starting now."

Pollard set down his briefcase to applaud. "Bravo, Counsel. Okay, I'm convinced, you're a true believer."

His smirk abruptly faded as his eyes moved over my shoulder toward the courtroom entrance. "Never say we didn't make you a fair offer."

Mayday and I both turned in time to see the Pope himself, Thomas Lewellen Stark, nod once in Pollard's direction, then push through the heavy brass doors.

The late Edward Bennett Williams, whom many regard as America's greatest all-around lawyer, once defended lobbyist and former Texas governor John Connally against charges of bribery, perjury, and obstruction of justice.

Fearing that a white, patrician millionaire might not cut the most sympathetic figure before an all-black jury in the nation's capital, Williams arranged, or so the story goes, to have former heavyweight champion Joe Louis stroll into the courtroom and shake Connally's hand in full view of the jury. Connally was acquitted on all charges.

Stark's appearance in Amos Spencer's courtroom was a variation on the same cynical theme. Mayday and I entered in time to see the three of them settling into the front row, and to witness Spencer's bailiff walk over to the railing and shake hands with the great man.

The buzzer sounded just as we reached our seats, and the court reporter wobbled in from a side door. Seconds later, the chambers door swung wide and Amos Spencer strode quickly to the bench, fresh-scrubbed and ruddy-cheeked, his black robes trailing like a smoke screen.

"All rise!" announced the bailiff, and all did, including, I noticed, the Pope himself. "The United States District Court for the Central District of California is now in session, the Honorable Amos Spencer presiding."

Spencer carried with him a stack of court files, which he dropped on to the bench with a resounding *bang,* causing the reporter to jump in her chair. Satisfied with that result, he wrapped his glasses over his ears and pulled the microphone close. His eyes swept the courtroom before settling on the unholy trinity, whose combined presence evoked first surprise, then a nod, and then an un-nervingly warm smile.

"Number one on calendar, Tazerian versus Hartford Allied Insurance Company, docket number 437622 ASRx. Continued hearing on application for temporary restraining order, preliminary injunction, and permanent injunction." He then looked to Mayday and me as we rose from our seats. "And order to show cause why monetary and other sanctions should not be imposed. Counsel, please state your appearances."

371

Pollard and Carlisle were first to the podium, leaving Stark to watch from his seat.

"Frederick J. Pollard of Plimpton, Simmons and Stark for defendant and responding party Hartford Allied. Good morning, Your Honor. It's good to see you looking so well."

Spencer smiled again, which must have set some kind of record.

"And you, Fred. It's been too long. How are JoAnn and the boys?"

"Very well, thank you. Little Freddy just started high school, if you can believe that."

Spencer shook his head. "My, my. Time certainly flies."

Seizing on a lull in the hugfest, I cleared my throat. "Jack MacTaggart and Marta Suarez for plaintiff Victor Tazerian. Good morning, Your Honor."

Spencer ignored this and took a long look at his notes. Pollard, meanwhile, had joined his hands behind his back, smiling like the teacher's pet waiting for his gold star.

"All right, we're here on plaintiff's application for a temporary restraining order and a preliminary injunction. Both sides have submitted further briefing. Mr. MacTaggart, let's start with your side's papers." He placed both documents on top of his stack. "First, the Suarez declaration. I will strike the following material *sua sponte* as either hearsay or without proper foundation. Paragraphs two, four, five, seven, and the last sentence of paragraph ten."

Mayday, alarmed, tore through her file to see what violence the old judge had just visited on our case. Pollard cocked his head and favored me with the same smirking grin I'd seen in the hallway.

"Next is the MacTaggart declaration. I will strike paragraphs two, four, and five on the same grounds."

He took the two declarations and tossed them down onto his clerk's desk. As the clerk stamped the documents into the file, Mayday began moving toward the microphone, but I caught her by the arm.

"Next we turn to the declaration of Donald Hudson Carlisle." Spencer looked up from his reading and zeroed in on Carlisle, who'd been hiding back by the rail. "Mr. Carlisle, don't be shy. Please step forward and state your appearance for the record."

Carlisle moved to the lectern.

"Donald Hudson Carlisle of Plimpton, Simmons and Stark for defendant Hartford Allied, Your Honor."

Spencer looked at him in a manner that reminded me, at least, of the way a butcher studies a side of beef. "Mr. Carlisle, how long have you been a member of the bar?"

The question sounded innocuous, but somewhere on the horizon, I saw a funnel cloud starting to form.

"Uh, almost three years, Your Honor."

Spencer nodded. "Three years. That's certainly long enough to know that when the court sets a filing deadline, counsel must adhere to that deadline. Is that a foreign concept to you, Mr. Carlisle?"

Carlisle shifted his weight. "No, Your Honor. But you see, we didn't schedule the deposition —"

Spencer cut him off with a hand. I felt a wind on my face, and the leaden smell of rainfall in the distance.

"The Carlisle declaration, having been late filed, will not be considered by this court." Spencer tossed the document not onto the clerk's desk, but onto the floor of the courtroom, in the open well between the bench and the podium. It landed with a sickening *thwap,* like a fish hitting the dock, and it lay there beyond rescue, its mouth open and gasping for air.

"All right, then. Having heard the arguments of counsel last week, and having read and considered the *timely* filed declarations of counsel, the court is now prepared to rule. Does the matter stand submitted?"

Now it was Pollard's turn to restrain his junior from approaching the microphone. "Submitted, Your Honor," he said, which was my cue to concur.

"Submitted."

Spencer again looked up at the four of us. Then he peered over our heads to where Stark was sitting in the front row. I glanced over at Mayday, who was gripping her briefcase so tightly her knuckles were turning white.

"Plaintiff's application for a temporary restraining order, a preliminary injunction, and a permanent injunction is granted. The court will sign the proposed order submitted by counsel, but with the following addenda."

Before he'd finished the sentence, Mayday had her copy of the order out of the file, her pen poised at the ready.

"First addendum. Any failure or delay on the part of defendant Hartford Allied in authorizing or paying for the referenced medical procedures will be deemed a contempt of court and will be punished accordingly. Should that occur, Mr. MacTaggart, you are to return to this courtroom forthwith, on an ex parte basis. But I assume that will not be necessary."

This last he said while looking directly at Pollard.

"Second addendum. In respect of the late-filed declaration of counsel, the court imposes a monetary sanction of nine hundred ninety-nine dollars on Donald Hudson Carlisle, payable to the clerk of court within ten days."

That, I recognized, was Spencer's idea of tossing a bone, since a sanction of a thousand dollars or more is automatically reported to the state bar. But Carlisle, failing to appreciate the largesse, pushed past Pollard to the microphone.

The ozone smell of electricity filled the air, and I felt the wind beginning to swirl.

"Your Honor, if I may be heard. The imposition of a monetary sanction under these circumstances is totally unwarranted. We scheduled —"

"Silence!" The old man practically levitated out of his chair. "The matter was *submitted,* Counsel! That means the time for argument has *ended!"*

Pollard steered Carlisle, pale and wobbly, away from the microphone. He then said to Spencer, "Our apologies to the court, Your Honor," which seemed to placate the old man, who relaxed back into his chair. Then Pollard stooped for his briefcase, adding,

"Notice is waived." And with that, both he and Carlisle turned toward the door.

"Not so fast, Counsel!"

Spencer's words froze them both where they stood.

The wind was blowing harder now, and papers began flying off the tables and swirling upward toward the high ceiling of the courtroom.

"Next on calendar, on the court's own motion, is an order to show cause regarding sanctions."

Spencer leaned over to speak with his clerk, who stood and handed back one of our declarations. The old judge adjusted his glasses and began to read.

" 'The senior medical staff in Connecticut carefully analyzed this transplant procedure and determined that it was both experimental in nature and unlikely to be of any therapeutic benefit to the insured.' Do those words sound familiar, Mr. Carlisle?"

And it was just then, as he opened his mouth to respond, that Carlisle's phone started to ring.

At first we all froze, as though a stink bomb had detonated in the courtroom. Carlisle tore open his jacket and silenced the phone midway through the second ring. By then, however, the bailiff was on his feet and moving toward the podium.

The wind was howling now, lashing our hair and tearing at our clothes. Mayday and I had to grab hold of the table just to remain upright.

The bailiff looked at Spencer, who'd turned a shade of red that even Crayola hadn't trademarked. He nodded once and the bailiff snatched the phone out of Carlisle's hand and carried it to his desk.

Spencer's face was still florid when, after a silent meditation, he'd composed himself enough to speak.

"For your benefit, Mr. Pollard, what I just read into the record was a quotation from Mr. Carlisle's argument when he was last in this courtroom. It now appears to the satisfaction of this court, based on the admissible portions of both the MacTaggart and Suarez declarations, that Mr. Carlisle's statement was" — he glanced at Stark in the front row — "mistaken at best. At worst, it was an outright fabrication. In any event, it was an unqualified representation made without any basis in fact."

Spencer pivoted in his chair, grabbed a book from behind the bench, and began flipping the pages.

"Mr. Carlisle. Have three years before the bar allowed you to become familiar with section 6068 of the California Business and Professions Code?"

Carlisle stared blankly, and after a moment of silent reading, Spencer found what he was looking for.

"Allow me to refresh your recollection. 'It is the duty of an attorney to employ, for the purpose of maintaining the causes confided to him, those means only as are consistent with truth, and never to seek to mislead the judge or any judicial officer by an artifice or false statement of fact or law.' "

After reciting the passage, the old judge closed his eyes, as if to further reflect upon its wisdom. Or maybe he was just counting to ten. Either way, he suddenly rose from his chair and hurled the book to the floor.

It landed with a thud beside the declaration, skidding all the way to the base of the podium.

"Read it, Mr. Carlisle!"

Carlisle scrambled for the book. The statute from which Spencer was reading had become lost in transit, so he began rifling the pages, his hands visibly trembling. But Spencer didn't wait before resuming his diatribe.

"You, young man, are a disgrace to your profession! And it's only out of deference to the fine reputation of your firm that I will resist my initial impulse, which was to remand you to the custody of the United States marshal. The circumstances do, however, compel the imposition of a significant monetary sanction."

Spencer shuffled through some of the papers on his desk before he found what he was looking for. When he spoke again, his voice was under control. Either the storm had passed, or we were now passing through the eye.

"In a case such as this, the question whether it is appropriate to sanction the lawyer or the client is a difficult one. You, Mr. Carlisle, failed the court in your obligation to ascertain with certainty that your representations were truthful. However, since it is inconceivable to this court that a member of your *fine* firm would fabricate such a story out of whole cloth, I must assume that ultimate responsibility rests with your client. The sanction, therefore, will be against the Hartford Allied Insurance Company."

I glanced over at Pollard, and saw on his face the look of a child whose puppy had just been torn from his arms and swept skyward to Oz.

"Therefore, having considered all of the facts and circumstances in this matter, the court imposes a monetary sanction, payable to Victor Tazerian in care of Mr. MacTaggart's office, in the sum of fifty thousand dollars. The sanction will be paid within thirty days. Plaintiff's counsel will give notice, and will prepare an order to that effect for the court's signature. Today, if possible. Good day, gentlemen. And lady."

Spencer was already on to the next matter by the time Carlisle, Pollard, and Stark reached the courtroom doors. The Pope's face was crimson, and Carlisle had either forgotten or decided to abandon his Black-Berry. I waited outside the gate while Mayday processed paperwork with the clerk.

We could hear Stark's voice echoing down the hallway long before we reached the elevators. The old man was gesticulating at Carlisle, whose head was bowed, while Pollard stood by with folded arms. They fell into an awkward silence as we approached, and we stood that way together for a small eternity until the tone chimed and the elevator doors slid open.

Mayday and I stepped in, but they did not.

The doors remained open for a measure while we stared at one other, the victors and the vanquished, across the humming threshold. Then, as the doors began to close, I turned and spoke to Mayday.

"I wonder if you can buy disaster insurance for something like that?"

18

Mayday, still giddy, leaned on a curbside mailbox while I phoned in the news. I had to shout to make myself heard over the traffic, and I wasn't sure if it was laughter or tears that choked Lina Tazerian's words, but their meaning was plain enough.

It was after ten by the time we'd recrossed Main, and I signaled for Mayday to wait up. I dialed Bowman this time, hoping to save myself a second trip downtown, but the call rolled to his voice mail. I didn't leave a message.

"Time for a quick side trip?"

We exited the parking structure, circling the block onto Temple. From there we cut up Grand, past the Music Center and Disney Hall, turning right at One Wilshire. The neighborhoods grew seedier as we crossed the Harbor Freeway and continued westward on Wilshire Boulevard, the main artery through the beating heart of old Los Angeles.

First we passed the swan boats floating in the lake at MacArthur Park, where today you could buy a bindle of heroin or a fake U.S. passport without ever leaving your car. Next came the art deco façade of Bullock's Wilshire, once the high temple of L.A. chic, recently reincarnated as a law school. Then came the site of the old Ambassador Hotel, long demolished, never having recovered from Bobby Kennedy's fateful visit in the summer of '68.

Between these faded landmarks, like moldy grout encircling vintage pink tiles, were the nail salons and video stores, the bail bondsmen and payday lenders; the myriad seedy testaments to the changing face of Los Angeles.

The signs on the storefronts segued from English to Spanish, from Spanish to Korean, and from Korean to a Cyrillic alphabet whose origins stretched to a point beyond my limited horizons. But all shared the common indignity of gang graffiti, the universal language of urban decay.

"You really know how to show a girl a good time," said Mayday as we passed an old man urinating into the gutter at Crenshaw. Mayday had grown up in La Jolla, a tony seaside enclave near San Diego, where inner-city grit meant tourists carrying last year's Prada bag.

"Don't be a snob. You see that building? That's my old office."

She leaned across the seat. "You're joking, right?"

"Nope. As a matter of fact, there were some pretty good lawyers in that building. In a courtroom, never make the mistake of judging an opponent by his address. Or by his law school."

"Yeah," she said, "I learned that this morning."

We made a left under the arched façade, and I parked near the open stairwell. There were three cars in the courtyard today, not counting the one on blocks, and one of them was an LAPD cruiser.

"This won't take a second."

I left her with the engine running and took the stairs two at a time. The door to Suite 210 was locked, as I'd feared, and there was no envelope or package outside, as I'd vaguely hoped. I banged a few times just to be sure, then returned to the parking lot.

"Sorry. False alarm."

"What is this place?"

"You remember Mrs. Everett's insurance claim? This is the adjuster's office."

We backtracked on Wilshire, but instead of following it out to the freeway, I veered left at Lafayette Park for the scenic drive through Silver Lake. I was in no hurry to get back, and I figured we'd earned the diversion. Or maybe I was trying to delay the inevitable reckoning with Tara.

Mayday already had most of the puzzle, so I gave her a few more pieces, including the deadly horse parasites, the non-IOLTA bank account, and the phone call to Sri Lanka. She stared out her window and studied the forming picture.

"I agree with Gabe," she finally said. "It doesn't add up. Even if you assume Jared is a killer, you wouldn't kill somebody to cover up a crime in which you're only tangentially involved. Not to mention a crime that's only one bank subpoena from being exposed."

"You don't think Jared is capable of murder?"

"At the risk of sounding like the serial killer's landlady, no, I don't. If Jared's a criminal, I see him more as the accessory type."

"Like a belt or a handbag?"

"Exactly," she laughed. "Stylish but not very useful."

"Okay then, what's the answer?"

She thought about it some more.

"I have no idea."

We crossed the Hollywood Freeway onto

Rampart, then jogged east onto Alverado Street, where a homeless man's shopping cart nearly sideswiped us at the light.

"For me," I said, "it all comes back to EVAgen. That's the big black spider at the center of the web. Tara says there's already an effective vaccine for equine viral whatever, so the company bio on Huang's Web site is probably bull —"

My cell phone interrupted, and I read the caller I.D. I set the phone in the cup holder and pressed the hands-free button.

"Gabe?"

"Mac? You got your head in a toilet?"

"I'm in the car with Marta. I've got you on speaker, if that's okay."

"Okay with me. Hey, Marta."

"Hello, Gabe. We were just talking about you."

"I know, we have your car bugged. Just kidding! Hey, Mac, guess what I'm looking at right now."

"The Dinsmoor autopsy report."

"Bingo. And are you ready for this? The cause of death was . . . cardiac arrest. Not a head strike, and not some mutant virus from outer space."

Mayday and I arched our eyebrows, placing quotation marks around Gabe's pronouncement.

"But there's hair on the cake. Because of the forensics, the ME ran a bunch of secondary tests. Bottom line, toxicology says that Dinsmoor was acutely hypoglycemic at the time of death. Off the charts, apparently."

"Okay, so what's it all mean?"

"Good question. At first they thought he might have O.D.'d on insulin."

"Insulin? Russ wasn't diabetic."

Mayday, the only premed major in the car, weighed in on that. "A large dose of insulin can cause a heart patient to go into arrest."

"That's right. Problem is, they rechecked every inch of his body, and they couldn't find any evidence of a hypodermic injection."

All of a sudden, the conversation was sounding eerily familiar.

"What about an environmental source, like food or drink?"

"Nope," he said. "Insulin doesn't work that way. If it did, you think diabetics would still be sticking themselves with needles?"

We rode in silence through Echo Park.

"Anyway," Gabe continued, "the coroner's in a tizzy over how to call it, especially with the media breathing down his neck. There's a press conference later today."

"There's a memorial service on Monday."

"Not a problem. The body's being released this afternoon."

We passed a foggy gathering of dreadlocks and dashikis beating African drums on the lawn. Mayday lowered the window a crack to sniff the air.

"What about the lungs?" she asked.

"What about 'em?"

"Nowadays, you can take insulin in aerosol form, like from an inhaler."

We could hear Gabe flipping pages of the report.

"Nothing in here about lungs or lung tissue."

"If it's not too late," I said, "maybe they should take a sample."

"If it's not too late," corrected Mayday, "have them take both lungs in their entirety."

"Okay," said the voice from the console. "I'll mention the aerosol thing to Melissa and see what they think. I'm glad I called."

"And Gabe? Anything new with Jared or Huang?"

"Parker's meeting with Dr. Wagner today. That should give him Huang and EVAgen, and EVAgen should give him the kid. Don't worry, the wheels are in motion."

"Slow motion."

"Patience, cowboy. And there's one other

thing. When Griegas took the housekeeper on a walk-through at Dinsmoor's house, she said there was a key ring missing from a hook in the closet. She said there was a little red-and-white float thingy attached to the ring."

"The boat."

"That's how they opened her up."

"Maybe the slip number was on the key ring."

"And maybe the gate code too. Problem is, the keys haven't turned up."

"Find the keys, find the killer."

"Thanks for the tip, Sherlock."

"I'll send you a bill."

Mayday calculated that if she worked through the lunch hour, she could get the sanctions order drafted and messengered to Spencer's courtroom by four. I dropped her off at the curb to give her a running start.

As I was signaling my turn into the parking structure, I had a sudden change of heart, and I accelerated back onto Union. And I suppose if I hadn't done so, I might never have noticed the tail.

It was a Lincoln Town Car, polished and black, with just enough tinting to hide the driver's face. Whoever it was, he must have been waiting on Union to follow me into the structure.

My route took us past the Pasadena police headquarters on Garfield, but being more curious than concerned, I drove on past, watching my shadow in the mirror. He tried to hang back and keep a car or two between us, but he hadn't much experience with this sort of thing. So to make it as easy as possible, I kept to the slow lane of the freeway, and when I approached the Oak Grove exit in Flintridge, I made it a point to signal well in advance.

The road leading to Fieldstone, normally a quiet cul-de-sac, was today lined with cars on both sides of the street. The guard shack was still shuttered, and a string of volunteers in green jackets waved me through, all the way to the big grass field they'd reserved for parking.

Instead of parking, however, I inched through a gap in the far hedge and continued on to the back parking lot, which today was crowded with trailers. A woman there tried to turn me around, but when I told her I was a guest of Miss Flynn, she directed me to an open spot in front of the bungalow.

I hopped onto a log and peered over the hedge into the parking field. The Town Car sat idling in the midday sun. I couldn't tell if he was looking for me, or waiting for a place to park, or planning his next move. Whichever it was, I executed a flanking maneuver around the hedgerow, then duck-walked behind the Lincoln to the front passenger door. I yanked it open and fell into the soft leather seat.

"Boo!"

Lim the butler nearly hit his head on the sunroof. He held a hand to his chest as if suppressing a heart attack.

"You frightened me, Mr. MacTaggart!"

"Sorry. Shall I hop out again and knock?"

I started to leave, but he locked a bony hand on my forearm.

"Wait! Please. Mrs. Everett sent me to find you. It's a matter of utmost urgency."

"Tell Mrs. Everett she can make an appointment like everyone else. Tell her I see horse killers on Tuesdays and Thursdays."

His grip tightened.

"Please, Mr. MacTaggart! You don't understand. It's a matter of life and death."

I turned in the seat to face him. "Not to burst your bubble, but the planets do not revolve around Sydney Everett." I pulled free from his grasp. "And as for life and death, tell her I said she's not qualified to judge the importance of either."

I rose to leave, but was stopped this time not by Lim, but by the press of cold steel against the back of my head, followed by the loud and unmistakable sound of a cocking revolver.

And it was Barbara Hauser's voice I heard next, from the seat directly behind me.

"When he said it was a matter of life and death, Mr. MacTaggart, I'm afraid he was talking about yours."

Lim, to his credit, looked no happier with the situation than I was. We were traveling westbound on Foothill, Flintridge's main commercial drag, heading toward Flint Canyon Road.

"I could be wrong, but I think there may be a law against this."

I'd addressed myself to the backseat, but got no response.

I twisted in the seat. Barbara Hauser wore an FRC ball cap pulled low over wraparound shades. She held the gun loosely in her lap with the hammer cocked, her finger alongside the trigger guard, in a way that suggested she might actually know how to use it.

"You ever shoot one of those things? They make an awful racket."

"I know," she said, gesturing with the muzzle. "Especially in tight places. Turn around, please."

I did as instructed, and watched the roadway ahead. Although he barely drove the speed limit, Lim held the wheel in a white-knuckle grip.

"It's odd to find you carrying water for Sydney," I said to the backseat, just to keep the conversation going. "I figured you two for cats and dogs right about now."

"This may come as a shock, Mr. MacTaggart, but you don't know everything. As a matter of fact, you don't seem to know a whole lot of anything." To this she added, "Not that Sydney and I haven't had our moments. But for now, let's just say that we share a common interest."

As we moved through the business district, a stretch of traffic lights promised to halt our progress every few blocks. From the backseat, Barbara read my mind.

"Don't even think what you're thinking," she said. "I'd hate to put holes in Sydney's car, but I will if I have to."

We soon turned south, into the labyrinth of shaded lanes that melded and funneled into Flint Canyon. As we approached the gates of Versailles, Lim touched a button on the overhead visor.

We bypassed the fountain and continued around to the back of the mansion, stopping at last at the base of a sloping lawn. As

Lim cut the engine, I heard Barbara lower the hammer and drop open the cylinder, and I turned to watch her emptying the bullets into a fanny pack open at her waist. She flipped the cylinder closed and presented the gun to me grip first.

"Here. You can hold this for now, as a show of good faith. I'll want it back later."

We exited the car together, and I followed Lim up the grassy slope. I slipped the gun, a nickel-plated .38 Special, into my belt.

Sydney Everett lay sprawled on a padded chaise, holding what looked like a tall gin and tonic. At her feet was a swimming pool, or what used to be a swimming pool, the water now brown and murky, the surface mottled with leaves and other flotsam.

"Hello, darling. So glad you could get away," she said before tasting her drink. "Do pull up a chair."

She wore big Jackie O sunglasses and a white silk robe through which the reinforced superstructure of a swimsuit was visible. Her feet were bare, and her scarlet toenails matched the talons holding the glass. Lim dragged chairs from the adjoining table, where a full bar was open for business, and he set them on either side of the chaise.

I took the seat nearest the bar, from which I looked across the parabolic landscape at

Lim, who'd perched attentively on Sydney's left. Barbara stood, her back to all of us, facing the pool.

"I do hope you'll pardon the rather unorthodox summons," Sydney began, gesturing with her glass. "But you've been very difficult to get a hold of."

I folded my arms.

"Lim dearest, perhaps Mr. MacTaggart would like a cocktail. He looks a little vexed, don't you think?"

Sydney seemed to be relishing the whole Sunset Boulevard routine that she'd choreographed, and all that was missing was the pet monkey. Then again, maybe I was the monkey.

"Oh my, he is vexed. But I do have to say, Jack, I'm the one who should be cross. Your public accusation not only mortified me, it also hurt me deeply." She took a long drink, the ice cubes clicking against her teeth. "It pains me to think you could have such a low opinion of me."

"What's on your mind, Sydney?"

She studied her glass for a long time.

"Four years ago," she began, "I did a very foolish thing. A terrible, terrible thing. You apparently know all about that. There's no excusing it, of course, but I will tell you that it was an extremely difficult time in my life.

Harold had died, and his sons had sued, threatening to take everything. It was humiliating, and it was frightening. I was . . . not myself."

Though her words were carefully chosen, her delivery was thick and deliberate, and I suspected the drink wasn't her first.

"Anyway, the house was tied up by the litigation, as were all of the bank and brokerage accounts. The only assets in my name were the clothes on my back and Creole."

At the mention of the horse, she bit her lip. Lim moved onto the edge of the chaise to comfort her.

"I'm all right, thank you, dear." She dabbed under the shades with a cocktail napkin and composed herself.

"As I said before, I make no excuses. Harold had a business associate in Nevada who was the sort of man who handled that sort of thing. I contacted him, and arrangements were made. I used the insurance proceeds to fund the litigation. Most of it went to your firm, in point of fact. And then" — she sighed heavily — "after the litigation was resolved, I received a call from Jared."

Barbara interrupted, turning away from the pool.

"Some goombah approached me at the World Cup in Vegas. Said he had proof that Sydney had paid to have Creole killed. For a mere five grand, he offered to sell me a tape recording. It was the best investment I ever made."

If Sydney was perturbed by Barbara's contribution to the narrative, she didn't show it. She just nodded her head and resumed.

"Barbara knew that Jared had handled the insurance claim, so she approached him with her . . . proposition. After a brief negotiation, we reached an accommodation. I agreed to help defray her competition expenses, and we agreed to purchase and campaign a new horse together. And not just any horse, but the best horse money could buy."

"And for a small fee," I said, "Jared offered to launder the blackmail payments through an account at our firm."

Barbara bristled. "Blackmail is a crime, Jack. Like she said, we had an arrangement, all legal and in writing. It included full sponsorship, shared prize money, and a fifty-fifty split in Hush Puppy's appreciation. We were partners, just like you and Jared are partners."

"Yeah, whatever. I get the picture. So what

brings us all to this happy place?"

Sydney spoke again.

"You said you had proof that I'd had Hush Puppy killed. I want you to know that it isn't true. I had nothing whatsoever to do with Hush Puppy's death. I couldn't. You must believe that. And you must realize by now that I have no reason to lie. Not anymore, certainly. And that's what brings us together."

"We want to hire you," Barbara concluded. "To find out who did."

I had a flashback to the scene in Russ's office where he'd tossed the same challenge into my lap two weeks ago. If Sydney was telling the truth — and I had the discomforting feeling that she was — then I was back at square one. Give or take my germ of a theory.

I addressed Barbara first.

"You're buying all of this?"

"You can't bullshit a bullshitter," she said, moving the sunglasses onto her ball cap. "I saw what Creole's death did to her. There's no way she could go through that again."

"What, she might fall off the wagon?"

"Look," she said, stepping closer, "when Hush Puppy died, I thought exactly what you thought, okay? So I confronted Sydney, and we had it out." She lowered the shades.

"She didn't do it. For one thing, and trust me on this, she's not that good of an actress."

I stood and walked to the water's edge. At the bottom, buried amid the muck and drifted leaves, was a folded beach umbrella.

"Why me? Why not hire your pal Jared and keep it all in the family?"

"For one thing," Barbara said, "Sydney doesn't trust him."

"Oh, yeah? Why not?"

Sydney gave a little shrug. "Call it a woman's intuition."

I returned to lounge side, propping a foot on my chair.

"You both seem to be operating on the assumption that Hush Puppy's death was no accident. And yet the board fired Tara on the grounds that it was."

The women shared a glance before Barbara spoke.

"Collateral damage, Jack. We couldn't have a hundred amateur detectives investigating a horse murder. No telling where that might have led. Don't take it personally."

"Oh, but I do take it personally. And I take being lied to personally. I even take being kidnapped personally."

Barbara looked to Sydney again. "I suppose we could reinstate Tara."

Sydney nodded. "If Jack will help us."

"Jack's not for sale, and insurance fraud is a crime. And so's extortion, Blondie, whatever you want to call it. And by the way, you two Dillingers left a paper trial that's about a mile long."

Barbara pointed a finger. "You're missing the point, Jack. I'll take my chances, in a courtroom if I have to. But whoever killed that horse fucked us both. So if you're too squeaky-clean to help us, then fine. We'll find somebody who will, and Tara can pound sand."

"Besides, dear," added Sydney, giving the cubes a shake. "Whoever did this to us played you for a fool as well, don't you think? You and that odious Mr. Bowman. Doesn't that stick in your craw just a tiny bit?"

What stuck in my craw was the idea of Tara being mixed up with the likes of Jared Henley and Brian Huang.

"All right. You hired me to handle your insurance claim, right? So that's what I'll do. Just don't think you're getting a free pass on Creole. It doesn't work that way."

Barbara turned again to the pool. Sydney sighed.

"All right, Jack. I guess I've always known I'd have to answer for Creole. If that's the case, then so be it. But I won't stand by and allow Hush Puppy's killer to go free because of my cowardice. That I couldn't face."

There was a quaver at the end, and Lim took hold of her hand. She set down her drink.

"Tell me, Jack. About Russell."

"He died over the weekend. On his boat. Right now, that's all there is to tell."

Sydney nodded. Then she turned away.

19

There were donuts and coffee in the barn office, and I helped myself to both while Barbara rummaged through a drawer in search of Jesse Vigil's phone number. We were soon joined by Margaret Carlton, who burst through the door like an ICE agent executing a no-knock warrant.

"That's it! I've had it!"

Barbara responded without looking up. "But you haven't had it lately, Margaret. That's part of your problem."

When the old hag noticed me in the corner, she froze.

"What are *you* doing here?"

I answered through a mouthful of Winchell's chocolate glazed. "I think she's looking for a phone number."

"Very funny," she said, tossing her purse onto the counter before leaving the way she'd come. "If you're looking for Tara," she said over her shoulder, "she's off until six."

Barbara jotted the number and tore off the page.

"Here. Tell Jesse I said hello. That's the number on top. The other one's my cell. Do me a favor and keep me posted."

"I tried posting once. It gave me a rash."

Barbara leaned on the counter. "If I were you, she's the first one I'd look at."

"Who?"

"Tara, that's who. I guess she thinks with Hush Puppy out of the way, she can ride that cart horse of hers to the Olympics. What a joke."

"I was at the Equestrian Center last week. Nobody was laughing."

"I was there too, but I wasn't riding. Come by on Sunday, and I'll show you how it's done."

As I crushed my cup into the trash, Barbara rose and held out a hand.

"Just curious," I said, handing her the gun. "What would you have done if I'd jumped ship on Foothill?"

She twirled it like a six-shooter.

"In that case," she said, blowing on the muzzle, "I'd have made you walk all the way home."

The lights were on in the bungalow, and I saw Tara's silhouette pass by the window. I retrieved my cell phone from the Toyota and checked for messages.

There were two missed calls, one of which was from Tara. I returned the other, and was patched through to Bernie.

"Mr. MacTaggart's office."

"Hey, it's me."

"Where have you been? Marta said you were right behind her, and people have been asking for you all day!"

"I was detained. What people?"

"Wait a minute," she said, and I could hear papers shuffling. "Okay. First a Patrick Bowman called. That was at one fifteen. Then somebody named Terina Webb called at two forty and said she was on deadline. I told her to join the club. Oh, and Veronica wanted me to remind you that Mr. Dinsmoor's funeral is at ten o'clock on Monday. She said there are no bagpipes on the program, whatever that means."

I smiled. "Toss Terina Webb and leave Bowman on my desk. And tell Veronica I'll be there as planned. Anything else?"

"Are you coming back today?"

"Yeah, but probably later. Go have a good weekend."

"I always do. Oh, and there's a surprise waiting in your office."

"What is it?"

"If I told you that, it wouldn't be a surprise. But I'll give you a hint. Jared's not the biggest prick in the office anymore."

I left the phone in the car, and I crunched up the gravel driveway. Stanley and Livingstone were lazing on the hood of my Wrangler, four yellow eyes following my approach with wary circumspection, questioning my trust and troth, my faith and fidelity.

"Mind your own business."

I took a deep breath. I knocked, and waited, and then Tara appeared in the doorway like a sunburst.

"Hello, stranger. My God, do I get a real hug?"

She did, and a kiss for good measure. She took my hand and led me into the living room where we kissed again, this time longer and deeper.

"I'm off until six," she said. It was more of a question than a statement.

"What time is it now?"

She hugged me tighter, her head on my shoulder, her body pressed against mine.

"I'm not sure," she said. "But I think the big hand is on the twelve."

The sun beyond the blinds had faded, and the room was dim and quiet.

"I have to go," she whispered, her breath

warm against my chest.

"Call in sick. Tell 'em you're exhausted."

She propped her head on a hand.

"I can't. There's too much to do. They need me."

"They fired you."

"I meant the horses. They need me."

"I need you."

"No, you want me. There's a difference."

I rolled to face her.

"First hear the plan. We'll set Margaret's car on fire, then we'll slip out the back gate. We won't stop until we reach the border."

"You're a very disturbed individual."

"No, I'm disturbing. There's a difference."

She rolled off the bed, taking the sheets with her.

"Do you want to shower here?"

"Can I just watch?"

"I'm not showering. I like the way I smell."

I pressed my naked self into a sitting position.

"How late do you have to work?"

"Only until nine, then I'm off for the weekend. Come to think of it, I guess I'm off forever."

She untangled herself from the sheets and shimmied into her jeans.

"Aren't we forgetting something?"

She made a face and turned to the dresser,

from which she extracted a clean T-shirt and held it up for inspection.

"I'm guessing Agnes from Enterprise is starting to get nervous. How about we return the Toyota tonight, then have Chinese somewhere in Alhambra?"

Still shirtless, she clambered onto the bed and straddled me, her little gold cross tickling my lips.

"You know what they say about Chinese. An hour later and you're hungry again."

We entered the clubhouse through the kitchen, passing through a little snack area that fed into a corridor. In the corner of the big fireplace room, a leather sofa and club chairs were grouped around a wide-screen television. Tara found the remote and sat.

"What channel?" she whispered.

"Nine."

She powered on the set and lowered the volume to two bars, enough to hear the broadcast if I sat with my ear to a speaker.

"Thanks," I whispered. "I'll see you later."

She kissed my head and slipped out the double doors to the patio. The doors sighed into place and locked behind her with a click.

I caught the tail-end of a brush fire somewhere on the coast, followed by ten minutes of ads and network promos. Then, after a brief return to the Action News studio, they cut to a live feed of Terina Webb standing outside a stone building I recognized as All Saints Episcopal Church in Pasadena.

I moved closer, adding a bar to the volume.

". . . will be held on Monday for Pasadena attorney Russell Dinsmoor, whose body was discovered this week aboard his sailboat in Marina del Rey. Today, the County Coroner's office released a statement."

They cut to a prerecorded segment filmed in broad daylight outside the coroner's office. Melissa the lab tech wore a white smock over her turtleneck, and she pushed her serious glasses onto the bridge of her nose. As she read into the bouquet of microphones, the whirr of camera shutters punctuated her remarks.

"The office of the Los Angeles County Coroner has determined that the cause of Mr. Dinsmoor's death was acute myocardial infarction, or a heart attack. Because, however, the crime scene investigation puts the official time of death at approximately seventeen hundred hours on Saturday, and because Mr. Dinsmoor's remains were exposed to the ambient marine environment for not more than six to eight hours, further tests are being conducted

to determine what other factors, if any, might have contributed to the cause of death. At this . . ."

Melissa continued reading, but her words were lost in a jump-cut back to the flood-lit façade of All Saints.

"Sources within the LAPD confirm that Dinsmoor actually died elsewhere, and that his body was likely moved to Marina del Rey approximately twenty-four hours after death. This was corroborated by Deputy County Coroner Melissa Takaguchi, and is the reason for the additional testing she just mentioned."

The screen changed again, this time to a fuzzy head shot of yours truly, which I recognized as a blowup of my old credential from the public defender's office. The shock of coming face-to-face with my younger self rocked me backward.

"In a Channel Nine exclusive, police sources have also confirmed that Jack MacTaggart, one of Russell Dinsmoor's law partners, is a beneficiary of Dinsmoor's estate, and now stands to inherit Dinsmoor's San Marino mansion. When we last reported on this story, MacTaggart was in the custody of the District Attorney's office and was being questioned about Dinsmoor's death. For Channel Nine Action News, this is Terina Webb reporting from Pasadena. Back to you."

I killed the power and slumped against the sofa.

The new biggest prick at Henley & Hargrove turned out to be a cactus. And not some little succulent in a glazed dish, but a five-foot saguaro in a cauldron-sized pot, blocking the nighttime view from my office window. Girdling the pot was a ribbon, and taped to the ribbon was a small white envelope.

The Hallmark card bore the words "Thank You" in a gold-leaf script. Inside, the handwritten message read, "Victor has driven his route for many years and has many friends in the community. Now his friends are your friends. Our family and our friends thank you for all you have done for us. *Shnorhakalutyun.* With our deepest appreciation, Lina."

"Gesundheit," I said aloud and set the card on a shelf.

On my desk were file-stamped copies of both of Judge Spencer's orders, along with a note from Mayday informing me that she'd personally delivered the restraining order to City of Hope.

Somehow, the elation I'd felt this morning seemed a long time ago.

I spent the next half hour with the day's

mail and messages, several of which were from Morris regarding the funeral logistics on Monday. The service was to begin at ten A.M. sharp, and all but a skeleton crew of staff were to assemble in the lobby at nine forty-five for the two-block procession to the church. Cancelation of prior commitments was encouraged. Statements to the press were strictly forbidden. Somber business attire was strongly recommended.

There was also a note from Veronica, requesting that I meet her at the All Saints rectory at nine forty. Stapled to the note was a clipping from the front page of today's *Daily Journal.* The article cited cardiac arrest as the cause of death, and while it gave the particulars of the memorial service, it made no mention of any homicide investigation.

I rang Bowman's office, but, as expected at this hour, caught only his voice mail. I didn't leave a message.

Next I dug out Barbara's note, and I dialed Jesse Vigil's number. When the ringing stopped, I heard a baby crying over the din of a television.

"Yo."

"Hello, is this Jesse Vigil?"

"Who wants to know?"

The man's voice was gruff, and maybe suspicious.

"This is Jack MacTaggart, from the Field-stone Riding Club."

There was a long silence, filled with rapid-fire Spanish from both male and female voices on the television. The audience roared at the exchange, and the sound of the crying baby grew louder.

"Hello, this is Jesse."

The woman's voice was young, and a little hoarse, like maybe she'd been shouting.

"Ms. Vigil, my name is Jack MacTaggart. I got your number from Barbara Hauser."

"Okay, sure. You got a job for me?"

"No, I'm afraid I don't. But I have a question about a job you did earlier this week, out at Fieldstone."

There was a pause while she shushed the baby.

"Sorry, mister, but I ain't been over there for a couple months."

It was, as Yogi said, déjà vu all over again.

"I've got some paperwork here that says you picked up a horse at the Chino Hills Veterinary Clinic on Monday and delivered it to Fieldstone. Is that not correct?"

"Wait a minute."

The baby's wailing receded, and I heard first the television, then an angry exchange between Jesse and her husband. When she came back on the line, it was without the baby.

"Monday was the twenty-eighth, right? Delivery on that job," she read from a written record, "was Jet Plane Laboratory."

"You mean the Jet Propulsion Laboratory? In Flintridge?"

"I guess. The place with all the guards and shit. Is there a problem or something?"

"No, not a problem. A white horse, right?"

"They're all green to me, mister."

"Do you remember who hired you for the job?"

"Some guy on the phone, I think."

The husband said something in the background that I didn't catch. "Oh, shut up!" was her response.

"Jesse, do you remember talking to anybody while you were there at JPL?"

"Just the guys on the loading dock is all. I wasn't there for but fifteen minutes. What's this about, anyway?"

"It's nothing. Thank you for your time. I'm sorry to have bothered you so late."

I started to dial Gabe, then set the phone back in its cradle.

I saw that I was traipsing into a jurisdictional turf war between the state and the feds that might take weeks, maybe months to untangle. Gabe would have as much

chance convincing a state court judge to issue a search warrant for a top-secret federal
facility as I had catching a ride on the space
shuttle. And by the time they'd sorted it all
out, any evidence we'd hoped to find would
have disappeared into a black hole.

And more important, there was Tara. Calling the cops or the DA meant handing over
the paperwork from Chino Hills, and I
wasn't prepared to do that. Not now anyway, just thirty-six hours before the biggest
ride of her life.

And maybe not ever.

It was nine twenty when I descended the
ramp to ground level. My Wrangler was
already waiting, idling in the empty darkness. I pulled alongside and lowered the
passenger window on the Toyota.

"We need to talk!" I shouted over the
rumble of both engines.

"I'm starving!" Tara replied. "We can talk
over dinner!"

"Last one to Enterprise buys!"

I rabbit-started, the rental car's tires
squealing on the smooth concrete, and
before she could react I was out onto westbound Union. The sidewalks were crowded
with strollers and shoppers, mostly couples
arm in arm, all of them backlit by the neon

glow of the restaurants and boutiques of Old Pasadena. I watched in the mirror as Tara closed from behind, flashing her brights in playful protest.

The city of Alhambra was maybe a twenty-minute drive if we stuck to the main boulevards. But rather than suffer the Friday night traffic, I blazed a circuitous trail, first doubling back onto eastbound Colorado, then south on residential back streets that wound through Pasadena and San Marino. Tara lagged behind, sometimes screened by other traffic, and since I wasn't sure if she remembered the way, I slowed to keep her headlights in view.

I must have been distracted, replaying the call to Jesse Vigil in my mind, because Tara was suddenly alongside me on Los Robles, a dark and twisting downhill stretch, and she surged past before I could respond. And then, just as I began to accelerate, a second car roared past, both of them blowing through the yellow light at Mission. I followed suit, running the red and catching horns from both sides of the intersection.

They were a hundred yards ahead when the second car, a dark sedan, swung wide to pass. As it pulled alongside the Jeep I saw the flashes, three in rapid succession, before I heard the muffled pops. Then, as both the sedan and the roadway curved, the Wrangler continued straight, like a freight train jumping its tracks. It bucked over the curb, throwing up a shower of sparks, and was swallowed by the shrubbery beyond.

The Toyota yawed as I locked the brakes, and it must have blown a tire as we bounced over the high curb, almost clipping a utility pole. I was out and running, through a broken fence and over a flattened hedge. When I saw the Jeep again, it was making furrows in a soft and manicured lawn, still inching forward like a juggernaut.

I reached the driver's side in time to open the door and unlatch the belt before the Jeep butted the house with a hollow *thunk,* a headlight popping for punctuation. Tara was limp in my arms as I carried her clear and laid her on the grass. I lifted a sodden hank of hair from the dark stream flowing down her face — a warm, wet ribbon that began somewhere above the line of her scalp. Behind me, footsteps approached at a run from the front of the house.

"Call an ambulance! Now!"

In the reflected glow of the single headlight, Tara's face was oddly serene, her eyes closed, her breathing slow and shallow. In her lap, tiny cubes of safety glass glittered like fairy dust. I tore off my shirt, and like some Satanic faith healer laying on hands, I pressed it against her forehead. Within seconds, the shirt was wet and sticky.

"Come on, baby. You can do it. Hang tough," I urged as much to myself as to her. After a minute, I felt a close presence behind me, then a gasp.

"Oh, my God," the woman whispered.

The lawn and the air above it were damp and cool, and soon I was shivering, all the while babbling sweet nonsense to Tara. The woman left, returning with a blanket that she draped across my shoulders.

"Thank you," I said without turning.

Somewhere in the near distance, from the dark corner of the yard where the Jeep had left the roadway, I heard a man's voice.

"Shit!" he called. "Helen, would you look at this!"

After what seemed like an eternity, I heard the sirens. They were distant at first but closing quickly, like cavalry topping the hill, their dissonant whines piercing the darkness, the strobes of red and blue soon coloring the lawn and the Jeep and the stuccoed walls of the house.

And then, as though responding to their clarion call, Tara's eyes blinked open. She winced as she tried to rise, her hand reaching for my wrist.

"Don't," I said quietly. "Help is here. You're going to be all right."

20

"A bullet?" asked the sergeant, this for the second time.

We faced each other in the bright fluorescence of the nurse's station. He was around fifty, short and compact, the jet of his mustache marred by a single streak of gray. He was making notes while his partner, a kid maybe half his age, eyed my bloody hands.

"I told you. I saw three shots fired from the other car. It was a dark four-door, like maybe a Taurus. Something American and nondescript."

He wrote in his pad. "I don't suppose you got the plate?"

I gathered the blanket around my shoulders.

"No, I didn't. I thought he was just trying to pass."

A nurse interrupted to hand me a folded shirt. It was the top half of a blue surgical scrub.

"Here you are," she said. "It might be a little tight."

She watched as I worked it, wincing, over my head and shoulders, then she nodded her approval.

"Thank you."

"Okay, we'll get a crime-scene unit on the Jeep right away," said the older cop, nodding to his partner. The younger man stepped away and spoke into a shoulder-mounted radio.

"I think I was the target."

"What?"

"She was driving my car. It was dark. We left from my office. We were probably followed from there. I think whoever shot at the Jeep thought he was shooting at me."

His tone was skeptical. "Any idea who'd want to take a shot at either one of you?"

"Yeah, maybe. Look, there's an LAPD homicide dick named Parker, Tom Parker, who needs to know about this right away. He works RHD downtown."

He stopped writing and looked at me, as though for the first time.

"Detective Tom Parker, LAPD robbery-homicide?"

"That's right. You might want to call him right now. He'll want to view the crime scene. He's a stickler about his crime scenes."

The older cop, whose tag read Carter, stepped over to confer with his partner. I walked to the counter and waited for the lone duty nurse, who'd been on the phone continuously since our arrival, to show signs of mandibular fatigue.

"Still no word yet," she said cheerfully, covering the mouthpiece with her hand.

"Look, all I need to know is whether she's gonna make it, okay? Just a thumbs-up. Can't somebody get that for me, please?"

She gave me a patronizing smile and turned her shoulder, the better to resume her conversation in private.

I looked around. Since no one appeared in immediate need of my counsel, I reached over and plucked Florence Nightingab's stethoscope from the counter, then backed casually down the hallway. After a dozen steps I turned on my heel, draping the instrument over my neck as I walked.

There were doors on both sides of the hallway that opened into the recovery rooms, this being the postoperative unit. But only a few of the rooms were occupied, and none of them by Tara. After a short distance, the corridor took a right-hand turn and I came to a set of double doors labeled AUTHORIZED PERSONNEL ONLY.

Beyond these doors were more rooms, and also more activity. I had entered the purgatory between the operating rooms and the postoperative ward — the place where the patients were carefully monitored as they awoke from their anesthetics. Nurses in full surgical dress bustled from room to room, pushing carts or carrying charts, while lights and tones blinked and chimed over the doorways.

In the first room I entered, three women in pink surgical scrubs, including caps, masks, and booties, gathered like germphobic craps shooters around the high rails of a bed. But the guy in the pit looked more stick-up crew than J. Crew, with heavy bandages covering where he might have been gut-shot.

In the second room, I found Tara. She too was attended by nurses, one of whom was bent over and whispering in her ear. She was deathly pale, a blue bandage covering the porcelain whiteness of her forehead, and she seemed to be drifting in and out of consciousness.

"How's she doing?" I asked nobody in particular.

Two of the women glanced up, but the third, who appeared to be in charge, said, "Excuse me, what are you doing in here?"

"If this is Tara Flynn," I said innocently, "the police sent me to get a report on her condition."

The head nurse rounded the bed and took hold of my arm, lecturing as she marched me to the door.

"You can tell the police that this is a secure area and that nobody without authorization is allowed in here. They ought to know better than that. You can also tell them that she's recovering nicely. It was a grazing wound that required some stitches, and she's lost a lot of blood, but she's otherwise fine and should make a full recovery."

Out in the hallway, she gave me a critical inspection, starting with my grass-stained sneakers and working north to the spot where my credentials should have been.

"Why is there blood on your hands?" she demanded.

"Oh, that," I said. "I just got out of surgery myself."

"Are you a doctor?"

"No, ma'am," I told her. "With me, it's just a hobby."

First I found a men's room, then I found some vending machines off the ground-floor lobby. I had two Almond Joys and a cup of black coffee that should have come with a label warning that it not be consumed more than fifty feet from an emergency room.

I found Sergeant Carter in the elevator lounge off the post-op unit, where he stood with his cap thumbed back, reading from his notebook to none other than Nick Griegas.

"There you are," said Griegas, who, being the detective, was the first to notice my approach.

"That's right," I told him. "Just released from the custody of the district attorney's office."

He raised both hands in mock surrender.

"Hold on, *ese*. I don't know where she got that shit."

Which didn't speak well, I thought, of his powers of detection.

The dispatch call must have reached Griegas at home, because he wore tan cargo pants and a blue denim shirt, the latter untucked to hide the pancake holster at the small of his back. He had his gold shield on a chain around his neck, which was more for Carter's benefit than for any safety reason I could think of.

"Looks like you two have some catching up to do," said Carter, tucking his notebook into a breast pocket. "I'm heading back to the scene. Any word on the girl?"

"She's gonna make it. The bullet grazed her forehead."

He nodded, then turned toward the elevators. Griegas watched his back until he was out of earshot.

"Why was she driving your car?"

"She's my girlfriend. I was returning a rental to the Enterprise office in Alhambra. How is the rental, by the way?"

"Beats me." He gestured behind me. "Let's sit over here and talk for a minute."

I followed him to the seating area and took the chair opposite. There were ragged copies of *Good House keeping* and *Family Circle* on a coffee table marred by graffiti tags. Griegas dug his own notebook from a pocket.

"Tara Flynn, like it sounds?"

I nodded. "She's the barn manager at the Fieldstone Riding Club. She lives on the grounds."

He glanced at my shoulder as he wrote.

"Dark sedan, four doors, possible Ford Taurus, no make on the license, right?"

I nodded again.

"Shooter?"

"I don't know. Could have been the driver, but I doubt it. Seemed like the muzzle flashes were too far to starboard. I think there was a passenger, but I'm speculating now."

Griegas wrote it all down, then looked up from his pad.

"Not a lot to go on."

"A crack shamus like you shouldn't need much."

He let it pass, probably figuring he owed me one.

"Okay, Jack. So who do you think is trying to kill you?"

"Does Parker have an alibi?"

He didn't smile.

"I don't know, Detective. But you can bet whoever it was also killed Russ Dinsmoor. Did Gabe tell you about Dinsmoor's visit to Caltech?"

He nodded. "We talked to Dr. Wagner this morning. We're checking out this" — he flipped some pages in his notebook — "this EVAgen company, but I'm not holding my breath. As for Brian Huang, he's a medical doctor in good standing with no priors, and he has security clearances up the wazoo."

"And his wazoo lives next door to Dinsmoor."

"Next door to you, you mean."

Okay, now we were even.

"Come on, Jack, don't get huffy. Somebody tried to kill you tonight, man. And when they find out they missed, they might try again. You thought about that?"

"I'll sleep easily, knowing you and Parker are on the case."

He started to respond, but was interrupted by his cell phone, which he pulled from a pants pocket as he stood. His ringtone was the theme from *Dragnet, dum de dum-dum.*

"If that's Parker," I said, "tell him I want my Jeep back. Tonight."

Griegas drifted toward the elevators, so I strolled back to the nurse's station. There were three women there, all new faces, and none with a telephone-shaped growth on her ear.

"Excuse me. How's Tara Flynn doing?"

"Are you a member of the family?" one of them asked.

"Yes, I'm her brother Jack."

She checked a chart on the counter, flipping the pages as she spoke.

"She's doing quite well. In fact, if you're available to drive her, she can probably be discharged this morning. You don't happen to have her insurance information, do you? We'll need that to finish up the discharge papers."

"You mean if she has no insurance, you plan to hold her indefinitely?"

"No, sir. I just meant —"

But before she could finish, Griegas strode

in from the hallway and hooked a thumb over his shoulder.

"Let's roll. Parker wants a word."

Which was fine with me, because I'd been waiting all night to have a little word with him.

It was after midnight when we reached the scene on Los Robles, where a couple of black-and-white units were still angled into the street with their lights flashing, poised to direct any hypothetical traffic. Uniforms were walking the pavement, heads down, following the beams of their flash-lights. Nearer the house, bright halogen spots on portable stands had been erected to il-luminate both the Toyota and the lawn beyond, and the entire corner was strung tree to tree with yellow crime-scene tape.

Griegas parked up the street, then badged us through the perimeter and signed us in on the log. They may not get much practice, but it looked like San Marino's finest knew how to run a crime scene.

A tire was indeed blown on the Toyota, and the angle of the wheel suggested a broken axle. There were two wheels on the curb and two still in the street, framing a trickle of dark liquid that puddled in the gutter.

Agnes from Enterprise would not be amused.

We stepped through the broken hedges, where a path had been beaten in the grass. Up at the house, the Wrangler now sat at the center of a klieg-lit supernova.

The crime-scene guys were packing their gear. At the top of the lawn, LAPD Detective Parker and San Marino PD Sergeant Carter were standing side by side with their arms folded, watching us as we approached. The big man wore slacks and a blazer.

"Tell me something, MacTaggart. How come whenever there's a shit-pile in this town, I find your footprints in it?"

"Maybe you have a nose for shit, but you're always two steps behind."

Carter pretended to brush something from his mustache. I asked him, "Did your people get anything off the Jeep?"

He glanced at Parker before answering.

"One bullet exited through the B-pillar. The others must have passed through the windows. The exit hole suggests a large caliber weapon, maybe a .44."

"Shell casings?"

He shook his head. "No brass and no slugs. But we're still looking."

I walked around to inspect the Wrangler, stepping carefully over the sparkling patch of broken glass and blood. It was an awfully big stain, I thought, for such a small woman.

The driver's side window was blown out of the frame, and there was a nipple hole the size of a silver dollar at the upper front edge of the hardtop, just behind the void that was once the passenger window. There was glass in the driver's front bucket, and papers littering the other.

"What about tread marks?" I called to Carter across the hood.

"None. There were transfers on the curb from both vehicles, but the only skid was from the Toyota."

Parker's eyes, colder than a stepmother's tit, watched me as I circled the vehicle. Carter excused himself and walked toward the Toyota, leaving me alone with the two detectives.

"You got a theory, MacTaggart?"

"I do. I think maybe you were dropped on your head as a child."

Parker's hands closed into fists. "Here's my theory, hotshot. I'm thinking maybe you staged this whole thing. To make it look like somebody's out to get you."

"Somebody is out to get me. And if he doesn't back off, I'm gonna drop him like a bad habit."

Griegas stepped between us just as Parker

erupted.

"You're dirty, MacTaggart! You may fool Montoya, but you don't fool me! I want some answers from you, goddammit, and I mean now!"

"You don't want answers," I told him evenly. "You just want me. Only I'm not the answer."

Tara was sitting up, a hint of color in her face, and the wide blue bandage made her look like the model for a Vermeer painting. *Girl with the Wounded Forehead.*

"Tara, these are Detectives Griegas and Parker. They want to ask you some questions."

Parker pulled up a chair. "You can wait outside, MacTaggart. This won't take long."

"Maybe she'd like to have her attorney present during questioning."

Parker hadn't expected that, and he looked to Tara, who nodded.

"All right, Miss Flynn, we'd like to ask you about your little accident. Any details are important, so please just take your time and tell us everything you can remember."

"Well," she began after a pause, "I remember driving downhill, and passing Jack's car. And then I remember the headlights of another car behind me, a different car, tailgating me. And that's pretty much it."

"You're sure it was a different car and not Jack's?"

"Yes, I'm sure of that."

Parker frowned.

"Do you remember the other car trying to pass you?"

She thought for a moment.

"No, I'm sorry. After that, everything's a blank. The next thing I remember is waking up on the lawn."

"What about sounds? Do you remember hearing any loud or sharp noises?"

"No, I don't."

Parker leaned back in his chair.

"Look, Miss Flynn. Can you think of any reason why someone would want to shoot at you?"

She shook her head, and winced. "No, I'm sorry."

With a glance, Parker passed the baton to Greigas, who spoke in a quieter voice. He must have played the good cop to Parker's bad so often that the role had become automatic.

"Miss Flynn, we're investigating the death of Russell Dinsmoor, who used to work with Jack. Had you ever met Mr. Dinsmoor before?"

She glanced at me.

"No, I never did."

"We're looking into the possibility that your accident is somehow connected to Mr. Dinsmoor's death. Can you think of any connection, any at all, between you and Mr. Dinsmoor?"

"Well, there's Jack obviously. And Jared Henley. He rides at Fieldstone, where I work. Or worked, I guess. Does that count as a connection?"

Griegas and Parker shared a look, then Parker resumed the questioning.

"What's your relationship with this Jared Henley?"

"No relationship. I was the barn manager at Fieldstone, and he's a member there. I've groomed his horse occasionally. Enzo is the horse's name. And we've spoken before, of course, but just chitchat. I really don't know him very well."

This last she said with her eyes closed, and I could see that she was fading.

"Can't we finish this some other time? She needs to rest."

Parker raised a finger. "What about a man named Huang, Brian Yee-Horn Huang? Ever heard of him?"

She opened her eyes again.

"Yes. He's also a member. He rides the school horses, so I don't really know him.

He's some kind of scientist."

"What are school horses?"

"They're horses owned by the club, that the members can rent. They're an amenity, for the newer riders."

"Try to use smaller words, honey, so Detective Parker can follow along."

Parker flushed.

"You said you *were* the barn manager at Fieldstone. When did you leave?"

"Actually, today was my last day working. I still live there, but I'll be moving next week."

"And if we need to get ahold of you after next week," asked Griegas, "how would we do that?"

"You can phone the MacTaggart residence," I told him, standing. "She'll be moving in with her attorney. We pride ourselves on being a full-service law firm."

Pink sunrise lit the distant mountains as I pulled into the circular driveway, alighted, and opened the passenger door. The orderly, an elderly volunteer, bent to lock the wheelchair in place and raise the folding foot rests. I gathered up the papers that littered the passenger seat, and then together we helped Tara out of the chair and into the Wrangler.

435

"Mind your head, miss," said the old man, gently shielding the crown of her skull. "We try to discourage repeat business."

The closing door clattered like a can of loose screws, and I saw the geezer eyeballing the bullet hole.

As I walked around to the driver's side, I sorted through the papers. There was the rental contract I'd salvaged from the Toyota, plus a receipt from the tow truck, plus the yellowed sports page from last Saturday's *Times*. And then there was the glossy program from the L.A. Equestrian Center Fall Classic.

The program stopped me. There on the cover was Tara's autograph, hastily scrawled in black Sharpie across the photo of a jumping horse. I studied the signature for a long moment, angling it toward the sunrise, and then I bounded into the driver's seat.

"Everything all right?" asked the old codger, leaning into the window frame.

"Never better!" I replied, firing up the Wrangler with a throaty roar.

I eased us into the empty street heading westbound toward the freeway, scanning the curb behind us for any vehicles that might be following. Tara's eyes were closed against the wind, and her hair lashed at the sides of her bandage.

"You're chipper all of a sudden," she observed.

I must have been whistling. Or maybe it was the bullet hole.

"I've had a revelation."

"Hallelujah."

"A whispered word, from God's lips to my ear."

"Don't keep me in suspense."

I leaned across the console.

"It's good to be alive."

She brushed a strand of hair from her mouth.

"It sure beats the alternative."

"What do you say we find a park and run barefoot in the grass?"

She reached over and placed her hand on mine.

"That would be nice, sweetie, but I'm a little tired just now."

As we waited out the light at Green Street, it occurred to me that Tara was shouldering a world of hurt, and not just the physical kind. Not only had she caught both a pink slip and a stray bullet, she'd also lost her last, best chance to flip a parting bird to the Fieldstone Drama Club, its board of directors, and Sydney Everett. And that, I suspected, despite everything else she'd been through, is what was paining her most.

"Hey. I'm sorry about all this. I know how important this weekend was to you."

She turned to face me.

"That's okay, because I've had a revelation of my own." She leaned closer. "There's important," she said, pausing for effect. "And then there's *important*."

I lifted her hand to my lips. "Where to now, m'lady?"

"Home, James," she said, closing her eyes. "Sam will be worried sick."

21

It was past noon when I blinked awake, Sam having failed to blow his traditional Saturday morning reveille. I felt beside me, finding only tousled sheets where the sleeping person of Tara Flynn should have been.

"Tara?"

I sat up and rubbed my eyes. Sunlight flooded from beneath the window shades, and kitchen sounds emanated from down the hallway.

"Tara!"

Footsteps. Then she appeared with a breakfast tray, Sam trailing happily behind her.

"I don't know what we were drinking last night," she said, pausing in the doorway, "but my head is killing me."

"Very funny. You're supposed to be in bed."

"If that's a pickup line, I've heard better."

She set the tray on the nightstand. There

was coffee and OJ, buttered toast and jam. She handed me a paper towel as she slipped back under the covers.

"I couldn't find any napkins."

Her bandage was clean and her color had almost returned. She kissed my cheek as she slid the tray onto my lap.

"Careful," I warned her, "a guy could get used to this."

She lifted a toast wedge. "That's the general idea, sweetie."

We ate shoulder to shoulder, and fed our leftovers to Sam. Then, as Tara moved the tray to the nightstand, I reached for my cell phone.

There was one missed call from this morning, from a number I didn't recognize. I hit Options, then Return Call, and listened to the distant ring.

"Hello?"

It was a woman, and her voice was vaguely familiar.

"Hello. This is Jack MacTaggart, returning a call to my cell phone?"

"Jack! How are you? It's Connie! Connie Montoya!"

I'd met Gabe's wife only once, at a legal seminar in Palm Springs, where the banquet dinner had led to drinks, and where the drinks had led to more drinks, and the next

440

thing we knew, the three of us were closing down the hotel bar.

Connie was a brunette, small and tempestuous, and a very funny drunk. A lawyer herself, she'd quit the practice following the birth of their twins. I remembered at the time thinking she was the kind of woman who'd either propel Gabe into the mayor's office or get him fired.

"Hey, Connie. Long time. How're the boys?"

"They're homicidal maniacs. They're out back, playing on the trampoline. That's what you need, Jack MacTaggart!"

"A trampoline?"

"No, children! When are you gonna settle down and make just one woman miserable?"

I smiled across the pillow. "Anything's possible."

"Gabe tells me you're up in Pasadena now? At a firm?"

"For now."

She lowered her voice. "Talk to Gabe, Jack. He's gotta get out of that office before it kills him, I swear to God."

"I will, I promise. Is he home?"

"Are you kidding? USC is playing Cal. If I hear that fight song one more time, I'll open a vein. Hold on."

She put her hand over the phone and called to her husband, who picked up on an extension.

"Mac? Hold on a second."

I heard some crowd noise and the oompah brass of a marching band before he lowered the volume.

"Sorry to interrupt," I said.

"No, no. I called you. I heard about last night. Are you okay?"

"Never better. My car's got air-conditioning, and my girlfriend's got a new haircut."

"She's gonna be okay, though, right?"

"If my cooking doesn't kill her."

"And no line on the perps?"

"Not unless you know something I don't."

Even with the volume lowered I could hear the crowd roar.

"Nick told me you got into it again with Parker."

"No big."

"He also told me about the news on Friday night, the six o'clock? That was fucked, man. I'm really sorry."

"Not your fault, buddy."

"Anyway . . . what's the Chinaman's name again?"

"You mean the Asian-Pacific American gentleman?"

"Yeah, him."

"That would be Dr. Huang."

"Yeah, Huang. Nick says they're checking him out."

"That's great. Do you think they'll question him before or after the Rose Parade?"

"C'mon, Mac. The journey of a thousand miles. Anyway, that's not why I called. I talked to Melissa Takaguchi this morning, about the lungs? And guess what?"

"Tell me."

"Marta was right. Insulin. A massive dose, in aerosol form. They think I'm a goddamn genius."

"You are a goddamn genius. You could make big money in private practice, you know."

There was silence on the line.

"Connie put you up to that, didn't she?"

"She worries about you."

"Private school. That's her latest thing. The boys can't go to Venice High. A bully might take their lunch money."

"You been inside a public school lately? You're safer at the Men's Central Jail."

"I went to public school. You went to public school. We survived. Adversity builds character."

"Now you sound like my father. And believe me, that's not a compliment."

"Wait a minute," he said, and the crowd noise swelled in the background. "Fumble recovery on the ten! Hooyah!"

"I'll let you go. Thanks for the update."

"No sweat. And hey! I know you don't want to hear this, but it sounds to me like you're pretty hot right now, and I'm not talking about Parker. You should find someplace safe to bunk."

"Trust me," I said, glancing at Tara, "my bunk is cozy. But I'll be careful, don't worry."

"I worry, Jack. You know me. That's what I do."

There was a muffled roar from the crowd, and the Trojan fight song began to trumpet. Somewhere in her kitchen, Connie Montoya was reaching for a knife.

I slid from the bed and opened my closet. "What are you doing?"

"I need to make a quick trip to San Marino. I won't be long."

"San Marino?" She was sitting up. "What's in San Marino?"

"A bunch of Chinese, apparently. I need to investigate."

"Try again."

"Oh, yeah. And Russ Dinsmoor's house."

"And what's at Russ's house? And don't say Russ's furniture."

I sat on the bed, working my socks.

"That was Gabe. The medical examiner thinks Russ was killed when a dose of insulin triggered his heart attack. I want to check it out, that's all."

She swung her legs to the floor.

"Let Detective Parker deal with it. That's his job, isn't it?"

She still didn't get it. Parker's rhino eyes couldn't see beyond me, and my old friend Gabe, however well-intentioned, was just a bird on the rhino's back.

"If I wait for Parker to do his job, there won't be any evidence left for a prosecution. And besides" — I kissed her head above the bandage — "there are options available to me that Parker doesn't have."

I grabbed a jacket from the closet.

"And what if this is all a big misunderstanding?"

"I suppose that's possible. Someone might have accidentally forged your name. Hush Puppy might have been misdelivered to JPL. Realizing the error, Huang might have gift-wrapped a fresh horse and sent it over. Then, when he wasn't invited to the service, he lost his temper and —"

"All right, all right. I get your point. But it's still a job for the police."

I dug Morris Henley's letter out of my

briefcase and folded it into my pocket. Then I headed to the kitchen for my wallet and keys, only one of which was on the counter where I'd left them.

"Tara?"

She emerged from the bedroom fully dressed, tucking her shirttail into her jeans.

"Where do you think you're going?"

"San Marino."

"Think again."

She stood akimbo. "Now you listen to me, Jack MacTaggart. I'm not going to lie around in bed all day while you go out and get yourself arrested. Besides," she said, a twinkle in her voice, "Sam and I are the only ones here who know where to find your keys."

I glared at Sam, who gave his tail a torpid wag.

"All right, you can come. But only if you promise to wait in the car."

We pulled into the driveway and parked nose-up to the garage.

"Wait here," I said, still unbuckling my belt when the passenger door closed behind her.

"Won't it be locked?" she called from the front stoop.

"Don't touch the knob! We'll go around back."

The house looked pretty much as I'd left it, minus the newspapers and mail. There was no crime-scene tape in sight, since that would have violated several San Marino zoning covenants. Which meant that whoever had raked the leaves and mowed the lawn had presumably left new prints all over the gate. So I opened it for Tara and followed her through.

In the backyard, I stopped to gaze up at the towering hedges. I pictured Huang somewhere beyond, mixing up nerve gas or dissecting neighborhood pets in his home laboratory.

"What is it?"

"Huang. That's his house. Or his hedge, anyway."

She looked at the hedge, then turned to take in the full sweep of the deep, sloping yard. Japanese maples blazed in waves of red and orange by the far fence, like a fire frozen against a backdrop of oaks.

"It's gorgeous," she said.

Someone had wheeled an old Weber barbecue kettle up against the back door, which meant, as I'd hoped, that the glass hadn't yet been replaced. There was a San Marino Police Department adhesive seal on the doorjamb, above a square of tan cardboard covering the broken windowpane. I peeled away the masking tape that held the cardboard in place.

"Your handiwork?" asked Tara.

"Looks like rabbit damage to me."

There was another piece of cardboard taped from the inside, so I punched it out and fumbled for the latch.

"Isn't this a crime? Like, breaking and entering?"

"Trust me, I'm a lawyer."

The seal tore loose as the door swung open, and we stepped into the dim expanse of the living room. It too was as before, right down to the dented hardwood and the ticking clock. The fireplace poker was missing, however, and the broken glass had been swept from the floor. Both, I assumed, had been bagged and tagged as evidence.

"The kitchen's this way."

Sunlight slanted through the windows, spotlighting the kitchen sink. Both the phone and the answering machine were missing, as was the water glass from the island. A funky smell permeated the room, and black smears and smudges marred every polished surface.

"What is it?"

"Fingerprint powder. Do you have those

gloves?"

Tara produced my rubber dish gloves from her pocket. They were banana-yellow on the outside and damp and clammy within. I stepped toward the refrigerator as I spoke.

"Don't touch anything with your hands, and try not to track on the floor."

As I opened the refrigerator door, a rotten stench assaulted us both, and I was transported for a queasy moment back to the coroner's basement. The fridge was fully stocked, and it looked as though nothing had been disturbed, let alone printed or bagged.

I sorted through the shelves, removing possible suspects and setting them in a row along the island. Tara was casting furtive glances at the doorways, so I talked to her as I worked.

"You know those Gary Larson calendars you get for Christmas? With the old *Far Side* cartoons? I saw one once that showed the inside of a refrigerator, with one jar holding a gun on another jar. Like a stickup, you know?"

"Uh-huh."

"And the caption read, 'When mayonnaise goes bad.' "

After assembling a dozen jars, containers, and zip-locked baggies, I straightened and closed the door.

"Okay, let's see what we've got."

"What are we looking for?"

"Some way that Huang could have delivered a lethal lungful of insulin to Russ on Saturday night."

I opened the first jar — grape jelly — and sniffed the contents.

"What if he just walked in and clamped an inhaler on his nose?"

"I don't think so. That would have meant a struggle, and it would have left marks. There was no evidence of either."

The jars and baggies were all benign, and the milk smelled only of sour milk. Come to think of it, I had no idea what insulin would smell like, so I searched for anything that reeked of chemicals or medicines. I held each candidate out for a second opinion from Tara, and each time she sniffed and shook her head.

"And then there was the phone call."

"What phone call?"

"Around nine o'clock on Saturday night, somebody called the house and let the message play all the way through. Then, when they were sure nobody was gonna answer, they hung up."

"Which means?"

"I'm thinking it means they'd set a trap of

some sort, then called to make sure it had worked."

"But you said the body wasn't placed on the boat until Sunday night."

"That's right. Which is why I'm certain Huang was involved."

She frowned. "How so?"

"Because Huang was indisposed, remember? On Saturday. I'm thinking they'd planned it all for Saturday night, only Huang had his little accident and wound up in the hospital. So they had to delay moving the body until Sunday night. Which meant they'd left Russ lying on the kitchen floor for a whole day, which is a risk they never would have taken unless they'd had no choice."

"Why they and not he?"

"Or she?"

"Or she."

"Two reasons. First of all, an inert body is heavy and difficult to move. There had to be at least two people involved, maybe more. And second, of course, is the phone call."

"Of course."

I set the last of the cartons back on the island.

"Huang was in the hospital, remember? You said until ten."

"More like ten thirty."

"Okay. So he couldn't have called Russ at nine. Which means an accomplice did."

"You mean Jared?"

I nodded. "The first call must have been Jared's job. That way, if the trap hadn't worked yet, and if Russ had answered the phone, Jared could have used some pretext for calling. Something office-related. Russ might have thought that odd, but not suspicious. Then Huang would have called a little later, and so on."

"Except that when Jared called Huang to report that the coast was clear, Huang wasn't home."

"Exactly. He was in the hospital, which meant a twenty-four-hour delay in moving the body, which in the end made all the difference."

"It did?"

I nodded again.

"Had they moved the body on Saturday night, then the body temperature, the rigor, and the exposure would have all been consistent. The cops would have assumed Russ had a heart attack on the boat, and the autopsy would have confirmed it. End of story, the perfect crime. But because of the delay, there was a mismatch in the forensics. And that's when it all unraveled."

"And to think," she said. "All because of a horse."

I returned the items to the fridge.

"Okay, what now?"

"The master bath."

We followed the hallway, and I recounted to her the story of the voices and the fireplace poker. In the master bedroom, the clock radio was missing, as was the broken lamp. In the bathroom, the mirrors and sinks were covered in powder.

I hooked the medicine chest open with a rubber fingertip, only to find it totally empty, the contents having been bagged and taken downtown. If this was the source of the insulin, it would be up to Parker's team to find it. And then to blame it on me.

"Oh, well," said Tara. "We could grab a late lunch and —"

"Shhh. Listen."

"Hello!" a voice called from the kitchen.

I peeled the gloves and stuffed them into my pockets.

"Come on," I whispered, and led her down the hallway.

In the kitchen stood a man. He was facing out toward the sycamore tree, and he turned at the sound of our approach.

He wasn't much taller than Tara, maybe five-six tops, and his face was shaded by the brim of a woven pith helmet. Beneath his chin, a surgical mask hung loosely from thin rubber straps. He wore a soiled smock or apron of some sort, and in his gloved hands was an old-fashioned bug sprayer, a silver rocket with a keg and plunger.

He smiled when he saw us, his teeth crooked and yellowed like old ivory.

"There you are!" he said, dipping his head in greeting. "So sorry to intrude, but my name is Huang, and I live next door."

22

Upright and in the flesh, Brian Yee-Horn Huang looked more like Dr. Ruth than Dr. No. But there was something unsettling about the gloves. They could have been gardening gloves, I suppose, but they looked unnaturally sinister, all black and rubbery with a pebbled surface and tight elastic cuffs. I edged myself between the spray gun and Tara.

"Hello," I said, forcing a smile. "You surprised us."

He barely acknowledged this, instead looking past my shoulder.

"Is that Miss Flynn? From Fieldstone?" The smile widened. "It's Brian Huang! I ride with Barbara Hauser! My, what a small world!"

"Yes, it is. Good afternoon," Tara said without moving.

"My goodness, what happened to your head?"

He pointed to the bandage with the nozzle of the gun.

"A near miss," I told him.

"An automobile accident," she clarified.

"Oh, dear. Not serious, I hope."

He stepped to the side and studied her from head to toe.

"And no other injuries? I'm a medical doctor, you know."

"No," she said. "Just a few stitches."

He returned his attention to me.

"You were . . . together at the time?"

"In a manner of speaking."

"How fortunate that you were not injured as well."

"Dumb luck," I agreed.

"Yes, you're a lucky man." He looked at Tara again. "For many reasons."

"My Uncle Louis used to say that you should place at least one bet every day. Otherwise, you might be walking around lucky and never know it."

"A wise man, your uncle," he said, showing the teeth again. Then, "Haven't we met before? Ah, now I remember! We shared an ambulance together. Surely you remember that?"

"I do remember. You looked taller on your back."

Tara kicked me on the foot.

"It's Mister . . . ?"

"MacTaggart. Jack MacTaggart."

He nodded, but made no move to shake hands. Instead, he shifted the spray gun into the crook of his elbow.

"I saw your car," he said, gesturing toward the garage, "and thought it prudent to investigate. We had a break-in here not long ago."

"Mr. Dinsmoor was my law partner," I told him. "We're handling his estate."

"I see," he said. "So sudden, his death. So tragic."

Tara put a hand on my arm. "You were friends with Mr. Dinsmoor?" she asked, keeping her tone conversational.

"We've been his neighbors for several years."

"We?" I asked.

"Yes. My wife and I, and our sons. I have three."

"Well, it's a lovely neighborhood," Tara said.

"Will the house be sold, Mr. MacTaggart? Eventually, I mean?"

"Why, have you got someone in mind?"

"Perhaps I do. An old home like this," he said, scanning the room, "with all of its original fixtures, would be very appealing to the right buyer."

"There are some who'd be reluctant to buy a house in which a person recently died, don't you think? Feng shui, and all that?"

He pointed the nozzle at my nose.

"Oh, but you're mistaken. I'm quite certain that Mr. Dinsmoor died elsewhere. On a boat, I believe. It's been in all the newsp—"

"Police! Hands in the air!"

Two cops came crab-walking from the living room, each holding a black Beretta with both hands. Tara and I did as instructed, but Huang, I noticed, turned almost casually to face them.

"Carter?" I said. "Is that you?"

Sergeant Carter peeked over the sights of his weapon. Then he straightened, lowering the muzzle to the floor.

"MacTaggart? What the hell are you doing here?"

"The question," I corrected, "is what you're doing in my house without a warrant."

"Your house?"

"That's right." I reached into my pocket for the envelope. Carter holstered his weapon and took it, reading both the letter and the photocopied enclosure. He removed his cap and scratched at his scalp.

"We had a neighbor call to report a break-in. She said one of the perpetrators was wearing a blindfold." He nodded at Tara. "Hello, miss. How's the head?"

"Much better, thanks."

He handed back the letter and turned his attention to Huang.

"And who the hell are you?"

"This is Dr. Huang, who lives next door," I answered for him. "He was just leaving."

Huang nodded. "Yes, I must return to my garden." He hefted the spray can. "So many pests this time of year. We'll speak again, Mr. MacTaggart, I'm quite certain. Miss Flynn."

He touched a glove to the brim of his hat, then turned toward the living room. Carter's partner followed him to the door.

"Thought I'd walked onto a movie set," Carter said, hooking his thumbs into his belt. "Bridge over the goddamn River Kwai."

"You know anything about that guy? Brian Huang? He's a Caltech scientist."

Carter shook his head. "I know his house, though. Used to belong to friends of my parents. They moved to Arcadia. Then when Arcadia fell, they moved up to Santa Barbara."

"You're a local then."

"San Marino Titans, Class of '76."

"You've seen some changes, I'll bet."

"None for the better, believe me."

I left Tara in Carter's care as I excused myself and walked down the hallway to the study. There was print powder on all the picture frames and tabletops, and the pipe and ashtray were missing from the side table. I took the photo of me and Russ, and I wiped it clean with my sleeve. A modest advance, I told myself, on my inheritance.

When I returned to the kitchen, I showed the photo to Carter.

"Did you know Russ Dinsmoor?"

He examined the face.

"No, not really. But my brother knew Rusty, the son. Before 'Nam, of course. They played baseball together."

Tara crossed from the window to put her hand on my shoulder. She looked paler, and very tired.

"Okay, let's go."

We were first into the backyard, followed by Carter and then his partner, who closed the door and squatted to work the latch. I looked at the hedge, knowing that Huang was up there somewhere, watching us.

Carter spoke as the two shuffling officers replaced the grill.

"What's with you and Detective Parker? You guys must have some kind of history."

"I was a deputy public defender once. Parker treats that like a felony prior."

He laughed. "I can see it. He's kind of a prick, you ask me."

I knew there was something about Carter that I liked.

"Hey, Sergeant," I said. "Don't take this the wrong way, but why the big entrance? Didn't you guys recognize my Jeep?"

"You mean the black Wrangler? Where?"

I passed the photo to Tara and trotted on ahead, up the path and through the gate to the front of the house. Everything there — the tree, the manicured lawn, and the garage — looked exactly as it had when we'd first arrived.

Everything, that is, except for the black-and-white police cruiser parked where the Wrangler had been.

In the final analysis, the call to Sycamore Lane wasn't a total waste for Carter and his partner. Once they'd taken our stolen vehicle report and radioed ahead for a taxi, they drove us out to the Starbucks on Lake Avenue and ordered two espressos to go, my treat.

Tara gave the cabbie directions to Fieldstone. She rode with her head on my shoulder, the framed photo cradled in her lap.

461

"You knew that was going to happen, didn't you?"

"What, the Jeep?"

"No. Dr. Huang."

"I allowed there was a possibility."

She was quiet for a few blocks, and I thought that maybe she'd dozed.

"What was in the envelope?"

"A letter, from Morris Henley. That, and an excerpt from Russ's estate plan. Russ left me the house and everything in it."

She sat up straight. "Jack! That's wonderful!"

"It would be, if I wasn't already a suspect in his murder."

The cabbie glanced at his rearview mirror.

"Oh," said Tara. "I see."

"Morris is the trustee, and he won't transfer title until I'm exonerated."

"By Detective Parker, you mean."

"That's one possibility."

"Jack," she said, taking hold of my arm. "Let the police do their jobs. You were right, Brian Huang is dangerous. He frightens me."

"Really? He pisses me off."

"I don't want you getting hurt, that's all."

I lowered my voice. "How could I possibly get hurt breaking into Huang's lab at JPL?"

"You're joking, I hope."

"Have you ever known me to joke about something serious?"

"They have guards at JPL. Guards with guns. You could get killed."

"Doing nothing almost got us both killed."

"Jack."

"Just listen for a second. You've ridden the trails all around there, right? Let me ask you a few questions . . ."

It was late afternoon by the time I'd tucked Tara into her bed. The day's show was over, but still the Fieldstone grounds teemed with activity. Grooms led steaming horses from the wash stalls out into the field. A rumbling front-end loader hauled a pile of manure from the barns. A water truck chugged slow circles in one of the warm-up rings. And in the roadways and parking lots, blanketed horses in thick leg wraps were being loaded on to trailers.

I passed through the commotion toward the main arena. In the parking lot, the vendors were stocking their booths for tomorrow's grand finale, while just beyond them, shaded by the big oak tree, the members of the Fieldstone Riding Club were gathered for afternoon cocktails.

Fieldstone, I'd concluded, was a drinking club with a riding problem.

A dozen or so spectators still lingered by the main ring, waiting to watch the professionals school their horses. Mounted riders milled at one end of the arena while a tractor-drawn harrow churned through the sandy footing. At the center of the vast ring, looking starkly utilitarian without their floral adornments, two lone obstacles stood side by side, a single and a widely spread double.

Once the tractor exited stage right, the riders untangled and began circling their mounts. All trotted at first, breaking one after the other into slow, collected canters, the hooves of the horses patterning the newly groomed earth like tracks in the first snowfall of winter. And then, as if by unspoken agreement, all the different patterns coalesced into two large circles; mirror images whose orbits joined at the center of the ring.

The riders shouted "Oxer!" or "Vertical!" as they turned off the railing and aimed at their chosen obstacle. After each horse had made several passes, the jumps were raised and the process repeated. Meanwhile, a second group of riders began gathering outside the entrance gate.

As my attention wandered from the horses to the spectators, a distinctive pair of forearms caught my attention, and I headed in their direction.

"Any patients of yours?"

George Wells looked up, surprised.

"Just the one. The dark bay with the socks. Name's Quentin des Hayettes. We're watching his left hock."

He studied the horse as its rider circled and took the vertical jump.

"Looks pretty good," he said, more to himself than to me.

"Who's the rider?"

"Her name's Cathy Lupo. She's from Middle Ranch."

"Any good?"

He looked at me again.

"They're all good. But she won't win tomorrow, if that's the question."

"Who will? Maybe I can get a bet down."

He returned to watching the horse.

"Probably Dos Santos, the Brazilian. Maybe Simms. Then again, I wouldn't bet against Barbara Hauser. That Havana's a hell of a horse."

The bay horse pulled up alongside the rail, and Cathy Lupo, breathing hard, called down to Wells.

"He feels great!"

Wells stepped through the bars and ran a hand over the horse's leg.

"I think he's all right. Give him a long cooldown, then cold water."

"Wish me luck!" she said, walking off while Wells resumed his place.

"She's a good kid. Nervous, though. It's her rookie season."

Other horses began leaving the arena, and the jumps were set back to the lower level. The next batch of riders took their places in the ring and started trotting their warm-up patterns. These included Diego Dos Santos, back from Belgium, and his handy little chestnut.

Diego wore a blue and green polo shirt with the word "Brasil" on the left breast. Across his back, DOS SANTOS was emblazoned in large gold letters.

I watched Wells watching the new batch of horses. His eyes seemed to follow the chestnut in particular. Or maybe it was Diego.

"What can you tell me about Brian Huang?"

"Huh?"

"Brian Yee-Horn Huang, M.D. and Ph.D."

He looked at me and shrugged. "I don't really know him."

"And yet you played golf together."

Now he turned all the way around to face me.

"That's right, we did. What of it?"

The horses had started over the jumps. I noticed that whenever it was the Brazilian's turn, all the other riders watched.

"I'm curious about his relationship with Jared Henley, that's all."

"Why don't you ask Jared?"

"I'd like your take. Did the two of them seem friendly? Do you remember anything they might have talked about?"

"Look," he said. "This sounds an awful lot like politics. And I make it a point —"

"Am I interrupting you studs?"

Barbara Hauser sat astride what might have been the most beautiful horse I'd ever seen, which in this crowd was saying a mouthful. Licorice-black and shining like polished obsidian, Havana had her head down, rubbing her bridle on the side of a foreleg.

"Hello, Barbara. How's the mare?"

Wells studied Havana's legs the way Tiger Woods studies a ten-foot downhill slider. I figured that if Wells had been around for Lady Godiva's ride, he'd have been watching the horse for lameness.

"She's ready, George. I just have a feeling."

467

"Maybe it's remorse," I suggested.

"You're so droll, Jack. Where's little Tara? I haven't seen Excavator all day."

"Probably still out on the milk run."

Forming a gun with her thumb and index finger, Barbara squeezed off a shot.

"You haven't called me yet. I'm disappointed in you."

"Stand in line," I told her.

She hiked her knee forward and reached under the saddle flap to tighten the horse's girth.

"They've posted the order of go," she said to Wells. "Field of thirty-one. I'm eleven, and Cathy's twenty." She looked at me. "Tara's twenty-five."

"And what am I?"

Ricky Ricardo's voice came from the other side of the railing. Diego Dos Santos had his helmet under one arm and his feet hanging loose from the stirrups. His hair was perfect.

"Last week's runner-up?"

He squinted at me, the dark eyebrows knitting into one, and his face reddened.

"You! Who allowed you in here? Where is the technical delegate? Where is the security?"

He tossed his head and spurred the horse forward. Barbara, meanwhile, fastened her chin strap and steered Havana toward the entrance gate, falling in with the next group of riders.

Which left me alone again with Wells.

"I'll say this about you, MacTaggart. You don't waste any time pissing people off."

"I know," I told him cheerfully. "It's my special gift."

23

The unfamiliar surroundings had no impact on Sam's internal alarm clock. I felt his weight on the edge of the bed and his nose wet and cold against my arm at exactly six A.M.

From out in the kitchen, I heard the sound of Tara setting dishes on the Formica counter. I staggered out of her bed and into her living room, buck naked and drowsy.

"It's alive!" she said, her hands moving to her face.

Her bandage was off, and for the first time I saw the stitches in her forehead, which had been shaved to around two inches above the hairline. She looked like a character in one of those *Star Trek* spin-offs, the beautiful daughter of a Klingon emperor.

"Better let Dr. Jack have a look."

I inspected the wound from above. It looked as though a fat purple caterpillar had paused momentarily on its journey from her left eye to the top of her head. The wound itself was only three inches long, but you could see that it had been very deep and very, very painful.

"I prescribe an immediate return to bed."

Tara had been asleep when I'd driven her Jeep to Bungalow Heaven, and she was still asleep when Sam and I had returned with our gear at bedtime. She must have risen at sunrise, because something good was baking in the oven, and she looked and smelled like she'd just stepped out of the shower.

"Do I have time to shower?"

She bent to the oven and peeked inside.

"You have exactly ten minutes. And enough hot water for five."

Tara frowned over the little campus map as I emptied my backpack onto her floor.

"This is insane, you know."

"I have it all figured out."

"Oh, yeah? Do lost hikers usually carry latex gloves?"

She had a point there, so I stuffed the gloves, along with the dog biscuit and the leash, into the pockets of my cargo shorts.

"And what about this map? How would you ever explain that?"

"I couldn't. That's why it's not coming."

"Then let's go over this one more time,"

she said, walking the map to the table and clearing away the last of her blueberry muffins.

Although Tara disdained the mission, she accorded its operational details the same reverence as Patton did plans for the invasion of North Africa. I flipped the map over without looking and sketched my coordinates on the back, narrating as I wrote.

"Guard gate. Huang's lab. Escape route one. Escape route two. Helipad. I've got it already."

"How long do you plan to be in there?"

"I'm figuring ninety minutes. If I don't have anything by then, I'll probably never get it."

"That should give me plenty of time."

I stopped packing. "Tara, please. We've been through this."

"That's right, we have. And involving other people is dangerous."

Which was true enough. But on balance, I knew I was right.

"I almost killed you once this week. That's once too many, okay?"

She stood, angrily.

"And what am I supposed to do? Wait here and bake cookies?"

"I assumed you'd want to watch the grand prix."

"You're treating me like a baby!"

"That's because you're acting like a baby!"

She stalked into the kitchen and dented some pans in the sink.

"Let me ask you a philosophical question," I said to her back. "If a man stands in the forest, and there's no woman around to hear him speak, is he still wrong?"

"It must be a terrible burden," she countered, "being right *all* the time!"

We were having our first fight, and the timing wasn't propitious. I'd heard somewhere that learning to fight well was one of the keys to a long and healthy relationship. Maybe it was Dr. Phil who'd said that. Then again, it might have been O. J.

"You said that Maritza's son can ride. Get him. End of discussion."

A line of cars snaked past the barns and the barricaded parking lot, and it continued clear past the guard shack and into the street. Volunteers in green walked the line, chatting up the guests and handing out programs. There were new pumpkins and fresh sunflowers everywhere, while the strains of classical music wafting from the main ring blanketed the entire grounds. And unlike the scene at the L.A. Equestrian Center, there wasn't a cowgirl or a corn dog in sight.

I loitered like a dope dealer behind a tall hedge while Tara approached the warm-up ring. Although the grand prix wouldn't start for another hour or so, the first riders were already out and in the saddle. There were four women on horseback, all in white show pants, all with their coats folded carefully on the white board railing.

I looked like Joe Backpack in my cargo shorts and T-shirt under a plaid flannel shirt, plus hiking boots and droopy wool socks. Tara wore jeans and a blue bandanna that covered the salient aspects of her new hairdo.

We'd chosen Calico Simms as our target. This was based on the order of go, and on Tara's inspection of the various horse trailers parked in the lot. Simms was third on the program, and one of the four riders already in the irons.

"Calico!" Tara called, hurrying up to the railing.

"Hey, Tara. What's up?"

"We have a small problem with parking. Okay if I move your trailer to the other side of the lot?"

"Sure," she said. "My stuff's in the dressing room in D barn. Keys are in the fanny pack."

I fell into stride beside her as Tara rounded the hedge and headed toward the club-house.

"Last chance to change your mind," she said tightly.

"I'll keep the one I've got."

"Then meet me at the trailer. I'll go and get Maritza."

The genius of my plan lay in its simplicity.

Tara would drive a horse trailer up to the JPL guard station, and ask if this was the entrance to Fieldstone. I would be hiding in the little tack room at the front end of the trailer, and Maritza Jimenez would be fol-lowing in her Volkswagen. The guards would direct Tara to turn around. Maritza, impa-tient, would honk her horn and refuse to back up. The guards, or so we hoped, would let Tara pull forward and make a U-turn around the station. Then, when the trailer was perpendicular to the station, I would jump out the blind side and run like hell. When it was her turn, Maritza would tell the guards in broken Spanglish that she was looking for the horse show entrance, and had simply followed the trailer.

My plan for exiting JPL was, on the other hand, problematic. The southern fence line, or so Tara had assured me, separated the

JPL helipad from one of the dozens of riding trails that veined Hahamongna Park. While the fence itself was ten feet of chain link topped with four-strand barbed wire, the stanchions at the top were canted outward, designed to prevent unauthorized entry. A swashbuckling barrister should have no trouble, I'd told her, scaling the fence from the inside and mounting the getaway horse that would be waiting at the appointed hour.

If the feds were in hot pursuit, my plan called for the horses to ride eastward, into the park and its labyrinth of trails, before circling back to Fieldstone. If the coast was clear, however, Fieldstone was a straight-shot gallop to the west, over a low hillock and through a concrete tunnel that ran beneath Oak Grove Drive.

What might transpire between the break-in and the breakout was anybody's guess. In the not-unlikely event that I were to be busted on the JPL grounds, my cover story was that I'd been hiking in the foothills and had lost track of Sam, my stalwart golden retriever. Thinking he'd perhaps slipped under this gigantic fence, I'd scaled the same without realizing I was entering into a top-secret federal defense installation. But Sam, that little rascal, would eventually turn up at the nearby riding club, lured there by the smell of grilling meats.

This alibi was hopelessly feeble, of course, and would probably land me at FBI headquarters in Westwood. This placed a high premium on avoiding capture in the first place. But, as I'd told Tara, the silver lining of being captured was that I'd avoid the galloping part altogether.

Calico Simms's trailer was a three-horse affair that was around forty feet long and fire-engine red. The trailer was connected to her matching Ford F-350 turbo diesel by means of a gooseneck hitch that locked into the bed of the pickup. A marvel of conspicuity, it looked like the rig Santa used to haul his reindeer down from the North Pole.

On the inside, the elevated prow at the front of the trailer housed a mattress, two pillows, and some folded bedding. Aft of the sleeping compartment was an eight-by-ten tack room, where I now sat in total darkness surrounded by buckets, rakes, whips, halters, helmets, ropes, bridles, saddles, pads, blankets, folding chairs, and an assortment of other equipment, products and devices about whose purposes I could only speculate. Thankfully, it was to be a very short drive.

After a bumpy descent from the parking lot and a pair of slow left-hand turns, we rode for less than a minute before stopping. I heard muffled voices, then a honking horn behind us. And then we sat.

Soon there were more voices, one coming from the passenger side of the truck, and then another, more insistent honk. Then the trailer rocked, as though a heavy man had mounted a fender to look into the back. This was followed by more voices, and what might have been the sound of laughter. And then we lurched forward over a speed bump, turning a slow arc to counterclockwise.

At noon on the clock face, the trailer stopped again and I jumped free, easing the door behind me with a quiet click. Then, while Tara executed a halting three-point turn of dubious necessity, I sprinted toward a nearby cluster of shrubbery. From there, winded more by adrenaline than by the weight of my pack, I watched from a crouch as the trailer completed its turn and receded into the distance. By then the guards had turned their attentions on Maritza, who harangued them like an angry fishwife while I slipped, undetected, into the inner sanctum.

The game was afoot.

The architecture of the NASA Jet Propulsion Laboratory covered the spectrum from post-Soviet industrial to Jetsons quasi-modern, the buildings having accreted over the course of several decades. The first I encountered was a three-story cube of tan brick and glass against whose western wall I flattened myself to check for closed-circuit cameras. The surprise of seeing none gave wing to a faint hope that the actual on-campus security might be lax, in light of the heavily militarized perimeter.

I pushed onward, moving from tree to building and building to bush like a truant who'd lost his clothes at the swimming hole. The campus, thankfully, was heavily land-scaped both by God and man, its rolling terrain webbed with shallow arroyos, nar-row roads, and winding paths. Plus, this be-ing Sunday, I expected little in the way of employee foot traffic, although, as Captain Kirk may once have observed, deep-space exploration follows no earthly calendar.

A tinny voice murmured in the breeze, followed by the faint but unmistakable strains of "The Star-Spangled Banner." I pictured Simms, and Dos Santos, and all of the other riders at Fieldstone sweating in their show coats as they awaited their turns in the ring. When the music ended, a patri-otic cheer rose up from the crowd.

And then, just as the cheer subsided, I heard the dog.

It wasn't a bark, exactly, but more like the anxious yelp of a large and excited animal straining against its leash. The sound came from behind me, where the path had curved. Up ahead the path curved again, completing a serpentine, and I hurried on without running. Then, in the shade of a large oak tree, I dropped off the path and picked my way down into a dry arroyo where I held my breath, watching the pathway above.

At first I thought they'd turned back. Then I saw the ears of a Doberman pincher moving like sharks' fins above the rim of the wash, towing what looked like a pallet of moon rocks with a burr haircut. With his navy shorts and baby-blue shirt, you might have mistaken the dog's handler for a muscle-bound mailman. Until you noticed the 9mm. semiautomatic strapped to his hip.

The dog was in full-alert mode, claws scrabbling on pavement, pulling so hard that its handler leaned backward as if bracing a gale-force headwind.

"What is it, boy?" he urged the dog. "Go get 'em, boy!"

The leash went slack as the dog stopped where I had stopped. Then it began circling, its head down and its stubby tail spinning like a toy propeller.

The ground where I stood was sandy, which meant leaving tracks if I moved up the arroyo. Not that it mattered, since the odds of losing the dog inside a fenced compound were longer than the last day of school. So while beast and man sniffed out their next move, I extracted the dog biscuit from my pocket and laid it carefully at my feet. Then I rock-hopped the wash and slipped up the opposite bank.

They came down the far bank like a landslide, to the accompaniment of crashing limbs and tumbling stones.

"Shit!" said the big man, sliding onto his back. "Whoa, boy. Hold on."

The dog, all sharp angles and bad intentions, dragged him to his feet and pulled him straight to the spot where I'd stood. There it sniffed a tight circle before clamping the dog treat in its teeth with an audible clack.

"What the . . . ?"

The big man jerked the dog backward. Then he choked up on the leash and brought it down hard on the Dobie's narrow rump.

"Bad dog! Bad!" he shouted, striking the dog again. The dog yelped and dropped to its belly, cowering.

"Stupid ass dog," he muttered, brushing the dirt from his shorts. Then he hauled the animal back to its feet and wrestled it down the arroyo, back in the direction from which they'd come. Each time the dog tried to turn, the man jerked it forward until finally, with a last fleeting glance in my direction, the dog gave up and heeled.

I moved on at a trot.

Huang's lab was a cinder-block shoe box set into the sloping hillside. Compact and sweatshirt gray, it could have passed for a compressor station, or maybe a water-treatment plant, but for two distinguishing features. The first was the bloodred trim on its two high windows, like barroom eyes staring back in the morning mirror. The second was the carved marble dragon standing watch in the entrance alcove.

I settled on a western approach, keeping to the tree line and climbing high into the hillside chaparral, then dropping straight through the fire buffer to the rear of the building.

The laboratory's back wall, like those on the sides, was solid and windowless, designed to withstand a brush fire from above. And while admirably utilitarian, the bunkerlike architecture winnowed my options to three.

The first, and maybe the most tempting, was to spit the bit and start for the rendez-vous point immediately. The second option was to use the dragon, assuming I could lift it, to flatten the laboratory door in a quick snatch-and-grab before dodging the flying bullets and racing guard dogs that the crash would likely attract.

After giving each their due, I settled on the third option.

Stripping to my T-shirt, I extracted leather gloves and a heavy flashlight from the backpack. I then rolled the flashlight in the flannel shirt and wedged both into the waistband of my cargo shorts before replacing the pack and donning the gloves. Keeping low, I circled the building and slipped into the alcove, and from there I reconnoitered my surroundings.

There were no visible signs of life, human or canine, and the only sounds were the beating of my heart and a muffled roar that washed over the treetops from the general direction of Fieldstone. I pictured Diego Dos Santos catapulting headfirst into a manure pile.

The door to the lab was a double-wide model, steel and windowless, definitely fireproof and possibly bombproof, with recessed hinges and heavy steel handles. Although there was no alarm or other security system advertised, it was abundantly clear that whatever Huang was doing in this building, he'd taken every precaution to do it in private.

I bear-hugged the dragon and rocked it forward. I figured it for between two and three hundred pounds — too heavy, even with two good arms, for the old smash-and-grab. So with a knee-flex and a straight back, I dragged it off the little porch and down the step, then hauled it another ten feet to the base of the near window, leaving a deep gouge in the gravel driveway.

I climbed to the window on a ladder of dorsal scales, and there, wielding the padded flashlight like a dagger, I punched in the glass.

Pain shot through my shoulder as I hoisted myself into the window frame, where I scooted sideways and dropped to the floor below, landing on a carpet of broken glass. And there I stood, waiting in the semidarkness for an alarm that never sounded.

The interior of the lab was a cavernous space of maybe two thousand square feet, framed by cinder-block walls and a bare concrete floor. And despite the fresh air and moted sunlight slanting downward from the broken window, the room was cold and damp, reeking of mildewed stone and powerful disinfectant.

The end wall, farthest from where I stood, hosted a pair of glass doors, dark and widely spaced, mirroring the room and its contents. And in the middle of it all, in the way that a boxing ring rises up from the center of a sports arena, stood a stainless steel table.

The operating table was huge — bigger than a standard autopsy table — with a drop spotlight above and a heavy steel vise at its head. From a place above the spotlight, power tools dangled like chrome stalactites on jointed steel arms. The open mouth of a drain, black and crusted, gaped in the floor below.

I shrugged off my pack to stow the flashlight and leather gloves, then buttoned up the shirt and snapped on the latex gloves.

There were four sets of file drawers on the south wall, each drawer marked with an alphabetic label. Inside the A drawer were hanging pendeflex dividers with handwritten tabs under plastic. The file headings ranged from Abacavir and Abbot Laboratories to AMA and Amprenavir. All of the drug name files held pharmaceutical literature, and in some cases articles that appeared to have been photocopied from textbooks or printed off the Internet.

In the B drawer were more of the same. So too the C and the D, and all of the rest, file after file and drawer after drawer, all the way down to the X-Y-Z drawer and a file labeled Zidovudine.

There was no file for EVAgen. Nor was there a Henley, a Horses, a Hush Puppy, or a Homicidal Maniac.

On the other side of the room, modular drawers held surgical supplies — a varied assortment of steel instruments, rubber tubing, glassware, gauze, syringes, latex gloves, and the like. Atop the counter, over a gap in the drawers filled by a rolling swivel chair, sat a new HP color printer and a tangle of cables, the latter suggesting that when Brian Huang went home to his weekend gardening, he took at least two laptop computers with him.

I consulted my watch. Fifteen minutes had elapsed since I'd dropped through the window. Ample time, I thought, for a Homeland Security SWAT team to have the lab fully surrounded.

There were two rooms behind the end wall, each with its own entry door of double-glazed sliders set into heavy steel frames. Each door had a nine-button keypad mechanism, and the door on the right had two decals affixed to the tinted glass at eye level.

One decal featured black angles on a red background over the word BIOHAZARD. The second was a triad design of purple on yellow above the word radiation.

This door was locked, thankfully, and the glass that hummed against my hand felt like the beer cooler at 7-Eleven. I retrieved the flashlight from my pack and held it overhead, training its beam into the blackness between the decals.

The room was deep and narrow, maybe ten feet by thirty, with a long modular table running down its center. The table was anchored at either end by stainless steel sinks, each with tall, looping spigots.

I played the beam from side to side, the light revealing tall glass cases and shelf upon shelf of glassware — test tubes and beakers of various shapes and sizes.

The second room was more than twice as wide as the first. Visible just inside its entry door was another wall that combined with the outer wall to form a sort of anteroom. Set into the inner wall was a sliding door identical to, and aligned directly opposite, the outer door whose glass my breath was fogging. And on the side wall between the two doors was a piece of stainless steel machinery in the general shape of a drinking fountain.

The inner glass returned the flashlight's beam, making it difficult to see beyond. But as I worked the light from side to side, I caught a polished inner surface that glowed in the way that a spoon reflects a dim radiance from deep in the dishwater. And vague, crepuscular forms took shape in the darkness.

The largest of these seemed to float in space, like a line of toy balloons in the Thanksgiving Day parade. And while I couldn't make them out exactly, there was something in their aspect that tugged uneasily at my cognition.

And then, with chilling clarity, I knew exactly what they were.

24

The problem of the outer lock was easily remedied, thanks to a steel mallet and a chisel-like tool borrowed from one of the supply drawers. And just as I was about to apply the same solution to the inner door, the drinking fountain caught my attention.

Only it wasn't a drinking fountain, of course, but some sort of electronic unit. The lower portion was a steel cube onto which a glass plate was set. Above this was a smaller, rectangular box that looked to have been sliced off the main unit and mounted six inches above. I passed the mallet head between the two, and the lower unit began to hum. Seconds later, a wave of purplish black light passed across the glass, like the action of a copy machine.

I set down my tools and placed a gloved palm on the glass. Now the light made two passes behind the plate, and with a sucking pop the inner door sprung wide, unleashing a breath of cold and putrid air into the anteroom. Hand to mouth, I stepped over the threshold and fumbled for the lights.

There were three carcasses in total. They hung from steel hooks in the center of the room, the ceiling lights casting neon rainbows on the oily sheen of exposed ribs. Massive and inert, like grisly piñatas molded for the *Dia de los Muertos,* their uniform decomposition suggested a shared and fairly recent vintage.

Even headless and limbless, flayed and disemboweled, I recognized them as horses. And one of them, I had to assume, belonged to Sydney Everett.

They hung by their haunches, their jagged necks suspended over a grated drain in the concrete floor. As I turned sideways to pass through the line, my shoulder brushed some jutting bone and spun one of the torsos, creaking, ninety degrees to clockwise. This, the low hum of refrigeration, and the pounding of my heart were the room's only sounds.

The walls were lined with stainless steel counters, and the counters were punctuated by sinks at regular intervals. There were also three refrigeration units, all in matching steel. A rubber apron hung on a dowel over a pair of black rubber boots. And in the room's deepest corner, beside a metal stool on rolling wheels, stood another file cabinet.

Unlike the ones outside, this cabinet was a fireproof model with a recessed deadbolt — more like a safe, really — and its three unmarked drawers were tightly locked. I retreated to the anteroom for a breath of fresh air and my trusty skeleton key.

The clang of steel against steel rang off the sinks and counters, its piercing reverb muffled only by the grisly curtain of meat and bone. After a full minute of pounding, I'd managed to separate the frame from the pop-out bolt by a quarter-inch at most. Hands on hips, I watched as my breath floated toward the open doorway in semaphores of whitish frost.

Out again in the fresh air, the main laboratory looked even larger than before, and somehow emptier for its size. I lifted the swivel chair up onto the operating table and hiked myself after it, detaching a polished steel Sawzall from its mechanical arm and lowering it gently to the table. Then I mounted the teetering chair, gripping the power cord for balance, and traced it upward to a strip of plugs set high on a crossbeam.

Back again in the meat locker, awash now in a shower of orange sparks, the Sawzall's tungsten blade made short work of the steel bolt, which hit the floor with a dull clack and skittered toward the drain. My shoulder throbbed again as I set the heavy tool into a sink.

All of the top-drawer files pertained to EVAgen, LLC. Up front was an organizational file containing various registration documents, including, I noted, the Statement of Information that Russ had obtained from Data-Check in Sacramento. Next was a thick file of correspondence between Huang and various investment banks and private equity firms — heavy hitters like Credit Suisse, Goldman Sachs, and the Blackstone Group. Then came an even thicker file of correspondence with U.S., German, and Swiss pharmaceutical firms, the letters transmitting various iterations of a lengthy confidentiality agreement. And last but not least, a file of patent applications.

There were a half dozen of these, some running to more than fifty pages if you counted the diagrams, flowcharts, and formulas attached as exhibits. The first was entitled "Method and Formulae for the Generation of Human Nucleoside Reverse Transcriptase Inhibitors Utilizing Genetically Modified Equine Arteritis Antibodies."

Checking my watch again, I stuffed both the organizational file and the patent application file into my backpack.

The files in the second drawer were labeled in spidery Chinese characters. The top document in each was a photocopy of an anatomical chart, a black-line drawing of a horse standing in left profile. Each chart was annotated with multiple lines radiating outward to the margins, where numbers and Chinese characters were scrawled, so that each of the diagrammed horses looked like an equine Saint Sebastian, or maybe the pony Custer rode into the Little Big Horn.

Even I could figure out that three of the files in the drawer must correspond with the three oversized briskets hanging from the ceiling. And it was in the last file that I found confirmation, in the form of the Release and Disposition Agreement from Chino Hills Veterinary Associates.

And so Hush Puppy's personal dossier joined the other files in my pack.

The third and final drawer proved anticlimactic. It held nothing but computer runs — bundle after bundle of agate-type data from a series of experiments or trials, each hand-labeled by date. I added the two most recent bundles to my swag pile.

I figured I had enough evidence in my

pack to indict Huang for grand larceny, and maybe a few Hail Mary's like animal cruelty or conspiracy to commit fraud. What I didn't have, however, was any evidence tying him either to Russ's murder or to the attack on Tara. But since I was due at the rendezvous point in five minutes, and since the JPL helipad was a good ten minutes away, I had no choice but to call it a day.

It was on my way back through the main laboratory that I remembered how Huang had pointed his spray gun in Tara's face. So I pulled a rubber glove and an empty test tube from one of the supply drawers, inserted the latter into the middle finger of the former, and clamped them both into the vise at the head of the operating table.

"So many pests," I said aloud, zipping up the pack and shrugging it into place.

And then I heard the siren.

First came a white Ford Bronco, its light-bar flashing as it skidded to a stop, showering gravel onto the overturned dragon. This was trailed by a golf cart bearing a muscle-bound mailman and a sleek black dog. Four men spilled from the vehicles and hurried to the lab.

All of this I observed from the tenuous safety of the tree line. Two of the security guys had their guns out and were circling the building, shouting instructions, while the third fumbled with a ring of keys. But it was the dog that had me worried, zigging to and fro, straining at the leash, dragging its handler from the stoop to the marble dragon and back again. And then, just as they'd all reassembled in the alcove and the double doors had swung open, the dog turned and looked right to where I was standing.

I battled my first impulse, which was to run like hell for the rendezvous. Even these muscle-heads would eventually think to unleash the dog, and when they did, I'd be a lawyer-flavored chew toy. So once they were all inside, I ran straight for the cart, slipping under the steering wheel and kicking the foot brake loose.

It was a beefed-up version of the standard golfing model, silent and electric, and after gathering some momentum, it shot down the sloping service road like a Tesla. I leaned into the curves and floored it on the straight-aways, passing bushes and benches and trash cans and trees, all of them blurring to white at the outer margins of the windshield.

I braked as the road curved eastward, skidding through a curb cut and onto a concrete pathway. Sun flickered on the windshield as the path devolved from pavement to gravel, then from gravel to hard-packed earth. Soon bushes were lashing the fenders, and I lost the path altogether, careening through brush and shadows before bouncing over a curb and back into sunlight.

This new roadway I followed westbound, past more darkened buildings and an empty parking lot, until it curved again south, down a long and winding hill. And there, finally, as the road began to level, a fence came into view.

I coasted to a stop at the curb. Before me sat a low brick building in the style of a Truman-era elementary school, with a Day-Glo wind sock hanging limply above the roofline. By the front entry doors was a statue — a ten-foot replica of the space shuttle orbiting a miniature bronze earth — and parked before the statue was another white Bronco.

There were two fences, actually, between me and my getaway. The first, fanning outward from the building's wings, was ten feet of chain link topped with overhanging stanchions of rusted barbed wire. The second fence, fifty yards beyond, was the one Tara had described, its stanchions canted outward toward the park. These were, I soon realized, one and the same fence — a continuous rectangle that enclosed the JPL helipad.

I checked my watch as a siren rose in the distance. I was five minutes late for the rendezvous.

I left the cart and ran to the base of the statue. Inside the glassed-in lobby was a lone guard in a radio headset, seated behind a console. Behind him, glass doors opened out to the helipad, and more important, to the outer fence beyond.

I sat on my heels and weighed some possible scenarios. All of them, however, seemed to end with me wearing a Doberman pinscher necktie. Meanwhile, beyond the trees, the siren grew steadily louder.

I hurried back to the cart. The Bronco was maybe fifty yards away, and facing in my direction. I pulled Sam's leash from my pocket and fitted the loop end over the accelerator pedal, running the clip end under the brake pedal and up to the steering wheel. Then I squared my shoulders and floored it, pulling slack as I went, wrapping the leash tightly around the wheel.

I jumped clear with ten yards to spare, running like hell for the base of the statue.

The impact wasn't great, and the cart just sort of glanced off the Bronco's front bumper. But the horn-and-lights crescendo of the Bronco's alarm was enough to register on the Richter scale.

The guard blew through the glass doors with his headset askew, the detached cord trailing him like a fuse. I was through the doors before they closed, then through the lobby and out the back, all before you could say *halicephalobus deletrix.*

The helipad consisted of a wide green lawn with walkways leading to two concrete landing zones, both demarked by sniper-scope circles, both currently empty. Opposite these and beyond the fence, a lone rider sat on a tan horse, with another horse ponied behind. I pointed to the far corner of the fence as I ran, to a spot outside the sight line of the lobby.

"Over here!"

I was on the fence and climbing before the rider could react. By the time I'd reached the top, the latex gloves were shredded and my hands were stained with rust. I hiked one foot onto the stanchion and pivoted, finding a handhold between the barbs.

"You're late!" hissed a voice from below, and I looked under my arm to see the extra horse below me, stamping and pawing the ground.

"Shit!" I cried to no one, dropping free and landing with a *hoomph* on the saddle, which, being of the western variety, had a very large horn. Through swimming stars I saw Enrique the groom watching me over his shoulder.

"Ready?" he asked.

I groaned in reply. And then we were galloping.

Enrique tested the water before spraying the horse's neck.

"I never seen that before," he said.

"What's that?"

"A horse make a grown man puke."

"You've never been to the track with my Uncle Louis," I told him, leaning back against the wall and feeling the sun on my face.

He hosed the last of Tara's muffins from the horse's mane and scraped its coat with a squeegee, fetid water sheeting onto the concrete pad where they stood.

After another minute of deep breathing, I rose unsteadily to my feet and patted the steaming animal on its haunches.

"That was fun," I said. "Let's do it again soon."

I limped for the bungalow. Tara, I knew, would be worried sick. Then again, maybe she'd occupied herself by hauling my things out to the Dumpster.

"Tara?"

The front door was unlocked, but the little house was empty. I deposited my pack in the bedroom and checked that my clothes were still in the closet. So far, so good. Then I found a water bottle in the fridge, limped back outside, and headed toward the main arena.

A roar rose up from the grandstand, and an amplified voice with a clipped British accent announced, "Rider number one-seventeen, Calico Simms, with no jumping faults and a time of forty-six point three-one seconds is our new leader."

Bright plastic pennants funneled me toward a table, where a green-jacketed attendant who should have been taking tickets was instead on her feet, craning for a look into the arena. I cleared my throat, and Margaret Carlton turned her orange scowl in my direction.

"Oh, God," she said wearily.

"But you can call me Jack."

"Just go," she said, waving me past as though shooing vermin from the basement.

I descended the concrete steps and hopped the railing before anyone could stop me. Not that anyone tried, since all eyes in the grandstand were now turned toward the entrance gate, where a slender rider in green loped in from the warm-up ring on a small-ish chestnut horse. Some sort of samba music echoed from the overhead speakers.

"Our next no-fault rider is from São Paulo, Brazil. Ladies and gentlemen, let's have another warm round of applause for the reigning Olympic champion, Diego Dos Santos aboard Eden du Boilary!"

While the crowd had a communal orgasm, I walked the railing to the place where I'd stood only yesterday, and from where I had a view back at the grandstand. I scanned the overflow crowd for signs of either a blue headscarf or an orange dog.

There must have been close to a thousand faces watching from under the canopy, plus fifty or so up on the patio, and a dozen more, mostly grooms and other riders, strung along the railing. Then Eden's hooves thundered past, and I turned my attention back to the course.

The jumps were huge compared to yester-day's warm-up, and there were more flow-ers on display than at a Mafia don's funeral.

Diego tripped the eye at a gallop and eas-ily cleared the first jump, then turned sharply to his left. I watched his hands on the reins, gloveless and delicate, moving in perfect sync with the bob and lift of the horse's head. He held the leather straps lightly in his fingertips, like a safecracker coaxing the tumblers into place. The chestnut's thousand-pound body seemed to turn or straighten, shorten or lengthen, in thrall to the slightest squeeze or release of those long, thin fingers.

The recital Diego was giving up front contrasted starkly with the naked force of what transpired behind. Muscles rippling, the little horse hopped and twisted, charged and coiled before launching himself skyward, tearing deep gouges and gashes into the soft brown footing. It was a breathtaking symphony of grace and strength to which the crowd responded with oohs and aahs and barely contained delirium.

They were fast and clear through six jumps.

The final combination featured a tall vertical and a wide oxer separated by a single stride. They made a tight turn to the first element, taking it at an awkward angle that left the horse's shoulders off-line, square to the outside railing. Diego tried to compensate by taking both reins in one hand and swatting Eden with his crop while yanking his head back toward the final jump. The horse reacted by launching himself like a missile, but it was an impossibly long takeoff, and the crowd, sensing disaster, let loose a collective gasp.

Horse and rider seemed to hang above the standards in weightless equipoise, sailing, stretching, *willing* themselves forward. And then gravity took hold.

The crack of Eden's hooves on the wooden rail echoed throughout the grandstand. The cups broke free from the standards, but still the pole bounced upward, wedging itself diagonally between the horse's legs, and they all came down together — man, horse, and lumber — forcing Eden's rear legs into a split. The horse tumbled forward, its body collapsing left while Diego bailed out to the right.

The crowd was on its feet. Eden, stunned, struggled to join them and trotted a halting jig along the rail. Diego, facedown in the dirt, rolled slowly and sat upright. He waved to the judges, and the crowd responded with a thunderous ovation.

George Wells was out on course, collaring the frightened animal. A groom dashed out to take the reins, and Wells immediately dropped to a knee to inspect the horse's legs. Diego rose stiffly and walked toward his mount, pausing to retrieve his fallen crop.

Wells and Dos Santos conferred for a moment, and they seemed to be having words. With a toss of his head, Diego lifted his foot into the stirrup and hoisted himself into the saddle, then turned Eden back along the rail. The crowd cheered again, but with notably less enthusiasm.

A tone sounded, and the BBC voice announced, "Ladies and gentlemen, your attention please. Rider number two thirteen, Diego Dos Santos, has been eliminated from the competition. Rider, please clear the ring."

By now the grounds crew had rebuilt the mangled jump, and Diego drew Eden to a halt between the two elements, head-on to the oxer. The horse fidgeted and Diego whipped him hard across the haunches once, twice. Then he turned and walked him toward the out gate, to uneasy silence and a smattering of boos.

Wells, livid, retrieved his binoculars from the dirt and resumed his place at the railing.

"The little shit," he hissed under his breath.

"That's what I call him," I said as I took my place by his side.

Music swelled and a cheer rose up and quickly turned to rhythmic clapping, like you'd hear at some kind of Euro soccer match. We both turned to see Barbara Hauser enter on the big black horse, her hair in a platinum ball at the back of her helmet, her red coat glowing in the sunlight. They were an impressive sight, and the hometown fans greeted them like rock stars.

"The next entry in our jump-off is from Flintridge, California. Needing no further introduction, please welcome back number one thirty-three, Barbara Hauser and Havana!"

The horse's name was lost in the swelling ovation. Barbara stopped, touched a gloved hand to the bill of her helmet, and began a slow clockwise canter.

Havana covered the course quickly and cleanly, her takeoffs exact and her landings sure. While Diego had brought a virtuosic flair to the proceedings, Barbara rode with metronome precision, every stride planned, counted, and perfectly executed. Even her face — steely blue eyes over a set and determined mouth — bespoke the bloodless detachment of a surgeon.

The tension built with every jump. By the fourth, the crowd had begun to gasp. By the sixth they were tittering with excitement, ready to explode.

Havana turned to the final combination at

a better angle than Eden, and she landed the first element square to the line. And then, after one explosive stride, they were over the oxer and clear.

All eyes turned to the digital clock, which had frozen at 45.21.

The crowd roared.

"Our new leaders, ladies and gentlemen, double-clear with a time of forty-five and twenty-one seconds, Barbara Hauser and Havana!"

There was bedlam in the grandstand as Barbara slowed to a trot and thumped Havana on the neck. Their path toward the out gate took them past our spot on the railing, and she beamed in our direction.

"It ain't braggin' if you can back it up!" she crowed, then turned and pumped her fist toward the rocking grandstand.

"Can I borrow those?" I asked Wells, focusing his binoculars first on the clubhouse patio, then on the grandstand below. The patio crowd was still up and clapping, with hugs and high fives all around. Down in the covered grandstand, the spectators were just settling back into their seats. There was a roped-off area with tables in the front row, and I scanned the faces above the floral settings.

At the best table, right on the center aisle,

sat Sydney Everett. She wore a black-on-white polka-dot dress with a wide black hat and gloves that rose past her elbows. She was flanked on either side by the two turkey-necks I'd seen on the patio. Sydney interrupted her commentary long enough to sip champagne from a flute.

I was working my way up the grandstand row by row when Van Halen's "Jump" boomed over the loudspeaker, and the Brit piped up again.

"Now entering the ring, ladies and gentlemen, our final jump-off competitors with a time to beat of forty-five and twenty-one seconds, entry number two-nineteen from Mill Valley, California, please welcome back Tara Flynn and Escalator!"

The crowd greeted them warmly, and there was a separate eruption of whistles and shouts of "Ándale, *Tara!*" from the grooms who'd gathered along the railing. I returned the glasses to Wells.

"Find what you were looking for?"

"I'm afraid so."

Tara wore her same lucky outfit of gold-on-black, accessorized today with dark Oakley sunglasses. Escalator was his usual self, snorting and throwing his head, acting as though he'd had other plans for the afternoon. Tara talked to him and stroked his neck, and then the tone sounded.

They trotted along the grandstand, with Tara studying the course while Escalator tried to unseat her. Then they stopped, backed three steps, and cantered off. The crowd, still energized by Barbara's performance, lapsed into reluctant silence.

"Good luck," said Wells as they galloped full out through the electric eye.

I focused my attention on Tara. On the flat sections of the course, she seemed to float above the saddle, weightless, while the big horse thundered and twisted beneath her. At the jumps, she appeared to throw her body ahead and wait for Escalator's powerful back to rise up and catch her. So steep were the landings that her head snapped forward like a crash-test dummy's.

Her riding style, to my novice eye, involved neither artistry nor precision, but barely controlled mayhem.

There were several tight turns on the course, and Escalator managed them well, but not as handily as Eden. And he was certainly fast on the gallops, but not, I thought, as explosive as Havana. But somehow, his unique blend of speed and size got him over the jumps and under the time, and the crowd, sensing this, began to stir.

The sixth jump, the setup for the final

combination, was a double-wide job with a water trough below. It required horse and rider to land, then execute an immediate U-turn back down to the vertical. The wide spread required a fast approach, but a fast approach carried you farther away from the final jumps. Diego had cut it too sharply, and he'd come in crooked. Barbara had hit it just right, but at the cost of a wider, slower turn.

To have any shot at the blue ribbon, Tara would have to find the perfect pace and then put Escalator on the perfect line. All while resisting his efforts to put her back in the hospital.

They came hard to the jump and cleared it easily, and Tara's head immediately turned to the jump behind her. For one stride, two strides, Escalator's momentum carried them out toward the railing. And he continued that way, stride after stride, until Tara slumped forward and slid awkwardly to the ground.

I was into the ring and running before the crowd could react. When it finally did, there were groans and shouts and a deep, collective gasp that seemed to suck the oxygen from the grandstand. I moved as in a dream, making slow-motion progress in the soft and sandy footing.

A couple of the grooms got to her before I did, and we all made way for Wells when he arrived.

"Her head," I breathed. "Check her head."

Tara was unconscious. Wells pinched off her sunglasses, then slipped a practiced hand under her neck and carefully unsnapped her helmet.

"What the . . . ?"

The wound had opened, but not very much, and a small trickle of blood ran from eyebrow to ear.

"Tara?" Wells entreated, and in response, her eyes fluttered open.

A group had gathered at this point, and the public address announcer was saying something to assuage the roiling audience. Tara blinked and looked from Wells to me and managed a weak smile.

"I must be in heaven," she said.

"Enjoy it while you can."

The fireplace crackled, and Tara snuggled deeper into the blankets. We were alone at last, after a long parade of visitors that had included one vet, two doctors, and three of the other competitors, none of whom was Brazilian.

"So," said Tara.

"So yourself."

"Tell me all about it."

I gave her a recap of my JPL adventure, leaving out some minor details, like the killer dog and the gun-toting guards. Even so, she was troubled.

"I know you don't want to hear this, but I have to say it. I love you, Jack."

"No, I like hearing that. Say it again."

"Please, let me finish. I love you, but you remind me so much of Keira that it frightens me. And I lost her forever, because she was reckless and headstrong and —"

"Tara."

Her eyes were shining in the firelight.

"Look at me," I told her. "I'm not a little girl. Nobody's going to come along and drive off with me, okay?"

She wiped her face with her wrist.

"Promise?"

I leaned in and kissed her gently on the forehead. "I promise."

25

Morris Henley wanted a word.

I heard it first from one of the secretaries in the parking structure, and I heard it again when I passed Nicky Petrov in the building lobby. And in a final confirmation that I wasn't imagining things, I heard it from Bernie before I could get my best suit jacket onto the hanger.

"I think he meant right away," she added.

I looked at my watch. Veronica Daley had almost certainly departed for the church, where I was soon to meet her. I needed this time to gather my thoughts for the eulogy.

"You haven't seen me all morning," I told her. "In fact, I called to say that I'm running late, and that I plan to go directly to All Saints. And now if you'll excuse me, I need some time alone."

She hesitated in the doorway.

"I've never had one before," she said, nodding toward the big cactus. "What am I supposed to do for it?"

"Check the newspaper every morning," I told her. "When it rains in Phoenix, water it."

Since the doctor had sentenced Tara to bed rest without the possibility of parole, I'd left instructions at the barn office that she not be disturbed. I'd also stopped at the clubhouse and asked Maritza to spread the word that nobody was to see Tara except the doctor. And finally, in an abundance of caution, I'd had a face-to-face with the newly resurrected Colonel Mustard, whose name was actually Mel, trading a C-note for his promise to call my cell phone should either Jared Henley or Brian Huang set foot on the Fieldstone property.

My next call had been to Gabe, from Tara's Jeep, setting up a post-funeral lunch date at the Parkway Grill, telling him only that certain documents relevant to the Dinsmoor case had fallen into my possession. He'd tried to cross-examine, but I'd said it was a long story, and one that was better told in person.

I was transferring Huang's files from my briefcase to my bottom drawer when Bernie buzzed on the intercom. I scowled at the receiver before picking up.

"I told you —"

"I know, I know. But it's Mr. Jackson, from downstairs. He left something for you."

She entered again, placing a thick envelope on the desk. "He said a fat man left it for you on Friday afternoon."

I glanced at the package, and I recognized the shape.

"You're gonna be late," she added. "Everybody's leaving now."

I checked my watch for the fourth time this morning.

"You go ahead. Just don't tell anybody I'm here, okay?"

Pat Bowman's audiocassette was labeled with the Everett policy number, the date and time of its making, and the inscription "MLIC CC Op. 47." I dusted off an old-model tape player from my credenza.

There was a prolonged hiss, followed abruptly by a robotic voice that recited the date and the Pacific daylight time, in English. Then a young woman's voice spoke in a lilting East Indian accent.

"Good afternoon, Metropolitan Livestock Insurance Company, this it Britney speaking. How may I assist you?"

She pronounced Britney like it had three syllables.

"Hello. I'm calling about the status of a policy, and I've got the policy number here if

you need it. The insured's name is Everett,
Mrs. Harold Everett, or maybe it's under Syd-
ney Everett."

"What is the policy number, please?"

"Hold on. It's 'C' as in Charlie, 'A' as in
Alpha, 99-12116. Need that again?"

"No, sir. May I please have your name and
telephone number so that a representative
can contact you with that information?"

"You can't tell me over the phone? I need to
know if the policy's still in force, that's all."

"No, sir, I'm afraid I don't have access to
that information here."

"And where is here, exactly? Is this India?"

"No, sir. But I will need your name and
telephone number in order to provide the
requested information to you."

"Okay. All right. The name's Henley. The
number is area code 626-5551910. Extension
210. You need that again?"

You could hear Operator Forty-seven's
fingernails as she tapped out her e-mail to
the old business unit in Los Angeles, in the
U.S. of A., neglecting to include the extension.

"No, sir, that is sufficient. You can expect to
receive a call from a Metropolitan Livestock
representative within the next seventy-two
hours. Is there anything else I may assist you
with today?"

"What have you assisted me with so far?"

"Well then, thank you for calling Metropolitan Livestock, and have a very pleasant day."

I stared at the machine for a long time as the tape hissed and the little spindles turned behind the hard plastic window.

Morris Henley's voice on the audiotape had taken the picture puzzle I'd so carefully assembled and sent it crashing to the floor. And I was on my knees now, metaphorically speaking, trying to gather the scattered pieces.

The spindles froze with an audible *click* that snapped me back to the present. I ejected the tape and returned it to its case, then added it to the files in my bottom drawer.

There were two news vans parked on the esplanade, and I spotted them just as Terina Webb spotted me. She wore a tailored black suit with designer sunglasses and a black headband that was straight out of the Audrey Hepburn playbook. As she closed the distance between us, I heard a dirge of organ music rising from inside the church.

"Jack MacTaggart! Terina Webb, Channel Nine Action News!"

I tried to ignore her, but she shadowed me step for step, her microphone thrust in my face. Over her shoulder, the doughboy cameraman angled for a shot.

"Any comment on the Dinsmoor murder? Can you confirm that you've inherited the Dinsmoor mansion in San Marino? What's your reaction to being labeled a person of interest in the investigation?"

Terina, I knew, was firing these scatter-shot questions so that if she got any kind of an answer, even a "no comment," she could cut and paste it to whichever question produced the most dramatic effect. I stopped at the foot of the church steps and turned to face her, waiting until the camera-man moved into position. She pivoted quickly, grabbing the back of my coat with her free hand.

"Good morning, Terina," I said, sounding convivial, "it's good to see you again. First of all, I want you to know how very much we appreciate your keen interest in Mr. Dinsmoor's death. He was a great lawyer and a great friend, and the L.A. trial bar is diminished by his passing. You'll be inter-ested to know that there's been a major breakthrough in the case, and our expecta-tion is that an arrest is imminent. That's all I'm at liberty to say for now, but stay tuned for a major announcement from police headquarters, either this afternoon or tomorrow. Now if you'll excuse me, I'm due inside."

She was momentarily speechless, and by the time she'd found her voice, I was out of her grasp and through the heavy wooden doors.

The vestibule was dark, the big church illuminated only by ruby daylight slanting through stained glass and by hundreds of candles that lined the side aisles and blazed from the elevated sanctuary. There, amid floral arrangements and a blown-up poster of Russ's smiling face, stood Warren Burkett, the immensely popular former mayor of Los Angeles. He was in the middle of uncorking a stem-winder, and a ripple of laughter rolled down the nave like the wave at Dodger Stadium.

I stood in back while my eyes adjusted to the sight of more than a thousand mourners overflowing the pews and lining the walls of the ornate church.

I accepted a funeral pamphlet from a doe-eyed usher. On the cover was the same smiling head shot that graced the easel up front. His Honor, meanwhile, had begun an elaborate joke that I'd heard before, about a fictitious visit that he and Russ had paid to the Vatican to hear a major address by the Pope. The story was meant to illustrate the width and breadth of Russ's renown. The punch line, when it came, would be, "Hey, who's that guy standing up there with Russ Dinsmoor?"

There were a few dozen faces I recognized in the audience. Most were lawyers, a few were clients, and the rest were area politicians great and small. There was also a cluster of state and federal judges, and when Amos Spencer saw me passing up the side aisle, he nodded his head in greeting.

At the front of the church was the entire Henley & Hargrove contingent, some with spouses in tow. Veronica Daley held a place for me in the second row, between herself and Marta Suarez.

"Where *were* you?" Veronica whispered, equal parts concern and reproach. "You're on right after Mr. Henley." She'd been crying, I could tell, by the handkerchief balled in her fist.

"I have a question. About the client trust account."

"You've got to be joking. Surely that can wait."

"I don't think it can."

Morris turned from the front row with a scowl.

"That account is audited every year, right?"

Before she could answer, the Mayor delivered his punch line, and a chorus of laughter rose to the vaulted ceiling.

"Yes, of course," she said. "The malpractice insurer requires it."

"So how might a ten-thousand-dollar shortfall slip past an audit?"

"Shh!"

Jared, his body fully turned, held a finger to his lips as Morris rose and crossed to the sanctuary, where he and the Mayor shared a manly clasping of shoulders. I noticed the closed coffin set crossways between the clergy pews behind them, its polished rosewood gleaming in the candlelight.

"I'm not the one to answer these questions," Veronica whispered. "Mr. Henley prepares the year-end financials. He meets with the auditors."

Russ would have known that, of course. And after he'd given the matter some thought, he would have wondered how the ten grand used to fund the IOLTA account could have disappeared from the trust account without raising a red flag. And while he was at it, he would have wondered why the files implicating Sydney were all but gift-wrapped in ribbon and waiting for me in Jared's empty office.

Morris stood at the podium now, his bald

head gleaming in the candlelight, and he eulogized his dearly departed partner with words like "integrity" and "friendship," his hypocrisy washing over the assembled mass like fog over the Golden Gate.

"Jack!" said Mayday, and I looked down at the crumpled pamphlet in my fist.

That's when the doe-eyed church lady beckoned me to join her in the aisle. There she handed me a cell phone, saying it had come from a young gentleman who was waiting outside, and who'd insisted it was of the utmost urgency.

And no sooner did she hand it to me than it started to vibrate.

I took the call while walking toward a side exit, memorizing the number that appeared on the little screen. The voice I recognized immediately.

"Mr. MacTaggart? I believe you have something that belongs to me."

"Is that you, Shorty? Where's my car?"

I pushed through the door and stepped onto the sunlit esplanade.

"I'm afraid that the whereabouts of your vehicle are the least of your concerns at the moment."

"I have no concerns at the moment, Huang. In fact, I'm kinda busy right now, so maybe we can do this later. At your arraignment, for instance."

I walked quickly as I spoke, alongside the church to the place where the news vans had been parked. From there I could see a pimply Chinese kid, maybe seventeen or eighteen years old, smoking a cigarette at the curb.

"I'll want all of the files you've taken, plus any copies you've made. My son is waiting outside the church. Go with him now, and do as he says. And please, Mr. MacTaggart, don't keep me waiting."

"First of all, I don't know what files you're talking about. Secondly —"

"I'm hanging up now. And when I do, a photo will appear on your screen. Study it carefully, Mr. MacTaggart. My son is outside waiting. You have sixty seconds, starting now."

The line went dead. And then, as promised, a color image appeared on the little flip-up screen.

It was a close-up shot of Tara. Her eyes were slits, as if she were squinting into a bright light. Her new bandage was askew, and her hair was disheveled, but she appeared to be unhurt.

Of course, it was difficult to tell for sure with her head clamped in a vise.

■ ■ ■ ■

The kid flicked the butt when he saw me approach. He was short and scrawny in baggy jeans and a white T-shirt, with morning-after hair and an elaborate tattoo coiling down a pencil-thin arm. He straightened and fixed me with the shark eyes he'd been practicing in the bathroom mirror.

He snapped his fingers and held out a hand. I gave him back the cell phone, and he stuffed it into his jeans. Then he glanced up and down the street before squatting to frisk me.

"Where's your phone?" he demanded, and I handed it over.

After he'd worked his way up to my shoulders, he turned into the street and gestured for me to follow. He walked like a gunfighter, his jeans sagging to half-mast, his arms swinging wide around back muscles that weren't there.

We crossed to a parked car — a Ford Contour, dark maroon — and he opened the shotgun door. I saw the two figures in the backseat before the kid shoved me in and slammed the door behind me.

The car was warm and stunk of body odor and garlic, and a sweet petroleum smell that

I recognized as gun oil. As the kid circled to the driver's side, I turned to the backseat, where his brothers slouched and waited.

The one behind me had black, shoulder-length hair under a red Geronimo headband. He wore a black leather jacket despite the heat, and he held an enormous revolver that looked like a .44 Magnum. The other, in contrast, was clean-cut in a Brooks Brothers suit and tie.

Once the kid was behind the wheel, we all turned to the suit, who seemed to be the oldest, and the one in charge. When he finally spoke, his tone was measured and oddly respectful.

"Hello, Mr. MacTaggart. We're so glad you could make it."

"The invitation was hard to resist."

"Yes," he nodded, "we thought it might be. Now, if you'd be so kind, please tell us where the files are that you stole from our father."

"In my office." I nodded. "Over there."

He looked through the windshield to the building, a corner of which was visible from where we were parked. He seemed to consider that for a minute, then nodded.

"All right," he said. "Here's what we're going to do. You and I will walk together. We'll retrieve the files and return here. If we're not back in ten minutes," he said to Geronimo, "you'll call Father. And just so we're clear, Mr. MacTaggart, unless my brother calls to check in with our father every half hour, someone very close to you is going to have a very bad headache. Do we understand each other?"

"Perfectly."

He opened the door and got out, and I followed his lead. We joined up on the sidewalk and started toward the office, looking like a couple of lawyers returning from a breakfast meeting at city hall.

"We weren't introduced," I said, walking more quickly than usual. "I'm Jack."

"And I'm Tommy," he replied without offering a hand. "Sorry to take you away from the service, but it was the one place we knew we could find you."

A dozen thoughts crowded my mind as we rounded the corner, jaywalking out onto Union. Like, for example, what it would feel like to wring Colonel Mustard's neck. And also, the fact that Tommy was short and soft, and that even if he was armed, which I somehow doubted, I could drop him whenever I wanted, either here in the street or inside the building lobby.

But what would that accomplish? I could ask Mo to call Parker or Gabe, but unless

Tommy and I both returned to the car in nine minutes, it wouldn't really matter.

"Your father's insane, you know. He already messed up once. He can't keep killing people to cover his mistakes."

I thought that might get a rise out of number one son, but he looked, if anything, more thoughtful than angry.

"You're right about that, but only to a point. Which is why we're counting on your full cooperation now. That way, nobody else has to get hurt."

Which was bullshit, and we both knew it. As long as I was alive, Brian Huang was a man at risk. More important, so was Morris Henley. And that meant I couldn't be alive for very much longer. And come to think of it, neither could Tara.

The lobby was empty except for Mo, who gave a nod as we passed. And other than Margot at reception, and maybe one of the girls in bookkeeping, both the eighth and ninth floors would be deserted as well.

I stepped into the elevator car and jabbed the button for eight.

"Relax, Jack. This won't take long, and everybody's going to be okay."

"In California," I told him, watching the numbers as we rose, "we have something called the felony murder rule. That means that if somebody dies during the commission of a crime, even if it's an accident, all the participants are guilty of murder. Even the chubby kid, sitting in back of the car."

He thought about that for a few floors.

"At first blush, that seems rather harsh. But from a public policy standpoint, I can see the deterrent value."

"What are you, a college boy?"

He nodded. "UCLA. The Anderson Business School."

We alighted at eight, and I key-coded us through the north hallway door. Now Tommy was on videotape, at least.

The floor was empty, and the only sounds were the ringing of unanswered telephones off in the distance. At Bernie's desk, the *Times* was folded open to the national weather page.

Tommy eyeballed my office while I sat and unlocked the desk. I removed the files, leaving Bowman's cassette tape in the drawer.

"Cal State L.A.?" he said, tapping the framed diploma. "I expected something more prestigious from you."

"Well, you haven't known me very long."

He examined the files, flipping quickly through each in turn.

"Copies?"

I shook my head.

"You're quite certain of that?"

"Trust me, I'm a lawyer."

"Put them in there," he said, pointing to my briefcase on the floor. I squatted to the task, while Tommy plucked the Hallmark card off the shelf.

"Shnorhakalutyun," he read aloud. "That's Armenian. Phonetic, of course. It means thank you, or blessings."

"No shit?"

"Good people, the Armenians. Very hard workers."

I rose and looked at my watch. I was guessing that around six minutes had elapsed since we'd left the car.

"Shouldn't we be getting along about now?"

"You're so right," he replied, removing his handkerchief and wiping his fingerprints from the card. He took the briefcase from my hand. "After you."

Out in the hallway, just as I'd turned toward the elevator lobby, he stopped and raised a hand.

"One moment, please. A small detour."

He led the way this time, like maybe he'd been here before, down to the end of the hallway and into the mechanical closet. There he went straight to the VCR machine and ejected the surveillance tape, which he slipped into his jacket pocket.

"We can't have that showing up on You-Tube," he said with a chuckle.

Back at the elevators, I checked my watch again.

"You're a smart kid. Whatever your father's up to, is it really worth putting his entire family on death row? I've never been there myself, but I hear the moo shu pork really sucks."

This seemed to surprise him, and he turned to face me just as the tone chimed and the doors slid open.

"Are you saying that you don't know?"

"Science was never my strong suit."

We descended in silence. In the building lobby, I nodded tightly to Mo and hurried toward the doors. Outside, the sunlight was blinding.

"My father," Tommy said as we strode together toward Union, "is a brilliant scientist. It's no exaggeration to call him the Fleming of his generation."

"You mean the James Bond guy?"

"I mean the man who invented penicillin."

We were approaching the corner now, with both the car and the church in view.

"Father will win the Nobel Prize, that much is certain. And he'll save millions of lives in the process."

"So what if he takes a few along the way, right?"

He stopped at the front of the car and faced me.

"That's right. What's the expression? You can't make an omelet without breaking a few eggs?"

Which was the wrong metaphor, given the cell phone photo, and the next thing Tommy knew he was pinned facedown to the hood. Seconds later, the Magnum was pressed hard into my ribs.

"That's enough!" Tommy said, smoothing his jacket as he rose. "Put him inside."

They escorted me back to the shotgun seat, and Geronimo climbed in behind. Tommy, however, remained on the sidewalk, and after all the doors were closed, he tapped on the window.

"It was good to meet you, Jack. My brother Johnny will drive you to your girlfriend now. Like I said before, if you cooperate, nobody will get hurt."

He walked to a Mercedes that was parked at the curb, and he tossed my briefcase inside. Then he and Johnny started their engines, and the last sound I heard as we pulled from the curb was the organ music swelling to a quiet crescendo from the church across the street.

26

We were northbound on Lake Avenue, across the Foothill Freeway and climbing toward the mountains. At around Washington Boulevard, I heard Geronimo flip open a cell phone. It was eleven o'clock on the dot.

"Tommy's on his way. Yeah, he's with us. All right. Yes, sir."

We were across Altadena Drive, heading into the do-rag archipelago of dump bars and liquor stores that littered Pasadena's northern boundary like jetsam left by a receding tide. A pair of teens in blue hoodies saw Geronimo's headband and threw hand signs at the car. Johnny flipped them the bird, then reached into the backseat for a brotherly fist-bump.

"Would you guys believe this is the second time —"

"Shut up!" Geronimo snapped, jamming the barrel hard into the base of my skull.

The kid glanced over, a lunatic smile on his face.

I watched the road, focusing now on the bigger picture. It was clear that Tommy, with his blue business suit and my briefcase, was headed to JPL. Since Tara was already there, I knew that wherever his brothers were taking me, it wasn't to attend any reunion. And once Huang had me, and Tara, and the documents all under his control, it would be game over.

Fortunately, he wasn't there yet.

At the top of Lake, the roadway curved and descended again into a warren of modest ranch houses, all of them set against the foothills towering above. This was the urban wilderness interface, the place where the developers ran out of real estate and the homeowners risked a mountain lion in the doghouse, or maybe even a black bear in the hot tub, in exchange for the city-lights view that stretched after nightfall all the way out to San Pedro.

The roadway flattened again, and we slowed at a flashing yellow light. There we turned north, past a debris basin and an open gate and into the National Forest.

The road was paved and narrow, and it hugged the cliff face, twisting and winding dizzily as we climbed. Many of the curves were without guardrails, and what guardrails there were had either been scuffed and dented or had long ago tumbled into the chaparral below. Now and then Johnny swerved to avoid rocks that had fallen, probably overnight, from the sheer cliffs above.

After a few minutes of climbing, we topped a low saddle and began another steep descent. On the back side of the mountain, the vegetation was denser and the trees taller, and I could see far below, above the pine tops, a Forest Service campground.

At the bottom we came to a fork. To the left lay a blacktop parking lot, secluded and empty, while straight ahead, beyond a second Forest Service gate, was an unpaved fire road. Johnny put the car into park and fished some keys from his jeans. The fresh air from the open car door smelled like pines.

"Almost there," said the voice behind me.

"Where's that?"

He leaned forward. "See that cabin?"

I leaned and looked. It was a ramshackle board-and-batten structure perched above the fire road, its façade obscured by oaks and heavy brush. A concrete stairway led from a sagging carport up to the cabin's ivy-strangled patio.

There were, I knew, dozens of these old cabins dotting the foothills. This one struck me as the kind of remote location at which they might film horror movies. Or maybe snuff films.

"Looks real cozy," I said as Johnny swung the gate wide and started back toward the car.

"Father uses it to get away and think. He says it reminds him of his boyhood home in China."

We pulled through the gate and turned into the carport, parking alongside a familiar black Wrangler with a bullet hole in the side panel. It had been backed into the deepest and darkest corner, out of sight of the parking lot.

"Nice little ride," said Geronimo, following my eyes. "You should take better care of it."

We exited the car together, the gun behind me at all times.

"You first," Geronimo said, nudging the small of my back. Johnny led the procession, up the stairs and through a wooden gate. There he fumbled with the lock, then hipped the cabin door open.

There was a postage-stamp kitchen cluttered with old lab equipment, greasy tools, and dirty rags. Beyond that was a threadbare great room with pea-green carpeting, where a wood stove had been set into the mouth of a charred fireplace. The furniture was early Habitat for Humanity, and the windows overlooking the fire road were clouded with grime.

If this was where Huang did his thinking, it was no wonder his mind was a mess.

"Want a beer?" Johnny called from the kitchen.

"No, thanks."

"Not you, fuckhead."

I sat on the couch as Geronimo backed into the kitchen, returning with two cans of Tsingtao in his free hand. He popped the lids and pressed the little tabs into the open mouths with a greasy fingertip.

"Here. You look thirsty."

We all drank in silence, and it soon occurred to me that the Huang boys were waiting for something. Johnny had opened a pack of playing cards, while Geronimo stood by the windows and peered out toward the gate, which, as I recall, they'd left wide open.

"Think they got held up?"

"Shut up."

I set down my empty can.

"Get him another."

"No, thanks," I told them.

"Get it," Geronimo repeated.

And by the time Johnny had returned with my second beer, all the pieces had fallen into place.

"Mind if I use my phone? I've got clients waiting at the office."

"No service up here," Geronimo said.

"How about a landline?"

He shook his head. Johnny, meanwhile, had shuffled the cards and was dealing a hand of solitaire. And then, halfway through the game, there was a crunching sound of tires on gravel, and Geronimo moved to the windows.

"Okay," he commanded. "Finish your beer. You'll be out of here in no time."

The patio gate opened, and a knock rattled the door.

Tara, when she entered, looked like she'd just awakened from a nap. She wore some kind of cowboy boots and jeans, and the same white T-shirt I'd seen in the cell phone photograph. Most important, she was alive and appeared uninjured.

"Jack?" she said vaguely, then stopped when she saw the gun. "What's going on?"

And in the doorway behind her, a figure appeared.

"Ask Prince Charming," I told her as I

rose. "I'm sure he'll be happy to explain everything."

George Wells surveyed the room, and he didn't look happy with what he saw.

"Brian said there'd be no guns."

Johnny thought that was funny, and even his brother had to chuckle at the vet's Boy Scout earnestness.

"Relax, Doc," he said, closing the door behind them. "We were just having a beer. You want one?"

I crossed to Tara, and I held her in my arms. She was none too steady on her feet.

"Are you all right? Come here and sit."

I walked her to the sofa, addressing Wells over my shoulder.

"How much does she remember?"

"Not a lot. I gave her a sedative at the house. She came to at the lab, but she didn't really wake up until the drive over."

"What are you talking about?" Tara demanded.

"A trade," I explained, examining her eyes. "I gave Huang his files, and he gave me you."

At this, Johnny snickered.

"Listen," said Wells, still standing by the door. "I know what you're thinking. But she was never in danger. The photo was Brian's idea, not mine."

"Fuck you, Wells."

Tara sat forward, her head in her hands. "Will somebody please tell me what's going on?"

"What's going on is that Wells over there has been playing Igor to Dr. Huang's Frankenstein. Blood-testing all the horses at Fieldstone. Probably at Santa Anita too. Is that where the others came from?"

Wells flushed, whether with anger or shame I couldn't tell.

"When they found out that Hush Puppy had the right antibodies, or whatever it is they were looking for, then George gave him a little taste of *halicephalobus deletrix.* Isn't that right, George?"

Tara lifted her eyes. "But I thought he was helping you."

"So did I, for a while. Until I realized he was front-running — that everything he'd ever told me, I would have found out anyway."

Tara turned to Wells, who seemed to shrink under her gaze.

"Go ahead, Doc. Break it to her gently."

Wells looked at the carpet. He swallowed hard.

"AIDS killed over three million people last year. Forty million more are HIV-positive.

In parts of Africa, the rate of adult infection is over fifty percent. Think about that." He looked up into Tara's eyes. "Have you ever cared for somebody dying of AIDS? Have you? Well, if you ever have, you wouldn't be looking at me like that. You wouldn't be judging me."

"So that's it," I said. "The cure for AIDS."

"Not a cure," he corrected. "A vaccine. Like the polio vaccine. Given to children, prepubescence. No side effects, one hundred percent effective. It's the scientific breakthrough of the century, MacTaggart. Imagine the first generation in forty years to live without the specter of AIDS haunting their lives."

"But to make the omelet, you had to break a few eggs."

He nodded. "Unfortunately. You see, stallions are viral reservoirs of EVA infection. But Brian discovered that one in a thousand is seronegative for EVA antibodies, yet still immune to the equine arteritis virus. Genetically immune. I helped him to identify these rarest of animals, and we harvested their bodies. Brian has perfected a technique for splicing their target genes into a new retrovirus. And once that retrovirus is introduced into a human host's genome, reverse transcription of HIV ceases entirely. It stops the virus cold, forever. It's absolutely brilliant."

"Harvested?" asked Tara.

"Racetrack rejects, mostly. Lawfully purchased, then humanely euthanized."

"Except that Hush Puppy was a little beyond their budget," I explained. "So Wells and Morris Henley set Sydney up for the fall. And then they set me up to push her."

Wells looked up again, angry.

"Come on, MacTaggart. Don't shed crocodile tears for that . . ." He turned pleadingly to Tara. "She killed Creole for the insurance. She had it coming, Tara. You of all people know that."

Tara put a hand to her forehead.

"Okay, let's go," said Geronimo.

"And what about Russ Dinsmoor?" I asked Wells as I stood. "Was he humanely euthanized? Or did he kick and scratch and fight to the bitter end?"

"I said, let's go!"

Wells's face was a blank. He turned from me to Geronimo and back again.

"Who's Russ Dinsmoor?"

I took a two-step launch off the armchair, hitting Wells chest-high. He did the backstroke out the front door, and we hit the patio together in a rolling bear-hug. Wells came out on top. He got off a hard right to my face. I head-butted him and rolled free, crawling on my hands and knees.

My head rang, and the patio was tilting at an odd angle. There was a commotion behind me, and I heard Tara scream, but the sound seemed to come from the far end of a tunnel. I staggered to my feet and almost went into the ivy.

When the fog finally lifted, Wells was standing with his hands on his knees, spitting blood onto the patio. Geronimo stood between us, halfway to the house, with the expectant grin of a Pelican Bay prison guard watching a shank fight in the exercise yard.

"Okay, MacTaggart," he said, gesturing with the gun. "You've had your fun. Now it's time to go home."

Tara brushed past and wrapped me in her arms.

"Who's Russ Dinsmoor?" Wells repeated, spitting again, only this time it came out like Hoof Wuff Dinfmo?

"Why don't you ask your pal Huang," I told him. "The great humanitarian."

Johnny led the way, while Tara and I followed like a pair of drunken sailors. Geronimo was behind us, leaving Wells on the patio to search for his missing teeth.

The vehicles were parked three abreast, with Wells's pickup nose-in next to the

Ford. When we reached the front of the carport, Geronimo extracted my keys from his pocket and tossed them in my direction. They bounced off my chest and landed in the gravel.

"You drive, and we'll follow as far as the lower gate. After that, you're on your own."

"Just like that?"

He nodded. "Don't ever say my father doesn't keep his word."

I moved to the Jeep and stopped.

"What about my cell phone?"

Johnny looked to his brother, who nodded. The kid tossed the phone, and this time I caught it.

I held the door for Tara, then circled to the driver's side. The Jeep sputtered and coughed, but it started with a roar.

"Why are they letting us go?"

"They're not," I told her. "And don't bother with your seat belt."

Johnny stood at the gate, and I watched in the mirror as he swung it closed behind the Ford. By the time he'd climbed in with his brother, I had a hundred-yard head start.

"This car has no brakes," I told Tara, talking quickly. "They think we don't know that, and that's our edge, so listen carefully. I'm gonna build as big a lead as I can. When we reach the top, I'll slow as much as possible, but we'll have to jump while it's moving. Hit the ground and roll if you have to, but get over the edge and down into the brush as fast as you can. Understand? Tara? They need to think we're still in the car when it goes over."

We were on the first long run leading to the switchback. The Ford was behind us and closing.

"It has to look like an accident, don't you see? Huang knows he messed up with Russ. This way, with us killed in a crash, he and Morris can frame me for the murder. They can say I was overcome with remorse, or some bullshit."

"Do you mean Jared's father?"

I nodded. "I was wrong about Jared. It was Morris who's partners with Huang, only Morris's share is in some kind of trust he set up for his son. I don't think Jared even knows about it. Only Russ figured it out. And when he started asking questions, they killed him. I guess they don't award Nobel Prizes to horse thieves. Get ready now."

As we topped out on the saddle, I eased off the gas and took the Jeep out of gear.

"Get down as far as you can, then wait for me to find you. Okay? Tara?"

"All right." She opened the door and

pivoted in her seat. The Jeep was already gathering speed on the descent.

"Now!"

I mashed the brake pedal, which dropped limply to the floor. I hit the pavement running, dry-surfing to a halt in the roadside scree. Tara landed and rolled gracefully, then disappeared over the edge. I followed her feet first, glancing over my shoulder just as the front end of the Ford crested the rise.

I tried to scramble, but the slope was steep and I rolled for around twenty yards, finally grabbing at some brush and snapping into a prone position. I heard Tara moving below me, and then the hollow *thunk* of the Jeep.

It landed and flipped, stern over stem, its little doors flapping like vestigial wings. It continued that way, crashing and tumbling down the hillside until it disappeared from sight, leaving a dust cloud and an eerie silence hanging over the canyon.

I lay flat and listened, my face and shoulder newly throbbing. Tara had stopped moving and was off to my left another twenty yards below. Up on the road I heard slamming doors and muted voices. Then the doors slammed again and the Ford drove off.

"Tara?"

"Here!"

"Are you all right?"

"I think so. I lost a shoe."

I got my feet beneath me and half slid, half scrambled to the sound of her voice. She was crouched on a narrow shelf around thirty yards from the bottom.

"Oh, Jack!" she said as I skidded to her feet. "Look at you!"

My left eye was completely closed, and my shirtfront was in ribbons. I untied my shoes, shaking the dirt and rocks from each in turn.

"We're gonna have to walk. How's your head?"

Her T-shirt was soiled, but she had no visible scrapes or cuts, and her bandage had remained in place. On one foot she wore a half-boot slip-on, while a dirty white sock dangled from the other. She bent and touched the side of my face, wincing before I did.

"You need to get to a hospital."

"I need to get to a telephone."

I removed my tie, winding it tightly around my bleeding palm. I was feeling pain from so many receptors that my brain couldn't process the data.

"If I remember right, there's a big housing development down canyon. We can wash up in the stream and follow it down." I looked at her feet. "I may have to carry you."

Off in the distance, we heard voices calling.

"They found the Jeep," she said.

We stood and watched as a column of oily smoke rose from over the ridge.

"Let's go."

We picked our way over jagged rocks and spiny yuccas. A silted arroyo marked the canyon bottom, and we followed it in the general direction of the parking lot. The footing was soft and sandy, and Tara managed. I found my cell phone and checked for a signal.

"Who should we call?" she asked.

"As soon as we can, we need to reach Mayday. Before Morris searches my office."

"Why? What's in your office?"

"The files I stole from Huang."

"But . . . I thought you said you traded them for me."

"I didn't say that. Did I say that?"

She stopped. "If the files are in your office, then what does Huang have?"

"Unless I'm mistaken," I said, turning to check our back trail, "he has a copy of Vic Tazerian's medical records."

27

The shower was hard and hot, and it stung like a swarm of yellow-jackets. And when I wiped the steam from the mirror, Rodney King was staring me in the face.

I had a baseball-sized bruise on my forehead, and my left eye was a thick, purple slit. The scrapes on my chest and knees were superficial, but the abrasion on my palm, and the gravel embedded within it, were another story.

When I came down the staircase in Mayday's bathrobe, a terrycloth number that reached to about midthigh, both she and Tara greeted me with wolf whistles.

"Eat your hearts out."

Mayday slid over and patted the couch. "Let's have a look at that hand," she said.

"Let's have a look at that nursing degree."

Tara had used the downstairs shower, and her hair was wrapped in a towel, turban-style. She wore her own jeans under some kind of peasant tunic of Mayday's that crawled with interlocking lizards in green and gold needlepoint. Mayday wore the same ivory blouse and navy skirt that she'd sported at the church, and each of the women held an oversized glass of white wine. Spread out on the coffee table were Bowman's tape, Huang's files, and what looked like the complete inventory of a small medical dispensary.

I took my place between them, tugging discreetly at the hem of my robe. Mayday went to work on my palm, starting with some sterile wipes that she tore from a paper packet.

"Did you reach Maritza?" I asked Tara through clenched teeth.

She nodded. "Sam's fine, but he had a little accident in my living room."

After scrubbing out the wound, Mayday applied alcohol to a pair of tweezers.

"This might hurt a little."

"As opposed to before?"

The tweezers hurt a lot, in fact, but I managed not to scream.

"Okay. Tell me exactly what happened."

Mayday narrated into my palm as she bent to the task.

"Bernie was gone, and nobody saw me. After I put the stuff in my briefcase, I went up to nine. There was a little reception thing going on in the east conference room. You know, coffee and Danish for the spouses. Hold still. Morris and Jared were there at first, but Morris left in a hurry."

"I take it my absence was noted."

She nodded. "Everybody was talking about you. Where did he go? Where is he now? I overheard Morris say that he'd met with you before the service, and that you'd seemed a little despondent."

Tara and I shared a glance.

"After Morris didn't return, I took a stroll past his office. His door was open, but nobody was there. Hold still, this one's gonna hurt."

"Hey-oh!"

The largest of the pebbles *tinked* onto the glass tabletop.

"There. Now a bandage."

By now my hand was throbbing worse than my face, and that was saying a lot. But the wound was clean and the bleeding was minimal. The doctor's daughter obviously knew her stuff.

"Anything else?"

She sipped at her wine before tearing open a roll of gauze.

"Well, as I was leaving to pick you up, I asked Margot if she knew where Morris had gone. She said he'd left for the day, but had given instructions that if a Detective Parker called, she was to give him his cell number. I assume that's not good."

She snipped, folded, and taped the gauze in place.

"There. How does that feel?"

I clenched and opened my fist. "Perfect."

"Those patent applications," she said, nodding to the stack of files, "pertain to anti-retrovirals. That's for HIV infection."

"So I'm told. Huang has apparently developed a vaccine for AIDS. He's already built a trophy case for his Nobel Prize."

"If that's true," she said, "that would be huge."

"How huge, exactly?"

"Put it this way," she said, gathering up her supplies. "Annual sales of HIV medications run into the tens of billions of dollars worldwide."

Tara, who'd been drying her hair, suddenly stopped.

"I don't care how much money's at stake. I can't believe George Wells would be part of a murder plot."

"I don't think he was," I told her. "I watched him on Sunday, after you fell, and he was surprised when he saw your stitches. And he'd obviously never heard of Russ. I think Huang and Morris only trusted him so far."

"Used him, you mean. The way they tried to use you."

Mayday lifted her glass. "I have a question. How did you know they'd release Tara before the briefcase arrived at JPL?"

I glanced at Tara before answering.

"I didn't. But I figured if they'd waited, we'd have been no worse off. I still had the documents. Worst case, we'd have made the same deal all over again. The cabin was a stroke of luck."

"No phone," Tara explained.

"It was only a matter of Wells getting over the mountain and out of cell range before my briefcase got to Huang."

Tara turned on the couch to face me. "We have the tape and the files now. Can't we just have them arrested?"

"We could, but you're forgetting something important. These records only evidence who killed Hush Puppy, not who killed Russ. And that assumes they're even admissible."

"Which is doubtful," Mayday added.

"Morris and Huang aren't stupid. If we come forward now, they'll lawyer-up in a big way, and there's a good chance they'd walk. Or plead down to some misdemeanor, like animal cruelty. I'm sorry, but that's not good enough."

Mayday refilled the glasses and walked the empty bottle to the kitchen.

"Okay, Mac," she said over her shoulder. "What would Russ have done in a situation like this?"

The parking lot at Santa Anita was a vast ocean of barricades awaiting the afternoon tide of racing fans. Gabe navigated his way to the stable area, and was able to bluff us past the attendant there with his DA credentials. We parked in the long shade of an equipment shed.

"Bring your tranquilizer darts?"

"I thought you said he'd cooperate."

"I said he might cooperate. He also might kick my ass."

"I'd say he already did that."

We found him not in the veterinarians' office, but in an outside barn aisle where, on bended knee, he examined the hoof of a whippet-thin thoroughbred. He looked up at our approach.

"Dr. Wells?" Gabe held up his creds. "Might we have a word?"

The vet lunged forward, like a sprinter out of the blocks, and before I could react he'd wrapped me in his blacksmith arms and hugged me to his chest, lifting my feet off the ground.

"Thank God," he said, rocking me back and forth. "I saw the crash on the news."

Tara and I walked the hundred yards or so from the barn office to the Fieldstone patio. It was a longer walk than usual.

"I still don't like it," she said, for maybe the third time. "It's too risky."

"Airplanes are risky. Eating shrimp is risky."

Sydney and Barbara were waiting for us under the portal. Both were smoking cigarettes.

"My God," Sydney said, examining my face. "If that doesn't heal properly, I can give you a name."

"Yeah," said Barbara. "One-eyed Jack."

"But you, Tara dear, look perfectly wonderful. I can see it now, short bangs will be *all* the rage next year."

"Are they here yet?"

Barbara nodded, stamping out her smoke. "They parked around back. The tall one's kind of cute."

"You'd like him," I told her. "He has his own handcuffs."

The clubhouse doors were marked PRI-VATE FUNCTION IN PROGRESS, and inside, seated around a table strewn with electronics, were Wells, Griegas, and Montoya, the latter two looking like caddies at Augusta National in their white Fieldstone coveralls. Parker, glowering by the fireplace, rounded out the field.

"Okay," said Griegas, blowing into an earbud receiver. "We get one shot at this, so everybody listen up. Jack, we need to wire you up. Tom will man the recorder from here, while Gabe and I will be hanging outside the office."

"Not too close. If Huang smells a rat, he'll spook."

"I smell a rat," said Parker. "I smell a pack of rats."

"When Gabe thinks we have enough for an indictment," Griegas continued, "he'll give me the signal. I'll detain the two suspects until Tom arrives, and then we'll take them into custody."

"Or we could execute this warrant," Parker said, fingering the paper in his jacket, "and take MacTaggart into custody now."

Griegas ignored his partner. "Anyway, that's the plan. Any questions?"

"The plan," said Sydney, savoring the word. "I so love a good *plan.*"

"Doc, you ready?"

"Huh?" Wells seemed to be elsewhere.

"Oh, sure. Ready."

I handed Gabe my cell phone and gathered up Huang's files, giving half to Wells. We sat shoulder to shoulder and held the files up to the camera. I smiled.

"Cheese, you little rats."

Alone inside the barn office, I paced.

I fingered the body mic taped snugly to my sternum. I watched through the blinds as Nick Griegas pretended to rake the same patch of ground he'd been raking for the past twenty minutes. And then I paced some more.

My text message, sent jointly to Huang and Morris, had been terse: "FRC barn office in half hour. Last chance to deal." Followed by the photo.

We knew from Mayday that Morris had left Henley & Hargrove in a hurry, just after the text. If he'd come straight here, he'd have arrived ten minutes ago. As for Huang, holed up in his castle keep, we knew nothing.

I checked my watch again. "Anything?"

Griegas shook his head without looking up.

"You missed a spot."

He gave me the finger.

I guessed that Tara, in the clubhouse with

Parker and Sydney and Barbara, was also pacing. And after everything I'd put her through, I really couldn't blame her.

Last I'd seen Gabe, he was pushing a wheelbarrow up and down the aisle in the barn behind Griegas, but that was five minutes ago. I think it was the most exercise he'd had in a while. He was probably resting.

As for Wells, he'd been allowed to do his rounds, but only on condition that he make himself available later. I don't think Gabe planned to prosecute the vet for his role in harvesting Hush Puppy, but he remained a material witness.

I checked my watch for the fifth time. I paced.

After another minute or so, Griegas stopped and touched a finger to his ear. Then I saw Gabe. He'd stepped into the sunny quadrangle to say something to Griegas, who nodded and began raking in earnest.

"They coming?"

Griegas nodded.

"Move away," I told him. "You look like a narc."

Griegas backed into the shadows, raking as he went, just as the Oliver-and-Hardy tandem of Brian Huang and Morris Henley strode into view.

Huang wore slacks and a white dress shirt, while Morris, ever the conservative, wore a vested wool suit.

I opened the door to meet them.

"You're late."

Huang brushed past me and surveyed the little room. Then, moving wall to wall, he began closing the blinds. Morris, meanwhile, paused on the threshold in the way that a wild animal, sniffing the air, approaches a cage.

"Where's Wells?" he demanded.

Behind his antique desk, with his shaved head and broad shoulders, Morris Henley cut an imposing figure. Here, somehow, he appeared diminished.

"He's around. With the files. He put me in charge of negotiations."

I closed the door behind him, leaning my weight against it.

"Negotiations?" Morris laughed as he turned; a short and nasty bark. "Let me tell you how things are, MacTaggart. Right now, Detective Parker and his partner are executing a search warrant at your home. And do you know what they're going to find there?" He ticked the items on his fingers. "First, Russ's briefcase. Second, the keys to Russ's boat. Third, a forged deed to Russ's house.

And fourth, and this is my personal favorite, a sample vial of FreshTex. Do you know what that is?"

"Aerosol insulin?"

Morris glanced at Huang. "That's right. And once I testify to your efforts to blackmail both Dr. Huang and myself, you'll be spending the rest of your life in prison. So don't talk to me about leverage, MacTaggart, because you have none."

"Two million dollars."

"What?"

"Each."

"Did you not —"

"Save it, Morris. Between the two of us, Wells and I can prove Jared's role in blackmailing Sydney, your role in forming EVAgen, and Huang's role both in a string of horse murders and a kidnapping. Add to that Russ's visit with Wagner, Huang's means and opportunity, and your motive. So if you want to get into a swearing contest with me, I say bring it on. Meanwhile, you risk cratering a billion-dollar pharma deal over four million bucks. Are you nuts? That's a rounding error, for Christ sake."

"It's a deal."

That came from Huang, who stood at the window peering out through the blinds.

"Like hell it is."

"Shut up, Morris." The little scientist turned to face us both. "Mr. Mac-Taggart makes a valid point. In the grand scheme of things, four million is not an unreasonable sum. A consulting fee, perhaps. After all, I need my files. And let's face it, Mr. Mac-Taggart has proven himself to be — how shall we say it? — quite resilient. That said, what assurance do we have that you won't be back again in a year's time, asking for more?"

"Look," I told them. "Between the two million from you and the proceeds from the sale of Dinsmoor's house, I'm set for life. And I don't want to spend the rest of it looking over my shoulder. So, we do this deal now, and I'm gone. I'll take Tara with me. To Kentucky, or maybe to Argentina."

"I don't like it," Morris said.

I addressed myself to Huang. "I just want to know one thing. It's been chafing my ass for two weeks now."

"And what is that?"

"How'd you do it? Deliver the insulin, I mean."

He smiled thinly. "Perhaps it's best that you don't know everything."

"I think I already know. It was the pipe tobacco. It was the one thing missing from the table in the den."

Huang regarded me for a moment, then nodded.

"I owe you an apology, Mr. MacTaggart. I believe I've been underestimating you."

"So tell me, how'd you do it?"

"Shut up, Brian," was Morris's advice, but the little egomaniac couldn't stop himself.

"Let's just say we were at a very critical juncture in our project. The patent examinations were underway, and the phase three trials were about to begin. Any hint of scandal could have — what's the expression? — upset the applecart."

"Brian!"

"So when Mr. Dinsmoor began his . . . imprudent inquiries, he received a little gift. His favorite tobacco blend, with a liberal dose of FreshTex. The packaging was hermetically sealed, of course."

"Until he opened it, and took a nice deep breath."

He nodded. "So it seems."

"And what made you think he'd trust a gift from you?"

The smile broadened. "Ah, but that's the genius of it. The gift wasn't from me at all. As a matter of fact, Mr. MacTaggart, the gift was from you."

My hands balled into fists.

"You little —"

I heard movement outside. I crossed to the door.

"Well, guess what, boys? I've got a little surprise of my own, for both of you."

I yanked the door wide and watched as the panic registered on their faces.

And then George Wells stepped into the room and started firing.

28

Huang saw the gun and threw himself to the floor as the first bullet hit with a thud, knocking Morris backward, spraying blood onto the wall.

The second shot ricocheted off the floor as I grabbed the vet's wrist with both hands, collapsing my weight onto his arm and taking us both down in a heap. We struggled there in a sort of rugby scrum, each leaning into the other, pawing the floor for leverage. I gripped his wrist and slammed it once, twice on the cold concrete.

The gun fired again and then clattered free, and I felt more than saw the wraithlike figure of Brian Huang hurdling us both and disappearing through the open doorway. Wells and I chuffed like horn-locked stags while Morris groaned and bled somewhere on the floor behind us.

"Let . . . me . . . *go!*"

Wells bellowed in impotent rage, and I felt

his free hand grip my shoulder like a vise, his thumb pressing deeply into the joint space. The pain cut like a drill, and the room began to swim.

"Police! Hands in the air, now!"

I rolled free and saw Griegas backlit in the doorway, his legs wide and his weapon drawn.

"Gun on the floor!" I shouted through the rush of wind in my ears. "Call an ambulance! He shot Morris!"

I rose to a knee and staggered upright, banging my hip on the counter. I saw Morris then, curled on his side by the file cabinet, a ruby pool spreading beneath him.

"Huang!" I pitched forward, pushing past Griegas.

"Wait, MacTaggart!" he called over his shoulder. Parker was outside now, breathing hard, his gun also drawn, watching his partner's back. Behind him, a crowd was gathering that included both Gabe and Tara.

"Where's Huang?"

Gabe pointed toward the back parking lot. "He took Wells's truck!"

"C'mon, Parker!"

The big man held a radio to his chest. "Forget it, he's too far gone. I'm calling a BOLO."

"Fuck that. I know where he is, and I

know where he's going. Come on!"

I started for the clubhouse. Parker hesitated, then yelled something to Griegas before following at a run. He moved like the linebacker he once was, powerful and compact, barking orders into his radio.

"Jack! Jack, don't!"

Tara's voice was lost in the patter of running feet and the squawk of the handheld rover. By the time we'd reached the Crown Vic we were both winded, but my head had cleared and the pain in my shoulder had quieted to a dull throb.

I figured that around three minutes had elapsed since Huang had fled the office. His exact whereabouts would depend on whether the back gate had been open or closed, locked or unlocked.

"He's circling the block, heading back to JPL. We can cut him off that way," I said, gesturing toward the front gate.

"You stay here!" Parker commanded, but I was into the car before he'd opened his door.

"Don't just sit there! Let's roll, come on!"

He started to protest, then turned the ignition, his arm flung across the seat back. When he threw it into drive, his tires squealed on the blacktop.

The Colonel gawked as we blew past his

booth and skidded to a stop at the curb cut. We both leaned into the windshield to scan the empty street.

"That was some fucking stunt back there."

"Yeah, but I didn't figure on Wells."

I saw the pickup first. It fishtailed onto Oak Grove, gathering speed again as it straightened.

"Here he comes."

Parker tensed, waiting, and then he gunned the big car forward, shooting us into the path of the pickup. Huang braked and swerved, clipping the Crown Vic's rear quarter-panel and spinning us to the curb.

"Shit!"

We hit hard, the rear bumper scraping concrete, and by the time we were moving again, the pickup was already passing through the checkpoint onto federal property.

Parker flipped a switch, and his siren started to wail. Then he snatched a radio handset off the dash.

"This is One-whisky-niner. We are code three from Foothill and Oak Grove in Flintridge in pursuit of a late-model Ford F-series pickup truck, white in color, with matching camper shell. We are proceeding northbound on Oak Grove Boulevard, over."

"Roger that, Detective," the dispatcher crackled in reply.

"You forgot to mention JPL."

"JPL?" He grinned crazily. "You mean this industrial park up ahead?"

Parker lowered his window and slowed the car, but not by much, and he badged the guards on the fly.

"LAPD!" he called, bouncing over the speed bump and roaring up the roadway, shouted protests from the guard station fading in the distance.

"I think you just bought yourself some paperwork."

"That's okay. Nick is good at paperwork."

He followed my directions to the bunker on the hillside, heads turning and fingers pointing as we roared through the now-busy campus. As Huang's lab came into view, we saw the white pickup angled in the gravel driveway, the driver's door open. Parker skidded in behind and cut the siren, unholstering his weapon.

"You stay here, MacTaggart, and I mean it."

"Sorry, Detective, but I can't do that."

He turned in the seat to face me.

"Has anybody ever told you that you're a real pain in the ass?"

The laboratory doors were open, but there

were no lights inside. Parker flipped another switch on the dash, and he grabbed the radio handset.

"This is the police! Come outside with your hands in the air!"

He opened his door and crouched behind it, his gun cupped in both hands.

"What do you suppose he's doing in there?"

"Destroying evidence."

"I was afraid you'd say that. I'm going in."

"I'm going with you."

"Not if I cuff you to the steering wheel you're not."

"You don't have time."

"I have time to shoot you."

I slid from the passenger seat and followed him to the rear of the pickup, and from there to the front of the building, where we flattened ourselves side by side against the wall. Parker had left his grille lights flashing, bathing us both in the red-and-blue strobes.

"It's one big room inside, with an operating table in the center. Against the far wall are two smaller rooms behind glass doors. One's full of drugs and chemicals, and the other's full of dead horses."

Parker nodded. "Okay. Glad I didn't shoot you."

He edged his way over to the corner and shouted into the alcove.

"Police! We're coming in with weapons drawn. Stand in the open with your hands in plain sight! Do you hear me?"

There was no reply. In the distance, rising up from the lower campus, the sound of sirens filled the air. Parker moved into the alcove and stood with his back to the door frame.

He looked at me and nodded, took a breath, then disappeared into the darkness.

The lab was cloaked in an eerie half-light. The window I'd broken on Sunday had been boarded over, and a single shaft of greasy sunlight spotlighted the head of the operating table.

"You want the lights?" I whispered to Parker, who was ten feet ahead, crouched behind a file cabinet.

"Fuck, yes!"

I found the box and flipped the switch, but nothing happened.

"Okay, Huang! This is Detective Parker of the LAPD! Come out with your hands in the air! Do you hear me? This is your last warning!"

Again there was no response. Parker moved in a low crouch around the table and toward the door with the decals. He held his hands like a penitent, the 9mm. pistol in place of his rosary.

"Talk to me, MacTaggart," he said. "I don't want to shoot you."

"At last, something we can both agree on."

We approached the door with our backs to the sidewall. As the adrenaline pumped my heart into my throat, I thought of how it must have gone down that day in Inglewood, with Parker and his partner Ray Rizzo. It was a hell of a way to make a living.

Parker moved past the decals and tugged at the door frame, then he stepped away from the wall and took aim at the latch. Two shots rang out, followed by sounds of breaking glass and the *cling, cling* of shell casings hitting concrete. The door, spring-loaded, hissed open about a foot. Inside was greater darkness, the cold air flooding the lab.

"You first," I whispered.

"Huang! Come out with your hands in the air!"

Parker waited a beat, then stretched his foot to hook the edge of the door. He slid it all the way open, then pivoted into the doorway, his body crouched and his gun leveled. He was a ballsy son of a bitch.

Parker relaxed, rising again to his full height. He felt for the switch, but it too was dead. He reached into his jacket and produced a little mag flash-light, the beam playing off the sinks and the glass shards on the floor.

He turned to me and jerked his head, and we stepped back into the lab.

We sidled over to the second door. The lock mechanism was still broken, but a metal eye hook, like you'd see on an old screen door, had been jerry-rigged onto the frame. The hook hung loose from the eye-bolt, but the door was tightly shut.

"He's inside," I whispered, and Parker nodded.

The sirens outside were audible now, and I wondered if Parker would stand down and wait for his backup. Problem was, the Homeland Security goons were just as likely to haul us away in cuffs as they were to arrest Huang.

Parker tugged at the door frame, then stepped back as before, raising his gun.

"Wait!"

I hurried to the supply drawers, and found my handy mallet and chisel.

"There's a solid inner wall. A ricochet could kill us."

He watched while I took a knee. I gave the chisel two good raps and the door popped open. I could see the drinking fountain inside, and the second door beyond it, sealed and dark.

"Watch this," I whispered, laying the chisel on the floor and stretching my arm for the glass plate. The unit hummed and the purple black light flashed, and the inner door hissed open.

"Oh, Christ," Parker gagged, ducking his nose in the crook of his elbow.

He shouldered past me with his flashlight. As he stepped into the anteroom, the sirens stopped and tires crunched on gravel. There were slamming doors and voices.

What happened next was a blur. A shadow passed between us, and there was a sudden rush of movement. Parker gave a wounded cry as he dropped the flashlight, tumbling forward into the darkness. The light beam rolled, raking the sidewall, and I bent to grab it.

"Gun!" Parker shouted, and suddenly Brian Huang appeared, rising to his feet over the fallen detective. He turned to face me, a defensive forearm lifting to his eyes as he cocked and leveled the weapon.

"Look out!" Parker shouted, and I dropped the light. A shot rang out as I sidestepped and set my feet, flinging the mallet into the darkness where Huang had last been standing.

There was a fleshy thud and a wounded shriek, and behind me, shouted commands and the sweeping arc of flashlights. On the floor, a metallic glint caught my eye, and I lunged for it.

"Don't shoot! Police officers!" Parker yelled as I rose to a knee with the pistol.

"Drop the weapon!" called a voice from the doorway, and just as I did, there came another blur of movement.

Huang appeared out of the darkness, his face a bloody mask, the mallet raised overhead with both hands. He screamed something in Chinese, spittle flying in the light beams. Then he rushed forward, still screaming, until a fusillade of gunfire knocked him off his feet.

I lay on my stomach with my ears still ringing, and in the sweep of the lights I saw Parker on his back, his gold shield held upright in one shaking hand, a large syringe jutting limply from the other.

29

The rain finally came.

At first, large drops that made slapping sounds on the granite markers, and then, when the skies finally opened, a cold and slanting deluge.

The wilted flowers bowed their heads, and the freshly turned earth grew slick and muddy before my eyes. On my lips, the moisture turned from warm to cold, from saltwater to fresh.

I flipped my collar and shivered. There were footsteps behind me.

"They told me I'd find you here!"

Gabe Montoya wore a belted Humphrey Bogart raincoat, and he carried a black umbrella.

"Check out the dates," I said as he shouldered up beside me, the rain drumming the fabric over our heads.

He squinted. "What do you know. Twenty years apart."

We stood for a silent moment, and then I squatted and touched the newest of the three stones, tracing the deeply carved letters with wet fingertips.

RUSSELL HALE DINSMOOR
LOVING HUSBAND
DEVOTED FATHER
REUNITED FOREVER

"C'mon," Gabe said. "Let's get out of here."

We walked together toward the parking lot. Gabe held his umbrella high, and our shoes made squeaking sounds on the newly sodden grass.

"How's Parker?"

"He's gonna make it, thanks to you. Turns out it was hali-whatever. They put him on massive antibiotics right away. He says he owes you."

"Tell him we're even. Finally."

Gabe's Volvo was parked alongside Tara's Jeep. They were the only two cars in the lot.

"How'd it go in Westwood?"

We were between the cars now, and at last I turned to face him.

"I was hoping you'd tell me."

"Well, let's see. They're holding the paper on Morris, of course. Wells is at County, where he's been spilling his guts out to Griegas. Get this, the guy has full-blown AIDS. He told Nick he wasn't gonna let those murdering bastards outlive him."

"A man of action."

"Oh, and they've opened an IA jacket on Parker."

That surprised me. Parker was a silverback gorilla, and his cowboy stunt at the JPL guard station seemed like small beer in the larger picture. I had to assume that the LAPD's Internal Affairs Division was just going through the motions, trying to assuage the feds.

"And the ladies?"

Gabe shrugged. "No one's very excited about an old insurance con, especially under the circumstances. They referred it to me for evaluation. I'm thinking I'll decline. Interests of justice."

He searched my eyes for some sign of approval.

"What about Huang's kids?"

"All in custody. Nick said the house was a fucking armory. Guns and ninja swords and all kinds of shit."

I nodded. "And?"

He counted his shoes.

"And, they gave the B and E to the U.S. Attorney's office. The Bureau's pushing it, but I have some influence there. Plus, it's got shitbomb written all over it. If I were you, I wouldn't lose any sleep."

I nodded again. Once I'd told my story to the FBI agents in Westwood, there'd been a debate over whether to book me there and then on breaking and entering, or to release me pending further investigation. An indictment, or even a preliminary hearing, would mean major complications with the state bar. But if the whole story behind Huang's little operation ever hit the press, many heads would roll, both here and in Washington. Plus, they were going to need my cooperation in the event that either Morris survived or the Huang boys chose not to plead.

Gabe was right, I wasn't overly worried.

"Where you heading now?"

"I was thinking of stopping to see Morris," I told him. "Don't ask me why."

"He's under lock and key. But I can get you in, if you don't mind the company."

It was the same post-op ward where Tara had been, and the same nurse behind the same counter had her same ear glued to the same telephone. I saw a flicker of recognition as we approached.

"Still waiting to see Tara Flynn," I told

her. She wrinkled her brow and looked at her chart, until Gabe stepped forward and flashed his creds.

"We're here to see Morris Henley. I know the way."

There was a teenage Explorer Scout on a folding chair in the hallway, a rover and clipboard on the floor beside him. He wore his little uniform with the neckerchief, and he may have been doing his algebra homework. He checked Gabe's ID against the approved-visitor list.

It was a large private room, with the bed angled into a corner. Electronic monitors were arrayed across the headboard, alongside IV bags and some sort of respiratory pump that wheezed in time with the rise and fall of Morris's chest. He had a tube down his throat, a tube in his abdomen, and IV tubes in both arms. There was also, I noticed, the telltale bulge of a plastic monitoring bracelet on his ankle.

Jared, startled by our appearance, looked up from his chair. Gabe still had his wallet out, and he flipped it open as he offered a hand.

"Hello. I'm Gabriel Montoya, from the District Attorney's office. And this —"

"Hello, Jared."

He looked at me, then turned back to his

father, ignoring Gabe's hand.

"I've already given a statement."

We stood at the foot of the bed, where I studied Jared's face in profile. It was, I realized, his father's profile.

"I'm glad you're here, Jared. I think I owe you an apology."

"Get out, MacTaggart. You're not welcome here."

We stood in awkward silence, listening to Morris breathe.

"What do the doctors say?" Gabe finally asked.

"Guarded. Whatever that means."

"Maybe they mean the kid in the hallway."

Jared leapt to his feet, overturning the chair. He stood trembling with rage.

I pitied him in that moment. He reminded me of something soft, like a snail perhaps, ripped from its shell. He'd lived his entire life shielded by the steel-plated armor of Morris Henley; first in law school, then in practice. And now he stared into a dim and uncertain future.

Morris must have realized that his son wouldn't survive long at the firm after his own retirement. And when he'd discovered Jared's complicity in the blackmail scheme on that first year-end, he'd protected Jared, hiding the records and cooking the books that might otherwise expose him. Then, when the EVAgen opportunity arose, he'd seized it for Jared's benefit, establishing a trust to partner with Dr. Huang. And, when Hush Puppy's death became exigent and the blackmail scheme offered the perfect vehicle for shifting suspicion to Sydney, Morris had made certain that Jared was out of the country, five tropical time zones away.

In that regard, at least, Russ had gotten it wrong. Morris Henley was a lion — a doting father who would do anything and risk everything to protect his runt cub. And here the cub stood, snarling over his father's body, as the dark shapes circled overhead.

"Come on," I said to Gabe. "I need some fresh air."

I saw her on the porch as Gabe pulled his Volvo to the curb. She wore a yellow rain slicker, and she sat with her back to the wall, studying something in her lap. From the sidewalk you'd have mistaken her for a little girl, her wet hair hanging in tangles that curtained her downcast face.

"I was just at your place," I told her, stamping my feet on the concrete. "I returned the Jeep. Sorry to keep it so long."

She watched the Volvo pull away.

"That's funny. I got a ride over here so I

580

could pick it up." She lifted the phone from her lap. "I just called a cab."

I slipped my key into the lock and Sam spilled onto the porch, whimpering and smothering Tara in kisses.

"Don't just sit there. Come on in."

She rose stiffly and ducked under my arm. Inside, Sam hurried off in search of a stuffed toy. Tara watched him, her hands thrust into the pockets of her raincoat.

"Would you like tea? Or maybe a towel?"

She shook her head, her eyes avoiding mine, and I felt a cold weight sagging into my bowel.

"I'm sorry I haven't called," she said.

"You got my messages?"

She nodded.

I peeled off my jacket and draped it on a chair. The house was dim, and cold, and I felt myself shivering. I would have built a fire, but I knew she'd be gone before the room was even warm.

She crossed to the mantel and studied the photo; me and Russ descending the court-house steps.

"Marta told me you quit your job."

I didn't answer.

"Why?"

"I don't know. I guess I wasn't cut out for life at a big law firm."

She turned, and for the first time looked at my face. My knees felt weak.

"I just —"

"Can't we — ?"

We both smiled, so very polite.

"You first."

She took a deep breath and let it out.

"This is so hard," she said, smoothing the hair behind her ear. "And I know it's not going to make any sense to you. I'm not even sure it makes sense to me. But the sight of you getting into that car, and driving away, and knowing I might never see you again." She shook her head. "I don't know. I thought I was ready for this. Ready for you. But . . ."

Tears scuttled down her face, falling onto the slicker. She pulled a ball of tissues from her pocket. "I'm sorry. I promised myself I wouldn't do this."

She looked at the tissues. Sam was at her feet now, foolishly expectant, his tail dust mopping the hardwood.

"I suppose it's a little late for 'I'm sorry'?"

She shook her head. "You don't have to be sorry. I'm the one who's the coward."

In the street outside, a car was honking. She patted Sam on the head.

"I should go."

The rain outside was sheeting. The taxi

shimmered at the curb, its exhaust billowing red in the glow of the taillights. On the porch, Tara waved to the driver and turned again to face me.

"What will you do now?"

I shrugged. "I haven't given it much thought. Maybe I'll hang a shingle. Maybe I can talk Mayday into joining me. Maybe I'll even catch a horse show now and again."

She looked down, and I think she might have smiled. Sam pressed his nose into her hand and she squatted, taking hold of his ruff with both hands. Then she stood and turned, walking quickly down the steps.

She was halfway to the sidewalk when she stopped, then turned and hurried back.

"This is so embarrassing," she said. "I just realized, I don't have any money. For the cab."

I reached for my wallet. After all these years, the bill was still there. Slightly discolored, its folded edges sharp as razors.

"Oh, Jack, that's way too much. I'll mail you the change."

I placed a hand on both of hers.

"Forget it. Just let it ride."

She studied my face, and the house behind me. Then she turned again, back into the rain.

ACKNOWLEDGMENTS

It is often the case that a first novel, like a first child, has many ardent benefactors. Happily for me, this is one such novel. Listed alphabetically, the following individuals deserve, and hereby have, my deepest thanks: Don Mike Anthony, Liv Blumer, Tom Colgan, Greg Donaldson, Dan Greaves, Katie Greaves, Jerry Held, Besty James, Dan Larsen, Lynda Larsen, Steve Madison, Sabrina Roberts, Margaret Smith, and David Snyder.

I would not be in a position to offer these thanks if not for the faith and tireless efforts of my agent Antonella Iannarino of the David Black Literary Agency, and the scrupulous labors of my editor Peter Joseph of Thomas Dunne Books. Both took a chance on a recovering lawyer, and for this I am in their debt.

All of the characters in the novel, and many of its closer settings, are entirely fictive. Of the latter, three require exegesis. Its name and location notwithstanding, the purely invented law firm of Henley & Hargrove bears no relation to Pasadena's Hahn & Hahn LLP, one of California's oldest and best-respected law firms, at which I had the great pleasure of practicing for twenty-five years. Similarly, and with the same qualifications, the fictitious Fieldstone Riding Club shares no correspondence with the storied Flint-ridge Riding Club, on whose board of directors I have had the honor of serving. Finally, while I have never set foot on the campus of the NASA Jet Propulsion Laboratory, I am reasonably certain that no diabolical plots are incubated there.

Lastly, I wish to thank SouthWest Writers for honoring this novel, while still in manuscript, as the Best Mystery, Suspense, Thriller, or Adventure Novel of 2010, and for honoring me with their grand prize Storyteller Award. With those small acts of beneficence, a career was born.

ABOUT THE AUTHOR

Chuck Greaves was born in Levittown, New York. He is an honors graduate of both the University of Southern California and Boston College Law School and spent twenty-five years as a trial lawyer in Los Angeles. *Hush Money,* his first novel, was named by SouthWest Writers as the Best Mystery/Suspense/Thriller/Adventure Novel of 2010, and won SWW's Storyteller Award. He lives in Santa Fe, New Mexico.